THE HANDICAPPER

THE HANDICAPPER

Robert Kalich

CROWN PUBLISHERS, INC.
NEW YORK

Copyright © 1981 by Robert Kalich
All rights reserved. No part of this book may be reproduced or utilized in any form
or by any means, electronic or mechanical, including photocopying, recording, or
by any information storage and retrieval system, without
permission in writing from the publisher.
Inquiries should be addressed to Crown Publishers, Inc.,
One Park Avenue, New York, New York 10016
Printed in the United States of America
Published simultaneously in Canada by General Publishing Company Limited
Library of Congress Cataloging in Publication Data
Kalich, Robert Allen, 1937–
The handicapper.
I. Title.
PZ4.K14525Han   [PS3561.A41653]   813'.5'4   79-25879
ISBN: 0-517-54024X
Design by Deborah Kerner
10   9   8   7   6   5   4   3   2   1
First Edition

To my brother Rick, without whom I never could have achieved this work, who taught, exhorted, criticized, guided, stuck by me, took my abuse, helped and helped and helped.

WITH RESPECT. WITH GRATITUDE.

And to my dear friend Harvey Ross, who combines business acumen with a poet's soul—an incredible combination, a fabulous man.

And to Abe Margolies, as my brother Rick says, "A Champion Among Men," who for me defined what the word friendship *means. For twenty years I've been blessed.*

THANK YOU, ABE.

I gratefully acknowledge the help of Harvey Litt, who helped for years; of Myra Ross, who sustained me with home-cooked meals; of Donny Burks, Rick's brother; of Michael Feldman, who started me off by bringing over a typewriter; of Melissa Joy, whom I once promised to write this book for; of Michael Roloff, who edited with creativity and zeal; of Deborah Emin, who made suggestions; and of Meghan Ellenberger, who traveled the last month of *The Handicapper*'s journey with me.

THE HANDICAPPER

David Lazar lived on the telephone.

"Hello, Eddie? Andy Steiman says his kids shot sixty-two percent against Creighton and eighty-one percent in the second half against Iowa. I'm betting against them. They're due to cool off. Especially tonight with the kind of tight man-to-man defense those animals at El Paso play. . . . Look, Arnie, I said I want fifteen and a half, not fifteen. Otherwise forget it. . . . Allie MacIntosh says his kids have been sluggish in practice all week, Eddie. He expects a poor performance tonight. It figures, Eddie—his boys have to be looking ahead to their game with Davidson Saturday night. That's the game that means something to them. I'm taking the seventeen. I think it's one of the best shorts all season. Remember, Eddie, I told you I power-rated the game at eleven this afternoon. . . . Hello, Doug . . . there's a game tonight I thought you might want to get down on. You can tell the Colonel to throw a couple of dollars on it, too. . . . Hello, Solomon, there's a game tonight. . . ."

David had millions of factors to consider, mounds of facts and figures to be dissected, synthesized, assimilated, and collated. Refinements had to be made long into every night.

"Hello, Max . . . I thought you'd want to know. I made the Georgia Tech game seven and a half tonight and the line is thirteen and a half. . . . Hello, is this Georgia Tech? . . . How's the game going tonight? . . . Thank you. Thank you very much. . . . Hello, Eddie. Roger called. He says— what? They really have Villanova at nine? Down here it's five and a half and in Indiana it's five. Listen. Do this—no, wait a minute—forget what Brantley said, take the nine. What can you get down for? . . . Is two thousand the most? Okay, I'll take the five for a nickel with my contact in Bloomington and the five and a half for the rest with some other guys. That gives us almost four numbers to work with. That's a fantastic edge. . . . It's worth much more than the two hundred in vigorish we're investing. . . . Yeah, I'm sure."

The phone never stopped working. He was in perpetual motion from 5:30 to 7:30 every night. Decisions . . . decisions . . . decisions. And then the gut-wrenching pressure of waiting up with his silver dollar clenched in his fist for the scores, and then telephoning around the country for the rest of them.

Every week David scrutinized his handbook, followed every rule, studied every game, power-rated every team. Every week he telephoned his sources, concerned himself with scouting reports, strengths and weaknesses, game plans, and guarded his selections from other people's ears.

. . . 1

1

I'VE GOT to get out, David Bernard Lazar thought as he sat at his desk in the Department of Welfare in Harlem. He looked around at his co-workers: Jewish misfits or blacks who had made it, Puerto Ricans who were content.

David stared at his desk piled high with cases for which he was filling out forms.

Doing social work, helping people. Offering tender loving care, as his supervisor would say.

David thought of his wife, Leslie, from whom he was separated. He still loved her.

He regarded with disgust two personal bills on his desk. He had just finished writing checks to cover them. Slowly he placed the checks in Welfare Department envelopes and began neatly printing the addresses. He knew them by heart—the Household Finance Corporation and the Beneficial Finance Company. When he finished addressing the envelopes, he thought to himself, "With these fuckin' installments paid, I now owe . . . God damn it, I don't remember." The phone on his desk rang. David picked up the receiver slowly.

"What's doin', Davy boy?" a voice inquired. David recognized Solomon Lepidus's warm, earthy greeting.

"Hi, Solomon," David said, and immediately felt superior to all his co-workers. None of them ever received a call from a Great Man. And Solomon Lepidus was a Great Man.

The Great Man continued talking to David. He quickly focused on the reason for his call.

"I want you to do this for me, Davy boy. Nathan Rubin's in town. He's staying at Sandy Rocca's apartment. Give him a call. Make up some kind of story to meet him for lunch. What I want you to do . . ."

Just then David's superior, the meticulous Walter Bloom, appeared. "David, excuse me. Can I see you a minute on the Brockington case? It's very important."

David motioned to Bloom that he had heard while Lepidus continued talking, outlining a proposal for action.

"Remember, Davy boy, tell Rubin I'm gonna be free later this afternoon. I want a game with him. And that I'm gonna make him some propositions that he won't be able to refuse. I'll be waitin' for you in my office. Give me a call."

David Lazar met Nathan Rubin at the Carnegie Delicatessen at five.

The first thing that David noticed as Nathan Rubin haltingly entered the perpetual neon of the deli was the multimillionaire's fingernails, manicured with cadaverish color. He saw one hand tremblingly clasp a knee as Nathan Rubin seated himself. The hand continued to tremble almost convulsively even after it had a firm hold on the knee.

The formerly dapper millionaire, one of the shrewdest and most feared men on the Street, seemed to be gravely ill. David was astonished. Rubin took his trembling hand off his knee and sat silently for a moment to let David take full measure of him.

"David, did I tell ya that while I was in Puerto Rico I beat Solomon for twelve thousand playing blackjack?" He halted briefly, "Ya see, I knew he'd go overboard."

"You're right, Mr. Rubin," David agreed. "Solomon doesn't know when to stop. He bets for the fun of it."

"Only suckers do it for the fun of it," Rubin retorted bitingly, sounding a lot more like the Nathan Rubin David used to know.

The never-ending rivalry between Nathan Rubin and Solomon Lepidus was legendary. It involved both business and gambling worlds. It was a ceaseless duel and could take the form of the most petty and vengeful altercation. At times the fights were literally over pennies.

David was only on the fringe of the contests. He compared them to a marriage coming apart. He saw how each man took advantage of the other's slightest fault, and then exploited it beyond the normal bounds of sanity.

Theirs was a life-or-death struggle between two rivals who could not, or would not, let go of each other. It was a struggle that not only involved millions of dollars but also the livelihood of thousands of people, many of them the principals' friends, though few people, if any, could claim Nathan Rubin as a friend.

If Solomon Lepidus was indeed a Great Man, David thought, Nathan Rubin was at least a strong runner-up. He had started with nothing and was reputed to be the richest Jew in America. His son Charley ran his empire, but it was Nathan who had forged it.

The empire included funeral parlors, modeling agencies, escort services, film companies and garment factories, plus assorted enterprises from diamonds and oil to loan sharking. His latest venture, begun in 1955, Nathan Rubin and Co., Inc., was a member of the New York Stock Exchange.

Rubin Escort Service was the one business Nathan Rubin still managed personally. It was an adjunct of the Rubin Modeling Agency, a natural outgrowth. It was the largest escort service in the United States.

Girls from all over the country were flown everywhere, for a night, a week, a party, a scene, a date. It was part of the Rubin underground. This was unwashed money, nontaxable, controlled entirely by Nathan Rubin.

Nathan Rubin was seventy-six. He was a bad loser. A man driven by greed. His great pleasure was to measure himself by the deals he could put across, by the profits he could strip from others, by the "trophies" he won. He was insatiable, ravenous, shrewd. He was Nathan Rubin.

"I didn't even worry when Solomon was up four thousand, David," Nathan Rubin was continuing. "Ya see, I knew it would turn around, and it did. He's a real sucker. A hell of a nice guy and good in business, but when it comes to gambling, he's like most guys, a grade-A number-one sucker."

"Are you really saying Solomon Lepidus is a . . . a patsy?" David asked with an edge in his voice.

"What do you know, kid—are you making a living?" Nathan Rubin snapped back.

David was beginning to feel uncomfortable. Keep cool, he told himself. He noticed a new ring on Nathan's pinky—it had a big cat's-eye set in it. There was a brand-new mole on the right side of Rubin's upper lip, which even his gray mustache couldn't hide. His forehead was chalky white.

"Mr. Rubin, why don't you and Solomon really have it out once and for all?" David suggested casually, with a laugh that sounded almost convincing even to his own ears. "It looks to me as though you two guys just keep toying with each other."

"Oh, we're just having fun. It doesn't mean anything." Rubin's right hand trembled as he lifted his cup.

This David was an odd fellow, Nathan Rubin thought; reminded him a bit of himself when he was young, except for one difference: David didn't have the killer instinct. He was a loser; a loser despite his energies, his talents; he was self-destructive; sentimental, the same thing; stayed on the fringes of the gambling world, never took the real plunge. Nathan Rubin couldn't figure it out. But it irked him that he even bothered to worry about the kid.

"I'll tell ya, David," he continued. "I've got an idea. I'm going to call Solomon at his office. If he's still there, maybe I can make him a proposition or two."

"I'll call him for you, Mr. Rubin, if you want."

"Do that, David, do that," Rubin agreed. "I'll clean myself up a little in the meanwhile."

As soon as David told Solomon Lepidus's secretary that Nathan Rubin wanted to come to Solomon's office, Solomon Lepidus was on the line. His voice was low-key and sober. "What do you think, Davy boy? How's the old man look?"

"Solomon, he's falling to pieces, he looks sick. You can take him," David said. "What do you want me to tell him, Solomon?"

"Tell him I'll play any game he wants. We'll talk odds when he gets here."

Transporting the fragile Nathan Rubin through rush-hour traffic to Solomon's downtown office proved surprisingly easy. The old fellow seemed to be reviving nicely at the prospect of a gambling session. Suddenly he was chipper, sputtering away about all the times he'd taken Solomon and sundry other "suckers." Yet when they reached Solomon's office, Nathan Rubin began trembling again. David felt reassured.

Behind his rosewood desk sat Nathan Rubin's old antagonist, Solomon Lepidus. His desk was cluttered with papers, contracts, memoranda, pens and pencils, and all the paraphernalia he surrounded himself with to conduct his business affairs. Besides the push-button phone apparatus handling two dozen extensions which squatted awkwardly amid the disarray, there were two other phones, one silver and one gold, each resting in open desk drawers with special safety locks on them to which only Solomon had the keys. Solomon himself presided in a well-worn high-backed maroon leather chair. The silver phone was applied to his ear.

Solomon Lepidus dominated this room, which was filled with the trophies and memorabilia of a lifetime. The emblems of success were all around him . . . pictures of the famous people he had known as well as pictures of those he loved. There were awards from civic groups, trophies from his cronies, and medallions from those who sought his favors. Here was a self-made tycoon with the air of a modest man. It was not easy to explain how Solomon accomplished this. It may have been that he was simply being himself.

David always found himself taking a deep breath when he entered

Solomon's office. It was a breath of delight mixed with awe and anticipation.

Solomon was busily engaged in a conversation on the silver phone. A variety of smiles darted over his happy face. His eyes danced. His earthy voice rippled through the room. It was a strong, secure voice which always gave a little bit more of itself than the occasion warranted. In that secure, mature voice there was also something peculiarly seductive.

Solomon put his hand over the receiver of the phone and greeted his visitors. "What's doing, Nathan boy? Make yourself comfortable. Be with you in a moment." Then he continued the telephone conversation. "Listen, Margot, I know it's important to you but I'd like you to think about finishing at Yale. You can always become a model. . . . What's your mother gonna say if I . . ." Solomon paused and listened.

"Is it really that important to you?" He paused again for a few seconds; then he said, "Hold on a moment, Margot." He considered the fidgeting Rubin, staring at him.

"Nathan, I want you to do me a favor. My daughter wants to become a model."

Nathan spurted out, "Whatever she wants. Let's get down to business."

"Don't you want to see one of her photographs first?"

"Don't have to, don't have to," Rubin grunted. "Stop wasting my time. I'll take care of it."

David gazed at the oil painting of Margot on the wall and said, "Mr. Rubin, she's almost as beautiful as Twiggy was. You'll see her on the cover of *Seventeen* in no time at all."

Nathan Rubin peered at the painting. He squinted and said more emphatically than before, "I'll take care of it, Solomon. You hear?"

Solomon roared into the phone, "Did you hear that, Margot? That was Nathan Rubin talking." He paused. "Yes, Nathan Rubin of Rubin Models. . . . Ha, ha. I love you too, hon. See you soon."

Solomon Lepidus stood up and stretched his hand across the rosewood desk. Trembling, Rubin shook it. Lepidus assumed the father's role.

"You know, Nathan, Margot's my daughter. I want you to make sure nothing happens to her. You know better than anyone what a dirty business modeling is. Things can happen."

Solomon paused and took a quick look at David. "Remember how that bastard Lou Cartel ruined Leslie's career. First he married her, then went around town telling everyone that their daughter wasn't his, and then he divorced her. The dirty bastard."

"Ahhhhh, come on, Solomon, stop bullshitting. It's water over the dam. Leslie wasn't ruined. David ended up marrying her, didn't he? And as for Lou Cartel, he ended up a gentleman."

Nathan Rubin turned to David. "You must be separated from Leslie just about a year now. Right, kid?" He didn't wait for David's answer. "And you don't have the money to support her or her child. Do you?" He peered at David, smiled to himself, and turned to Solomon.

"I told you Cartel's a gentleman, Solomon. He must be sending Leslie a chunk of dough. He's the one supportin' the kid."

Rubin turned back to David Lazar, whose face was red with anger. "Ain't I right, sonny?"

Before David could respond, Solomon interrupted.

"Listen, Nathan, stop picking on Davy." He rose from his chair, walked to Nathan and put his arm around him. "And just remember, Nathan, Margot's my daughter. You know what I mean, Nathan?"

Rubin shook free of Solomon and spoke sharply.

"Sure, sure, Solomon. I'll watch after her like she was my own grand-daughter." He paused. "I promise you, Solomon, nothin's gonna happen to the kid."

David Lazar could remember how his wife, Leslie, had almost been destroyed by Lou Cartel after Lou had made her "the Cartel Girl." Leslie had been the same age as Margot Lepidus at the time.

Perhaps it hadn't been Nathan Rubin's fault, but he certainly hadn't helped her after Cartel was through with her. Rubin would have consigned her to his "escort service" if David hadn't come along.

David didn't quite understand why Solomon would trust his daughter to Nathan. Perhaps some things were above and beyond their lifelong contest, perhaps "family" was safe. Perhaps Solomon had a bottom line hold on Nathan when it came to family matters.

"Well, let's get down to business," Rubin grunted.

Solomon nodded, returned to his desk, and eased into the high-backed leather chair. He grinned at Nathan Rubin, who still stood restlessly in front of the desk, his hands clenched in his pants pockets and his weight on the balls of his feet. Like a shaky old man, David thought, just barely holding on . . . or, he almost thought, like a cat with its claws still in.

"Sit down, Nathan boy," Solomon said. "Be comfortable. Particularly if we're gonna talk business."

Nathan's eyes narrowed, focused on Solomon, as he took hold of the chair next to David and pulled it to the other side of the desk. He didn't look any more comfortable sitting than standing. Solomon smiled at him and nodded.

"Okay," Solomon said. "Now here's the story. I've been bettin' with you for twenty years now, and losin' to you for twenty years now. . . ." He grinned. "All but on them Boone College basketball games, of course. . . ."

"Yeah, yeah," Nathan cackled. "I know that. Now tell me, Solomon, what's your new proposition?"

"Take it easy, Nathan boy," Solomon said. "I'm gettin' to it. Now I don't know how much I've lost to you"— Nathan screwed his eyes up and looked up at the ceiling as if it were a ledger sheet; Solomon quickly cut him off—"and I don't care. That's not what's important. I know you probably think I'm a sucker, but what you don't understand is that you never got to me. I got to you because you never got to me, even with all the money you've won."

"Yeah?" Nathan said. "So what am I doing here?"

"Because I want to try to get even with you, once and for all. And if I don't"—Solomon chuckled—"maybe that would get to me."

"I don't care about any of that," Nathan said, but David saw him lean forward in his chair, pick up a pen from the desk, then almost drop it a moment later as he tried to scratch down some figures.

Solomon looked over Nathan's bent head at David, smiled at him, and nodded. David smiled back, pleased that Solomon had acknowledged his part in the setup and confirmed his observation of Nathan's shaky state. "Lemme see, Solomon," Nathan said. "I figure that if we play for everything you lost to me in twenty years, we got to set the line to—"

"Don't give me the line, Nathan," Solomon interrupted again. "Just hear out the proposition. I'll play you every game we ever played except the casino stuff, and play it with you right now, every game for half an hour. . . ." They didn't even shake on it.

Solomon had David get out the cards and the dice, instructed his secretary to hold all calls, and swept his desk clean in one motion.

The session began quietly. They gambled with $100 bills as if they were circulars being handed out to passersby on Times Square. They started by playing cards, first blackjack, next gin rummy.

Nathan kept screeching out one proposition after the other.

He counted his money during each and every game. And after each victory his sly, peering face creased in a smile. He was crouching, twitching, glaring at Solomon, studying the odds, rattling the dice, clutching the currency, shuffling the decks, barking out bets.

Solomon Lepidus took it all, graciously asking a question now and then, observing, asking another question, offering his antagonist mineral water, catering to him, purposely making a little mistake now and then which Nathan Rubin would seize upon.

David Lazar had never seen Nathan Rubin so frenzied. He had been right; the man was clearly falling apart.

Solomon seemed to pity his old antagonist. He had lost hundreds of thousands of dollars to this man over the years, and it had never really mattered to him. He'd always recovered in other areas, he didn't fight for every penny. He knew how to turn his losses into eventual winnings, David felt. He sensed that Nathan Rubin was basically penny-ante in hysterical miserliness.

David felt that Solomon Lepidus had overcome the desperation of his childhood poverty and that Nathan Rubin hadn't. Lepidus was part of the world. Nathan Rubin was still fighting as if the whole world were at his throat.

Lepidus glanced over his shoulder at David and called, "Hey, Davy boy, stop daydreaming and get Nathan and me some Cokes. And, Davy," Solomon said affectionately, "get one for yourself. Here, take some singles."

Three hours later, Solomon and Nathan were still at it, Solomon acting as gruff and warm as ever, Nathan his usual surly self. They had been gambling without pause, and Nathan Rubin was ahead, but not by much.

David could tell that Nathan was annoyed with himself. Solomon, on the other hand, seemed to be feeling good. He was relaxed. Nathan had pounded away at him, with the dice, with the cards: Each game had been taut, tense, meaningful. Now there was a lull.

Solomon sat behind his desk, Nathan Rubin directly in front of him. David sat against the wall, the oil portrait of Solomon's daughter Margot hanging above his head. Rubin lit a cigarette and puffed nervously. Solomon remained calm.

David took a silver dollar out of his pocket and flipped it in the air a few times, catching it in his perspiring palm. Rubin glanced over at David flipping the coin. "Hey, Solomon, I got an idea."

He walked over to David, grabbed the silver dollar from his hand, and immediately started to pace off twelve feet from the wall with the portrait on it. He marked the polished spot he had paced off with the heel of his shoe. Then he walked back to the spot beneath the painting, made David get up, lifted the chair out of the way, and placed the silver dollar one inch from the wall, directly beneath Margot's portrait.

Nathan's idea was to pitch quarters to the silver dollar. They'd each have 250 tosses at the coin. For each quarter over eight that hit and stayed on the target, he'd give Solomon two-to-one odds on a $10,000 wager; anything under that number he wanted five to one.

Solomon looked at the portrait, apparently lost in thought. It appeared he wasn't going to go for the wager.

Nathan Rubin said, "I got to go to the toilet, Solomon. Think it over. I don't want you to say I cheated you."

When Rubin had left the room Solomon said, "Yes, Davy boy, he's trembly all right. I can't figure it out. Never seen him like that."

"I don't quite trust it," David said. "His mind's as sharp as ever."

"But his mind's gonna go too."

"Solomon," David said, a bit afraid of the intimacy of what he was about to say, "I wouldn't trust him with Margot either."

"Don't worry, Davy boy. Nathan's no fool, he's gonna do Margot and me a good turn and then make me a proposition someday and cash in on the favor. I'll tell Margot all about him and his operation. She catches on fast. I'll tell her just enough so she won't get hurt by him."

"There are other modeling agencies besides Nathan's," David said. "Maybe she won't get to be a star quite as fast, but with her looks, if that's what she really wants to do, she can make it on her own."

"Davy, making it on your own is fine if that's how you're brought up. I didn't bring Margot up to make it on her own. I made it on my own, but if I had the choice . . . Well, there are other ways too. And I can make it easier for her. Besides, all the other agencies are as bad as Nathan's. Here I've got control, and with the others I don't."

When Rubin returned Solomon said, "Is this what you mean, Nathan, that I only have to touch, or lean against, or fall upon the silver dollar with the quarters I toss eight times in two hundred and fifty throws to break even, and you're going to give me two to one each time I land on the target after I hit the first eight?"

"That's right, Solomon, and I toss after you."

Lepidus leaned to his right and opened the bottom drawer of his desk. He lifted a large brown envelope filled with paper money to the top. Carefully he counted out some bills, put a note into the envelope, and put it back into the drawer.

"I'll be back in a second," he said as he left the room and walked into the outer office. There he opened another desk drawer, pulled a petty-cash box from a secretary's desk, counted out thirteen rolls of quarters, replaced them with the bills, locked the cash box and desk drawer, and returned to his office.

Rubin was waiting at Solomon's desk. He divided the quarters into two equal piles and counted them again. Then, with a serious manner, he once more paced off the twelve feet and again marked the waxed floor with his heel.

Rubin walked back to where the silver dollar lay. He pressed his hand to the parquet floor, took a quarter out of his pocket, and slid the quarter slowly over the smooth waxed area.

"You want to wax the floor, Nathan, be my guest."

Rubin, peering up at Solomon, stood tall and cackled again. "You never know where you're going to find an edge, Solomon."

A challenging smile appeared on his face. The silver dollar sparkled in the fluorescent light, ready for the assault of the quarters.

"I've never seen this, Solomon." David laughed. "As a kid I used to pitch nickels and dimes, but this is—"

Solomon interrupted, "It's the same thing, Davy boy."

Rubin tapped his knuckles on Solomon's desk and chortled. "The only difference is the numbers, right, Solomon?"

Solomon smiled and replied in a raspy voice, "That's correct, Nathan."

Solomon Lepidus was first. He removed his jacket, rolled up his shirtsleeves, flexed his right arm. Holding the quarters loosely between his thumb and index finger and laughing, he tossed them at the silver dollar, chattering all the time he did so.

Nathan Rubin, like a hawk, counted each toss, and kept score by scratching a mark on a large yellow legal pad.

David Lazar clenched his teeth. He cringed with a surge of resentment as he thought: Why they? Why not I? Nathan Rubin is one of the wealthiest men in America. Solomon's one of the most powerful. . . . But why not David Lazar?

Sometimes we reach a crossroads. Things suddenly come together. Romantics can shed their softness; idealists can see life's crassness; dreamers are splashed with blood.

Lazar's eyes were riveted on the contenders. He could hear Rubin's snide crack: "What do you know, sonny? Are you making a living?" He could hear Solomon's advice: "First you make a living, Davy boy, then you live your life."

The soul of David Bernard Lazar hardened as he watched these two tired old men on their pitiful field of battle. In their way they were trying to meet the universal challenge of surviving.

Long enough he had floated in the aesthetic fairy-tale world, long enough he had paddled around among dreams of writing a great novel. He had lived the part of the gambler-loser long enough. He had been a second-rate civil servant long enough. He had been a failure as a husband; he had been dead broke long enough. Here he was, anonymous, powerless, while these men of power played at coin tossing.

Why they; why not I? I swear I'm going to change. God damn it, I'm going to make money. Yes, I'm going to be rich, I swear!

At the twenty-ninth toss, Solomon landed a quarter on top of the silver dollar. It quivered but stayed on top. He jumped into the air and grinned from ear to ear.

"That's one for me, Nathan boy!"

Nathan Rubin glared and muttered to himself.

At the sixty-fourth toss, Solomon again hit the silver target.

"That's two, Nathan boy!"

By the two hundredth toss, Solomon had succeeded six times. He was beaming; he considered himself a winner.

Nathan Rubin was silent. He had the legal pad in his dry hand, and as the next quarter caromed off the wall onto the silver dollar and spun off, he called out in a cold, piercing tone, "Forty-nine to go, Solomon, and you still need two to break even."

By the 224th toss, Solomon had for the eighth time succeeded in having a quarter touch the silver dollar. And after each hit was officially recorded on Nathan Rubin's pad, David's job was to take the quarters off the silver dollar and hold them.

David now held eight quarters in his perspiring palm, and Solomon still had twenty-six quarters to toss, and any one of them that leaned, touched, hit, or held onto the target would be worth $20,000.

Solomon turned to David and winked. "Twenty-six to go, Davy boy. . . . Whaddaya say? Want to be my partner?"

David just sat still, clutching the quarters, nervously waiting for Solomon to toss.

Solomon started tossing again. The first five coins didn't even come close. His concentration increased, and the coins edged closer to the target. On his 241st toss, a quarter skirted the silver, rolled over it, did an about-face, and rolled back and missed by an eyelash. Solomon grimaced. Nathan Rubin didn't even flinch. On Solomon's 246th flip he leaned a quarter on the silver dollar. He jumped into the air and roared.

"That's twenty big ones for me, Nathan boy!"

On the last toss he missed by a mile. He smiled, laughed, walked around the room, patted David's head, punched his arm, and slapped Nathan Rubin on the back.

Nathan Rubin removed the cat's-eye ring from the pinky finger of his left hand and placed it on Solomon's desk. He knocked with his knuckles on the desk, spit in his left palm, rubbed his hands together, and grabbed a fistful of coins. He placed one quarter firmly in his left hand and delicately rolled it against his thumb and index finger. Then he got ready for the throw. He inched closer to the target, crouched, and leaned forward. His hand was steady, his concentration enormous.

By his fiftieth toss, Nathan Rubin had successfully hit the target four times. Each time the quarter hit and rolled off he jumped in the air and cursed and howled. By his 158th toss he had already reached the break-even mark of eight. By his two hundredth toss he was ahead $40,000.

Solomon whined out in a thick, husky voice, "Nathan, you got to give me a chance to get even. Let's do this. You got fifty more throws. I say you can't hit the mark more than five times. For each time you hit the target over that number I'll give you forty thousand. Anything under the five I want twenty. Is it a deal?"

Nathan Rubin grabbed his legal pad and started calculating. He muttered to himself as he figured. At last he looked up. He counterpropositioned: "This is what I'll do, Solomon. Anything over the five I want forty big ones. Anything under, I'll give you ten." He hesitated. "And if I hit the target five times, I collect too, I want ten thousand. Ya see, I figure the odds this way . . ."

Solomon twitched, laughed, shook his head, and agreed.

The veins on Nathan Rubin's forehead bulged. His face flushed and grew tense; his body was taut.

His first toss hit the silver dollar, rolled off, and fell on its back against the wall. His second toss came within inches before falling on its face. On his third toss, he successfully hit the target but the quarter caromed off, fluttering within an inch of the silver dollar before flopping to its side. It was phenomenal, but by the thirty-eighth toss Nathan Rubin had reached the bull's-eye the necessary five times. This left him twelve tosses, and with each one, he could make himself $40,000.

Solomon Lepidus twitched and squinted and was sweating blood.

Six tosses later Nathan Rubin leaped into the air as his quarter rolled onto the silver dollar, rotated around it, fell on top of it, and finally came to rest smack on its belly.

Nathan Rubin screamed and screeched, "It's a winner, Solomon! That's forty big ones you owe me." Then he composed himself. On his next-to-last toss Nathan Rubin scored again and won another $40,000. Immediately he hurried to the desk and his yellow pad and totaled his winnings. In a toneless voice Nathan Rubin said, "Solomon, you owe me . . ."

Solomon winced.

When they were about to leave, Nathan Rubin noticed the quarters still scattered on the floor.

"Hey, Solomon, don't you think you should put them quarters away?"

Solomon shrugged his shoulders. "Ah, leave them, Nathan. One of the girls will find them in the morning and get a bonus for being early."

Nathan Rubin glared at Solomon as if he were crazy. He wheeled and rushed to the coins, stooped down, and started scooping them up and stuffing them into his pockets. After a while his pockets were bursting with coins, but Nathan Rubin was still scooping.

David was lying on a bed in his parents' apartment with his hands behind his head. A cold chill ran through him.

Was it all premeditated? Was he duped? Was he a "sucker"? Was Solomon . . . ? The hand shaking in the restaurant . . . Rubin had removed the cat's-eye from his *left* hand. It was his right hand that had shaken when he lifted his cup of coffee in the deli—*his right hand!*

David started to dial Solomon to tell him what he had recalled, but he put the phone down. An hour later he still couldn't sleep. Finally, he telephoned Solomon.

"What do you mean, Davy boy?"

"It was his right hand that shook, Solomon. His right hand!"

Solomon remained silent for a few moments before saying in a strained voice, "That s.o.b. is a genius. He's the best in the world at setting you up." He stopped. "Just remember," he ordered in a voice more composed, "how he took me, and thank your lucky stars how cheap the lesson was for you. Do you understand, David?"

"Yes."

"Good, then let's drop the subject."

2

DAVID BERNARD LAZAR'S thoughts descended into his world, the real world of his life as a failed husband, frustrated civil servant, gambler, loser. He fought with himself and he thought: Am I like most other people? Did I start to die twenty years ago? Earlier? Who am I? . . . Who am I?

David's mind continued to whirl, and, as always, he retreated to his notebook, which he then called his Handbook and Prayer Book. He wanted to take some notes, but, flipping through the pages, he came upon a self-assessment he had written a long time ago:

"I am six feet and one-half inch tall and I weigh one hundred and seventy-eight pounds. As a boy my hair bleached blond in the sun; later it became tawny and now it's straight brown. I have murky, brown bedroom eyes, a good-looking but not dangerously handsome face, softening muscles and a belly that has a hint of a pot, and I can tell that in a few more years I'm going to have a jowl under my chin.

"But that's not how I picture myself at all. I see myself as a wounded insect circling and buzzing in rage and indignation. I see myself filled with anomalies and contradictions, extremes of emotion, and overly reasonable thought. Crouching, twisting, straining, snarling. I'm gloomy and troubled and violent and tender too; ferocious and self-conscious. I'm beleaguered by an erratic brain that bubbles and spins and thunders and groans. I maintain a torturous balance between the extremes of feeling and intellectuality, and I'm a mystic too. I glorify virgins on pedestals, either by frenetic and ecstatic stirrings or in a quiet mood of reverie and tranquil acceptance of the miraculous cherry. But of course I'm a cynic too. I put down the virgin and the bitch and condemn the passivity of the triangular sex. I say the clit is dead, but in that I am an optimist. I say long live wanton fanciful liberation and I drink my fill of it but think it degraded. And I am querulous and mean-tempered and gloat a great deal over ephemeral accomplishments. At those times my twin brother usually reminds me that I am only grandiloquent and egocentric, a blowhard, and sometimes he goes a step further and calls me sentimental, and then I am good-natured and subdued for a while. And I am a coward one day and madly valiant the next. One day I move forward, the next I retreat. One day I love the whole universe and see the masses as children, and the next I curse everyone and see them as roaches. I hate all their aspirations and all their scurrying. Is that glory? I drift on and keep going to my welfare job in Harlem for what seems like my hundredth year; clock in, clock out, day by day, week by week, like any other civil servant, a mere social worker earning $315.81 every two weeks. Why? Why? I continue to exist on a gleaming, red-eyed float and dream of winners and glory and changing all my tomorrows in one fell swoop. And believe it or not, I love my wife, and want nothing more than to be an artist, and I don't only want golden coins. . . ."

He tossed the loose-leaf notebook aside in disgust and thought, "God damn it, I haven't changed one bit in thirteen months." And then he remembered the day his marriage began to go sour. It was May 1, 1969. . . .

He had stepped toward his wife, Leslie. She was wearing a flimsy blue bathrobe, hair loosely tossed over her shoulder. She looked beautiful, magnificent, to him. He reached out. She cringed. "Don't touch me, David. Leave me alone." He headed for the door. "And don't forget to take your silver dollar," she screamed after him as she flung it at his head. He ducked and it ricocheted off a coffee table and rolled under a chair.

Tiny Jennifer had heard the commotion and trotted into the room. She was sleepy-eyed, adorable in David's eyes. She spotted the silver dollar under the chair and crawled there to pick it up. "Here's your lucky silver dollar, David." She gazed up at him, smiling, the coin much too large for her small soft hand. He walked over to her, stooped, and kissed her on top of her head as he took the silver dollar out of her hand.

"Look at the silver dollar, Jennifer. Look closely. It's smiling," he said. Jennifer peered at it. "See, Jennifer, how it's smiling. It always smiles for me."

Jennifer looked up at him and pouted, adorably, he thought. "Oh, David," she said, "why are you always teasing me? I'm no baby anymore." He looked at her five-year-old face, grabbed her, lifted her off the floor, kissed her neck, and hugged her tightly. He carried her into her bedroom with his hand under her tush and carefully placed her back into the bed. "Remember, darling, the silver dollar will always smile for us."

He walked back into the living room. Leslie stood there, puffing on a cigarette. She removed it from her mouth and hissed, "Your gambling has ruined my life. Do you realize that, David? You've ruined my life."

The phone rang. Leslie answered it. "It's your 'friend,' that bookmaker Johnny."

David walked over, grabbed the phone, and yelled for Leslie to hang up the extension. In a bright voice he said, "Hi there, Johnny."

"Look, David," Johnny cut in, "Tafuri said he ain't gonna wait another week. You either come up with the money by Friday or—"

"You bastard," his wife broke in, "you swore to me last night you were through with gambling. You lousy liar. . . . You—"

"Get off the God damn phone, Leslie. God damn it, Leslie, hang up."

"Listen, Johnny, I'm going to see my friend Solomon Lepidus next week. He'll lend me the money."

"Look, Lazar, you don't owe it to me, I'm just the runner. It's Nino Tafuri, understand. It's Tafuri. And he don't want to wait."

David hung up and Leslie came into the room.

"David. I can't take this life anymore. You have to stop gambling and start being responsible." She kept talking and talking, telling him to stop dreaming, to stop writing, until he couldn't take it anymore.

"God damn it, Leslie, I'm not going to quit."

Leslie became hysterical. David tried to soothe her, took her to bed, and made love to her. They fell asleep, exhausted. But something wasn't there anymore.

David remembered that phone call.

"Hello, David, this is your mother. Leslie called your father and me last night. She upset us terribly. What's the matter, darling?"

"Nothing's the matter, it's just a money problem. You know how Leslie is, she makes everything a big deal."

"How much money do you need your father to lend you, David?"

"David, this is your father. I'm an Orthodox cantor. I have to sing in shul tonight. I can't afford to irritate my voice. Listen to me, David. I'll give you five hundred dollars. That's all I can afford. Why don't you ask your friend Solomon Lepidus to help you? You keep telling me what a big shot he is. How rich he is."

And he remembered his twin brother, in his apartment with him. Doug was on the phone with Solomon Lepidus: "I just don't know what to do, Solomon. You know I'd do anything for David, but I already gave him all the money I have. It's not enough. He's in trouble. Real trouble this time, Solomon. I just don't know what to do."

It was May 20, David remembered, and he had gone to see Solomon

Lepidus. Maxine, Lepidus's secretary, directed David into the mammoth office. There was one other person there. He was a tall man with a sliver of a mustache and a full head of curly gray hair. It was the fellow Solomon used as a baseball handicapper, Mustache McDuff. McDuff had spread a baseball schedule over Solomon's desk and was leaning over, pointing to certain games on the schedule.

"The games circled in red I want you to bet two thousand apiece on, Solomon. The games circled in blue, one thousand." The handicapper hesitated. "You know, Solomon, I feel kinda bad the way we've been going. This is got to be the worst start I ever had." He shook his head. "I know I'm not picking fifty percent. I don't understand it."

Solomon looked at McDuff and stared him down. Then he grinned and placed his arm around the handicapper's shoulder. "Are you crazy, McDuff? I'm having a lot of fun. That's all that matters. Now stop worrying about how you're doing. Just keep handicapping. Things will turn around. You'll get a hot streak going. Lepidus is backing you. You don't have to worry about a thing."

McDuff beamed. "You're great, Solomon. Do you know that, Solomon? You're really the greatest." Solomon smiled, finally looked up, and noticed David. He roared, "What's doing, Davy boy?"

David couldn't say a word. He started to stutter. Then he began saying crazy things about Leslie and his marriage and then somehow he was talking about the money he owed Nino Tafuri and all the other bookmakers he knew.

Solomon walked over to him and took a wad of bills out of his pocket. He counted out $4,200. Quietly he said, "Here you are, Davy. Give it to Tafuri's runner, Johnny. And don't worry, I spoke to Tafuri myself, and all of them other bookmakers of yours too. But let me tell you something"—he laughed—"for a small-time gambler you sure have plenty of bookmakers. Anyway, Davy, don't worry. . . . I straightened all of them out. No one's gonna touch you. No one."

Solomon Lepidus put his arm around David's shoulder. "Listen, Davy, you aren't to make another bet. Understand?" Solomon shoved David in the ribs with his fist. The phone rang. "Who is it, Maxine?"

"It's Nathan Rubin, Mr. Lepidus. He says he has a proposition for you."

"Tell him I'll call him back in fifteen minutes."

The phone rang again and again. Solomon roared, "Maxine, tell everyone I'm out."

Five minutes later Maxine had another call that couldn't wait.

"It's Leslie Lazar, Mr. Lepidus."

Solomon picked up the telephone. He spoke as convincingly as he could. He reminded Leslie that he'd known her since her father had first brought her up to his office when she was fifteen and she wanted to be a model. He reminded her how he had made her a cover girl through Nathan Rubin and one of the most successful models in New York.

Solomon tried even harder than David himself to convince her that David could be a different man. Then he ordered David on the phone. "Tell your wife that you've changed. That you're going to work for me. That you're never going to gamble again. That you're giving up gambling. That you're giving up all that bullshit about being a writer."

David walked over to Solomon's desk, picked up the phone, and quietly said, "Listen to me, Leslie. I love you. I don't want you to leave me. Believe that. But I'm not going to take any damn job that—"

She hung up in the middle of the sentence. Right in the middle.

A half hour later Solomon was saying, "You're crazy. First, you got to make a living. Then you can live your life. Now, listen to me. This is what you gotta do with Leslie. . . ."

Before David left Solomon Lepidus's office he felt like a new man. Solomon was the only person in the whole city he knew could make him feel like that. But when he got home . . .

"Get out of my life. You've ruined my life. . . . Get out. . . . Get out. . . . Get out. . . . And never come back. You gambler. . . . You loser. . . ."

David met his "best friend" Johnny for the last time late at night in front of the Winter Garden theater.

"Got the forty-two hundred dollars, Lazar? Tafuri is still waiting for it."

"I got it," David said, obviously upset. "You know as well as I do that I got the money from Solomon Lepidus."

"Just give me the cash and no more bullshit."

David took the envelope out of his jacket pocket. Johnny grabbed it, ripped it open, and put the wad of crisp new bills to his right ear and clicked them off. Then he counted.

"Yeah, that's right, Lazar. There's forty-two hundred here." Johnny turned to Lazar. "I'll be talking to you, Lazar."

"No, you won't. That's it for me, Johnny, I'm through."

Johnny looked over his shoulder and said, "You'll be back, Lazar. You'll be back."

And Johnny disappeared into the crowd. Even the slight limp, by which you could spot him blocks away on a clear street, became instantly indecipherable among the throbbing legs and feet of the late-night crowds.

And David started walking and kept on walking.

He walked into a sewer with blinking lights. He entered the Times Square area, a human cesspool. He walked by dance palaces where for the price of a ticket tired-legged bags pushed out saggy breasts to make a few dollars by holding up the longing and the aching, offering lukewarm heat. Here clean-shaven sailors, pallid bankers, palsied accountants, and shaking teens roamed the sidewalks.

David walked along Broadway, past the seedy movie houses. His mind awhirl, he turned west on Forty-second Street and north when he reached Eighth Avenue. He walked past porno dealers and peep shows, past the massage parlors, the nudie photo booths, and book and girlie-magazine stands, and the sundry other sellers of sex and drugs who populate the area.

He walked by crazies yelling at no one, at everyone—just walking with twisted bodies and twitching heads and blinking eyes and shouting to God and to all their yesterdays. He walked by pimps in gaudy uniforms of leather and suede and jewels and the blades of their trade. He walked by dopers and alkies and winos and stoop-shouldered men, hunchbacked women, syphilitic bums sleeping in hallways, and other rag-clothed sickies shaking and shivering and spilling over in the black corners of dank cellars. He walked by a crazy pissing on the street. He floated into one of those raunchy topless-bottomless pits and sat down within touching distance of the topless and bottomless ones and he ordered a drink and he watched them flaunt their nipples and their slits in front of him. He watched them smile at him. They would sit down on the stage within an eyelash of him, spread their legs wide, and play with themselves until their clits protruded like an infant pygmy's penis. He watched every dissolute low-bred stare, every glare of disdain. He watched these women with their magnificent contempt.

David went to a telephone booth and dialed Kim Colby. She was the highest-paid fashion model in Nathan Rubin's agency, an intimate friend of Nathan's, an acquaintance of David's.

"No, David, I can't see you tonight. Odette and I are busy."

After he finished his drink he drifted back onto Eighth Avenue with the miniskirted painted magdalens in high heels and teenaged streetwalkers in skin-tight pants and knee-high boots. He walked by men in drag, and the cocksuckers and the sodomites. He walked past the mounted police on the beat, doing nothing, seeing nothing, as pimps chased down their livelihood. He walked by two hookers who were trying to hustle some fuzzy-cheeked boys.

It was very late when he arrived at his parents' apartment. The movers had already carried his possessions out of his and Leslie's apartment back into his parents' home.

David was formulating a plan. A cause. A quest. He had resolved to show Leslie that he could make money, big money. He was filled with resolution, shedding every weakness, down to essentials, ready for the fray. David Bernard Lazar had decided to become a handicapper.

3

IT HAD BEEN thirteen months since David had learned to manage, to maneuver, by squeezing around boxes and climbing over furniture. He was living in his parents' apartment, in the room his mother still called "the twins' room," a room with three bleak walls and a fourth occupied by two large and unsightly windows overlooking an ugly fire escape and the grated and padlocked bedroom and kitchen windows of Mrs. Emma Polanski, octogenarian widow, who had lived alone for the last twenty years.

David's room contained the same two sturdy beds of his youth; the same beat-up dresser Doug and he had used, the same friendly mirror on top of it, which was now too low for his adult height; the same giant bookcase they shared with the very same black paint suffocating the wooden pores.

The bookcase was adorned by his mother's dusty set of the *Encyclopaedia Britannica* and by her even more dusty bric-a-brac junkshop treasures. The dust was to be expected, as the room had been used primarily for storage since Doug moved out in 1961, the year of Mantle and Maris. The walls were still bannered by the same New York Yankee World Championship pennants of 1947, 1949, 1950, and 1951. The windows still held fragments of the stick-on decals of all sixteen major league teams of those wonderful hero-worshipping years.

Also on the wall opposite the closets, just like yesterday—but it *was* yesterday here—were the 1951 color photographs of the twin rookies Willie Mays and Mickey Mantle, and another of the lordly Joseph Paul Di-Maggio. Though faded, yellowed, and browned, their photos stubbornly remained in their original places.

In this overcrowded storage room there were also two closets, both exuding camphor and stuffed with his mother's trinkets, booty derived from her compulsive raids on Klein's, Alexander's, Macy's, and Gimbels—the forgettables of her exasperating, smothering, obese existence.

Everything was crammed and packed, closeted and compressed to capacity by pushing and tugging and shifting, the products of a dozen obsessive shopping sprees a year.

To these bulging closets and to that billowing room was added David's marriage plunder. Two thousand books, cartoned and sealed. Now lifeless and dumb, piled to the brim, like coffins vaulting silently up from the bedroom floor in a jagged line, each column of boxes looking as if a book avalanche were inevitable. Each carton, taped and indexed by David's own hand, was now deposited on every bit of floor space. At the time he thought, For how many years? Or was it, perish the thought, forever?

He couldn't move in with his twin brother; that was one thing he couldn't do. Doug had a fabulous one-bedroom rent-controlled apartment with a terrace overlooking all of Central Park. Privacy is more important to a bachelor than anything else, and even though David and Doug had shared girls in their youth, David did not share Doug's fervent Saturday-night expeditions, his dream and chase of big-titted and bigger-assed Latin women picked up at the Corso, the Lorelei, the Caborojeno, and other more sordid retreats of the city which Doug frequented but told David little about.

Yes, Doug was still living the adolescent dream. David now and then reverted to it too, but a steady diet of tit and ass wouldn't fit into his plans; not even watching his brother excited him. For these pursuits, Doug needed a place of his own.

So all David had left was "the twins' room," and fitting, too, since what he was doing was starting life all over again.

He had opened but one book carton, the one with pens and pencils, papers and toiletries, a pocket radio and Sony TV and his Smith-Corona. These were the resources needed for his everyday survival as well as his sanity.

The other cartons would remain taped, until, and if, he survived this penal colony and regained his freedom. He was aware that his aspiration for freedom—that is, freedom from gambling debts—might take years. His clothes were squeezed into a wardrobe carton which rested in the space between the twin beds. The carton had been slashed at the top so that suits and jackets and coats could be removed, with another gaping wound at the bottom for shoes, socks, underwear, and shirts. That had been his only unpacking. And when he had unpacked, the realization of his separateness left-hooked into his belly and he had cried like a baby. In this cramped prisoner's universe he would work. And dream. . . .

He began studying all the major league rosters in the 1970 editions of the American League Red Book and the National League Green Book. He also started checking box scores and gathering information on all the current starting pitchers' performances and on anything else that he thought useful concerning the two-month-old baseball season.

One afternoon he ran over to Ed Kashman's pharmacy to rap with him about the season.

Ever since David was a little boy, "the Kash-Man," as he liked to call him, had been gambling on baseball, basketball, and football, and no bastard of a bookmaker had ever knocked him out of the box. David respected that, and he genuinely liked Ed. He was a man's man, with a gruff no-bull-shit approach to everything, and now, though he was almost sixty, you could still feel his life-loving vibrations whenever you were around him. He had a strong pleasant face, a double chin, broad shoulders, a barrel chest, and Popeye's muscular arms. He could easily have been mistaken for an ex-jock. During all the years David had lived in the neighborhood he had never missed one single day at the pharmacy.

As soon as David walked in he spotted "Kash-Man" behind the counter, waiting on a Puerto Rican woman. He looked up and winked at David and then hurried to fill the lady's prescription. David sat down across from the public pay phone, in the same beat-up chair that Ed used during the day when he would sun himself in front of the store. As soon as Kashman finished with the customer he walked over to David in that jaunty swagger of his that David had admired since he was nine. "Hiya, kid," he said with affection.

"Hiya, Kash-Man. You look as if you're in good enough shape to be playing third for the Yanks."

"I've been working out at the club. I still play a pretty fair game of handball, ya know. I beat the hell out of a guy yesterday."

"I'll bet he was older than you," David teased.

"He was a guy in his thirties and was just like you, a wise guy. He thought he would have an easy game, wanted to lay me two to one that he'd beat me. Boy, did I beat the pants off that wise guy."

In good humor, trying to sound perplexed, David said, "What the hell took you so long with that nickel-and-dime sale? I need you to catch me up on the baseball season. How have you been doing, Ed?"

Kashman's face changed expressions, and all of a sudden he was serious. "I've been getting buried. Them bookmakers have been knocking my brains out all season. I haven't collected once. Every Monday I got an envelope waiting for them that could choke a horse." He paused. "Did you hear the Yankee game today?"

David shook his head.

"The Tigers were ahead seven to four going into the last of the ninth, and with two out and nobody on, Murcer and White get on, and then that scumbag Gibbs hits one out. Can you believe that? Gibbs! . . . He can't hit his way out of my telephone booth and he pinch-hits a homer to tie it up."

"Well, go on, Kashman, you still haven't lost it."

"Don't get smart, kid," he shouted in an irritated voice. "Just listen. In the tenth Hamilton comes in and intentionally walks Kaline to load the bases, but then the son of a bitch strikes out Cash and Northrup. Geez, that guy is tough on left-handed batters. In the bottom of the eleventh some kid name of Kilkenny wild-pitches the winning run in from third with two out and a two-strike, no-ball count on Roy White. I tell you I've been running into bad luck all season. I'm jinxed or something. I'm taking a rest." He slumped into his chair and continued muttering to himself.

How many times had David heard Ed Kashman say that? That he was going to take a rest. That he was quitting. But the following week, or a month later at most, he was right back in action. David must have empathized too much with Kashman's story. It shook him up. He felt chills and his palms were sweaty. He was thinking of how many games he had lost just like that when Ed interrupted, "How have you been doing, kid?"

"I haven't done a thing all season. I haven't made a single bet since I separated from my wife. I'm still paying off debts that I accumulated during my marriage."

"Geez, kid, she seemed like a nice girl to me. What happened?"

"I guess I just picked too many losers, Ed. After a while she couldn't take it anymore."

"That's too bad, kid." His voice reflected genuine concern.

Flippantly David said, "I came in here for you to give me your professional opinion on how the season's been progressing. After all, Kash-Man, no one knows the game like you."

"Don't be a wise guy. You know I don't go for that kind of bull."

"Come on, Ed, how have Lolich and Palmer been pitching? Are Seaver and Koosman doing a good job? Give me a full report. I haven't watched a game in weeks."

"Didn't I tell you a thousand times that pitching don't mean a thing? Screw Connie Mack and his 'pitching is ninety percent of the game.' He never *bet* on a ball game. The only thing that matters is the price. It's the price that you make a living on, not the pitcher. I've seen more wise guys go busted betting pitchers than you can count. Guys have tapped out on all of them . . . Hubbell, Feller, Ruffing, Spahn, Ford . . . I don't give a damn who's pitching against me, just as long as they make the price wrong. You've got to take the price if it's out of line. It's the only chance you've got. I'll bet against Tom Seaver every time. The prices are ridiculous. You had to put up nine dollars to five to make a bet on Tom Terrific today. Nine to five! Geez, with that dog club he's with, he's lucky if he gets two runs to work with. The Cubs were a hell of a dog. Get all that hero worship out of your head, kid. There's no room in this racket for sentiment. When you put your money on the line you stop being a fan. The only way you're not going to get knocked out of the box during the season is by sticking to dogs. You get the faves," he said and sighed, "and you'll go busted." He stopped. "Remember, it don't matter who's pitching, Tom Seaver or Jim Palmer, when they give you a price that's out of line, take the short end every time."

Ed walked to the front of the store to get a pack of cigarettes for a customer. When he returned, he said, "You know, David, I've been around the game my whole life. I've seen more freakin' chalk players than you've got hair on your head. And every one of them guys that play the favorites think they know something. They know nothing. They all go down eventually. None of them can stand up to the prices they have to lay." He paused. "Take my advice, kid, stay out of trouble. Don't go asking for a pitcher's line. You want to bet a pitcher's line, bet against the pitchers."

David started to mention a system he had been thinking about.

"And stay away from all those bullshit systems you're always hearing about. None of them is worth a plugged nickel."

From the back of the store came a pathetic whimper.

It was Kashman's wife, Maggie. He had dedicated himself for the past ten years to ministering to her daily needs and had virtually kept her alive by his devotion.

Ed Kashman had yesterday's virtues. Marriage was for richer or poorer, for better or worse. As a youngster David had had a great deal of respect for the relationship of Ed and Maggie, but now it was one that he only pitied.

"I'll talk to you tomorrow, kid. I've got to take my old lady home."

"You should have her hospitalized, Ed. She looks like hell. Besides, she's going to drain you the way she's deteriorating. I've had a lot of clients with the same kind of problems. None of them ever got any better."

"Ah, she's not that bad, kid. I give her a few tranquilizers and she's quiet as a baby. Besides, I just wouldn't feel right about putting her in one of them places. You know how bad they are." He stopped and sighed. "I couldn't do that to her. You don't know how it was, kid. We had a lot of good years together. You know, until Maggie got sick she was a beautiful girl." His voice was wistful.

David started walking toward the door.

After a long pause Kashman yelled out, "Remember what I told you, kid, forget all that bull about pitchers and systems. The only thing that's important in this racket is getting the price, and remember, it's a mitzvah to beat a bookmaker. And give my regards to the cantor and to your mother, David." There was deep respect in his voice when he said "the cantor."

"Okay, Kash-Man, I'll see you tomorrow." As David walked out he could hear Maggie: "Eddie, where are you? I don't feel well, Eddie...."

When David arrived home he started going over baseball statistics. It was almost a daily routine. Hitting, pitching, fielding, the whole bit. By the time he finished he was bleary-eyed and dizzy. Around midnight, after soaking himself in a hot bath, he got into bed and watched Emma Polanski through his bedroom window for a while. She was preparing for bed. In a way, he was fascinated by her. He found a prim grace, a guileless dignity, a certain haunting harmony in her. Something that was magnificent and tranquil and beautiful.

When Emma retired David lay back with his arms behind his head, his fingers intertwined, and reflected on what it was that had turned him on to sports and why it was that he had such self-confidence in his knowledge of baseball and basketball, in his understanding of all their meanings and rhythms.

He first saw Mickey play when he was a brooding, blond rookie of nineteen. The first time David saw him at bat, Mick smashed a ground ball straight at the Philadelphia Athletics' shortstop, bespectacled Eddie Joost. It was unbelievable, but by the time Joost threw the ball to Ferris Fain, the first baseman, the Oklahoma Comet had already flown by. No one had ever spike-run those ninety feet faster. He was timed in 3.1.

Then David saw Mickey strike out with a lightning-fast perfect swing. The next time that Mick came up he crashed the ball. It moaned and soared and winged its way to the bleachers in right centerfield, and dropped one hundred feet beyond the stadium's 407-foot mark.

As for Willie, David saw him catch and dance and run and laugh and love a ball and glove and a pair of spikes the way no man had ever done before or since. He saw him spank his first off Warren Spahn in the old Polo Grounds, the ball clearing the left-field pavilion. Willie had been punished, chastised, humiliated, and collared by the crafty veteran pitchers that entire month. He had wanted to run away and hide, but with paternal Monte Irvin and wiley Leo Durocher as his mentors, Willie was resurrected. "The Amazing One" went on to smile and laugh and destroy the opposition.

Mickey and Willie, art and poetry, music and dance. Both gave David's adolescence its meaning. Both held David more powerfully captive than any president or general or rabbi or statesman or scholar ever could.

David's memory traveled back to the first day he attended Central Park High School, and how, in his first official class, he took a seat next to a skinny black boy wearing bifocals. They soon became inseparable. A month after he met Noah Weldon, Noah announced casually that he was going out for the basketball team. David did a double take and laughed. He had seen some of the guys on the Central Park team scrimmage during his gym class, and they looked like pros. Most of them were big and physical and street-tough. Noah was so much smaller and frailer than most of ther that David couldn't accept the fact that he was really going to try out. He just didn't look like a ballplayer, with his thick glasses and slight frame. Besides, he was too sensitive, too intelligent, and much too soft. He had grown up in a quiet rustic community in North Carolina. He didn't know the first thing about street gangs, shivs, Harlem, or any of a million and one things these ghetto-spawned youths absorbed by the time they were ten. For a week David tried to talk him out of making a fool of himself by trying out for the team. But Noah was never fazed. He remained quiet, determined, confident.

David remembered teasing him, calling him "Mars Man," because of his big head, and calling him by his middle name, Judy, which he hated.

David remembered telling him how he thought some of the guys on the school team could play in the pros, but not once in the weeks that followed did Noah ever volunteer a comment. And whenever David questioned him about the progress he was making in the tryouts and scrimmages, he would only shrug or mumble or change the subject.

David recalled the day Noah told him that he had made the squad, and how shocked David was and how thrilled. David remembered watching him warm up before the first game of the season of 1951 without having any idea that he was going to play. After all, David thought, Noah was only a sophomore and most of these guys were juniors and seniors, and on the varsity from the previous season. If he had been the seventeenth man, it would have been no surprise to David. In fact, the seventeenth man that year was Noah's friend Arty Garcia, and he went on to become a good college player. There was talent on that Central Park team.

Noah Weldon not only made the squad, he made the team. He was the playmaker, the backbone, the wheel, the very best. He wore number 67 and he played the "city game" as if he were born to it.

By his junior year Noah Weldon was selected for first team All-City. David asked him to get him the job of team manager, which he did, and David was able to see every scrimmage and every game. He kept all the stats and got close to most of the guys. More important, he got to know the inside of the game and learned its technicalities—the psychology, the sour grapes, the fears, the disciplines, the coaching strategies, the blackboard play, the special kind of courage it takes to be a basketball player.

And then in November of 1953, in Noah's first game during his senior year, tragedy struck in the ugly form of Big Jake Lupko, a hatchet man from Vocational High. Noah was in the air, soaring wildly and beautifully to the hoop, when Big Jake crucified him. Ligaments and cartilage in his right leg ripped. David saw it happen, and he was heartsick. For weeks he couldn't forget Noah's screaming and writhing on the gym floor. He had to have an operation on his leg, and afterward, when David visited him at the hospital, it was he who cheered David up.

Noah was able to play again, but he never was the same. The quickness and the flair and the transcendent talent were gone. One hundred and fifty basketball-hungry universities withdrew their scholarship offers, so he went to a small college in upstate New York, and he played some, but without inspiration.

As David continued to muse over what had turned him on to sports, his mind journeyed to a day when he himself was in college.

The date was January 9, 1956, and again he found nourishment and affirmation for his sports-loving feelings. This time the super-player was the most perfectly balanced force ever to step on a basketball court. Oscar Robertson. He had a rhythm and beauty and perfection to his game that never, but never, could be improved. The splendid O, from Cincinnati. The Big O made his New York debut at the old and intimate Madison Square. He went against a stubborn, tenacious Honey Russell-tutored Seton Hall five, a pirate team which had as one of its leaders Barry Epstein, a kinky-haired fellow from Brooklyn. Barry, the Pirate, against Beautiful O, the Bearcat.

Barry, a former star at Brooklyn's Lafayette High, had been honored during his senior year with All-City status by the Brooklyn section of the New York *Daily News*. Now a sophomore, he was ready to uphold the city's banner. He had been psyching himself for a month for this game, according to his coach's newspaper quotes, ever since he had learned that he would be the one to have to hold the young and highly touted Goliath of the Bearcat five. And so, in front of 16,500 empty seats, Epstein had his comeuppance. Of course, before the night was over every member of his South Orange five might also say, and with much truth, that they had been equally responsible for "holding" O to a Garden-shattering record of 56 points.

They were buzzing at halftime in the old Garden lobby, a lobby that has never been duplicated, and for city-born basketball freaks like David, never could be. It was intimate and friendly. Today's modern nuclear-age structures are not the same. The old Garden lobby gave them time to palaver and debate and argue with passion. "Who's better? . . . You don't know the game, man, he can't go to his left, ya dig. . . . He can't hit the boards. . . . He can't shoot."

He recalled going with his parents to Klein's Hillside in the Catskills, every summer from the time he was five until he graduated from high school. He recalled how even at that early age, he, not Doug, had pleaded with his parents to let him stay up once a week so that he could go watch the Borscht Belt basketball games. How excited he became, and how he loved those games. The games were played by professional stars like George Mikan, Dolph Schayes, and Bob Cousy, and others of like talent.

David remembered looking forward eagerly to every one of those summers in the mountains, hero-worshiping all those great players, seeing so many of those games.

David's thoughts wandered among the champions, the idols of his youth.

He was almost dozing off, ready to sleep, seeing the wondrous imagery of Oscar and Noah flash through his mind. And along with those flashes other flashes were ignited, other moments of greatness stirred within, moments even earlier in his childhood stirred by "the Yankee Clipper" and "Stan the Man" and "the Splendid Splinter," and in basketball by Bob Cousy, Tom Gola, and Elgin Baylor. And in boxing by Sugar Ray Robinson. They were all there in his memory.

And then David's mind traveled back to Klein's Hillside again, and he recalled the young Lazar twins, Doug and David, watching an old man running around the basketball court, sinking two-hand set shots, one after the other. The devil-may-care attitude of this man intrigued David. The man looked at least thirty years old and should have been worrying about making a living. Instead he seemed thirty years young, and the look on his face and the agility of his body projected a character that couldn't care less about anything in the world but that bouncing ball.

David smiled as he remembered Solomon Lepidus inviting him and Doug to shoot baskets with him. As David lay in bed, he realized that Solomon's frequent quote, "Sports is the common denominator among people," really proved true in his case. For that incident started a lifelong friendship between David and Solomon.

And then, finally, as always, David's mind wandered, and Leslie Kore was there.

"You don't know how to love anyone, David. You don't love me. You're in love with yourself. Can you understand I have needs too? I need someone to think about me. You're a monster."

"I'm not a monster, Leslie, I'm an artist, and I have my novel to worry about. It's the only thing that's holy. The rest is ugly, Leslie. Ugly!"

"So I'm the rest? I'm ugly? Don't you know you're killing me? I do love you. I do try. I'm not your enemy."

"Don't bother me, Leslie. I'm writing now. Get out of here."

And in the stained recesses of David's mind, he saw Leslie whimpering and racing into the bedroom and falling on the bed. . . .

"I hate my life. I hate this fighting."

And David saw Leslie continuing to sob, looking defenseless, like a child. And he felt his heart going out to her, and he heard himself saying, "I'm sorry, Leslie. Please don't cry. You know I can't stand it when you cry. Please, it's me. I'm half out of my mind. The book's almost finished, and inside my head, all I keep thinking about is, What happens then? What happens if it's rejected? What then?"

And David saw himself on the bed next to Leslie, placing his arms around her, and he heard her whispering, "Tell me you love me, David. Please, David, tell me you love me."

And he heard himself saying, "I love you, Leslie. I love you."

"Then hold me, David. Hold me." He held her and gave her a Librium and after her eyes closed he rushed back to his typewriter.

David kept hoping things would get better. He felt they really did love each other. But as soon as he began to gamble and lose, he stopped giving anything, and there was so little left to receive. He went into blind rages. He needed more. He needed to be an author, full-time, and he needed success. He needed to be somebody. Without success, he was wanton and cruel.

Ultimately, when he couldn't stand himself any longer, he'd lie down next to his wife, and he'd touch her, and put his arms around her, and whisper to her that he loved her. He said he was sorry for the things he had done. He'd try to stop himself from thinking.

But a day later . . .

"What are you thinking, David? Talk to me, David. What do you feel, David? I love you, David."

And by the next morning, or in a few days or at the most a few weeks, he'd again begin to fester and the cruelty would begin to ooze.

"Don't bother me, Leslie. . . . Get out of here. . . ."

She talked gently: "Hold me, David."

She shrieked: "You don't love me." He cringed. He thrashed her with verbal abuse, with screaming, scowling, and lying. She pleaded. He weakened and quivered whenever he saw her lying there in such condition. He recognized then that he had gone too far.

Then and only then would he lose his anger and love her a little.

David recalled another time after Leslie and he had separated.

"Leslie, can I spend the weekend with you? Can I? Please!"

"I made other plans, David, I'm sorry."

"How could you?"

"I didn't want to."

"Why did you, if you didn't want to?"

"You know why."

"Why?"

"I'm not involved with anyone, you don't have to worry about that."

"Why, then?"

"I was afraid you'd pressure me. I need to relax, David, and to do that I have to stay away from you. I'll tell you what, David. Why don't you come over on Sunday?"

"There's a game, Les. . . ."

"Please come over, David. We can spend the entire day together. Jennifer will be with my mother. Please."

When David arrived, Leslie asked him to join her in the bedroom. The first thing he noticed was that the kitchen radio was blasting with the obliterating sounds of a hard-rock group. Years before, she had listened to Bach or to Horowitz playing Chopin. She used to take pride in her classical-record collection. Both David and Leslie loved to listen to Mendelssohn and Schubert.

"Leslie, shut off that noise."

"I like it, David."

"Are you serious?"

"Even the names are pretty. Cream, Vanilla Fudge. I adore Jimi Hendrix."

Before David was able to ask even one of the thousand questions he had saved, Leslie was undressing him. There was nothing wanton about the way she did it. It wasn't as if she were going to devour him. It was as if that was the only activity scheduled for the day. There wasn't any enthusiasm; it was a perfunctory ritual, programmed and mechanical.

She drew David over to the bed and leaned over and started kissing and licking his belly. Before he could put up even the slightest resistance, his penis was stiff and in her mouth. Leslie was fantastic at that. One hour later, after her thighs had stopped undulating against his, Leslie was still moaning. "Please don't rush, don't rush, David. David, you're fantastic."

She had been drinking, and the boozy smell and taste excited him again. Again their bodies collided and they slid and bumped and pushed their way to another climax. "I want you, I want you," Leslie breathed at him, and the smell again turned him on. "Make me suffer, don't rush. Please, David, don't rush."

To David, the experience was no more than an exhausting sexual encounter. It was not tender. There was no compassion or even desire, but rather a kind of cruelty. It was a torturous assembly-line ritual that lacked meaning and was completely impersonal.

And the next day:

"I know you love me, David. I know you've changed for the better. But I'm afraid that if I take you back you'll take me for granted again. You'll revert to how you were. You'll accuse me and judge me and make me feel miserable. I'm afraid to take the chance, David.

"Your brother has damaged us a great deal, David. You have to admit that. He always hated me. Everything's taken its toll . . . the gambling . . . the fighting . . . the lack of money. I worry about bills all the time. I don't care about anything, David, not even Jennifer. I thought with you out of the house I would feel less pressure, but it's worse. I don't know what to do. I'm scared to death. I'm not twenty anymore, David, and I have a five-year-old daughter. I have to live in the real world. I've made too many mistakes already. I wish I could just go away. If I didn't have Jennifer, I'd disappear. . . . Oh, how I'd like to just escape."

"Let's try, Leslie; all I ask is to be with you. Nothing else is important. Please, Leslie, I know I can make you love me again."

"Give me time, David. I'm still scared of you."

David continued to push her, but again he went too far, hit a raw spot, and set off a new tremor.

"Leave me alone. . . . Stop pressuring me. . . . You're a fool, David. Didn't you once tell me that only a bad gambler doesn't cut his losses? Take your loss. I know it hurts, but it's better than waiting for me. I'm afraid of you. Leave me alone."

Each of Leslie's mercurial changes—one minute violent, the next passive; one minute involved, the next detached; one minute heartening, the next hurting—affected David more deeply than the one before. Each time new hope awakened, and then was crushed. Each time he'd feel more exasperated and helpless. Each time he'd become more and more convinced that it was all over, that Leslie despised him and would never take him back. But at other times he was almost as sure that she had no other place to go, that he was her only anchor, and that because of her desperate need for security, a husband, she'd return. Unless she found someone better, she'd continue to keep him on a string, not out of maliciousness, but out of an instinct for survival. He began to resent being held on that string. It finally reached a point where all he heard in her voice was loathing, and all he sensed in her heart was guile.

RON NIVENS, stockbroker, was David's closest friend, one of the few people he confided in and depended upon for a helping hand. Nivens had patiently heard almost every detail and painfully witnessed almost every battle during David's years of marriage. He was intimately aware of David's gambling problem as well. Of all the men David had ever known, he thought Ron the most perceptive. Nivens understood fully that every moment of a marriage was pregnant with possibilities, that every manifestation—pain, anger, affection, boredom—could be reflected in the voice or by a shrug or a smile. He never failed to notice anything. Furthermore, Leslie adored him. During the last two years of the Lazar union he was the only friend David had whom Leslie enjoyed being with. And he was one of the few friends they still shared.

Ron admired David too. David's attempts at writing were "heroic" to him; his gambling an "existential experience"; his behavior with Leslie "romantic"; his social work in Harlem "humane." To Ron Nivens, David Lazar was an existential man, Broadway Dave, Mr. New York.

"Listen, Ron, I don't want to use a divorce as an ax over Leslie's head, but I do want to pin her down so that I know where I stand. Seriously, Ron, I'm a wreck. If she won't try, a divorce will be the next best thing. Please call her and tell her that both of us have suffered enough. That now we both have to try to understand each other and take care of each other. If she still refuses to try, there's no way to go but divorce."

"David, a divorce will cost you."

"Forget money, Ron. That's unimportant. . . . And, Ron, before you start talking about divorce, make sure Leslie doesn't want to try."

Ron Nivens called Leslie and scheduled a meeting. They'd all meet for dinner. David and Ron went over every detail. David drilled him on why Leslie didn't have to feel insecure about money: "A real man is never poor, Ron, he can only be broke."

David emphasized how frantic and overwrought Leslie had become, how she couldn't withstand any pressure. He prepared his defense in terms of what he anticipated Leslie's onslaught would be. While he was doing so, Ron also lectured him about his limited income and the necessity to give up his gambling. Ron needed to hear David say, "I haven't been gambling, Ron. I'm much too heavily in debt for that," before he'd tell Leslie in good conscience that David was willing to try.

David Lazar didn't smoke and he didn't drink. So while he waited for Leslie and Ron to arrive at the restaurant, he had nothing to do but sit authoritatively at his table for three and stare down the cynical waiter. He was there fifteen minutes before he heard Ron's familiar prep-school voice addressing the maître d'. He heard Leslie add a comment. Already she sounded combative.

David watched her as she and Ron approached his table. He watched the people nearby pause and study them, the haughty model, the modest broker a step behind her. For a moment, David felt proud of the attention she drew, then noticed the people turning back to their companions and smiling—what an incongruous couple—and for the first time he wondered if he and Leslie had appeared to be that incongruous, too.

She slid into the booth seat opposite him, and he caught her perfume. He remembered her tone with the maître d', and he prepared himself for the worst.

Ron explained the office crisis which had made him late in meeting Leslie.

Leslie then called the waiter and ordered a whiskey sour. David watched her carefully. After the waiter served her, she took a few sips of her drink and her face softened. Ron fell silent and turned toward her. Leslie looked at David for the first time and said, "I want you to know, David, I'm only here because Ron asked it of me as a personal favor. I had to use a baby-sitter to keep this appointment. Can you give me ten dollars for her? I really can't afford it."

"Don't worry about it," David said sourly.

"You don't have to become nasty right away, David," she said sharply. "I wouldn't have asked you if I didn't need it." She took another long sip of her drink.

David began to feel that all the elaborate preparations were going to waste. He looked across the table at this beautiful woman and felt she was a stranger, as if he were out of place. It was an unhappy feeling. Yet the strangest feeling was not that he suddenly felt as if he were a loser, but that, at the same time, she made him feel alive.

Ron laughed a little and said, "Well, I guess you both know why I asked to meet with you this evening." David and Leslie both stared at him. Ron looked at the tablecloth, abashed.

David thought, The buzzer's just rung, but we're off to a bad start.

Ron Nivens's knowledge of Leslie and his balance between their points of view was unique. It was almost as if he were androgynous. For the first hour, he squirmed in and out of trouble. He tried hard to understand and be fair to both of them. But nothing helped. There were moments of insight, instants of tenderness, but most of the time, once he managed to get both of them talking, there were only accusations.

"You say David has an artistic temperament, Ron, and David says it, and his damned brother says it, but none of you say he doesn't have any special talent—except for making my life miserable! He and Doug both defend themselves by developing philosophies to justify their actions." She stopped as a waiter came over and she pointed a finger at her empty cocktail glass. The waiter nodded and disappeared. Leslie added, "David would rather call himself an artist and destroy his life than compromise his so-called values for me. And as long as his brother's around to influence him—"

"Doug didn't influence me to marry you, Leslie," David said. "You know that. I chose to marry you, and I'm still choosing to try to work things out with you."

Leslie said nothing, but she did look at him, and David was encouraged to smile at her. He added gently, "But you have to admit you've tried to castrate me, Leslie, and as far as Doug's concerned, you've always been paranoid about him." Her eyes narrowed and she snapped her head away from him, pointing a finger.

"There he goes again, Ron! He's the one that's paranoid! Castrate him, my God!" The waiter came back with her drink, and she continued, "I know that's just Doug again. The man has a diseased mind. He's over thirty and he's never had a healthy relationship with a woman in his entire life. He's the one operating David's mind. He has him believing that sleeping with eighteen-year-olds is freedom and that I'm the one 'castrating him' and taking away his freedom."

"David cares for you, Leslie. Not the way you want him to care, but he cares," Ron commented.

"He cares for no one at all, Ron, except perhaps his brother." She took a sip of her drink. She looked at David through the corner of her eye, and then, quickly, returned to Ron. "What kind of love is it, anyway?" she said, softly. "I remember once I had to have a boil lanced. I couldn't lift my arm, I was in such pain. I begged David to take me to the doctor, but he refused. You know why?" She smiled bitterly. "You know why? He had a bet on a ball game, and it was more important for him to watch the game. I'll never forget it."

She lit a cigarette and stared into space. "All those ball games. I remember if anyone called during a game, he'd hang up on them or bark, 'She's not here,' and I'd be standing right there. He'd glare at me as if it were my fault my friends called. How do you think I felt?"

Before Ron could say a word, David reached across the table and took her hand. "What's the good of all this, Leslie? You know I apologized, you know you said you'd forgiven me." Leslie took her hand away to light another cigarette.

"I was afraid to bring my friends home, Ron, but you should have seen the people he allowed to come into the house. Did you ever see the scum he deals with, Ron? They're horrible people." She paused. "How many times has he sworn to me he'll stop gambling? How many times has he lied? I've lost all faith in him, Ron. I'm afraid to try."

"But Leslie, David's not gambling now."

"I know that, but who's to say he won't tomorrow?" Leslie passed a furtive glance in David's direction, and he glared at her. She flinched. "Do you know, if you weren't sitting here, Ron, I'd be afraid to talk like this."

David shrugged his shoulders as if to say, Leslie's crazy, Ron, see what I mean? That gesture refueled her.

"That gambling scum had him terrorized, Ron. They called in the middle of the night. He was always afraid to answer the doorbell. I had to lie all the time and say he was out."

David turned toward Ron. "I never allowed myself to get hooked to an office that was Mafia-connected, Ron. Those guys do break your legs. But believe me, Ron, I was never afraid of being hurt. That's only Leslie's paranoia at work. I needed some money to pay off a couple of bookies. Big deal."

Leslie countered, "You needed the money so they wouldn't stop your credit. So you could gamble again." Leslie was on the edge of hysteria. She glared at David. He could see the venom spilling over now.

Ron broke them out of the clinch. "But Leslie, that's all in the past. David's given me his word of honor that he'll never gamble again."

"His word of honor." Leslie snickered.

David intervened, "Come on, Leslie, let's stop all this. No one ever threatened me physically and no one ever stopped my action. Besides"—

David shrugged—"Ron's right. What's the difference? I've stopped gambling, haven't I?"

Before Leslie could answer, the waiter appeared and asked if everything was all right. Ron complimented the food. The tired-eyed waiter smiled and disappeared.

David took advantage of the time out to say his planned opening line: "As far as I'm concerned, the only thing I want to do is get our marital situation straightened out and get back to my writing. That's why we're all here, isn't it?"

"He means get back to where we were before, Ron." She shook her head. "Maybe you think our problems were only because of David's gambling, Ron, but that's only part of it. He just said he wants to get back to his writing! But you know he's not an artist. He's just clinging to childhood ambitions his mother instilled in him. And now," she said bitterly, "Doug reinforces them."

She called the waiter over and ordered another whiskey sour. She did so in such a way that it seemed as if she were born to give orders. "He refuses to grow up, Ron. To reconcile himself to his limitations. He's never been successful as a man or an artist."

"You have to have more faith in David, Leslie." Ron hesitated a moment. "Take Doug, for instance. Now, I admit they're extraordinarily close, but don't forget they've shared their entire lifetime together. All their dreams. And both of them have the same personality. They're both artistic." The word made Leslie wince.

"They're both sick, Ron."

"I admit Doug can be obnoxious, Leslie, but he's also an unusual person." Leslie snorted, and Ron raised his hand, said, "Let's be frank, Leslie. The way you're talking you sound as if you've made up your mind to divorce David."

"I didn't say that. I want to remain separated for now. You should understand, Ron. You know how David is. It's more important for him to buy books and gamble than for Jennifer to have shoes. What kind of man is that, Ron? No, wait, let me finish." She put out her cigarette and folded her hands in front of her. Her voice lowered. "I did have faith in David once, but I'm afraid now. I'm afraid." She paused and deliberately said, "But I never said I wanted a divorce."

Ron looked as if he didn't know what to say. David shook his head.

"You don't want a divorce," he repeated bitterly. "That's right. You just want to keep me on a string, don't you, Leslie?" Leslie shot one fierce look at him and turned to Ron, who'd raised his hand again. Too late.

Before Ron could say anything she shrieked, "Now *he* wants a divorce, is that it? Let him support me, then. What kind of alimony is he willing to pay?" She gulped her drink down, lit a cigarette, and said,

"David's living with his parents rent-free, he doesn't have one real expense, and he still doesn't send me anything. Is that fair?"

"Come on, Leslie," David interrupted. "Cartel is sending you enough child support for Jennifer to support the three of us."

She wouldn't look at him. The only feelings David had were contradictory. He fluctuated between feeling beaten and feeling hatred. She wouldn't look at him. "Ron," he said, "I'm going to leave. I can't take any more." Leslie did turn to him then, looked at him hard and with loathing.

"See how it is? He can't take the truth. He was never there when I needed him." She glared at David, and he at her, both of them smoldering. It was obvious at that moment how much they despised each other.

Leslie pointed a finger at her husband and screamed, "You're nothing but a cheap compulsive gambler. You're no man, you're scum."

David's reply was violent. It had been welling up inside him. He screamed, "I can't take any more of this." Ron turned pale and began to cringe and sink lower in his chair. Leslie, seething, continued to point her finger directly at David.

David continued howling. "Who the hell is she to put me down? I don't give a damn any longer. Screw this shit, I'm through." He reached into his pants pocket and pulled out a $10 bill and threw it at her. "Here's the ten dollars for your baby-sitter."

He turned to Ron. "Thanks for trying, Ron, but it just isn't worth it."

Leslie started screaming and calling David names. She picked up what was left of her drink and flung it at him. It splashed against the side of his jacket, and David wanted to punch her. Instead, he stood up and pushed her hard and she fell to the floor. Everybody was watching; the waiters didn't know what to do.

Ron, who was still slumped in his chair, now tried to get up, but somehow he got himself tangled in the tablecloth.

David walked out of the restaurant, and, as he did, the last thing he heard was Leslie screaming. "He's no man, Ron, he's scum. Scum." Ron, the foiled mediator, was still fumbling with the tablecloth.

5

TWELVE INDECISIVE MONTHS had passed since David Lazar had resolved to become a handicapper. Many complications had joined to prevent him from achieving that goal. But the basic plan, the battle plan, as it were, had remained unaltered. His determination was not one iota less. For once, he was not counting on any of his old friends for help.

His built-in hero worship, especially of professional athletes, had been abandoned. Hero worship was kid stuff. It had no place in the life of a professional gambler. As a gambler you watched for the edge, the flaw, as it were, of every margin on every price. Your feelings had to be squeezed dry. You had to come of age. Sports and money, that was the combination that made his business. It was a sober marriage. It could be a profitable one.

At night, he devoted himself utterly to his thoughts on gambling. There was no room now for Leslie or for Jennifer. He thought of players, of teams, of coaches. He brushed up on the lingo of the gambling world.

Then one restless night he hit on the keystone for his master plan. He would put together a gambler's handbook, a basic text, an operating manual. He would fill it with the wisdom of the gambling world, the kind of knowledge and know-how and guidelines that might lead him to the top of the mountain.

When he awoke he was firmly resolved. He was graduating to the one profession he felt qualified to enter: professional sports gambling. He knew what he had to do. He had to relearn his craft and gain compensation for all the undisciplined, obsessive-compulsive, Leslie-drained years of his life. His credo: Play only to win. He vowed to work as hard at gambling as his mentor Dostoevsky worked from October 5, 1886, when he started to write *The Gambler*, until he completed the novel on October 29 of the same year.

Dostoevsky worked in a frenzy because he had incurred gambling debts and was forced, for a small advance, to assign the rights of all his future works to cover debts.

Dostoevsky—that same beautiful soul who had the will to defy the rationalists with his frightening cry against reason: "To me two and two are five."

David had to make sense out of the chaos of gambling figures, odds and prices, and calculate with precision and predict with certainty at least some of the games that were put on the board for the nation's interest. By using his will, desire, fanaticism, his own methodology and approach, and by revamping his character, by cultivating and refining his ability, he would be able to make more sense out of stats and figures than any other bookmaking professional.

It seemed such a simple plan: to gear one's intelligence to spot the flaw, the error in the professional point spread and price line.

It was simple, and yet, to the best of his knowledge, it had never been done. If anyone *had* done it, or was currently doing it, it certainly was one hell of a well-kept secret. Maybe the closest was Champ Holden, the famous old-time college basketball handicapper, but the only thing he had ever announced to the public, as far as David remembered reading, was his famous dictum, "Never under any circumstance lay points on any college team that is playing away from home."

To the fellow who believed in generalities it made sense—in fact, as a rule of thumb it made sense—but what if you stop abstracting and generalizing, if you stop looking at everything in mass, and stop thinking of things in their aggregate relations? What if you start attending to detail, and start examining minutely the innumerable variables, the millions of combinations? What about the hundreds of games every season when teams are 1- and 2- and 3-point favorites and win by 10 and 15 and 20 or more while playing on the road? That, too, as well as everything else, had to be examined.

He was confident that he could do it if he allowed himself sufficient time to prepare. His four objectives were clear—*to make money, to beat the system, to show Leslie, to be a winner.*

In all of his years following sports, every once in a while a game stuck out for David like the proverbial sore thumb. Not that it was guaranteed to win, of course not, but it was wrongly priced, it was badly quoted. This was the miscalculation he wanted to magnify. If he had picked out a few winners every year, mainly in college basketball, then there must be many more he had overlooked, due to either ignorance, lack of concentration, lack of information, or his don't-give-a-damn attitude.

From now on he was going to build his life on the premise that he could locate these games the way a scientist finds bacteria under a microscope. He was building his premise not on any magical gift or feeling that he could pick winners at random, or by instinct, but rather on the singular fact that he had the ability to work and to train himself to find out everything he could about *every* game and *every* player and *every* roster and *every* situation and *every* factor that could possibly influence a game. Picking winners at random every day, or every other day, is impossible. Finding the flaws in the line, and eliminating those in his character—*that* was possible.

He would hone himself so that his character was bone; train himself so that his discipline was iron; steel himself so that his patience was unyielding. He would work and work to create a handbook that synthesized every system, every approach, every rule, every definition, every method. He would understand every flaw, every emotion, every statistic, every conceivable technique. And he began with what he knew best, baseball and basketball. Everything else he disregarded. He felt he knew as much about those two sports as any player, coach, manager, gambler; as any man alive. He stressed that this didn't mean that he could pick winners. He was no longer a fool, or a man deluded.

What it did mean was that he would try to evaluate and understand every ramification so that he would be able to create a perfect price or line. There wouldn't be a game played that he couldn't create a number for, and his numbers would be more accurate than the figures of the Vegas sharpies. He would know when and how and whom to bet. The rest would still be up to Lady Luck, and he would still have to hope that the lady wasn't a barracuda. He'd bet his soul that his gambling would never again be determined by anyone else's prices. He wouldn't be losing by giving in to a bookmaker's line. He wouldn't be playing with the sentiments and emotions of yesterday.

Yesterday . . .

Doug Lazar had been talking about gambling on college basketball when David interrupted. "Listen, Doug, this whole basketball point betting system. You know as well as I do. It's simple. The linemaker in Las Vegas makes a line. He sends it out across the country. The bookies pick it up. Quote it to us gamblers. One team is two, another three, another six or twelve, and so on. And then it's up to us gamblers to make a decision whether or not we think the favored team is that many points better than the opponent. If we think it is, we bet the favorite to win by more than the amount of points quoted. If we think it isn't, we bet the underdog to lose by less than the points quoted. Of course on a push—that means a tie, Doug—no one wins or loses on a push."

Moments later David was saying, "Of course some guys think there's an edge in power-rating games for themselves, but that's a waste of time. I save myself a lot of effort by just pickin' up the Gold Sheet on the newsstand. It's a handicapping sheet. It gives the power ratings for every college team in the country. Most of the time, though, I don't even check the sheet. You see, most of my bets are made because of my own personal feelings about a game. If I feel strongly about it, I'll bet it."

"What about the vigorish?" Doug said in a voice revealing his irritation. "It can eat you up."

"The eleven dollars you have to put up on every ten dollars you invest isn't going to kill you, Doug. All you have to do is pick fifty-three winners in a hundred games to overcome it. That doesn't sound very hard, does it?"

"Damn it, David. It just isn't that simple. Gambling is the toughest business in the world to make a profit in. And as for evaluating every team and making your own power ratings, I think it makes a lot of sense. I think you should only make a bet when you find a large discrepancy between your opinion and the bookmakers'. You mentioned that you've been betting as many as twenty-five or thirty games on a Saturday night, correct, David?"

"That's right, Doug," David barked. "Maybe more."

"That's crazy. I don't care how good an opinion you think you got. You wager on that many games and the vigorish has got to kill you. Besides, David, your opinion isn't that brilliant to begin with."

At this juncture Doug's girlfriend at that time, Esther Aroni, made eye contact with Doug and smiled, then lowered her voice till it became almost seductive in its friendliness. "Doug, I still don't understand what power ratings are. Will you explain it to me, please?"

Doug was flustered. "Well, Esther, they're arbitrary numerical weights determined by a formula that includes records, statistics, and whatever other factors the rater feels are necessary to rate the teams."

"Ya see, Esther," commented David, "that's just like my brother; he's making it sound like a damn textbook lesson. Believe me, all he means by it is that you gotta take everything into consideration including the kitchen sink. Correct, Doug?"

Doug muttered, "Just remember, David. I don't care how good an opinion you think you got. Gambling is still the toughest business in the world."

As David constructed his gambling philosophy he became even more aware of the dangers within his character. He knew he would have to control his emotions. He would have to learn to live within a framework that was safe and secure, a structure which couldn't explode in his face. He needed to spot every one of his weaknesses, understand all his flaws, evaluate all his strengths. Everything would be considered, every precaution taken.

He began jotting things down. He felt before his study could even begin, all his characteristics had to be labeled. They'd be guides for his work. For example, that he might be a born loser, and couldn't win, was scribbled down. He continued jotting. "Must eliminate anxiety: the *must* feeling; the unknown. That feeling that today is the only day, that there is no tomorrow. That horrible, horrible feeling of panic, of feeling rushed, of feeling as if you were jumping out of your skin while waiting for the phone to ring and the bookies to return your call. That feeling of being unable to get through before the game has started, before post time. That need to dial and dial and dial. All the time becoming more compulsive, more piqued, more irrational, more unable to prevent yourself from making the wrong choice, the irrational plunge."

He also contemplated the ecstasy, the feeling of winning, the happy moods, the opposite of ennui—the feeling that it's preordained, your destiny to win. Feelings leading to the keenest dangers. The times when your body and your brain feel electrified, when your involvement surpasses any experience you've ever known. It comes on the days when you watch a game; on those days when the game comes down to the last second, the last pitch; on those days when you win at the buzzer, in the last of the ninth. On those days you soar!

David began to list meticulously each of these thoughts in his loose-leaf handbook. He planned to take weeks, months if necessary, to create the guide.

Then he would prepare and wait for the right game and the right price and the right number and the perfect opportunity.

These were the things he mulled over and assimilated and began absorbing. Somewhere he wrote down: "The only time you can win money by gambling is when the money isn't sandwiched to dread. If you take a chance on a game (and it doesn't matter how perfectly the game figures on paper) with money that matters to you, that was derived from your sweat, your blood, for bills, debts, food, rent, other essentials, you definitely risk destruction." From the moment he wrote that into his book he reread it until he had it branded in his brain. He swore his bets would be based on precise evaluations, and after his first small-risk investments, every future investment would be with the same small-risk amount until he was in a position to play with the bookmaker's money or show a profit. Once he collected, or once he was behind or ahead, he would make it a rule to re-evaluate. His rule would be that when the money was profit, and still in the bookmaker's wallet, it could be "played with" so to speak, but once it left his bookie's pocket and was transferred to his hands, it was his. Procedure then would dictate for him to start all over again with a percentage of his own bankroll.

Artistic creation is the adventure chosen by the best in man, and so the artist takes no short cuts. But gambling is the adventure chosen by the worst in man, and so the gambler wants the sure thing.

Gambling is the art of the wounded and the haunted and the faithless. Its fascination lies in that terrible continuous wrenching tension between ascending and descending, the love of life and fear of the finite, unbearable aloneness and the indifferent universe, affirmation and negation.

The gambler as artist wants to climb to the peak of the highest mountain. He longs for the infinite, and so, as with the artist, with each daring step he might plunge to the abyss, and each of those treacherous steps is an adventure, a risk. In that risk, however, and only there, lies the freedom of the gambler's life, the meaning, the creation, the light, and though not always beautiful, that, too, is art.

For the first time in David's life he was convinced beyond a doubt that he had a chance for success. He had been frustrated by Leslie, frustrated by losing, frustrated by the arts, by his job, by the system, by middle-class poverty, by his lack of achievement, by his lack of fame, by his lack of talent. Now he felt he was entering an arena where he had a chance to be more than anonymous.

HOW DO YOU *define what a twin relationship is? It's consummate acceptance. The burden of living without boundaries and quietly understanding that whatever, wherever, however, whenever, your twin is there. It's belonging. It's trusting, loving, fighting, leaving, and returning. It's knowing your twin's mind all the time. Being linked by a larger force. It's sharing everything and questioning none of it. And questioning all of it. It's forever.*

David Lazar could hardly wait to visit his twin brother Doug to tell him of his gambling plans.

"David, for the past thirteen months you've been telling me the same thing. And each time you'd make some headway, you'd weaken, call Leslie, or the bitch would call you, and your head would get screwed up all over again. And don't you think I know what happened last month? Ron Nivens called. He told me the three of you had dinner. That you're still involved. You haven't changed at all in the past year. Damn it, David, you haven't even unpacked. Besides, even if you weren't still involved with Leslie, you'd never beat gambling. You're no different from all the other shmucks who go broke betting."

Doug's remarks hurt, but David didn't reply. This time he wanted to learn from rather than reject Doug's comments. This time he wanted to absorb everything—and record what was useful in his handbook. He felt that in the long run he could benefit from Doug's lecture. This time he listened.

"You'll have to pursue every bookmaker you've used with a fanatical commitment. You'll have to be an obsessive avenger." He looked at David and sighed with resignation. "Let's face it, David, it's just another fantasy of yours. You lack what it takes."

Doug paused. His eyes became alive with intensity, and when he spoke his voice shook with deep hatred. "Now if it were I and I wanted to gamble, those bastards wouldn't have a chance. I wouldn't borrow the money. You have to hate those animals and hate losing as much as I hate the fact that I can't write.

"Every time I sit down at the typewriter nothing comes out but a lot of junk. Sometimes the pages sound as if I were lecturing a philosophy class." He started to snicker as he said ruefully, "Someone sure did a hell of a job on me." Then with a tinge of envy: "At least when you write it's cathartic. At least you pour out what you feel. With me, I'm always bottled up."

Doug stopped talking and walked out on his apartment balcony. It overlooked Central Park and Fifth Avenue, and if your eyes swept left you could see the skyline of Central Park South. David followed Doug outside and said, "At least you admit I have a few strengths."

Doug shot right back, "But you still have a million weaknesses. Just look at your relationship with Leslie and your gambling. They both reveal the same thing—your weaknesses. To be a professional gambler you'll have to become exactly what you're not, a winner."

With mounting irritation, David said, "Look, Doug, I'm trying to tell you I'm going to dedicate myself completely."

"Just remember, David," Doug said, "every time you go to the telephone to bet you gotta make sure it's a perfect bet. If you don't control yourself every second you're dead." He paused and reflected. "That's a kind of sickness you'll have to have. You have to love money as much as you love Jennifer. You got to treat every dollar as if it were your own child. If you can't do that you don't have a chance."

David interjected, "This time it's going to be strictly business."

Doug continued pounding at him. "If you want to make it a business you're going to have to consider the larger aspects of why you're gambling. It's got to be more than because you're bleeding and have a need. As far as I'm concerned, all this talking is bullshit until you can prove to me, and more important, to yourself, that your gambling's no longer dictated by compulsion. Without doing that it's a waste of time to discuss it any further. The handbook you mentioned is a great idea, but do it, don't just talk about it. Otherwise you might as well join Gamblers Anonymous right now with all the other idiots who thought they could pick winners and get rich quick."

Doug calmed down, but David continued to talk about his ideas, and slowly Doug became convinced of David's sincerity.

"It's not such a stupid idea if you really are going to take gambling seriously," Doug said. "You certainly know sports. But remember, you gotta remind yourself every day what gambling did for you in the past. It served the same purpose as Leslie did," he added bitterly. "It turned you on. It was just another sick way to make you feel alive." He reflected a bit, then said, "You know the first thing you should drill into your head—that the stimulation you get from gambling never lasts longer than while the game is on, and that it poisons the best part of you for a lifetime. The second is that the difference between winning and losing, between success and failure, can be an inch. One lousy inch. Remember Cal Ramsey and Satch Sanders? What was the difference between their abilities? In college everyone thought Ramsey was the better pro prospect and a much better talent, but he was an inch or two shorter than Sanders, and they didn't want six-feet-four-inch forwards in those days, so he was cut, while Satch, because of that extra inch, went on, and eventually made himself into one of the best damn defensive forwards in the pro game."

"When Ramsey got cut it wasn't only those couple of inches, Doug. In those days every team in the NBA had a quota on black players. Who'd they keep instead of him? Some white guy who couldn't hold his jock."

"It doesn't matter if that's true or not, that's not my point," Doug continued. "All I meant is that there weren't any great differences in talent, and it's the same in everything. If you worked as hard at writing as you did at draining yourself by compulsively gambling, maybe you'd have been a pretty good writer by now. But you never had the guts to work at it. You were always sloppy, and you never took the time to go over your work. You never had the love and faith in yourself that was necessary. It's that extra commitment that I'm talking about. That's what it takes." He stopped.

"And drill this into your head too," he continued. *"The only validity in betting any single game is that there is no validity.* The only chance you've got is to build an approach that works for the long run."

Doug's phone rang. It was Solomon Lepidus. When Doug hung up he returned to the terrace and started telling David about a deal he was trying to put together with Lepidus that could make important money.

"I'm telling you, David, the only thing that could screw things up for me is if Solomon keeps losing with that creep McDuff. Do you have any idea how much cash he's lost following that guy? Damn, he'd be better off even with you touting him."

"Don't worry about Solomon," David said sarcastically. "Worry about everyone else."

For a while they both remained silent and just stared out into Central Park, watching children playing in the meadow and the cabs maneuvering through tunnels.

In spite of himself, David burst out, "You know, Doug, I'm the one who has to live with Mother and Dad. I'm the one who sees that damn oxygen tank at the side of her bed, and her holding in the pain and the fear and trying to act as if she's perfectly okay. I'm the one stuck up there in a room filled with cartons. I'm the one who's in debt up to my ears, not you."

"Stop all that whining," Doug snapped. "You put yourself in that situation, I didn't. That's just what I mean about you—you don't have the guts to face the fact that you screwed yourself up. The flaw is in you—not in your situation."

David calmed down when he realized Doug was making sense, and David asked him to get back to gambling, and when Doug returned to that discussion David was attentive. He consciously held back his insolence, his counters to Doug's excoriating remarks.

David tried not to interrupt—he wanted to hear everything. He wanted to nail every truth into his skull, again, and over again. Doug was as astute as anyone in his understanding of the problems of the gambler. He might not be a compulsive gambler himself, but he knew, as a twin knows, the problems David had. David even began to take notes as if he were attending a lecture class. Doug spoke slowly, and David was able to copy down everything. Some of the things he scribbled down he later put into his notebook.

"I'm confident I can do it, Doug. I've already started planning. I started to tell you, but you cut me off. I started outlining every piece of information I could possibly think of that might influence a game or a price or myself as a person. Before I'm through I'm going to know everything there is to know about baseball lines, and then I'm going to start studying basketball. And I'm going to know every bookmaking office in the city. Which ones take large bets. Which raise the price on you. Which change the points. The limits they allow. Everything. I'm going to know everything it takes to gain that extra inch. Everything."

Doug smiled noncommittally as he said, "You'll have to work on that handbook then as if you were writing *Moby Dick.*" He walked over to one of his bookcases and pulled Melville's book off the shelf. "Do you think Herman knocked that whale out in a year? I'll bet it took him almost his entire lifetime to get it straight. It might take you ten years before you begin to show a profit, but whatever it takes, don't ever give in to your compulsions. The only shot you have is to reconstruct your personality completely. Until you do that you can't touch a phone or think of making a bet. I can't say that too many times. You've got to remain a virgin and then, when you're ready, you've got to become a whore."

Doug and David had been talking for more than two hours. It was almost three in the afternoon when the doorbell rang. It was Morty Lefko, the Colonel, as they affectionately called him. He was the last of the great peddlers; he would buy and sell, in quantity, anything from cheap perfumes to expensive Audemar Piagets. He was also Doug's next-door

46 . . .

neighbor, their good friend, a sort of man-child who never moved, never grew, never changed. He was a caricature, a lovable relic. But that didn't diminish the Colonel's essential truth: "Boys! Anything a woman says above a whisper is offensive to a man's ear."

The Colonel strutted in with his melon face, inevitable cigar, hearty chuckle, and husky greeting. He had the ability to make you relax and laugh. "Women? They're killers, that's why they live five years longer on the average than a man. They don't do anything all day but complain. It fulfills them. It's their true nature. They're all murderers."

The Colonel could charm the hell out of you when he was speaking. But it wasn't his expertise in oratory that made him so genuine and so charming. It was even more than his cheerful manner. It was something innate. He was a genuine original. You immediately took a liking to him. He made everything he said almost believable. He had an incredible flair for bringing the most cliché-filled verbal fossil to life. "Boys! At best a woman is only a small part of a man's life." From anyone else it would have sounded as if the man was a simpleton, a numskull. Coming from the Colonel, it sounded as if he were a sage.

As soon as the Colonel entered, the room filled with warmth. He was attired in his early-afternoon uniform, an extra-large, all-white terry-cloth robe tied loosely around his middle; underneath the robe, baby-blue silk pajamas; around his throat, a dark navy-blue ascot; on his feet a pair of fur-lined Gucci slippers. He removed his cigar from his mouth and solemnly flicked the ashes into one of Doug's ashtrays, making certain all the while that Doug noticed his precision. David's brother had trained him to do that. Some of their biggest disagreements in the past had been over ashes the Colonel had let fall on Doug's Aztec rug. Many times Doug had barred him from the apartment for a day or two as punishment.

"I can only stay five minutes, boys. I've got a three-o'clock appointment at the office. I'm already late."

The Colonel had trained his lovely wife, Rebecca, to clock in at his office at 9:00 in the morning, but he himself considered it indecent to tend to business before 2:00 in the afternoon. He preferred to remain home and parade his 260 pounds of self-admired, ice-cream-and-cheesecake-filled nudity until noon. He also considered it uncivilized to answer his telephone before he was out of his bubble bath, and no one ever enjoyed more the simple pleasure of soaking in a steaming hot bubble bath. It was a ritual he performed without fail every morning. By the time the water had been emptied from the tub he looked like a beached whale.

The Colonel shook his head and steered his bulk to port, anchoring himself in Doug's most comfortable chair, "You guys are lucky. You're both bachelors. Marriage, it's death." He chomped on his cigar a few times before removing it from his mouth.

Trying to conceal a smirk, Doug said in a droll manner, "Come on,

Colonel, you know the truth—your wife wants that beautiful body of yours. And you haven't screwed her in months. With that little pecker of yours it's hard enough, but lately I've been hearing rumors that you can't even get it up. Is that the truth, Colonel?"

The Colonel quickly changed subjects. "By the way, Douglas, you made a terrible mistake the other day. Please don't ever discuss with Rebecca my business dealings with Isaac Pizer, or anyone else. You should know better than that. You can't tell a woman your business. They never understand."

"You're nuts, Colonel," Doug asserted. "Most of the women I know are sensitive and have talent besides." Doug stopped for a second to wink at David. "As for Leslie, all that she was good for was giving David an erection. And as you know, Colonel, that means nothing."

The Colonel chomped hard on his cigar. "Ahem . . . your brother doesn't understand anything about women, David. After all, the only thing he likes to do is lolly."

"What's wrong with lollying, Colonel? You like to eat it up also, don't you, Colonel?"

"Tits and asses aren't everything, Douglas."

"Are you crazy, Colonel?" Doug asked.

The Colonel switched his attention. "David, he doesn't understand what you had. Don't let him upset you. The fact that you always wanted to fuck her, that she could always get you hot, that's fantastic. How many women can do that for a man?" He shifted his legs and massive frame in his chair and set himself for Doug's retort. Doug got up, walked toward him, stared at him, turned, located the director's chair next to his desk and dragged it to where the Colonel was sitting, and sat down.

"You're crazy, Colonel. Leslie was nothing."

The Colonel blinked and in a shocked voice said, "You're out of your mind, Douglas. Leslie is gorgeous! What a female! A cat! I remember the first time I met her. The way she slithered around and purred. I wanted to throw her a little fuck myself."

The Colonel stuffed his cigar back into his mouth and in a more sober voice said, "You both know what I think of marriage, and as far as intimacy, there's no such thing with a woman. We all know that. But a pussy hair can pull a battleship, you know. Whoever doesn't admit that isn't much of a man." He hesitated. "You know, when my ex-wife Shirley walked out on me she left me in such a fog I couldn't screw another woman for years. I gave my whole business away for nothing. That Isaac Pizer, some friend. He bought everything I had for a nickel on the dollar."

The Colonel hesitated again and then said sourly, "I ran away and lived in Paris for three years. Pissed away everything I had at the casinos. When I finally returned to the States I was dead broke. I had to borrow ten thousand from Solomon Lepidus to start again." He nodded his head as he recalled the experience and then pensively said, "I admit I'm just a peddler, Doug. I grew up in the East Bronx and pushed fruit and vegetable carts as a boy. I'm not an educated man like you. I'm only a graduate of Morris Evening High School, and at that it took me six years. But I can understand what David's going through. How he's suffering. Women haven't any sensitivity at all, Douglas. They're monsters, not human beings."

And then, as if by electrical shock, the Colonel vaulted out of his chair and squealed, "Oh my God! What time is it, Douglas? I just remembered. I have a three-o'clock appointment."

Doug, in a mischievous voice, answered, "It's only three-forty-five, Colonel, you've got plenty of time. But if you want, I'll call Rebecca and tell her you flooded the bathroom or something."

David quipped, "Are you kidding, Doug? It's only a business appointment the Colonel's got, and business is for whores. Right, Colonel?"

"Absolutely. I only wish I was a scholar like you, Douglas, or as talented as you are, David. Two geniuses. . . . Both of you can do anything you want. Me—my whole life I had to waste time peddling for a living. What else was I ever prepared to do?"

The Colonel switched the subject to baseball and to those teams he was considering betting that day. David grabbed the *Post* off Doug's desk and flipped the pages until he reached the sports section. He found the probable pitchers, and Doug and the Colonel huddled around David.

Then Doug interjected that David was seriously thinking of going back into gambling. The Colonel gazed at David with a quizzical expression on his face, and David felt some pressure to explain himself.

"I'm going to do it right this time, Colonel. I'm going to take advantage of my knowledge. I'm going to pursue gambling as if I were Nathan Rubin. From now on I'm going to make it my business."

Immediately the Colonel became enthusiastic. "Fantastic, David. It's a great idea. I always said you could make important money gambling if you put your mind to it. This country has more gambling now than ever before. Just the other day the *Wall Street Journal* had an article on gambling on their front page. The right guy could make a killing. Do you have any idea how much is wagered on the Super Bowl and on the World Series? Billions! It's unbelievable!"

The Colonel offered to stake David to $1,000, and to talk to some friends of his to get him started. He suggested Isaac Pizer, a successful businessman in the jewelry trade, a fellow David was somewhat attracted to, and with whom he had had dinner more than once. He remembered how each time when it came to paying the bill, Pizer would take out a $100 bill and flaunt it in front of the waiter.

With great effort the Colonel got up from his chair and walked onto the balcony and gazed at the view. A few minutes later he and Doug and David started talking about Nathan Rubin—how the old man fought you for every dollar; how he cried like a baby for every dollar; how he might spend $200 on you for dinner and a night on the town, and then rob you of $1 in business the next day; how he had gone to Las Vegas with Solomon Lepidus a month before and won over $10,000 at the blackjack tables; how Solomon had lost the same amount shooting craps.

Doug interrupted the Colonel and said, "It's amazing how similar Solomon and Nathan Rubin are, isn't it, Colonel?" The Colonel reflected for a while before answering and then said, "I'm surprised at you, Douglas. Solomon's no Nathan Rubin. They might have similarities, but they're worlds apart. Solomon's a human being." He stopped, shook his head and said with heartfelt respect for Solomon, "Solomon's no Nathan Rubin."

David soon began to relate some of his own Nathan Rubin anecdotes to the Colonel and Doug.

"The other day I saw him with that lowlife Sidney Feld. I'll bet you didn't know this, Colonel, but Feld told me personally that Nathan Rubin owns more than a few of those topless bars on Broadway. Did you know that, Colonel?"

"No, I didn't. You know, David, that Sidney Feld is quite a character in his own right. I see him at my club sometimes. He drinks much too much now, but ten years ago, he was the best poker player in the country. No one could beat him. Nathan Rubin backed him and they took every card shark in the country. Now I understand he's broke and a runner for Fat Tony Giardello. Is that right, David?"

"I didn't know he was connected with any office, Colonel. I always thought he was booking my action himself."

"Maybe he is on his own," the Colonel muttered. "The guy who told me about him bullshits a lot."

"It could be true, though. I wouldn't put anything past Feld. He'd do anything for a buck." David remembered Feld's son, Arnie, with whom he had some dealings in the past. "And his son's even worse."

The Colonel again repeated he probably could get Isaac Pizer and some of his other cronies to stake David to a few bucks.

David answered the Colonel as honestly as he could. "I don't think so, Colonel. I wouldn't feel right. Besides, I don't want to be obligated to anyone, not even Solomon Lepidus, and you know how I feel about him."

"Suit yourself, David, but if you need any help just let me know. And don't listen to Doug. That Leslie of yours is fantastic."

"You're crazy, Colonel," Doug interrupted. "She's false."

The Colonel broke in. "Don't you remember your Schopenhauer, Douglas? He said the prime virtue of a woman was dissimulation."

Doug looked at the Colonel incredulously and said in a shocked voice, "You're right!"

"Of course I am," the Colonel said. "That's something I learned from you, Douglas."

Before leaving, the Colonel made one last request. He asked Doug to call his office and tell Rebecca that he was detained, but that he was on his way, and, if possible, to have his 3:00 appointment changed to 4:30.

With the Colonel's departure, Doug turned to David again. "You know, David, the Colonel throws a lot of sludge, but his idea isn't that far-fetched. If you had one good year and made a couple of thousand, say three or four, with his ability to promote he'd make it sound as if you were Jimmy the Greek. I bet he could get you staked by Nathan Rubin and Isaac Pizer and some of his other friends to four or five thousand."

They walked to the elevator and as they waited in silence David thought over all that Doug had said that afternoon. He realized that his brother's criticisms didn't distress him because for the first time in thirteen months he was totally able to accept that point of view. Of course, the hard part wasn't in agreeing. It was in carrying out what had been suggested. And David was sure that he could.

For the first time in thirteen months David Lazar was absolutely confident he could gamble successfully.

7

MAXINE, Solomon Lepidus's secretary, guarded his privacy and exercised discretionary authority over incoming calls and visitors just as a mother allows only certain strangers to pick up and cuddle her baby. She motioned Mustache Harry McDuff to enter Solomon's office.

"You can go in now, McDuff," she said. She did not say "Mustache McDuff." That would have been beneath her. She allowed Solomon forms of address of that kind, but only as a kind of indulgence.

Mustache McDuff had been waiting in the reception area for well over forty minutes. While he had been waiting he had watched dozens of people enter and leave the office, but his impatience had been tempered by apprehension and by his attempts to formulate a plan for how he was going to tell Solomon that he was about to stop handicapping for him and that he was going to start handicapping for Nathan Rubin.

Was he simply going to bow out? Claim that he was a loser who was doing his friend Solomon more harm than good? Would he admit to his face that he was going over to the enemy's side?

He weighed the pros and cons between deception and forthrightness and still hadn't decided what to do when Maxine gave him permission to enter Solomon's office.

McDuff had known Solomon since adolescence, been in his employ for the past five years, been carried by him even longer. But Solomon had had a thing going with Nathan Rubin for as long as he could remember, and it seemed to McDuff that he had become something of a pawn in that power struggle. Or was it an ego struggle? He didn't know what it was about, it didn't really make sense to him. As far as he was concerned, he would have handicapped for both men as long as neither of them minded. But whatever it was, it didn't really concern him. What did concern him, ultimately, was the opportunity. For years he had rejected the onslaught of Nathan Rubin's propositions to handicap for him, and for years he had explained to Nathan Rubin that he couldn't, that he was obligated to Solomon, chained to Solomon for as many reasons as a son is to his father.

Rubin had never let up. It was almost flattering, the way he kept making new and better propositions, sweetening the pot until it became nearly irresistible. And with each new proposition Nathan put to Mustache McDuff, McDuff's own financial situation had deteriorated. It was as if each of Rubin's overtures was perfectly timed. Each came right after McDuff had suffered some setback or other. First, it was losing Isaac Pizer as a client, a minimum loss of $8,000 per year. Then there was the year his wife had to enter the hospital and needed home care. Then, last month in fact, he had lost his shirt to Sidney Feld in a damn poker game. He still couldn't figure out how Feld had been able to read him so well. After all, they had never met before this particular game, and the game had been played on his own turf.

Now Nathan Rubin had made him a sterling proposition. McDuff would handicap baseball games for him. Nathan would put up all the money and McDuff would receive 15 percent of all winnings, if winnings there were, at the end of the season. Of course that included the World Series.

That was fine with McDuff. He'd always done well on the big games. And Nathan Rubin, like all bettors, would want to take a bigger-than-average shot on them. The one proviso Nathan Rubin had made was that McDuff would have to stop handicapping at once for all other customers, including Solomon Lepidus. What Nathan Rubin did not appear to know was that Solomon Lepidus was the only customer McDuff had left. All the others, and there had been half a dozen high rollers at one time, had pulled out in the past two years.

Mustache McDuff's handicapping had shown no profit in the past five years. Besides, there were other factors aside from greed that influenced McDuff's decision. The most important of these was his wife, Marsha. She had given him an ultimatum. She would leave him unless he started to make a decent living.

As Mustache McDuff entered Solomon Lepidus's office, he noticed David Lazar sitting unobtrusively in back, taking notes in a loose-leaf notebook. There was also a beautiful olive-skinned woman whom he thought he recognized as Esther Aroni, standing next to Solomon at his desk. But as soon as Esther caught sight of McDuff she left Solomon's side. She had never felt comfortable in McDuff's presence, nor had he in hers. Still, she gave him a brief smile as she walked over to David and whispered in his ear. David grinned at Esther and said something McDuff couldn't make out. It must have been amusing, because Esther broke out in a laugh.

Esther Aroni bent over and kissed David on the lips, a soft friendly kiss, stood straight, and waved to Solomon, indicating that she was leaving. Her body, her face, her loveliness were overwhelming. She walked to the door and David followed her and they kissed goodbye once again. Mustache McDuff envied David that kiss, but immediately felt better as he muttered under his breath, "She's got to be that Israeli bitch who ruined Doug Lazar, the kid's twin brother."

"Remember, Esther," David said, "if you call Leslie, don't mention what we talked about. Okay?"

Esther smiled and nodded. When Esther smiled, her eyes closed just a little bit. Her lips touched each other and then opened slightly. Her whole face became perfect.

McDuff watched David return to his chair. He had never liked Lazar. He reminded McDuff of the worst defects in himself. Lazar was a gambler, a dreamer, a loser; a man like himself who was always at the edge of bankruptcy, financially and maritally. The picture of his own wife flashed across McDuff's mind. He was as hooked on her as on gambling. She'd had herpes for as long as he could remember. The damn woman couldn't shake it. She Frenched him as deliciously as ever but he couldn't go down on her anymore; he lived under some misapprehension about the transmission of viruses. And he loved to eat a woman. Especially his own wife.

McDuff took out a pack of cigarettes and anxiously drew one, offered the pack to Lazar, and said, "That's the girl who destroyed your brother, isn't she?"

"How do you know that?" David shot back.

"Solomon's always talking about her. He told me she destroyed a friend of his. Knowing Doug, that could only be he."

Lepidus was talking into his phone.

"I'm telling you, Nathan, you should build an apartment building, instead of wasting such a fantastic location on a parking lot. You could get top luxury rents for a building in that location. . . . First thing I have to know is if the property is paid for or do you have a mortgage on it? . . . You have it free and clear. Good! Now, will you allow me to work with the property as your contribution to the project? I'll do the rest, and we'll be equal partners. . . . You don't have to put up one dollar, Nathan boy."

While Mustache McDuff chain-smoked, David Lazar flipped the pages of his loose-leaf book, making notations now and then and underlining certain passages.

McDuff continued to contemplate how he'd break the news to Solomon Lepidus. Yet the more he thought the more uptight he felt. He knew Solomon. He didn't love Solomon, as it seemed most men did. But he knew him. And this awareness made him believe that Solomon could be as tough and ruthless as Nathan Rubin. Perhaps worse.

"What's that, Nathan?" Lepidus screamed. "You must be crazy. Mustache McDuff ain't going to handicap for you. He's my handicapper. How many times do I have to tell you that, Nathan? He's mine."

McDuff nervously rubbed his mustache with the thumb and forefinger of his right hand. Whenever anything went wrong he rubbed it that way. A month ago, unbeknownst to him, in that damn poker game with Sidney Feld, it had cost him almost everything he owned. The gesture was an unbreakable habit, just as his wife's herpes was incurable.

"McDuff, I saw that move to your lip. What does it mean, McDuff?" Solomon Lepidus said in a well-controlled voice. Mustache McDuff froze.

"I'll call you back, Nathan," Solomon said curtly. "I got some business I got to attend to."

Solomon stared straight at McDuff. His eyes bored in on the target. David Lazar looked up from his loose-leaf book.

"I'm on the spot, Solomon. Rubin gave me a deal I can't turn down. You know how it is, Solomon. Business is business. Besides, my wife's insisting that—"

"Your wife! What the fuck do you mean, your wife? Do you realize who you're talking to?"

McDuff's hand gave a quick swipe to his mustache, and then another, and then another, so that it looked as if he were trying to scratch the pencil line off his face. He began to back away from Solomon Lepidus's desk until he was just a few feet away from the door. "I got no choice, Solomon. With you I'm down eighty-eight thou."

"*You're* down," Lepidus roared. "What the fuck, are you crazy, McDuff? It's my money you're losing."

"I know, Solomon. But I can't make anything until you get in the black. And you cut my bets to two dimes a game. And . . ."

Solomon stepped out from behind his desk, squinted at a scroll on the wall for a moment, a scroll which had printed on it in large script: TO EVERYONE'S BEST FRIEND: SOLOMON LEPIDUS.

"You know what, McDuff, maybe it's a good idea if you started betting five thousand a game for a while. What the hell, I'm having fun. And if you feel your luck's gonna change, I'll go along with you. After all, I never was a guy to hold anyone back. If you think you're gonna start winning."

Solomon Lepidus paused briefly. "On the other hand, McDuff, if you feel you want out, if you feel you'd rather go to work for Nathan Rubin . . . well, yes, in that case, McDuff, if the case comes down to that, I'm not going to stand in your way. After all, as you say, business is business."

Solomon shrugged and walked over to David Lazar and pulled the loose-leaf book from his lap. "See this, McDuff? David's taking notes all the time on handicapping. This is his—what do you call it, Davy boy?" Solomon flipped the pages until he reached the title page. "Handicapper's Handbook." Solomon smiled. "Someday David also wants to be a handicapper. Don't you, Davy boy?"

David Lazar looked up at Lepidus's benign face, and felt amused. "That's right, Solomon," he said. "And I'll tell you one thing for sure. If I had eighty-eight thou to play with, you wouldn't see me losing. And you wouldn't see me leaving."

Solomon gave Mustache McDuff a brief glare and then said, "You know, McDuff boy, maybe it's a good idea if you went to work for Nathan Rubin. It'll be a fresh start for you. Maybe you'll get lucky. Maybe." He smiled. "Come here now, McDuff. Let's shake hands and call it a day."

McDuff cautiously approached Solomon Lepidus. He didn't know exactly who was quitting whom. Solomon grabbed him by the shoulders as soon as he was within reach, pulled him toward himself, and gave him a bear hug. Then he pushed him away.

"Give my regards to Nathan Rubin, McDuff boy. In fact, I owe him some money. Would you mind doing me a favor and bringing it over to him?"

Solomon Lepidus reached into a desk drawer and pulled out an envelope. He ripped it open, looked inside, and then tossed the envelope over to David Lazar. "Count out ten thousand, Davy boy." Then he turned back to McDuff. "I really think you're doing the best thing for the family, McDuff." He paused, then said, "Come here, McDuff."

McDuff again approached Solomon. Solomon again reached out and grabbed him by the shoulders. He looked directly into the man's eyes. Pulled him toward him and gave him a tight hug. "God bless, McDuff, God bless."

David Lazar slowly counted the bills, all of them brand-new $100 Franklins. "It's ten thousand, Solomon," he announced. "I counted it twice."

Solomon Lepidus walked over to Lazar and grabbed the money.

"Thanks, Davy boy." Then he handed the bills to McDuff. "Take care, McDuff boy. Take care."

An instant later Solomon Lepidus reached for the phone and returned to business. "Pete, I'm glad I got you before you left the bank. . . . Pete, I want to build a twenty-seven-story building in the best location in New York. . . . I'm investing a million dollars in the form of land, and, Pete, it's got no encumbrances on it. All I need from you is a construction loan. . . . Well, this is a thirteen-million-dollar project, Pete, and I need up to twelve million at its height. When the building is finished, I'm sure I can get a takeout mortgage to relieve your loan."

As soon as Solomon finished his call, he said, "Let's get out of here, Davy boy." And minutes later they were walking uptown. Neither of them said very much at first, but after a few blocks David began, "I heard you on the telephone, Solomon. How come you're going into a real estate deal with Nathan Rubin?"

Solomon smiled. "As usual, Davy boy, Nathan thinks he's taking advantage of me. And in a sense, from his viewpoint, he is. You see, Davy, if I bring off this deal I'm putting him in a position to make millions of dollars on a one-million-dollar investment.

"However, looking at the situation through my eyes, it's a terrific opportunity for me. I have a shot at making the same amount as Nathan with no investment but my ingenuity."

Solomon poked David in the ribs and pointed across the avenue. "There's Betblood Willie, Davy boy. I haven't seen the son of a gun in months. He musta got lucky and won some parlays."

David asked, "How did Willie get to be called Betblood, Solomon?"

"When we were kids, Davy boy, Willie never worked. All he did was bet parlays all the time. Now in them times no one worked, so we didn't think of him as a bum. It was only after the Depression ended and we all got jobs that we realized Willie was a degenerate."

David persisted, "But Solomon, how did he get the name Betblood?"

"That's easy, Davy boy. Every time he goes broke and needs a couple of bucks for one of his sure-thing parlays he sells a pint of his blood."

At that very moment Betblood spotted them and rushed across the street, as haggard as ever. "Solomon, I haven't been able to get over to see you for two months. Do you mind paying me retroactively?"

Solomon frowned, smiled, reached into his trouser pocket and took out some money. He scrupulously counted out $71.25 and handed it to Betblood. "Here's your rent money to the penny, Willie boy." He paused. "And don't ask me for an extra two dollars whatever you do. You'll only blow it on a parlay."

Betblood grabbed the money, shrugged, and rushed away, disappearing around the corner.

Solomon once more reached into his trouser pocket. "Here's for the cab, Davy boy," and he handed David a $20 bill, and as he did so a chauffeured Lincoln Continental crawled to a stop alongside them. Solomon walked over to the car and as the uniformed driver opened the door for him he turned toward David and smiled. "That son of a gun Betblood. Some character, ain't he, Davy Boy?" With that he entered the car.

ALTHOUGH IT WAS an unusually hot June morning and although David was drugged with tiredness from his previous night's session, he had to get himself together to go to his desk at the welfare office and hit the field to check out a pending case.

After a ride to Harlem on the M-20, a ride that did little to assuage the tender state of his psyche, he walked through Mount Morris Park, one of the great junkie retreats of the city.

As David entered the welfare applicant's building he immediately noticed ripped-out mailboxes in front of the corridor, and then, as he walked inside, he saw a young black woman sitting on the steps in the back of the hallway. She had a glassy-eyed look and it was obvious that she was a junkie and high.

David stared at her. How different was he from her? He, too, had been out of control, both with Leslie and with gambling. He was always going against the odds with both. He looked at the woman and thought, There's nothing I can do to help her. It's the same thing up here in Harlem—here I'm against another set of odds in an arena where oppression is literal, where life is really a gamble, with all the odds against you, and addiction is one of the few ways out.

He continued staring at the woman as she nodded and smiled. Help her? He had to help himself. He had to get out of here. And then his mind wandered. . . . Could he ever be a successful gambler? In gambling you had to be inhuman. You had to be disciplined and lock your teeth and grind and grind. He'd been out of control, compulsive, on the brink, all his life. He wrecked himself as a gambler, just as that woman on the steps had wrecked herself as a human being. He took a deep breath and studied her. She was leaning against the stairway, caressing a splintered wooden step with her palm. On the step was garbage and next to the garbage a dog's stool.

The young woman started to rock herself and hum. She placed her arms around her body. Somehow her blouse unbuttoned and he could see her breasts bouncing unhappily within. He could see the brown coronas around pointy nipples. He gazed at her for a while and then he closed his eyes. "I got to get out of here."

The woman walked up to him and took his hand and motioned for him to join her on the stairs. He did. She started talking to him, but he wasn't concentrating on her words. She put her hand on his thigh. He tried to push her away, but she kept grabbing at him and telling him that she'd give him stuff and get him high.

"I'm not an addict," David responded. The woman seemed amused at what David said, smiled, leaned against him, and rested her head in his lap.

She started kissing his neck, whispering in his ear over and over, "Come with me, let's go to my place, I live right upstairs. I got some good shit, come with me." He felt that if he didn't control himself now he would never be able to.

The woman stood up and pulled him toward her. She placed her hands on his chest and slowly slid them down his body to his thighs, and then she started unzipping his fly.

On her face, David saw Leslie's want. He felt himself losing control. It was impossible for him to stop her. He felt overwhelmed and joined in. He pulled her down beside him on the stairs and forced her head down and pushed his penis inside her soft moist mouth. She started lifting herself up and down slowly, tightening her lips and the insides of her cheeks around his penis. She continued moving her mouth and tongue and lips from the base to the tip of his swollen joint, and he could feel the wetness and the suction and the warmth. He felt himself getting excited; he closed his eyes. He was aware of the footsteps before he opened his eyes. When he did look, he threw himself back against the stairs, seeing two black men, their faces shining and eager. Their eyes shone with hate. The woman hadn't heard them. She continued bobbing her head, her fingers clutching at his waist. He stared at the two men.

"Hey, baby, whatcha got there?"

The girl lifted her head in alarm, lips shining, twisting against his leg. One of the men grabbed her by the hair, turning her head back, and bashed her face with his knee. David leaped up, conscious of open wetness, embarrassed, weak, unable to think. The other man's burly shoulders tightened under a work shirt, and his face gleamed with delight.

The girl screamed. It was a choking sound. David dashed for the bright doorway, down the corridor. Again the girl screamed. One of the men grabbed at David's arm. He tore free. At the same time, the other one was kicking the girl in the stomach. She lay in a heap on the dusty floor. David fell to one knee. A new man peered into the dim hall, his face twisted with alarm.

"Get a cop," David yelled.

The man ran.

They were beating at the girl. She looked broken, a jumbled heap of rags. David was on his feet again, trying to zip up his fly, running. One of the blacks shouted at him and ran toward him.

David burst from the corridor doorway into the sunlight on the street. There was no sign of the man whom he'd asked to go for the law. He ran blindly, panting, frenzied inside, and then he was rushing down the subway stairs, a dark tunnel of dust and newspapers. A train waited at the bottom. David rushed in, then sat shivering. His mind was a blank. There was only fear.

When he got home David went directly to his room and locked the door. He was still shaking, and as he shook he repeated to himself over and over again, "I got to get out! I got to make it! I got to get out!"

The next morning was as sweltering as the previous one, and David broke out in a sweat walking through Harlem.

On East 105th Street David visited a client, Blanca Calcursi, and after discussing her strung-out son he left the tenement.

His next visit was with Madeline Rivera, a sixty-three-year-old crippled woman who had been raped and robbed. She had no money for food. He had $8 on him; he gave her $6. He stopped in front of a building on Third Avenue. Junkies were loitering in the halls; a wino was sleeping at the curb. An old woman with a wrinkled face was standing there. "Will you please help me across the street, young man? I'm afraid I'll fall. I'm dizzy from the heat."

"You shouldn't go out on a hot day like this," he said.

"But I like to go out," she said, and nodded her deeply wrinkled face to accent her conviction. She reminded him of his mother. "David, darling, the sun is shining. Go out and play." David moved on and passed a fire department, 4th Division, Engine 59, Ladder 43, and a moment later passed the Church of the Holy Agony.

David made his last visit for the day to Leroy Bannister, child abuser, at 1796 Third Avenue. With that assignment completed he rushed out of the stinking apartment and down the stool-stained stairs and hurried through green and red lights to catch the subway that would speed him out of Harlem, and as he did he thought to himself, I want to change the world by my writing. What a laugh. Not even the great writers did that. He remembered something his twin brother had said to him earlier in the week. "It is only after we kill all our passion that we can make it work for us."

On Friday afternoon, after browsing in a bookstore, David went for escape to a bar, where he spotted Sidney Feld sitting in a corner. Sidney Feld was an unattractive man. He had a small, untrustworthy face whose complexion shifted from chalk white to sanguine. He had weak, sneaky eyes, cheeks with patches of whiskers, hair covering somber hollows. Under his chin there was black-and-gray stubble. He had large agile hands, with long piano-shaped card-shuffling fingers—half-moons perfectly rounded, fingernails trimmed faultlessly. The clothes he wore were in the very best tradition of Miami Beach and Las Vegas, of the Fontainebleau and Caesars Palace. His voice and manner were at times surly, at other times dour.

"Hey, Sidney . . . over here."

"How you doing, Lazar?"

"Geez, Sidney, this is a coincidence. I've been going to give you a call. . . ." David told him that he was beginning a book on gambling and wanted to talk to Nathan Rubin. He had tried calling Rubin's office, but had not reached him for more than a week. Since Feld had always been so close to Rubin, he would appreciate it if Feld could arrange for an interview with the old man.

"That weasel! He'll offer you every propostion he can think of. They'll all sound like sure things, but he'll end up robbing you blind. Every proposition Nathan Rubin gives you will be double vig and a tease. I don't know what a college guy like you wants to fool around with a weasel like that for. You'll never get the best of Nathan Rubin, Lazar. He's made more green beating college guys than he has beating bookmakers. And if he doesn't beat you, if he loses, he'll cry like a baby and pull claims on you. And I'll tell you something else, Lazar—he don't lose very often. He gets leverage on everyone. He even hustles half a point on the line from Tony Giardello, and you know how tough Fat Tony is."

David interrupted Sidney and told him that he didn't want to make Nathan Rubin any betting propositions. Feld didn't believe David, or maybe he wasn't really listening. He went right on talking. It took David a while to focus on the fact that Sidney's mind only worked on that one track, but as soon as he did, his patience improved.

"Sidney, I know all about Nathan Rubin. I've been around him long enough. Look, Sid, the only thing I want to do is talk to him. I'm doing a book on gambling, and I selected Nathan Rubin because he's from another era, an era of real gamblers. And besides, Solomon Lepidus said it would be a good idea for me to call him."

"Solomon Lepidus told you to call him?"

David lied and said he had.

"Why didn't you say so?" Sidney paused and thought for a few seconds. "Look, Lazar, when I talk to Nathan I'll tell him Lepidus asked it as a personal favor, and I'll tell him how tight you are with Lepidus. How'd you ever get so close with a man like that, anyway?"

Abruptly David said, "Nathan knows I know Solomon. Anyway, why should that make a difference?"

"Well, you gotta understand Nathan Rubin, David. For the longest time now, he's been looking to take Lepidus. It's not that he hasn't beat him, 'cause he has on ninety percent of the propositions he's made. But that damn Boone College, the one he's the benefactor of. It's his Achilles heel. Every basketball season he wagers Solomon on them man to man. And for the last nine years he's lost every bet. He's steaming. He's looking for a way to get even with Lepidus. Now maybe he'll figure he can use you to scheme up a proposition to beat him with. I'm sure he'll get together with you now, Lazar, but just remember, he's a weasel!"

"Can you get me to him this week?"

"I don't know. For the past two weeks he's been in Houston with one of them oil barons on some real estate deal. From there I think he's gonna helicopter over to Boone. He mentioned something about arranging a job for some old friend of his that's moving to Boone." He paused. "But I think he's due in the city by Tuesday. He's also got a thousand deals going for him right here. Now remember, Lazar, when you're with him, be careful, or else he'll rob you blind. He did it to me. No one knows this, but I owed that weasel a lot of money about ten years ago. There was no way I could pay him back, and when he started screaming for his money like a maniac I had to give him my house to clear up the debt."

"How the hell can you remain friendly with a man like that?"

"That's the way Nathan Rubin is," Feld said, his tone revealing just the slightest tinge of anger. "He just hasn't any soul when it comes to money. He's still a friend of mine, though. It was my mistake and it cost me. Now, take this number down. It's his home number in Palm Beach. It's unlisted, so don't lose it. And here's Sandy Rocca's number. Write it down too. Most of the time Rubin stays at Sandy's apartment when he's in New York. Now remember, Lazar, let me talk to him first, and don't forget what we made up about Lepidus. A little larceny don't hurt. Besides, Lepidus will back you up if necessary, won't he?"

"That's no problem, Sidney."

"Good. And remember, Lazar, if you want to start betting again, give me a call. Now how about buying me a drink? All this talking's made me thirsty."

Minutes later David dialed Solomon Lepidus's private number. Solomon spoke in a friendly but harsh voice.

"Hold on a second, Davy boy, I'm on a long-distance call. . . . Hello,

Nathan, Pete Henry, my account exec, consented to give us the bridge loan at ten percent interest. We're putting up the property and the bank's putting up the money to start our construction. Oh, Nathan, I guess I don't have to tell you, you can take the interest payments off of your income tax. Do I, Nathan boy? . . . What am I gonna do now? I'm gonna hire Kirkman and Watson to monitor the building. They're the finest experts in the real estate field, Nathan boy. . . . Of course they'll do it. The rent roll is gonna come to over three million a year. Besides, Jerome Vogel is chairman of the board. He's a personal friend of mine. I'll keep you posted, Nathan boy. Take it easy. . . .

"What's doing, Davy boy?"

"I've scheduled a meeting with Nathan Rubin."

"What for?"

"I want to learn as much about gambling as I can from him."

"You'll never get a square deal from that snake. He'll throw you a curve on everything, and he'll want to protect himself on five sides. You better be very careful, Davy boy."

"But I only want to learn about gambling from him."

"That's okay for now, but later on you'll probably get involved in a deal with him, so just make sure you're careful."

"Don't worry, Solomon. I'll be careful."

"What else?"

"Well, last Friday, up in Harlem, I had an emergency—"

Solomon interrupted, "Anything new with Doug?"

"Nothing, really. Everything's about the same."

"Tell him to give me a call. There's something I got to talk to him about."

They continued to talk for a while, and Solomon focused in on anything and everything to do with business, David's business, the Colonel's business, everyone's business. He kept abreast, always asked questions, always pumped for more and more. It wasn't long, though, before two long-distance calls cut the conversation short.

He told David to take it easy. That was as much his trademark as "What's doing?" and "You don't understand, Davy boy," which he must have said a million times since David had first met him. And what was it David didn't understand? "Solomon, just because you made millions doesn't mean you aren't a bankrupt."

"Like how?"

"Like not knowing your children, not spending time with your wife, not having a free minute to relax, like having to keep busy, and rationalize and justify and manipulate, like—"

"You don't understand, Davy boy, you don't understand!"

Before Solomon hung up David thanked him for the tickets he had given Doug and him for the heavyweight championship fight between

Jimmy Ellis and Joe Frazier at Madison Square Garden. They had been ringside, $75 each. They had been on Solomon. That, too, was Solomon.

Nathan Rubin peered at Mustache McDuff. "Ya see, McDuff, you've been picking nothing but losers. I'm behind over ten dimes, and I just started with you. You know how it is. I just don't like to lose. And we're not even into the middle of the baseball season. And that's your specialty. Football was never your strong point."

He paused and tapped his cat's-eye on the Ming vase on the coffee table. "I'll tell you what I'll do. If you want to put up the ten thou you cost me, I'll make a new deal with you. What do you say, McDuff?"

"I don't have ten thou, Mr. Rubin. I left Solomon because of you. You promised that you'd go with me all season. I lost a lot more for Solomon and he didn't drop me. Anyway, we've just started, Mr. Rubin, we've been betting the pitchers, the best pitchers and you get the best lines, so there's nothing wrong with betting the best pitchers if you get the best line, the best pitchers are gonna be in shape come late July or August. You just got to stick with me a bit longer, I'll turn it around." And he rambled on and on, frantically stroking his mustache, until he was almost on his knees, begging.

"Ya see, McDuff, it just ain't possible. You've cost me ten thou. Things change. I just don't see where I can make it back with you. Your handicapping ain't all it should be. I checked you out pretty thorough with some friends of mine. You haven't had a winning season in five years. You cost Lepidus a fortune, but that Lepidus is a jerk, the biggest jerk in the world when it comes to gambling. Lots of businessmen are suckers. Lepidus is just a bigger sucker than most."

Rubin's face turned dead sober. "He forgets that his right hand had to kill to get it in the first place. Well, Mustache, you got to kill with both hands. Yeah, otherwise they gonna kill you; right-handed killing is for men like Solomon Lepidus."

McDuff continued to plead, playing what he thought was his ace card, over and over. "I left Solomon Lepidus for you, Nathan. You were after me to handicap for you for years. I made an enemy of him for your sake. Do you know what that means? Do you realize what you've done to me?"

Nathan made no attempt to control a snickering smile. "I just don't understand you, McDuff. You can't use that against me. That was your decision. The only thing I did was make you a proposition and you took me up on it. And you didn't have to."

It began to sink in that he, Mustache McDuff, had been taken, that he'd been a pawn in a ploy to get him away from Lepidus at any cost. At the cost of Mustache McDuff. Because it had been Lepidus's gain to lose him.

"I can't go back to Lepidus," McDuff said. "You know that, Nathan."

He stopped. "You're a son of a bitch. You play with people's lives, Nathan. People are just chips to you. That's worse than people being just numbers, Nathan. Nathan, you're the devil."

Nathan continued to snicker, but as he continued to listen to McDuff his snicker turned as close to a broad smile as his pinched face could manage. The phone rang, and someone picked it up.

"It's for you Nathan," Sandy Rocca called from another room of the spacious apartment. "It's Sidney Feld."

McDuff raised his thumb and forefinger to his upper lip. "You, a friend of Sidney Feld's? You . . ."

Nathan Rubin's grin grew even wider and he cackled, "Do I know him? What, are you crazy? He's been on my payroll for years. Sidney and I go back a long way." He paused. "Incidentally, McDuff, you should really do something about that habit of yours. Every time you touch your mustache like that it's gonna cost you. You know what I mean."

The bile in McDuff rose to the surface. He remembered the poker game. Now he knew why he had lost. His face contorted, and he lunged for Nathan Rubin. He grabbed him around the neck and started squeezing. The vase on the coffee table plunged to the floor. Sandy Rocca, hearing the crash, rushed into the room. He saw Rubin on the floor, Mustache McDuff on top of him. He quietly walked over, took a revolver out of his holster, and swung the butt, hitting McDuff perfectly on top of his skull. McDuff slumped over.

Nathan Rubin cackled, "The creep almost killed me. Get him out of here. And make sure you pass the word around, Rocca. I don't want him to be able to get down anywhere. I don't want him to handicap for anyone. I don't want him to make a living. You understand, Rocca. Pass the word around."

As soon as Mustache McDuff had been removed from Rocca's apartment, Nathan Rubin reached for the telephone. But he put down the receiver when he noticed that he had nervously misdialed the same number several times. Once he'd calmed down he reached Josh Turner in Paducah, Kentucky.

"Hello, Josh. I've arranged for you to sell your farm. You're going to get a God damn good price, leave it to me. I've also arranged for that job clerking that we talked about. You're expected by the end of the month. When you get there, look up Sam Boone at the college, he'll help you find a place to stay. Now listen to me, Josh, and I don't want no back talk. Ya see, I'm wiring you some money through Western Union. It's just something to tide you over until I finish off the business with the farm. Now I got to go. I'll call you later. I'll be staying at Sandy Rocca's if you need me. Goodnight, ol' friend."

Sandy Rocca peered at Nathan Rubin. He didn't ask him who Josh Turner was. He didn't understand the bond between the two men. Nathan

Rubin had never discussed it with him and Rocca somehow knew that he should never ask.

Mustache McDuff was on the phone with Solomon Lepidus. He had been trying to get through to him for days, but with no success. Maxine kept intercepting the calls. Mr. Lepidus was out of town or otherwise engaged. But finally McDuff did get through.

"I don't know if you know what happened with Nathan Rubin, Solomon. Anyway, what I want to do is go back to being your handicapper."

Solomon Lepidus knew all the facts. He knew everything Nathan Rubin had accomplished. McDuff was washed up. He couldn't bet. He couldn't get outs. He couldn't pick winners. He couldn't pick losers. He couldn't get handicapper clients. Rubin had put out the word. No one that Solomon knew would buck Nathan Rubin. No one.

"You wanna come back, McDuff boy. Geez, according to my way of thinking, you've never been gone. I'd love to have you. We always had fun, didn't we? You're a hell of a handicapper, McDuff. Just remember that. I understand what happened. Business is business. But sometimes things don't work out." Solomon stopped as Maxine interrupted him. When he was back on the phone he said, "I got a long-distance call, McDuff. I can't talk now. Why don't you give Nathan Rubin a call later tonight, McDuff? Tell him I'm taking you back as my handicapper. Tell him I'm giving you another eighty-eight thou to play with." He lowered his voice until it was very friendly. "Will you do that for me, McDuff?"

Mustache McDuff, though he realized that something was not altogether kosher, that he probably was still a pawn in a game he did not entirely understand, loved Solomon Lepidus—at least for the moment.

"You're the greatest, Solomon. Do you know that you're the greatest? Thank you, Solomon. Thank you."

"I got to go now, McDuff. Take it easy."

After Mustache McDuff made his call to Nathan Rubin, he tried calling Solomon Lepidus for two weeks. But every time he called, Solomon was either out of town or otherwise engaged. Finally McDuff, with his wife bugging the life out of him, his financial position nonexistent, his ego destroyed, took a job. He became a taxi driver.

When Solomon Lepidus found out, he made it his business to take McDuff out to dinner. McDuff didn't refuse. On leaving the restaurant, McDuff was given a choice. "I'll tell you what I'll do for you, McDuff," Solomon said. "I'll give you a couple of thou if you contact David Lazar. Make friends with him. See what kind of work he's doing. See if he's really got it in him to be a handicapper. Or if he's all talk. If he's only a gambler. You find that out for me, McDuff boy, and I'll be very grateful. Whaddaya say?"

9

AS SOON AS David Lazar walked into the Harlem welfare office, he was told by a terrified co-worker that the assistant to the director wanted to see in his office at 9:15 all male employees who worked on the third floor.

David attended the conference. In a somber voice Bruno Edgecombe issued a warning. He said there was some wise guy in the office who was using too much toilet paper. An hour later when David went to the toilet he noticed a memorandum taped to the inside of the booth:

MEMORANDUM
DATE: June 6
TO: Staff
FROM: Bruno Edgecombe—Assistant to the Director

   The custodian has mentioned that we are having serious overflow of the commodes due to excess use of toilet paper and insufficient water pressure on the third floor to release the valve and force the paper through. He suggests that after using the commodes, if staff would hold the flush lever down a few seconds, allowing the water pressure to build up, this will allow sufficient water to funnel through and release the valves and force the waste through. If this is not done I will be forced to take stern measures that will insure . . .

Immediately upon returning home David called Nathan Rubin. Rubin said that he would be glad to talk to him but that under no circumstances could David use his name in his book or in any way identify him. He said that in the next three months he'd have plenty of time, as he'd be residing in New York during the week and staying at Sandy Rocca's Fifth Avenue apartment. On weekends he'd be flying down South to be with his appetizing Hungarian-born young wife at his home in Palm Beach.

The first appointment David made with Nathan Rubin was at one of his favorite hangouts, the Café des Artistes.

Rubin wore a topcoat even though the sun was shining and the temperature was in the seventies. When Rubin shook David's hand he crushed it. His pants were baggy, but pressed with a razor crease, and the cuffs were the one and a half inches demanded. He had withered lips and eyebrows the color of blackboard erasers smudged by chalk, high cheekbones with all sorts of coloring, ranging from colorless to pink to blue to ruddy to red-crimson and aching mauve; each shading was dependent upon the time

66 . . .

of day, his energy level, his mood, the conversation, his involvement. He told David that his blood was always chilled and that was why he wore a topcoat, and immediately upon hearing him use the word "blood," David responded as if it were a psychologist's word game and thought to himself, Nathan Rubin—cold blood.

Nathan Rubin played constantly with his huge hands, rubbing them and twining his bony fingers, and then unclasping them and playing a drumbeat on the table. And during those first minutes together, when the conversation was icy, he didn't twirl his fingers on the table much, but rather he raised his left arm in order to brush his hand against the side of his temple. In the next several minutes it also became evident that his left leg was raised perceptibly above his right, and quivered ever so slightly. David carefully dropped a menu and when he stooped down to pick it up he looked under the table and saw that it all started from the ball of Nathan Rubin's left foot, which was lifted two inches off the ground.

Before ordering, and since he wanted to break the ice, David said something about Sidney Feld which he was sure Nathan would find amusing. When Rubin chuckled, David noticed that his gums were deteriorating and his front teeth were porcelain-capped. After they ordered their food David explained to Nathan Rubin that he was not interested in gambling himself but only in preparing a guide to sports handicapping; that his intention was to address himself to that hypothetical gambler *out there.*

But as soon as Rubin started speaking to David in that high-pitched cackle of his, he relaxed as if David were his protégé and as if David were going to gamble himself. For a while David tried to correct him. Then he stopped trying and gave up. He thrashed over everything David said about sports and found linkages to gambling in every comment he made.

Nathan pounded away to make his points. Soon David became completely entranced by Nathan's comprehensive knowledge of gambling. He was imaginative and cunning, and his remarks revealed an absolute ruthlessness when it came to human values, a disdain for poverty and a contempt for losers. It was obvious that David Lazar could learn a great deal from this man.

After that first luncheon date, Nathan Rubin and David began meeting everywhere: at restaurants; at Sandy Rocca's apartment in the Buckingham Towers; at the Colonel's office; at the Chrysler building, in Solomon Lepidus's private office. David averaged about two hours a session with him and saw him at least three times a week during that first month.

Nathan always wore a carnation in his lapel, a bow tie with polka dots, a gold watch and chain adorning his vest. Always with twitches and winks. Always behaving in a manner both vibrant and abrasive. Many times he'd become irascible when David asked him a question which he considered naive. Many times he'd shout to illustrate.

Once, in a Chock Full o' Nuts where they had stopped for coffee, David inadvertently mentioned that money had never meant much to him in the past, and Rubin flew into a rage. He pulled from his breast pocket a wad of bills, there must have been at least $10,000, and he waved them in front of David's nose and screamed at the top of his lungs. The other customers just stood frozen to their spots, gaping. At other times he'd pound his fist on a table or a desk or stamp his feet.

Many times Nathan would speak about women he had known in the past, and sometimes about Kim Colby and Odette Bashjian and other young women he knew in the present. He spoke of them as if he were depraved. At times his mind was recondite and enormous; always it was computerized and omnivorous. Many times he reminded David of an elf, other times of a gnome, other times of evil itself. Each time David was with him the younger man culled every tidbit of information he could. Every conversation went into his loose-leaf notebook, and within a month he had enough raw material to begin a guide to sports handicapping.

"This racket isn't easy, kid. Each year you have to start off by evaluating what each team picked up, lost, dropped. What vets are gone. What new players are around. What rookies can help. What trades have been made. And then you got to start figuring a million other angles. But there still aren't any guarantees. Hard work doesn't always work. Wouldn't you rather stick to being a social worker, kid? Ya see, this racket isn't for college boys."

"Mr. Rubin, I'm only going to write a book on sports gambling, I'm not going to gamble. Can I see you again tomorrow?"

"Okay! Say, kid, here's a fact for your book—the suicide rate in Las Vegas is the highest in the entire country."

"You know kid, you can't become a good gambler until you've gone broke a few times."

"Are you kidding?"

"Don't be silly. No one's going to hold that against you. It's the only way to learn. It makes you tough. You gotta be tough to be a successful gambler, kid."

"The thing a gambler must understand is the importance of managing money. He has to give himself plenty of room for leverage. If you have five dollars you should be making a basic bet of five pennies. That's about the percentage of your capital you should be playing with. And your basic bet should never be increased when you're behind. Only when you're winning. There are games that are worth double and triple bets, but that should be taken into consideration before you set up your scale. Everything has to be scaled perfectly, kid, like a blueprint."

"Do you think I give a damn about the athletes? They're here today and gone tomorrow. Kids come and go like the change of seasons. Twenty-two-year-old boys who were All-Americans in college can't even make pro squads half the time. They're all just jocks who can jump, throw, hit and be hit. They'll all fumble and double-dribble and screw up a game for you. Remember that, kid!"

"Don't get so involved that you can't walk away from a game. Nothing is outstanding until the game is over and you got a W. Don't ever get caught up in the hocus-pocus of believing a team can't lose. You do that and the next thing you know you've lost control. Now, if you were Solomon Lepidus, that would be something else. He can afford to bet the whole board and be emotional. But most guys can't, and I don't like to."

"When you're winning you should never stop. That's when the smart gambler pours it on. You gotta be able to stand up to the pressure, and pressure means betting big money. It's an art you might have a genius for, kid. Then again, you might be better off being a social worker."

"Mr. Rubin, did you ever feel scared when you called a bookmaker?"
    "That's what they want. Ya see, they want to rattle you so that they'll have the advantage. Don't you think every bookie knows that when you lose your poise you're more likely to make a mistake, bet more than you should, take the wrong price, even the wrong club? The whole trick is not to panic. To always keep your wits. Not to let anyone rush you or hassle you. If they ask you to hurry up and make a bet or if they tell you they don't have time to give you all the prices, you tell them to go screw themselves and hang up. They'll give you the complete line next time; they want your business. And always make them repeat the line. Bust their chops a little. Make it a game. Don't ever get uptight. Keep cool. Make them curse you under their breath. Remember, kid, most of them are nothing but guys who have no other way of making a living. Half of them can hardly read and the other half never have to."

"I lost one of my biggest offices last week. Angelo Scarne was knocked out. I hope he'll be back in business for football. He'll have to be more careful and he'll have to start paying off a lot more bread. I think he was paying about five hundred a phone. But that just wasn't enough. I think the going rate for an office that size is something in the neighborhood of sixteen hundred a week. In New York you pay the highest for protection. Otherwise, the vice squad is sure to bust you."

"My God, Mr. Rubin, sixteen hundred a week—are you sure?"

"I'm sure!"

"Whenever I was placing bets in the past, Mr. Rubin, I always found the offices I dealt with so damn busy it would take me an hour to get through."

"What a guy should do is have his bookie call him at a designated time. He should make up a schedule and stick to it. You want to give your readers a tip, tell them to read Andrew Carnegie's principles of good management; study time-and-motion principles. You know, kid, you can lead a horse to water but you can't make him drink. Don't think I'm giving that much away."

As soon as Mustache McDuff identified himself on the telephone, David Lazar knew something was wrong. The man had never, but never, greeted him with anything but disdain. Indifference had been a courtesy. Now Mustache McDuff was sugaring him up. "Let's get together, Lazar. We've got things to talk about. Handicapping. Broads."

David felt repelled by the conversation. The man was ignorant and uninteresting, and the most uninteresting part about him was that he was a loser. Still, David didn't hang up on him. He pumped him for information. Picked his brain for about twenty minutes, and then realized that there wasn't anything worth picking. But in those twenty minutes Mustache McDuff had told him all he knew about handicapping. Then he began repeating himself, saying the same thing over and over: "Baseball's my game, Lazar. I can beat that racket. I know the pitchers."

"Everyone knows the pitchers, McDuff."

"It's not a question of knowing, Lazar. I just know them better, you know what I mean?"

"Not really, McDuff. Anyway, if you can beat it, how come you're down so much? How come you haven't scored for Lepidus or Rubin? How come you . . ." Are a loser, David Lazar thought, but said, ". . . have been doing so bad so long, McDuff?"

Mustache McDuff had been following Solomon Lepidus's orders. He was trying to get along with David, but he had been weakened by Solomon Lepidus, toyed with by Nathan Rubin, given ultimatums by his wife. Now he lost whatever control was left.

"Fuck off, Lazar. Who the hell are you anyway to talk to me like this? I called you up because I wanted to help you. Solomon told me you were trying to learn the handicapping game. I wanted to help. I don't need the kind of shit you've been throwing. Believe me, Lazar, you'll never be the handicapper I am. Never."

It took just a touch of extra control, but David Lazar kept his cool. First he digested the facts. Mustache McDuff had lost for Solomon Lepidus five straight years. He had been dropped by Nathan Rubin. He was driving a cab.

"You know, McDuff," he said, "it's not that I think I'm going to do better than you. It's just that I know I couldn't do worse if that's what I wanted to do." And with that David Lazar hung up the telephone, flipped open his Handicapper's Handbook, and got back down to work.

Mustache McDuff was incensed. He knew he'd blown it. What was he to tell Solomon Lepidus? That Lazar, too, the lousy social worker, didn't want to have anything to do with him. When he called Solomon Lepidus he said, "That kind don't know the first thing about handicapping, Solomon. Believe me, he won't make a dollar."

As the weeks passed by and as David's Handicapper's Handbook continued to grow, he kept jotting down the sayings of Nathan Rubin.

"You know how many bookies there are in this country? At least three hundred thousand, and less than fifteen percent of them pay the fifty dollars necessary to get the gambler's stamp. The IRS can't do a thing about it. Out of the ten thousand arrests for gambling every year, ninety-five percent pay a fine of one hundred dollars or less. Does that sound to you as if organized crime has to worry about law enforcement?"

"It ain't like the old days, of course. Ya see, the rackets guys are no longer the only people you can deal with. Today, most independents like Dominic Denucci out on the coast, and Allan Klein in Miami, run pretty clean operations and don't use strongarm methods."

"As far as New York goes, there are a lot of nice independent guys taking book. Just warn your readers to stay away from the Brooklyn offices. Those gangsters from Brooklyn still believe in doing things the old way."

"The worst weakness you can have as a gambler is to think of money as an abstraction. You have to always remind yourself how real it is. You know what a good trick is? When you telephone in a bet to always have the amount you're betting in your hand. That way you know it's real. I did that for years."

"Mr. Rubin, what was the biggest bet you ever made?"

"It was, let me see . . . probably the hundred thousand dollars I wagered on the first Super Bowl game. Green Bay covered the spread easily. That's how a big bet should be—easy. If you don't win easy, it shouldn't have been a big bet. I loved that Packer club. I was sure of that one."

"Any others, Mr. Rubin?"

"Another one I remember took place a few years back. I made a bet with Harry Richardson and Scarface Sicily. It was on Sandy Koufax when he went against the Yankees in the Series. I forget the year but I remember he struck out fourteen or fifteen batters. I remember he even struck out that preacher boy, Bobby Richardson. Koufax, ya see, kid, he was something special. I go back to . . . well, just about to the beginning of the century. Koufax, he was the best. Even better than old Lefty Grove. He was one guy I didn't worry about laying a price on. I just worried about betting enough. But guys like that come around once in a lifetime. The others are all mortal. Koufax, he was one of a kind."

"Mr. Rubin, you'll give anyone a sporting proposition on anything, right?"

"If I don't have an edge I wouldn't even consider making a wager. If a guy wants to play by my rules I'll take a chance. No other way."

"Mr. Rubin, last night I picked up a girl at Elaine's. You know, that uptown literary bar. She reminds me a lot of Kim Colby."

Before David could continue, Nathan Rubin leaped from the table. "I just remembered, I got another appointment. Come with me, David. We can share a taxicab."

He picked up the check on the table. It came to $17.55. He reached into his trouser pocket and pulled out a roll of freshly printed $50 and $100 bills. He stuffed the wad of rubber-banded bills back into his trouser pocket and searched his other pockets for a small bill. In his jacket pocket he found a soiled $20 bill. He clenched it in his fist as he waved his arm in the air and impatiently looked around for a waiter. "Waiter," he screeched. "Waiter!" And when no one responded immediately, his voice rose in decibels. "I'm in a hurry, God damn it. Where's the waiter? Waiter!"

David casually advised Nathan Rubin that the bill was $17.55 and that he could leave the $20 on the table. Nathan Rubin glared at David and continued to scream. "I want the waiter. God damn it, I'm entitled to my change, ain't I?" And again he screamed, "Waiter . . . waiter!"

The waiter finally appeared, a young blue-eyed college boy, clean, tanned, and preppy-white.

Nathan Rubin handed him the check and the soiled $20 bill. "Hurry up back with my change. Hurry up," he repeated as the waiter began to move. When the young waiter returned with the change, Nathan Rubin snatched it from his hand and counted it. Then he handed him a tip. "Here's a dollar for you, waiter," Nathan Rubin cackled authoritatively. He eyed the waiter up and down. "Go buy yourself a tennis racket, kid—you sure as hell have the spick-and-span look of a player." Immediately Nathan Rubin looked back over his shoulder at David. "Now come with me, sonny. Hurry up, hurry up."

As the two men were traveling by taxi to Nathan Rubin's destination, David said, "That girl I met last night, Mr. Rubin."

Nathan Rubin jerked his head toward David. "Who? What girl?"

"The girl I met at Elaine's last night, Mr. Rubin. Her name is Saskia Verdonck. I saw some photos she has. I think she'd be one hell of a model."

Nathan Rubin peered at David. He began to chuckle as if he knew something David didn't. "You know where I'm taking you, sonny? I'm taking you over to Kim Colby's. She's the number-one model in the whole country right now." Nathan Rubin paused. "Did you meet Kim's roommate, Odette Bashjian, David? She's quite a looker herself."

"Don't you remember, Mr. Rubin? I met them over a year ago when you were negotiating some deal with Solomon and you asked me to take both of them to lunch."

Nathan Rubin snickered. "The two of them are something, ain't they, sonny?"

Yes, both of them were something, both were beautiful. Kim, cool, lithe, and so clean-looking one could almost smell generations of New England starch in her clean skin, and Odette with her Cleopatra profile.

David remembered Kim's telling him over lunch that day what a good relationship she and Odette had. "We never cruise gay bars," she had said. "We never think of each other as a number." And David thought of the ravages beautiful flesh is heir to in the flesh markets of New York.

As soon as Nathan Rubin entered Kim Colby's apartment he reached into his jacket pocket and took out two gift-wrapped little boxes. One he tossed to Kim and the other he handed to Odette. "Here's a little something for each of you," he cackled.

The two women smiled at each other and excitedly began stripping the wrappings off the boxes. When they discovered the gold Bueche-Girod watches inside they ran up to Nathan Rubin and hugged and kissed him.

Rubin chuckled and said, "Fix me a drink, Odette. You know David Lazar, don't you, Kim?"

Kim turned to David, graciously walked over to him, extended her hand, smiled, and said, "It's nice to see you again, David. How's your handbook coming along?"

As David was about to answer, Nathan Rubin glared at Kim. "Kim, get David that book on gambling I left here the other night. I want to give it to him to study."

Kim left the room to get the book, and Nathan Rubin turned toward David. "Sorry, sonny, this scene ain't for you. I'm gonna have to ask you to leave as soon as Kim comes back with the book."

Kim returned with the book and handed it to David, saying, "Are you staying, David?"

Nathan Rubin immediately announced, "He's leaving, Kim." And with that he walked to the door and opened it for David. Kim smiled and said, "Maybe tomorrow night Odette and I will run into you at Elaine's, David."

"I'm still not hanging out that much, Kim. As I told you, all my time is taken up by the handbook, and I still got my wife, Leslie, on my mind."

Kim Colby smiled as she said, "Things change, David. Don't they?"

David walked toward the door and Nathan Rubin said, "So long, sonny. And don't forget to read that book." He chuckled. "It's your homework for tonight."

With that he slammed the door and walked back into Kim's living room, and as he did so, Kim adjusted the dimmer switch very low and called for Odette.

When Nathan Rubin returned to Sandy Rocca's apartment he was wide awake, but rather than force himself to sleep he called David Lazar.

"Hello, sonny. I just wanted to tell ya, you can bring that little girl you were talking about over to my office tomorrow. If she's anything like Kim Colby I'll be able to do something for her. You can tell her . . ." He snickered. "Tell her Nathan Rubin is always interested in assisting a pretty girl." His voice rose to a metallic cackle. "Ya see, David, I'm not as bad a guy as most people think. Anyway, it's getting late. I'll see you tomorrow. Tomorrow I'm going to tell ya about a friend of mine, David, Harry Richardson. A pretty interesting guy. Ever hear of him?" Before David Lazar could answer Nathan Rubin said, "Goodnight, sonny," and hung up.

That evening David tried to read the thick book on gambling Nathan Rubin had given him, but his mind kept turning to Saskia Verdonck, the young woman he had met at Elaine's.

"One thing that worries me, David, is this New York air. It does terrible things to one's face. Blemishes appear. I'm going to make my living with my face, David. Don't laugh, it's very serious. My face will make my fortune. The air is very important to me. When I was a little girl I had a big dog, Oliver, and he was my friend. We walked together in my father's orchard and I told him stories about how I was going to come to America and be a model. Become very famous. I grew up in Bergen, which is thirty miles from Amsterdam. A village of three thousand, I think. My father sold apples, pears, plums, black and red currants." David smiled to himself as he recalled the voice of Saskia Verdonck. "My father also had a greenhouse and grew strawberries. He sent them in baskets to market where the grocers came and bought produce. My father also grew lettuce, cucumbers, and tomatoes in his greenhouse."

More and more David thought of the evening he had spent with Saskia.

"When I came to New York I tried to call my friend from the airport, but I could not reach her. I had nowhere to stay, so I went to the Chelsea Hotel. I asked for the cheapest room. Very expensive. Twenty-five dollars. Don't you think twenty-five dollars is very expensive, David? I called my friend again and again. Finally I reached her. She told me to come over. I took my suitcase; no one helped me with it. They are nasty people, Americans, I thought. I felt like leaving America then, but now I have fun. David, do I make you laugh? Do I say something funny?" David Lazar pushed Nathan Rubin's textbook on gambling aside and reached for his telephone. He dialed Saskia Verdonck.

Saskia had arrived from Amsterdam with the morning mail. She had large hips and an incredible pout on her voluptuous lips. She grew on David Lazar in forty-eight interrupted hours; her age, twenty-one; her charm, curiosity blended with a smile; her ease with men; her intensity. Anyone listening to her immediately understood her need to make it, her need to succeed. Relationships with men would not stand in her way. Though they would be fully enjoyed. Sensually enjoyed. Saskia's face was precious, a cross between Liv Ullmann and carnal sin. Her body, blessed by those flawed hips—"I'm on a diet"—was magnetic.

When David Lazar brought her to the Rubin Modeling Agency, it was his intention to introduce her to Kim Colby, and, of course, Nathan Rubin. He would allow the two of them to discover her; enjoy her. And Saskia would enjoy her success. "I want to model. Be successful. Make my mother proud of me. I want to have lots of money. And buy presents for my friends. I want to be famous, David. Very famous."

Kim Colby smiled as soon as she saw David. She ran up to him and kissed him fully on the lips. David took both of Kim's hands and held her away from him. He knew where she would touch him next, and he didn't want to be touched. "This is Saskia, Kim, the girl from Holland that I was telling you about."

Kim's eyes immediately focused on the young woman. In one sweeping motion she appraised Saskia. "The hips got to go, David. The face is marvelous, but"—she shrugged—"the hips won't be of any use to her outside of a bedroom."

"Is Nathan Rubin around, Kim?" David anxiously asked.

"He stepped out for a while. He'll be back after seven. We're going to dinner. Why don't you join us?" Kim smiled. "Maybe we can all have a scene." And as Kim made her suggestion she moved her body in front of Saskia and blocked her out of David's view.

David took Kim by her shoulders and guided her to the side. "I'm taking Saskia to dinner. I just wanted her to be introduced to you people. We'll wait to see Nathan Rubin, then the two of us are going to split."

"Whatever pleases you, David," Kim said. "You know what you want. You're not a little boy."

David took Saskia's hand and walked across the room and sat on the couch, Saskia beside him.

"Close that button," David ordered in a whisper, and Saskia obeyed his command.

They thumbed through a current issue of *Penthouse*. Saskia's eyes kept flashing to the door. She was impatient, waiting for Nathan Rubin, who could make her a model. Kim Colby paraded back and forth, not knowing how to gain David's attention.

Minutes later, a young woman entered the office, and as soon as she did, David rushed over to her, kissed her on the cheek, took her hand, and forgot the other two beautiful women in the office. It was Margot Lepidus. Immediately they became engrossed, and she spoke to David about her father, her reasons for leaving Yale, and the modeling jobs she'd done. "It's so exciting, David. The whole business is crazy, but I can't get enough of it right now."

As Margot spoke to David, Saskia kept thinking how she might capture the men who could do something for her career. The competition, she realized, was tremendous. The women were as beautiful as she was, if not more beautiful. What could she do? Her brow furrowed, her eyes narrowed, her pout sucked on a cigarette as she observed David, Margot, and beautiful Kim Colby.

And then Nathan Rubin strode into the office, looking all his years. Saskia, for an instant only, had a disappointed look on her face. Then she put out her cigarette and opened her full lips in a smile. Without waiting for David, she pranced over to Nathan Rubin's side.

"Hello, Nathan, I'm Saskia. Did David tell you about me?"

A few days later David again met with Nathan Rubin.

"Tell me about Harry Richardson, Mr. Rubin."

"He ran the biggest bookmaking operation in the country. I don't know, but he might still be at it somewhere. I haven't seen him in years. He was located in Vegas, right next to the Sahara. His partner was Scarface Sicily for a long time, but all Scarface ever did was stand around and look mean.

"Harry was the whole operation. A lot of guys called him a lot of funny names. Mr. Cool, the Commissioner, the Champ, the Bible, the King Fish, Harry the Great, Rich Harry . . . he must have had a hundred labels.

"I called him Numero Uno. Ya see, he became a legend to the ordinary bookies and to most of the in crowd out there. He was the best at making odds and spreads. The sharpies took his word as gospel. He never bet money, he bet numbers. Of course when he went up against a wise guy like me, he'd adjust his line . . . but he had faith in himself. The main strength the s.o.b. had was that eleven-ten! You take that away from any of them bookmakers and they got no edge at all. I'll tell you this, though—Harry Richardson was pretty damn good. Maybe not as good as they all said, but pretty damn good. He knew numbers. What he liked to do was throw his numbers out to guys like Sandy Rocca and Champ Holden, guys who really knew their sport, and let them bet into his outlaw line. Then he'd adjust it and hold it until Doomsday. Once his line was set he'd send it out to the regional offices all over the country, and they, of course, made their necessary adjustments depending on where they were dealing from."

"From what you say, Mr. Rubin, he sounds no different from most of the other guys. I don't see why his system was flawless. He could have been beat. Take that eleven-ten away and he wouldn't have been so special."

Nathan Rubin slammed his hand down on the table, knocking over some coffee. "Never underestimate the strength of that eleven-ten," he insisted. "It allowed him to take on all comers. He never had to be afraid of anyone's opinion. He didn't believe in wise guys once he set his line. He'd take anything you'd throw at him. Numero Uno had nerve, kid, but more than that he had that eleven-ten!"

"What makes you think he's out of business now, Mr. Rubin?"

"Well, ya see, in 1961 Bobby Kennedy stopped interstate gambling. Without that Richardson couldn't get to his customers. The Feds were on to him and he was being watched all the time."

David kept quiet, but he thought, "If I ever want to place bets interstate, there must be a hundred ways a nobody like me could do it without arousing suspicion." The way Nathan Rubin was peering at him made him feel as if he knew exactly what he was thinking.

David Lazar remembered his first meeting with Nathan Rubin. It was when he was still in college. He was standing in the lobby of Madison Square Garden when he spotted Solomon in animated conversation with Rubin. Rubin was going a mile a minute, with his face close to Solomon's, trying to dominate the taller man's attention. He was completely oblivious to the crowd around them. To David's surprise, when he walked within hearing distance, they weren't discussing the game, but were working out a business deal.

"Ya see, Solomon," Rubin shouted, "I'm willing to allow you this mitzvah for three hundred thousand, all cash, only because you're a close friend." David was astonished when he heard Solomon answer.

"I like the proposition, Nathan boy, but I don't want to pay three hundred thou cash. . . . Let's do this. I'll pay you four hundred thousand on a payout basis." David distinctly recalled Nathan Rubin's gainful grin as he shook hands with Solomon on the deal.

As David closed his eyes, he vividly recalled Solomon strutting to the other end of the Garden lobby to join his wife, and Nathan Rubin frantically motioning for another man to join him, and when the man did, hissing, "Ya see, Sandy, I sold the restaurant to Lepidus just like I said I would. Only a miracle can make it a paying proposition. Ya see, Sandy," Nathan Rubin said in a triumphant, high-pitched cackle, "I told ya, Solomon Lepidus is a sucker!"

As soon as David returned home that evening, he telephoned Solomon and asked him when he could see him.

"If it's urgent, Davy boy, you can see me at seven-thirty tomorrow morning."

"Seven-thirty?"

"That's right, Davy boy. Every day of the year, including Saturday, I'm at my office from seven-thirty to six at night. It's the foundation of my business life, and the one big secret to a business is to watch it closely, minute by minute, hour by hour, day by day."

As soon as David arrived at Solomon's office he blurted out, "How did you let yourself be conned by a rattlesnake like that creep last night?"

"Calm yourself, Davy boy, and sit down," Solomon replied as he chewed on his bagel and sipped his coffee. "Have some coffee and a bagel and listen carefully so that, when I'm finished, you may also have an antidote to administer to snakebites from the many Nathan Rubins crawling around today.

"First of all, I examined the statements for the restaurant . . . pretty good. All I have to do to make the restaurant worth a million is to push the volume over a million a year. I can do that by bringing the food and liquor cost down ten percent and by getting some honest and loyal help. And I'm also gonna put in a three-piece band and repaint and redecorate and change the food to the best money can buy. I'd rather people walk out saying, 'He is expensive, but it sure is great food and atmosphere.'

"That's on the positive side. On the negative side, let me show you how I protected myself. If I gave Rubin the three hundred thousand cash and the place went bad, I'd lose it all, since I gambled all of it. However, if I give him four hundred thousand to be paid over ten years, I'm only gambling as long as I keep going. That way if things go bad I only lose my first yearly payment of forty thou and interest, instead of three hundred thousand. That, Davy, is a nine-to-one shot the snake is unwittingly giving me. Now, Davy boy, knowing me, can you really see me passing up odds like that?

"And another thing, if it does lose, I bought it in my corporation's name, and with the tax bracket I'm in, the loss will be cut down by seventy percent." Solomon smiled knowingly.

"Let's make this a project of ours to watch over the next year, Davy, and we will then judge who was the conner, and who was the conned, Nathan Rubin or me."

David often wondered why Nathan Rubin was so cooperative on the handbook. After much thought, he began to suspect it was more than the fact that Nathan wanted to use him to proposition Solomon Lepidus. Perhaps Nathan Rubin was living his life over again through him. He was affirming his life. Justifying it.

10

AS THE WEEKS went by David's handbook began to grow and take shape. He began to envision it as something alive. He planned his chapters cautiously while continuing to research relentlessly. He added and he removed information. He constantly refined.

He purchased and read every book, magazine, and newspaper he could find that had anything to do with sports handicapping. He analyzed and underlined everything of importance, synthesized and memorized every fact and rule that he could. He extracted everything that he thought might help.

He stayed up until he was exhausted every evening—pondering, studying, recording, typing whatever fresh material he had culled or thought of that day onto new white sheets which were then placed into his swelling handbook. Every piece of information, every statistic, every conversation that had to do with gambling.

During July, David's focus on what to gamble, as well as his relationship to Nathan Rubin, changed. They met for lunch, and as soon as David greeted Nathan he noticed Rubin had a whitlow on the middle finger of his right hand, and immediately Nathan started complaining of a felon on his toe. After he finished with his complaint he squeezed the pus from his finger and began speaking in that rapid machine cackle of his.

"We've been talking for almost six weeks now, David, so let me give you some advice. If I were going to select a sport to gamble on I certainly wouldn't pick baseball. I'd specialize in college basketball. Baseball's too exposed. The prices are always correct. You can never catch a wrong line.

"In baseball and every other professional sport, as well as college football, the bookmaker and the general public have all the information in the world from which to draw an opinion, because nothing escapes the media.

"But in college baskets almost everything escapes. The bookies have almost nothing except the opinion of the linemaker, who has the impossible task of handicapping almost two hundred games in a six-day week. The linemaker errs on some of those games, kid. He's got to!"

Nathan Rubin untwined his bony fingers and fiddled with some sugar cubes and then commented, "Besides, remember, kid, baseball's not a numbers game—you always have a much better chance when it's a point spread rather than an odd."

He deliberated for a moment and sipped some coffee before continuing, "If you were betting yourself, kid, I'd tell you to stick to college baskets. I can see there you might have an edge. You know, kid, sometimes by the way you talk I think this book you're writing is a lot of hooey. I think you've been pumping me all along because you want to wager."

He looked at David, and David could feel Nathan's eyes boring into his, crumbling him. David became tongue-tied and stammered a confession.

"You're right, Mr. Rubin, I'm not really writing a book on gambling. I ... I mean, I am, but it's for me, not for the public. The only thing I'm interested in doing is preparing myself so that I'll know all there is to know about gambling correctly. I hope that doesn't upset you."

As David made his confession he noticed that the corner of the left side of Nathan's mouth was twitching. Nathan Rubin smiled engagingly. "I'm kind of glad. I always thought so, ya know." Glancing at his watch, he said, "I'll see you Thursday, David, but then I won't be able to see you for a week or two. I have to leave the country on some business. When I'm back, the two of us should get together with Solomon. I want to make him a few propositions anyway."

Instinctively David said, "Mr. Rubin, I'll be glad to help you if I can, but I won't get involved in swindling Solomon Lepidus. I love that man, Mr. Rubin, I love him."

The expression on Nathan Rubin's face didn't change, but his eyes narrowed and he broke into a sour chuckle. After a few moments he tried to assuage David. "Don't worry, David, I'd never ask you to do anything to take Lepidus."

Nathan Rubin then began to tell David about his son, Charley; about the estate he had in Sands Point for which he'd paid over $2 million; about the grounds, the pool, the furnishings, the art work, and the twenty-two bedrooms; about the bungalow colony where the help lived, the yacht that he kept on the Sound; about his hobby, ornithology—he had six rooms filled with birds—about the twenty or thirty houseguests that Charley entertained every weekend, the thirty-four servants who were trained in the South; about the woman he was married to; about the security on the premises; about the brokerage house he ran; about his children, one of them a girl of seventeen, Patricia, who had left home.

"Patricia's just like any of these kids today. You can talk to them for an hour, and then, if you say just one wrong thing, they'll run away. They have no ego strength at all, they won't stand up to you, they'll just run away."

Then Nathan Rubin told David of a party his son, Charley, was giving in his home the coming weekend. He told him of the tent that was being set up to house four hundred people for dinner. He mentioned that the cost would run around $30,000, but it was worth it, Nathan said, as it was for Charley's younger daughter's sweet-sixteen party. He told David his daughter-in-law's dress cost $5,000, Cynthia's $3,000. Each of them to be worn one time. Upon finishing the dispensing of all the gaudy details, Nathan Rubin asked David if he'd like to attend the party.

"No thanks, Mr. Rubin, I don't think I'd fit in."

"Don't be silly, David. As far as that goes, there isn't a person alive who fits in." He chuckled. "The trick is to be able to do it anyway." He paused. "Say, David, why don't you bring Margot Lepidus?" He paused again, "Yeah, that's a good idea, bring Margot!" He stopped again. "If you can't arrange a date with her, I'd like it if you brought that Dutch girl from Bergen. There's something about her. What's her name, David?"

Nathan Rubin insisted David go to the sweet-sixteen party. He went so far as to order and pay for the suit David wore. When David arrived he saw a sumptuous estate filled with art works hanging unobserved on a hundred walls, thousands of books dying on shelves, ten thousand stuffed birds, barracudas in beach chairs surrounding a monstrous pool, and saunas where youngsters were getting high.

People were standing around sipping drinks, picking at food, speaking in whispers about politics, free markets, buying and selling, tax write-offs and foundations that actually gave away nothing.

It was mind-boggling. Nathan Rubin kept bugging him, in subtle and not-so-subtle ways, about a proposition he had that he wanted David to help him foist on Solomon Lepidus. He offered David a large piece. It was just about the biggest opportunity for making money he had ever had. David said, "I love that man, Mr. Rubin, I love him."

At the very same time Nathan Rubin was offering David Lazar an opportunity, he was also offering Saskia Verdonck her chance.

"Ya see, Saskia, I believe in diamonds and gold, not in the stock market. I believe in real estate too. Ya see, Saskia, it's forever, not like modeling." And as Nathan Rubin spoke, he never once removed his gaze from Saskia's face, which was wonderfully alive and cheerful. But his peering eyes had first been attracted to her lips. He realized how much he was attracted to her because of those heavy lips. He thought of his mother, a submissive, frightened woman with a sour face and small, thin lips that were dry and quiet. Saskia's lips were slightly parted now, so that her white teeth showed. Those perilous lips told Nathan Rubin that she had a hunger for life, that she was impatient to succeed. And as Nathan Rubin peered at Saskia's lips, she spoke.

"But those girls who model for your agency, they all look the same to me. Walking toothpaste ads, with their blond hair. All sisters, none of them different, Nathan." She smiled at Nathan Rubin. David admired her. "I'm not interested in real estate, Nathan, I'm interested in being a model."

David took her hand. "You're delightful, Saskia. Delightful." Saskia squeezed David's hand and continued to gaze with a gamine's artfulness into the twinkling eyes of Nathan Rubin, who continued to fondle her calf.

Item by item David reviewed the opulence he had seen at Charley Rubin's home. And he did not forget the proposition Nathan Rubin had made to him. For days he considered what Nathan had said about baseball and basketball wagering. All the time he was turning over baseball statistics and theories in his mind.

One thought kept intruding—all baseball games have odds. Always, yes always, the odds are correct. That gives the bookmaker a consistent edge. How do you overcome this bookmaking edge? David scribbled down a variety of ideas. He studied a dozen systems. He even applied the "Top Bottom" system of the roulette wheel. He considered every other system he knew, every theory.

He began to do more paperwork than he had ever done before. He went over teams, rosters, records, wins, losses, and streaks. He checked every stat and figure he had, each one of his many rules, his maximizing and minimizing principles, everything; and he kept coming to the same basic conclusion. *The prices are always correct and all the knowledge in the world can't buck that.*

College basketball is all numbers, David thought to himself. It's a *point-spread* line, not *odds* as in baseball's dollar line. I have no sentiment or romantic attachment when it comes to taking points against any team in the country—you don't have to win, just fall within the number. There lies a great difference, both emotionally and practically, between investing in baseball or baskets. Definitely worth further exploration.

"Ya see, the difference is simple, kid," Nathan Rubin had told him. "In football the linemaker only has to study about six hundred games, while in baskets he has to know what's happening in over four thousand. That's just too many problems for the linemaker to be right all the time. A good handicapper would have a hell of a shot by picking his spots in college basketball. The bookie would be nothing more than a target. But as I said, to do it right a guy would have to be a hell of a handicapper and he'd also have an impossible task in trying to get down any important money. In fact, the days you could make a real killing in anything are going."

By the end of July David had made a decision. Baseball was out. He just didn't think he could beat the sport. He knew every roster, every earned run average, every batting average, every flaw in every player's game. But all his information and all his knowledge didn't mean a thing.

Nathan Rubin was correct and his twin brother was correct. Baseball just didn't give you enough of an edge. Luckily he had found out after only two months of concentrated research and with zero dollars invested. Maybe someday he'd write a book utilizing all his information, but what did it all mean now? Nothing. Zilch. It didn't give him an edge. The linemaker knew the same facts.

If there was a flaw in the bookmaking business it had to be found in college basketball. David began to devote himself exclusively to the study of college basketball every afternoon and every evening. During the first week in August, he started gathering all the stats and schedules of the past ten years. He started collating all the games played by more than 250 teams; all the lines; every piece of information. It wasn't easy to get those records, but he did—he made it his business to.

David studied *Basketball News, Sports Magazine, Sports Illustrated, Sports Action,* old issues of *Smith and Street College Basketball Yearbook,* Dell basketball magazines, and every other basketball publication he could get his hands on. He wrote to each one of the more than two hundred colleges in the country that bookmakers put an official line on. He advised them that he was writing a new book on basketball and that he would appreciate any information they could funnel his way through their promo and publicity departments. He started gathering literature, in bundles. He started collecting the telephone numbers of radio stations, TV stations, newspapers, wire services, dormitories, field houses, arenas, every school in the National Collegiate Athletic Association, coaches and players—anyone and everyone he thought he might someday call; who might have, or someday have, some information on the university that he was researching.

He studied statistics by the hour: points scored, points given up, margin of difference, winning and losing records, heights of players, depth of the squads, shooting percentages, the number of team turnovers. He wanted to know everything else, right down to what team had a water boy and what he looked like and what his telephone number was and how much information he could give David. The more he studied the more he wanted to know, and the more he learned the more certain he became that Nathan Rubin was correct.

There were errors in the official Vegas line, and he wanted to be able to pinpoint all those errors from now on. He was sure that sometime, somewhere, in some honky-tonk of a college basketball town, some Johnny-come-lately would have the measles, or stub his toe, or screw up in the classroom, or have a fight with his girl, or make a deal, or hate the coach, or cause a black-white rift, and David wanted to make it his business to know when and where and how and why and everything else that might influence a new, more accurate line.

The Vegas line—a piece of sludge. A bummer. David Lazar's line—up to the minute. A winner. He'd have the perseverance and the discipline to stay right on top of everything throughout the entire year, maybe for ten years.

By the middle of August David realized that he was working through a project that might take him another six months to a year or even two. There was no way of telling when the first profit would be realized, if ever, and, for him, profit would come only after he had paid back all his many creditors. He had just finished preparing a financial statement, which was placed in his Handicapper's Handbook. It showed, as any Dunn and Bradstreet report would, his assets and liabilities.

Assets: A job which gave him an income of $322.58 biweekly take-home pay.

Liabilities were as follows:

1. A loan from the Household Finance Corporation. Total remaining to be paid, $939.24. Installment payments of $52.18 for the next eighteen months.

2. A loan from the Beneficial Finance Corporation of New York. Total remaining to be paid, $1,738.00. Installment payments of $79 for the next twenty-six months.

3. A loan from the First National City Bank. Total remaining to be paid, $2,480. Installment payments of $80 for the next twenty-six months.

4. A loan from the Chase Manhattan Bank. Total remaining to be paid, $1,520.00. Installment payments of $76 for the next twenty months.

5. A loan from the Municipal Credit Union of New York. Total remaining to be paid, $3,555. Installment payments of $79.58 for the next forty-five months.

6. Loans from Doug. Totaling $2,000, and that was owed in full, and would not be asked for nor paid back until and when and if David was with assets.

7. Personal loans from Ron Nivens. Totaling $4,800, made during the crucial period of his compulsive-gambling years. Ron, like Doug, would have to wait until killings or at least bullet wounds were made into the bookies' pocketbooks for the collection of any part of that sum.

8. Loans from his father. Totaling $8,000, made over a period of thirteen long-suffering years of gambling malaise. Loans made because of jams, crises, depressions, lies, and promises to quit gambling. Loans made because of losing streaks and Mickey Mantle strikeouts and Oscar Robertson misses and Willie Mays double-play balls and by any and everyone else who has ever made a double dribble or a bobble or put on a pair of rubber sneakers or black leather spikes.

9. Loans from his mother. $1,000. Of all the loans, this one was the most painful. It was money she had saved for a trip—one that she didn't take, and because of her health probably never would. This was something David had to live with day and night.

The gloomy accounts payable figure totaled up to the frightening reality of $26,032.24.

"Telephone numbers," David's good friend Solomon Lepidus would say. But David searched for a silver lining and found one. His fixed installment payments came to only $366.18 per month. "Oy vey," his parents would say. Without rent payments to make, little food to purchase, no marital obligations of a legal nature, and with only telephone, subway, bus, sports publications, postage, newspapers, and dry-cleaning costs to concern himself, he calculated that he could play, when the time was ripe, with $50 as a base bet, and from there work his way up from the minor to the Nathan Rubin major leagues.

In the past, he had bet as much as $500. In bookmaking parlance, $100 is known as "a dollar," and when you graduate to $500 you are wagering "a nickel," and by the time you have won the "Phi Beta Key" and are wagering $1,000, you are, in the vernacular of the bookie, wagering "a dime." Forget it! A minuscule $50 would be David's bet when he was ready to begin.

David pondered. Could it be that those friendly "dese, dem, and dose" guys knew something about human psychology? Were Johnny and Sidney and Nino Tafuri and all his other "best friends" really no more than Madison Avenue con men? Has their shrewd argot sold the big bettors, seduced them with euphemisms such as dimes, nickels, and dollars? Would using a real vocabulary have put a prophylactic on the balls of the gambler? Would it have awakened him to the reality of what he was doing?

In any case David planned not to use codes and jargon in his bet calling, because it just might have given another valuable, perhaps decisive, edge to the bookie. He planned to hold every dollar he wagered in his hand so that it might never become a stillborn abstraction. David promised himself he would never relate to money as an abstraction again. And in the dark of those August nights he whispered, "Liabilities twenty-six thousand thirty-two dollars and twenty-four cents."

On one such evening David looked out his window onto West End Avenue and saw Emma Polanski getting ready for bed. She turned him on to his studies and he closed the ledger on debts and began to work on rules and regulations again, and tried to exorcise through introspection each and every mistake, obsession, compulsion, and Freudian slip of his past.

He dwelled upon bets he had made—from Stanley Dancer's Su Mac Lad in the late fifties right on up through to Tom Terrific and the World Championship New York Mets of 1969.

David worked with numbers and figures and percentages and volumes of basketball magazines and guides and encyclopedias and books that were at his beck and carton-crammed call. He studied every conceivable handicapper's publication and every tout's comment. He learned of the born losers and of the reasons why. He began to study systems. He remembered a conversation with Nathan Rubin.

"Mr. Rubin, is there any system you know that's infallible?"

"There are guys who have died with systems and others who have lived by them. Ya see, it's according to a guy's personality. If you want to learn about theories, I suggest you do some heavy reading. Get your hands on Mort Olshan's *Winning Theories of Sports Handicapping.* From that book you'll learn a great deal about theories. Of course, that doesn't mean you'll pick any winners, kid."

The next day David purchased Olshan's book and began to outline parts of it in his own handbook. That evening he finished working at 11:30 P.M. and instead of masturbating he went out and picked up a young woman at a singles bar. A half hour after meeting Marilyn Spencer he took her home. They fell into bed almost immediately after entering her apartment. In the afterglow she said, "Isn't it amazing that I knew the size of your cock before I knew the color of your eyes." David never saw her again.

The next day when David got home from the field after visiting Louise Ramey and discussing the numerous housing violations in her apartment—rats, vermin, roaches, garbage in the hallways, no hot water, no steam, broken windows, lighting fixtures either damaged or exposed, banisters fractured, gaping holes in the ceiling and floor—he again studied Mort Olshan's book and came up with a list of checkpoints which would eventually be taped under his telephone. At the same time, he began to brand, to burn, all of the checklist into his brain.

Later that night he studied his handbook over and over and compiled the numerous events and situations that must be considered, whether they might have an effect on the outcome of a game. He began to list the questions for which he must find answers: Is the coach announcing his retirement? Is the coach being fired? Is he quitting? Has the coach invited any young high school phenoms to watch the game? If so, he is recruiting, and will most likely try to have the club give its top effort in order to impress the high school boy.

Is the game of personal significance to the coach, such as an anniversary game for his fifth, tenth, fifteenth, or twentieth year at school? Is he going for his twentieth win of the year? The fiftieth of his career? Is the game on national TV? Regional? Is the game of importance in the conference race? Is the game significant to the team for a post-season tournament berth? Will there be any ceremonies at halftime? After the game? Any honors being given to players, coaches, alumni? Is there going to be a dance on campus after the game that the players are attending? Is the team playing a school it has beaten badly on the road? Is it a game with a revenge motive? Is there anything at all about the circumstances of the game which will motivate the players to a super effort, or which will cause a sub-par effort? Are the referees known to the league? Are the refs local guys? Are the refs above suspicion?

When he finished writing all of this into his handbook it was almost four in the morning, and before he put his head on the pillow to close out another fatiguing day, he remembered Nathan Rubin's advice: "When you're tired and doing bad it's the easiest thing in the world to give up and die. Anybody can do that. It's a lot harder to go on living and to try. That don't only go for betting, ya see?"

And because of Nathan Rubin he wearily got out of bed and wrote himself a memorandum—to find out every answer to every question. To start tomorrow! And then, as he put his giddy, dizzy head to rest, he whispered to Nathan Rubin, "I know what you mean, Mr. Rubin, I know what you mean."

As he lay in bed flares went off in his head and he thought of the peculiar nature of baseball. He thought of the prices he'd laid in the past on Drysdale and Spahn and Marichal and Seaver and he shivered and bundled up in his blanket and felt wounded and raw. He felt confident that he would pick at least four out of ten basketball winners, and with that percentage, and money management, he was certain he could beat the game of hoops and dribbles and the 11–10 and the system and the bookmaker and perform the Kashman mitzvah. Then he remembered that tomorrow he was scheduled to meet Nathan Rubin for lunch, and once again he dragged his aching body out of bed, this time to place his loose-leaf notebook and pen next to his keys and wallet so that in the morning when he awoke, still aching and tired, and grabbed the M-20 to go to work in a fog, they would all be there and he wouldn't have to worry about having forgotten them.

Tomorrow he would be with Nathan Rubin. He smiled as he saw himself furiously scribbling more Nathan Rubin gems in his scuffed, marked, and stained blue loose-leaf notebook. And then the last flare went off in his head and as it descended he thought to himself that he would have to start working on his own rules and regulations for wagering on basketball in the next day or two. Finally, he fell asleep, content.

He woke up after only two hours. It was 6:30 when he started typing into his handbook principles of money management. At 8:00 in the morning he telephoned Doug and asked him to explain exactly what he meant by maximizing and minimizing.

"What do I mean by maximizing and minimizing? It's very simple. No long-winded explanations. Just this. When you're ahead you put out like a nymph, and when you're behind you cross your legs and say no like a virgin.

"That's it, nothing more, and I don't care if you bet shorts, favorites, pitchers, teams, players, home courts, craps, cards, touchdowns, baskets, flats, trots, hardball, or what time Emma Polanski sets her hair. Just maximize when you're ahead, minimize when you're behind. It might be a year before you have your winning streak, but when you do, you'll end up with plenty of pussy. Now let me go back to sleep. That girlfriend of mine, Carmen, kept me up until three in the morning."

He noticed the clock and the hour and he rushed to get dressed, since he was already late for work. Two hours of sleep last night—was it Friday already? Maybe during the entire work week he had had as much as four hours of sleep on any given night. But he did not feel tired; on the contrary, he felt invigorated, and he looked forward to lunch and his meeting with Nathan Rubin.

"You know, Mr. Rubin, in college basketball I'd take the points a lot faster than I'd lay 'em. The favorites don't always cover. That's something I always felt certain about when I was betting."

"You should work on that, kid. If you got an instinct for spotting live underdogs in college basketball, it's a big edge. Champ Holden useta feel that same way. He'd never lay points on a team playing the road, and he'd love to take points whenever he could." Nathan Rubin chirped, "Champ Holden made a hell of a living as a college basketball handicapper, kid."

And as Nathan Rubin said that, David thought: Champ Holden couldn't possibly have had my vision, or my appetite or my ability. If he made a living, and he did, I could make a million!

"Is Champ Holden still around, Mr. Rubin?"

"He's out of action now. He's eighty-two."

"Mr. Rubin, would it be possible for you to introduce me to him?"

"I'll see what I can do, kid."

A week later David finished his rules and put them in his handbook. They would remind him of what he must not do during the college basketball season. That is, from November 15, approximately two weeks before opening night, until April Fool's Day, when the season ends in a grand finale with the NCAA championship game. Yes, it is a short fiscal season. It has a six-day week. More than 99 percent of the games are played on Monday through Saturday night. Almost never on Sunday. Sunday would be his one day off. His preamble stated: DO NOT READ ANYTHING BUT GAMBLING AND BASKETBALL MATERIAL. NO SOCIAL DISTRACTIONS. That included not going to the ballet with Ron Nivens, or to the movies or theater with Doug, not having dinner with Solomon Lepidus and the Colonel, or spending time with Roger Brantley and all his other friends in small talk. His third rule was: NO WOMEN. (Well, maybe on Sunday.) He would try not to make exceptions here, and, of course, this would be difficult, since it included several women he'd only recently met and found quite interesting. One was a beautiful Rubin model, Stefanie Toliver. She looked like a manikin, quite sharp with a marvelous body.

David was in training for the biggest fight of his career, and all his energies, just as Rocky Marciano's or Joe Frazier's, would be forged by steel-hammered dedication. He thought to himself: I've been tested and depleted by losses enough. I don't need any more females interfering.

He told himself that no girl, woman, femme, Ms. in the history of his life had ever made him a penny. He could definitely be an ascetic between November 15 and April 1—except maybe on Sunday. Then he thought to himself that he would never again enter any relationship that had a single iota of hate/fuck attached to it.

He thought he now knew what was of value—laughs are of value, good talk, something as solid as holding hands and passing smiles, definitely. His fourth rule was: NO WRITING. Aesthetics, creativity, spiritual quests were only for the courageous and geniuses and the few who were whole. He might still be broke, but at least he had found a new cause. He had also resolved: NO CASEWORK outside of the barest essentials—he didn't want to get fired. This hurt. Because whatever else he had been, he was always a damn good social worker. It never impressed Leslie; in fact, she resented his giving such tender loving care to "the people." That, too, had to be put aside during the college basketball season.

David looked out of his window. He stared at the sweltering black August night, and he thought a silent litany. He pledged to his new vocation not to quit nor to give it merely a halfhearted try. He picked up his handbook, and he held it close as one might a prayer book, and he felt it to be his refuge, his comrade, his steady companion, his very last resort. Right then, in the quiet of the sweltering night, he realized that he'd be gambling more than just money, he'd be gambling all that he was.

11

THE DAY AFTER Labor Day David noticed that a new batch of workers had arrived at the Harlem welfare office. They were mostly youngsters just out of college. Two, especially, stood out from the rest, not the average black or the dull spastic gray that usually enlisted in the civil service ranks. They were little more than a boy and a girl.

The boy had a cheerful look and appeared to be from out of town. The girl also looked like an out-of-towner. She was not beautiful but beautiful. It was strange, but she seemed to be a swan who had once been an ugly duckling. As David gazed at her he was reminded of fresh clean linen. For some reason he instinctively knew that she wasn't at all like Leslie, but had probably been the kind of child and young teenager who hid in her mother's lap and turned crimson at the sight of a boy. He continued watching her as she talked to her supervisor, her arms folded purposefully across her full bosom. When she finished he noted her awkward gait as she walked to the elevator and the way she bowed her head and kept her eyes riveted to the floor. Her body did not have an affected feminine sway. To him it was obvious that she was shy and still adorned with a gawky long-legged youth. She was unaware of her bloom; her self-consciousness glowed.

The boy was in the training unit with her. He joined her happily in the elevator. David envied him. He recalled when he had first started working for the department. He remembered the indoctrination he had gone through, and he thought that they must have just gone through a similar two-week training period at the Welfare Training Institute. He contemplated quietly how nice it would have been if he had met a girl like that then.

His mind and eye wandered, and he saw his supervisor, Walter Bloom. He walked to his desk and they spoke for a while, and then out of the corner of his eye he saw the same girl walking across the hall, and he mentioned to Bloom that of all the women he'd seen come and go in the office in the past ten years, this was the first one he'd noticed who seemed worth dating. Bloom looked up and spotted her as she came through the corridor and marveled at her slender but beautifully proportioned body. Then he shook his head and muttered, "She doesn't look Jewish, David. She's not for you." At that moment, David received an unexpected telephone call from Leslie.

90 . . .

"Hello, David. What are you doing? You must come over, I have to talk to you. I need you. Can you be here in an hour?"

Her voice wasn't soft or calm. She used a guileless anxious whimper. David told Bloom that he had to go to the field.

Bloom reminded him with a hint of authority that he was the "emergency worker," and that he was obligated to stay in the office the entire day.

Once a week each member of the group was obliged to cover the units' emergencies and remain in hell between 9:00 and 5:00. David walked over to the cashier's cage and negotiated an advance. You could buy a soul in the welfare department for $5 on any given day.

He snatched his field book and his Handbook from his desk, left the office, rushed to the subway, placed a token in the turnstile, passed through, raced down the stairs to board the Woodlawn Express which was pulling into the station, jumped on, found a seat, and started reading his Handbook. But he couldn't concentrate. He started to calculate how many stops it was to Leslie's.

Then a grim sight bore in on him. A quadriplegic woman was navigating an oversized skateboard foot by foot through the crowded subway car. The woman's face shone in the bright lights. David could not keep his eyes from her. She had an oval-shaped, even cherubic, face. She was singing, in a voice heard above the subway noises, a well-known religious song. To David it sounded like "Amazing Grace." The woman's torso took on its own light as she laboriously maneuvered her way through the crowd. Slowly she picked her way forward.

David stared at the dismembered body, at the severed place where it came to a stump. It was harnessed tightly to pine planks which were nailed to roller-skate wheels. The longer he gazed the more pity he felt for the singing woman, and soon he needed to flee from his own discomfort. In fleeing he began to scan dozens of passengers on the subway car. He noticed many had never turned their heads, and others who had kept their faces buried in books, magazines, and tabloids, and still others who gazed blindly ahead seemingly at their own grim realities. And he gazed at an old couple who, as if enacting a ritual, gingerly dropped a nickel and a dime into the singing woman's cup before returning their attention to the Bibles on their laps.

In his vest pocket David searched for change, but failing to find any, he impulsively reached his hand into his trouser pocket and pulled out his wallet. A photograph of Leslie, dog-eared from much handling, fell to the floor. After lifting the photograph from the floor, David removed the largest bill from his wallet and leaned toward the singing woman.

Concealing the $20 bill from the other passengers, he carefully crumpled it into a small ball and then stuffed it into her tin cup, which was hanging like a cross from a frayed string line around her bosom. As he did so the cherubic singing woman continued to push her way along the car.

Leslie didn't say anything when she opened the door; she attacked. She undressed David, stripped and rubbed and cried and scratched and bit and clawed and writhed and sucked and clung. She screwed her way out of anxiety into oblivion. Then she rolled over with a tear-stained face. David noticed a half-empty bottle of Jack Daniel's on a night table. She had bourboned her way through the night. Within minutes she was asleep and David was alone, confused, and dejected. He tried not to stare at her as she lay there in the nude, but he did just the same. He winced as he felt a spark still throbbing in his testicles.

As he got dressed to leave he felt a sense of hovering futility and he bent over and tried to kiss her, but as he did, he noticed her shudder, pull away, and then he realized that she had only used him for a chaser. David didn't leave.

When Leslie awoke, she smiled and pulled him down on her bed. She lit a cigarette, inhaled, and blew a foggy gray smoke ring into the air. By the time she finished her cigarette a glazed look had clouded her face and she was saying in a submissive voice, "I couldn't love anybody that way again, David."

She reached for his hand, held and caressed it. She purred softly and wept a little. The tears trickled down her cheeks. He kissed them away. He touched her breasts with his fingers and then slowly began to work his hand between her thighs. He stopped there, slowly rubbing his palm against golden moss and gently pushing two of his curved fingers into the moist crevice. She began to moan and tremble. He took her face and placed it over his penis and almost at once her head began bobbing up and down.

Some time later she stretched out languorously and seemed kindled by a new and sweeter abandon as she whispered to him for the first time in many long aching years that she was willing to try. He knew it was sick, but he was impaled by years of grief and torture and he wanted to pay her back for all the humiliations.

"I don't know, Leslie."

The telephone rang, and she answered it. While she chatted he walked into Jennifer's room.

He remembered being in his den, working on a manuscript. He had a beard at the time. There was a light knock on the door and a tiny voice: "David, let me come in, please, let me come in." It was sweet Jenny. She wasn't more than three years old at the time.

"What do you want, Jennifer?" he said, opening the door.

She looked up at him and smiled and said, "I want to pull your beard."

He remembered continuing to work while Jennifer stayed in the room pulling at his beard, and he remembered Leslie walking in and placing her hand on his shoulder and bending over and kissing him and whispering, "I love you, David, I love you."

"Me too," Jennifer said. He remembered laughing and laughing. It was delicious. His eyes moist, he walked out of the room and announced to Leslie he was willing to try.

When he returned to his parents' apartment, David scribbled several questions he wanted to ask Nathan Rubin. He tried to study and jot down some notes for the handbook. But his mind was preoccupied, and he couldn't concentrate. He realized that Leslie was getting to him. Depressed, he called his twin brother. He knew he could count on Doug to say at least half of what David thought himself.

"Damn it, David, even before you married Leslie you wanted a divorce. It stopped being romantic right after she met Lou Cartel."

"Then how come we still have such a fantastic sex life?"

"That goes way back. That bitch messed your head up. All that platonic sludge. Years of it. Cartel Girl. You didn't know whether you were coming or going. All that juggling she did. Keeping you around. 'David, Lou Cartel means nothing to me.' Dropping you when she decided to marry him. Coming back when he ditched her. She needed you. The more confused it becomes, the more desperately you try to prove to each other that you love each other, through your lust! Besides, with a bitch like that, what other way does she have to relate?"

David hung up, despising himself for being so weak, for feeling about Leslie the way he did. Still, he knew there was another half, another reasonable half to his emotions, and he knew whom to call to hear it: the Colonel.

"Don't be silly, David. Being crazy about a woman like that is always the right thing to be. That's why you love, you have a soul, you're a poet, you can be hurt. Doug might not understand how you feel, but I do. It's beautiful to feel so much about someone."

Thanks to the Colonel, David fell asleep with his spirits brightened.

Leslie didn't return to sleep. She kept remembering. . . . Holding David's hand on the street outside of her parents' house. Reciting sonnets over lunch; attending classical concerts and the ballet; listening to him quote the aphorisms of Nietzsche, and speak longingly about the big novel he'd write someday. She kept remembering David's tenderness and shyness, and she kept remembering Lou Cartel: "You need a man's strength, Leslie, and you need security. . . . After you sleep with me, you'll know the difference between a boy and a man.

"Besides, I've decided to make you the Cartel Girl. You're going to be the most famous face in this city, Les. . . ."

And Leslie remembered the way Lou glowed when he gazed at her, and how she felt soft and safe when he talked to her; and she remembered: "Leslie, I don't want to hear another word about that college boy. Make up your mind. It's either me and a modeling career, or . . ."

And Leslie remembered how wonderful David was when she was at the bottom: "Lou's claiming Jennifer isn't his child, David. He ruined my career, and now he's refusing to give me alimony and he won't pay child support. I'm all alone, David. I'm frightened." She remembered how supportive he was; how patient and strong. How he helped her and loved her. And she remembered the first time they slept together after all those "friendship years." How exciting, how intense it was. And she remembered their marriage. . . . David locking himself in the bathroom with his silver dollar and his pocket radio and constipation and guilt. The radio on as low as possible so that she couldn't hear; listening to the radio while he held his breath and clenched his silver dollar so hard that his hand turned beet red and indentations appeared which throbbed and remained swollen for hours.

She recalled David losing a tough game. Storming out of the house and onto the street with nowhere to go but to Maxwell's Plum for a drink. She recalled being at Madison Square Garden with him and David too nervous to sit beside her, leaving her and pacing in the empty balcony with only the vacant rows of wooden seats as his companions. She began thinking that he must be insane. Three thousand in attendance for some no-meaning college game and fifteen thousand silent seats and her husband up in no man's land screaming, pacing the floor, clenching his silver dollar, and praying to heaven for a basket or cursing to hell for a miss.

She remembered David's hiding in the Garden john so he couldn't hear the game or see the game or get the score. Killing time on the toilet so he wouldn't have to watch. She recalled David's returning to his seat next to her, saying he was sorry, and staying a minute or two before losing his ability to stand the pressure, walking out of the arena and up to Seventy-second Street and Broadway and inevitably about-facing and timing it to the minute so that he'd be back to see the last live-or-die torturous seconds.

As Leslie lay in bed she found herself hearing David's voice. . . . "God damn it, Leslie, jet-setters are dancing in the in discos. Nathan Rubin's son is entertaining his friends in a mansion right out of Fitzgerald's *Gatsby* on Long Island Sound. And he's no more than I am, Leslie, and he does exist.

"Solomon Lepidus is pissing away thousands, and Bellow and Mailer have made it big. People are enjoying themselves, Leslie: holding hands, loving, talking, kissing, living. But I'm trapped with you and taking the M-20 back up to Harlem."

She found herself sobbing and whispering, "David, I can't live like this. I'm too insecure. I'm sorry, David. I can't."

* * *

He didn't hear from Leslie for a few days. Then she called him at his office. "David, I've made up my mind. I'm going to divorce you. I'm flying to Mexico."

He could not believe it. Several moments passed before he said, "I don't want to divorce you, Leslie. You're my wife. I want a reconciliation. I love you."

She insisted.

He slumped down in a hard-back wooden chair, and co-workers on each side of him began to stare. Paying no attention to them, he half-sobbed, half-whispered into the phone, "I can't live without you in my life, Leslie. It just wouldn't be the same. I need you. I need Jennifer. Please, Leslie, tell me what happened."

"Nothing's happened, David. I just realize that it's impossible to start over again with you."

"You're wrong, Leslie. We're good together. There isn't a thought you or I have that we haven't shared. You know everything there is to know about me, every feeling I've ever had. And it's the same way from me to you. I know every inch of you. Every mole, every dimple. We love each other, Leslie. . . . Leslie . . . are you listening?"

In a calm voice she answered, "I can't take the kind of life you have to offer. You live in two, or even three, worlds at the same time and I can't live happily in any of them. Your life is writing, and being a social worker, and gambling. None of that is for me, David. I need something else."

"But . . ."

"I need someone who's stable, David."

He had that feeling in his stomach, one which came whenever he felt he'd never see Leslie again. Like a madman he slammed down the phone and ran by Walter Bloom, down the stairs, and out of the building.

While on the subway, David couldn't stop thinking about Leslie. He remembered a day when she'd asked him to get her a pack of cigarettes.

Those were their platonic years. They were in David's Fifty-sixth Street pad and a blizzard had been raging over the city for the past several hours. As all transit systems were shut down, Leslie was forced to remain in his apartment for at least that evening. He knew she would be there, that he would have her all to himself. He felt ecstatic.

Leslie asked David to get her some cigarettes though she knew that would demand his going out into the mean weather. He raced into the storm, plowing into knee-high drifts. He stumbled and slid through the snow and finally, almost breathless, reached the corner store. He was the only customer. A couple of packs in his pocket, he challenged the storm again and finally reached his door, but only after much leaping, stumbling, and falling. Later he learned that the snowfall measured the greatest in the city's history. He had reason to remember it.

For the entire half hour he had been on his errand, David's stomach had knotted, while his heart, from all the exertion, had pounded relentlessly. However, as soon as he opened the door and saw her waiting, he felt like laughing. She smiled, and immediately, despite his encounter with the storm, he felt warm.

"What's the matter, David? Why are you looking at me so funny?"

"You're so beautiful," David stammered.

"Oh, thank you." She smiled. "By the way, David, can I have a shirt or sweater to wear around the house, and do you have an extra bathrobe? I don't want to ruin my dress."

He felt overwhelmed, so happy he began laughing. He couldn't touch her, and he was too reticent to tell her how much he loved her. He didn't know what to do. Nervously he started flipping his silver dollar. When he looked at it, its face seemed to be smiling too. He mentioned it to Leslie, and she took it from his hand and gazed at it. She smiled and agreed. He pulled an anthology off a bookshelf and read aloud sonnets of Shakespeare; a little later she was reading to him Blake's "The Lamb," and she referred to him as her little lamb, and he glowed.

The storm continued for days. After she left, he kept his shirt and sweater, the ones she had worn, under his pillows for weeks. Her scent was inside them. At that time theirs was a platonic relationship; but still, it was fantastic, hearing her voice, her way of smiling at him and calling him "a little lamb," her loveliness, her lyricism, her sensuality, her perfection. . . .

When he arrived at Leslie's apartment he pleaded for at least two exhausting hours.

"You've ruined my life. I hate you for what you've done to me."

She walked to her desk and scooped off the top a batch of bills and held them in front of his face. "I don't need words, David, I need money!"

Just then the doorman buzzed on the intercom advising that Warren Landau, a friend of Leslie's, was on the way up. In what seemed like seconds to David, Landau was at the door. Leslie opened it. Angrily she shouted, "Warren, please help me. David refuses to leave my apartment. He's being impossible." She turned toward David and shrieked, "I want you to leave here right now."

Landau walked toward David and politely asked him to leave.

David answered back, "I'm not leaving. She's my wife. I want to fuck her. Do you mind?"

Landau started arguing, telling David that Leslie didn't love him anymore. That it was foolish to make a scene. That she had made up her mind to divorce him and that he should please act like a man and leave her alone. That he had caused her enough grief and aggravation already. David could hear Leslie screaming in the background.

Warren glared at him through steamed glasses.

"Get him out of here, Warren, get him out!"

When Landau put a hand on David's shoulder, something snapped in David Lazar. He swung wildly at Landau. The blow landed solidly on Landau's jaw. It stunned him.

Again and again David hammered Warren with wild punches, until Landau went down, his smashed glasses skidding off to one side. Blood was spilling from his mouth and from a cut above his left eye.

Holding his hands to his face, he screamed in agony, "My eye! My eye! You've blinded me." David felt exhilarated and at the same time frightened. He started walking to where Leslie was standing. She was shouting at the top of her lungs, "Animal! Animal!"

As she saw David coming toward her she crisscrossed her arms against her breasts and covered her face with her hands. The look on David's face was menacing, ten times worse than in the restaurant incident.

Leslie was sure that David Lazar had gone berserk. He pulled her arms apart, grabbed her throat, and with all his hate, strength, and fury, he squeezed. For a few seconds, just a few, he lost control. He could feel the life being choked out of his wife, and yet he continued tightening his grip. He could see her face turning purple and the veins bulging against the skin on her forehead and temples.

Landau tried to get up but groped for a coffee table and fell back to the floor. David heard him yelling, "You'll kill her! Let her go! You'll kill her!" Hearing the word "kill" snapped something inside David back into place, and he let go of Leslie's throat. At that moment he was aware that if a few more seconds had passed—and he hadn't stopped—he'd have murdered his wife.

Leslie started gasping for breath. "You bastard! You . . ."

With all David's remaining strength he grabbed her by the nape of her neck and flung her across the width of the room. She crashed into a wall mirror, and it splintered. David felt the capacity for murder oozing out of him. Leslie ran to the front door, hoping to call a neighbor.

David got there first and pulled her back into the living room, where Warren Landau was still down on his hands and knees, bleeding profusely.

Leslie began screaming again. David glared at her, his face reflecting the loathing he felt at this whole affair. Leslie caught the look and froze. David realized there was a smear of Warren's blood on the white llama rug under his feet. He could also see what appeared to be a three-inch gash above the man's left eye. Leslie's screams had subsided to spasmodic sobbing. Suddenly he felt panicky and began shaking all over. He didn't know what to do. He found himself running out of the apartment, racing into the damp air. He ran around the corner and down the street. The farther he ran, the calmer he felt.

He spotted a public phone and dialed Leslie's number. She answered. He told her to get Landau over to New York Hospital. At first she didn't say anything, then she screamed, "I'm divorcing you! Do you hear me? David! I'm divorcing you!" Then the phone slammed down.

12

LESLIE WAS QUICK to fly to Mexico and divorce David. Then he tried to shake his foul mood by keeping busy. One evening he went over to Ed Kashman's and watched *Mogambo* on television. "God, Ava Gardner was the sexiest woman in the world!" Kashman said.

"Nobody is as sexy as Leslie," David answered.

The next evening David had dinner with Doug. While they were eating Doug seemed especially excited. He kept talking about a deal he was trying to put together. He kept stressing that they were equal partners as always in everything, and that if one of them made it, both would. Of course, as of yet, nothing had materialized. But down deep, Doug believed he'd make it, and they'd share in everything.

David believed in Doug. He remembered during their growing up years thinking: Why can't I be free? . . . Be left alone? . . . Be me? . . . Is he me? . . . Am I him? . . . We're the same. We're not different, if he makes it, I make it. What's the difference who succeeds? . . . I'll show him. I'll make it first. He's nothing. I'm better. . . .

He remembered girls he dated speaking to Doug for hours and never realizing it wasn't David. How many times did he hear it: "I can't tell you two apart." They shared parents, dates, birthdays, suits, foods, movies, friends. Even their haircuts were done by the same barber. It's time we stopped sharing, he thought.

Doug was the "Good" twin, David the "Bad." David knew Doug was stronger, more disciplined, and wiser. But just the same he couldn't keep himself from interrupting Doug and talking about Leslie. Almost immediately Doug cut him off. "David! All this God damn self-pity of yours is disgusting! Don't you see how ridiculous you are?"

"What about you?" David shouted. "All you ever do is bullshit about making it and running off to South America and writing a great novel—but you never do it. You know why you never made any important money in business with all your million and one schemes? It's because you can't give yourself with a full heart to any of them. The truth is, you're a bigger cop-out than anyone. As for Leslie, I'm talking about my life, and if I'm boring you, that's too damn bad."

David's remarks hurt Doug, and an awkward silence ensued. Soon afterward, they parted.

After the divorce, David forced himself to return to the ascetic life. He stayed home and worked on his handbook through all hours of the night. Day after day he caught catnaps on the M-20, in the office, on the subway; found other ways to adjust to his all-consuming commitment. He received invitations to dinner; he refused them all. He looked in the mirror and saw—a civil servant, a frustrated author who couldn't make a living by writing, and a gambler.

Weekends came and he thought about Leslie. He tried to force himself to exorcise her, but he couldn't. He felt her spreading and assaulting his memory; spreading and affecting his self-denials; spreading and tormenting his new and hard-won dedications; spreading into a constant monologue which intruded itself upon everything he did and was.

Damn her, I can't let go. . . . Damn her. And he still felt lost. Damn her! . . . Damn her! . . . Damn her! . . .

Every time the telephone rang he felt a shock. She would never call. In his sleep he tossed and turned. When he awakened, he turned to his handbook. Deep within he couldn't believe it was over. Not for one minute on any given day. That was impossible. He couldn't believe that she would be able to say "I love you" to another man. Their relationship was different. It was more than others knew. He couldn't ever love another as he loved Leslie. She gave him an erection even when he just spoke to her on the telephone. Someday she'd contact him and he'd be there. Someday her true feelings would return and she'd be able to face them. She'd be haunted by them. What if it took years? Would it give him pleasure? Satisfaction? Make him sad?

One day when the telephone rang, it was Sidney Feld, half stewed, out of his mind. David hung up on him. Seconds later the phone rang again. This time it was Champ Holden, calling to confirm their appointment, and as soon as David finished with him the phone rang again. This time it was Saskia Verdonck. She suggested that he come over, but he told her he had a lot of work to do. She told him that she'd have a surprise waiting for him. Staying with her for the weekend was a young girl she had met through Nathan Rubin, Ursula Knutson, and she too was beautiful. She put Ursula on the phone, and her voice purred and chimed as Leslie's had a long time ago. He said he would come over.

After that weekend David took the M-20 bus back to the office and learned that Walter Bloom was being transferred to the Melrose Center in the Bronx. No reason was given, just a memo from downtown advising of the transfer.

For the first time in all his years in the welfare fraternity he agreed to attend a going-away luncheon. Bloom was the only one for whom he would have endured that. He sat next to Beryl Reed—"I had to run all the way from the subway to the time clock this morning." David pictured young Beryl running to Mommy, Daddy, school, church, machine, always running. "I'm afraid they're going to penalize me by charging my lateness to my annual leave. Do you think they'll do that, Mr. Lazar?"

David nodded. Beryl Reed continued chattering.

David moved over to Walter Bloom. Hymie Rosenblatt came over, "You're lucky to be getting out, Walter. I hear Melrose is air-conditioned during the summer."

David moved over to Vern Blender, the union representative, and John Fagan, the office's young revolutionary. Fagan was wearing his uniform: long hair, beard, faded jeans, sandals, leather vest, and T-shirt with a lollipop decal, the words "suck me" ironed on. He was reading *The Unionist* and studying a rate-increase chart and gleefully telling Blender that he'd be getting a biweekly increase of $4.83.

"What kind of Yippie are you, John?" David said. "If you want to work for money, go get a job and make money. If you want to work here, work for the free time, and maybe in your spare time help some people."

Vern Blender kept telling David how the union was fighting for a ten-dollar-a-week raise. David told him he had never joined the union. He looked at David as if he were Benedict Arnold. Willis Knox talked about medical benefits, and about Mrs. Fitzmorris, who had retired to collect her pension three months earlier and had died over the weekend.

Then Clem Allen mentioned the new young woman David had noticed. "Did you get a look at that new chick, Lazar? Man, did you ever see a finer woman in your whole life? Man, if there's one thing I dig, it's a thin woman with big boobs."

Balding, under thirty, Arthur Fink, the assistant office manager, came over with a worried look on his face. "I have to ask you something, Lazar. You're a man who gets around. Where should I take my girlfriend for her birthday?"

"Take her dancing, Arthur."

"I don't dance," he squeaked.

"Fake it, Fink!"

Harry Epstein came over. "I've lost a fortune in the market, Lazar," he whined. "About six hundred dollars."

Shortly thereafter, David returned to Bloom's table. He took Bloom's hand and said earnestly, "I'm going to miss you, Walter. We've been together a lot of years."

"That goes for me too, David, and if you like that little girl, take her out. I wanted to apologize to you for the way I spoke the other day. Don't worry that she's not Jewish. The truth is, that day I felt uptight—is that the expression, David?"

David smiled. "That's the expression, Walter."

"Oh, before I forget, good luck on your handbook. I hope you become a great handicapper. David, I meant to ask you, *vot* is a handicapper?"

David laughed and became boisterous. "It's the name of the game, Bloom. It's pitting your brain against bookmakers. It's calculating numbers and matching point spreads and culling information in the middle of the night. It's picking winners, Bloom—picking winners!" David grimaced, became deadly serious. "It's getting out of this godforsaken place, Bloom. It's getting out!"

Bloom shook his head and said, "You might be a genius, David, but you're still a little bit meshuga." He smiled. "But who isn't?" The smile left his face as he gazed at David and took David's hand and clasped it in his. "Take care of your clients, David. Remember, you're all they have."

David's face showed that he was becoming perturbed.

"David, when you want to be, you're a wonderful caseworker. Don't think that's unimportant."

David couldn't take any more. "Thanks, Bloom, but I got to cut out now. I'll call you next week to see how you're doing."

As he started to leave, Hymie Rosenblatt caught up with him. Removing the cigar from the middle of his face, he said, "I tried talking to that new girl, Debbie Turner, this morning, Lazar, but I couldn't get anywhere."

"Hymie, how many times do I have to tell you? You'll never make it with a woman under twenty-five until you get rid of those baggy pants of yours and those white shoes."

Hymie's eyes opened wide. He stared at David with a quizzical look as if to say, "You're crazy."

David went over to Doug's place to meet an old friend, Roger Brantley. When he arrived a girl who couldn't have been more than eighteen was leaving the apartment. She was skinny as a sword and had a terrible case of acne.

David removed a key from his trouser pocket, unlocked Doug's door, and entered. He found Brantley half undressed. He was no longer the emaciated black shoeshine boy he had been as a teen. He had put on about forty pounds and sported an afro. His rotten teeth were a thing of the past, too. Now he had a handsome set of dentures and caps. His clothes, though, remained those of a shoeshine boy. He wore tattered jeans, sneakers, a knickerbocker T-shirt, and a frayed-at-the-cuffs windbreaker, the kind that could be picked up at any army surplus store. The windbreaker was tossed over one of Doug's director's chairs.

Roger was devoting his entire concentration on his afro with his pick comb, but as soon as David mentioned seeing the girl, he compulsively started talking. He said her name was Ellie Kaufman and that he had picked her up in front of the Garden a few weeks back. He had first spotted her one evening going into Penn Station on her way home. He told David that she was living with her parents in Roslyn and that her father was a dentist. He also said that he had promoted Doug into letting him use the apartment by telling him that Ellie would fix him up with a friend.

Roger smiled. "Shee-it! Your brother's the greatest. He bullshits a lot, but you know him. When it comes to chicks, he's out of his mind."

Roger then proceeded to ask David the same kind of questions that he always asked when it came to white women. What did he think of Ellie? Was she sexy? Would he want to make it with her?

It wasn't long before David found himself interrupting him. "Roger, that's not what I want to discuss with you. I need information on as many players and college teams as possible. With all those college scouts and coaches you've been dealing with, you can get me more inside information than anyone. I want to know every kid who has a chance to make it on a college varsity. Every kid who's a sleeper. Every freshman who's been red-shirted. Every junior-college transfer."

David looked straight into Brantley's eyes. "You're the only guy who can do it for me, Rog—you're tighter with more ballplayers and coaches than anyone in this freakin' city."

Brantley broke in. His voice was ghetto cool. "What is this shit, man? You going to start gambling again?"

"That's exactly what I'm going to do, Roger."

"You're crazy, man, you can't beat them. I told you years ago you should have saved your money the way a bee stores honey. All that tension you had, what was it all for?" He shook his head. "Nothin', man, nothin'! You would've been better off drinkin', smokin', or snortin' coke. Shee-it, man, gambling ain't no better than shootin' dope."

"It's going to be different this time, Roger. I'm going to approach it like a business."

"Shee-it, you're either going to get mixed up with the underworld or the law, and neither of them mess around." Brantley paused, nervously playing with his pick. He continued, "Shee-it, if you ever borrow from a shylock and don't pay back, you'll be in real trouble. You know what them guys do to you? I've seen it happen. When I was shining shoes as a kid in Brooklyn I useta have them for customers. I've seen how mean them cats can get. You'd be foolin' around with the worst kind of trouble if you start dealin' with them." He shook his head. "Shee-it, you're crazy, man. No wonder you lost Leslie. No guy ever had a finer fox, but you blew her because you're a fool." He paused. "You're a bigger fool for wanting her back. Let me tell you something. Loving a woman that don't love you back is like bouncing a basketball without air in it." .

David suppressed a smile. Roger's beautiful street-rich language never failed to impress him. "Skip the advice, Roger, and tell me about some of the players you think might be sleepers."

It took considerable effort, but David finally persuaded Brantley to assist him. The complexion of their conversation changed.

"You know who I should get you to is Eddie Zeno. He runs the Mr. Tom tournament for high school All-Americans in the Philly area. He's also into gambling and he does some agency work on the side. You two might be able to work something out."

David made an appointment to go to a Knick-Philly exhibition game with Roger on Saturday night. Zeno was supposed to be driving into New York to see the game and to talk to Roger about some high school phenom in Brooklyn. It was a good time to meet. Roger started rapping to David about Sky Davis, a boy who had dropped out of high school in his sophomore year and whom he had been helping ever since.

"I had Sky in junior college all last year, and now I got him into Western. When the season starts that club will beat anyone in their conference. I also got Tony Willis of Jefferson into Western, and between Tony's rebounding and Sky's doing the rest, that club's going to be tougher than shit. Sky's mean, David. I wouldn't be surprised if he leads the whole motherfuckin' country in scoring. Shee-it, last year in his first game at San Pueblo he got fifty-one. I just spoke to Johnny Anderson this morning— he's the coach. They're going crazy over Sky. They think he's going to be super!"

"What about Tony Willis, Rog? Won't he resent Sky's getting all the press?"

"Shee-it, Tony's an animal, but you gotta realize he idolizes Sky. He'll do anything for him. Shee-it, that's why I got Tony into the school. He got a great attitude. And next year I'm getting Billy Duval from Boys' High into Western. Shee-it, with him doin' the playmaking, Western will be as tough as any team in the damn country."

Roger walked out onto Doug's terrace. The seasons were changing and the trees vacillating between colors: brown, yellows, reds, oranges, greens all fusing. Roger didn't notice—he turned wide-eyed toward David.

"Shee-it! I'm already talking to more agents than I want to. They won't leave me alone, man. My phone never stops ringing. Shee-it! My wife, Cheryl, should be getting paid. She's become a damn answering service. I guarantee you within two years Sky's the number-one draft choice in the whole motherfuckin' country." Roger frowned. "I just hope he don't fuck up with too many white bitches down there."

"Roger, that's enough on Sky. Concentrate on what I want for a second."

"Shee-it! No sweat, man, stop worrying." Roger grinned. "Just be at the Garden Saturday night."

Eddie Zeno turned out to be a dream. He lived on the Pennsylvania side of the Delaware River, in New Hope. His office was in Philly. He had fat jowls, thin lips, a jaundiced complexion that gave his face a sallow glow, and a soft smile, and, most important, he had hard-core basketball facts.

They talked during the game, and Zeno told David that he had a master's degree in psychology from Bradley University. David responded by telling him how his twin brother, Doug, had gone for his doctorate in clinical psychology but had had to drop out when he was leveled by Esther Aroni. At that Zeno smiled and said, "Women, they can be even more devastating than gambling."

After the game, Roger, Eddie, and David had dinner at Chinese Village, a restaurant only a couple of short blocks away from Madison Square Garden. They rapped until a little past midnight, when Roger split for his home in Bed-Stuy in Brooklyn.

Several minutes later Eddie and David grabbed a cab. "Fifty-third, between Park and Lexington, driver. The Brasserie." That made David snicker. It was Cancer City to a T. It's making it, gloss, surface, a balloon to everywhere, a float going nowhere. It's voyeurs, panderers, scene players, *parlez-vous français*, all the dandy bullshit. It's eating your guts out every time you see a beautiful pair of tits you'll never have. It's staring at the girl and being ignored. It's cheap food at expensive prices; ugly ladies wearing resplendent gowns and smelling nasty, and innocent young things with straight and frizzy hair, in jeans and silky shirts, smelling pretty. It's menus like Toulouse-Lautrec posters, and it's help scurrying around as if they cared, but you know they don't. It's the Brasserie. It's walking in from the black of the street through a revolving door, stopping on that two-by-two center stage at the top of the stairs and saying to yourself: "I want to be seen, and I want to see everyone." It's waiting on line for a table. "I'll wait for one in front," and then turning to your date and saying, "Don't worry, hon, Jeanette knows me for years." It's being seated with circumstance and pomp; a bottle of wine, hamburger Basque, onion soup, eggs Benedict and Florentine. It's spending money, wasting time, stuffing your belly, doing nothing. It's every Saturday night, more dead than alive.

They entered the Brasserie through its main entrance, the ever-present inexorable revolving door. They entered and immediately were whooshed inward as if boarding a Lexington Avenue express at rush hour. They were shoved and squeezed against throngs of anonymous night people, and while waiting as they did for a table, Eddie gawked and David fumed.

When they finally were seated, Eddie and David ordered coffee and hamburger Basque, and continued talking about college baskets until four in the morning. When it came to the inside stuff ("You're wrong, David, the nation's best college basketball official isn't Steve Honzo, it's Irv Brown"), Eddie Zeno proved to have even better inside dope than Nathan Rubin. He had scouting reports on every good high school player in America, as well as on most of the collegians. His annual Mr. Tom game was the most popular high school all-star game in the country. He had sole jurisdiction over everything, and he took the game seriously. Very seriously. He explained to David how he had bird dogs all over the country scouting the youngsters, and that he listened to every coach's opinion, and viewed as many of the players as he could personally during the course of the season before making his final selections.

The idea for the Mr. Tom game had been Zeno's own invention. He had conceived it as a charity game and sold it as such to the Philadelphia *Examiner* in 1963. The *Examiner* financed everything. All profits went to The Children Need Love, a large local charity. Eddie's cut came from the live gate. All in all he averaged about $8,000 a year in profit from the game.

Of course, as far as David was concerned, the best part of everything was that Eddie Zeno was a gambler: like David, nothing really big; like David, he had never done well. Because of that and his other credits, David figured it would be a natural for them to hook up. And when David told him of the contacts he had and the handbook he was preparing, Zeno was as enthusiastic as David was to work something out.

David suggested that once the season started he call him every day at precisely 3:00 in the afternoon. David reasoned that way they'd be able to talk as long as they wanted without being hassled about placing their bets and getting lines. They'd be able to compare information and go over the power ratings for the games on the board, and discuss them at length.

David planned for Eddie to call a second time at exactly 6:20 P.M., at which time they would compare the Philly line against the New York lines. Then they'd exchange opinions again, as well as discuss any new developments, such as hot games.

Whichever one had the best line on any particular game they liked would proceed to call in the bet. The second call, David calculated, would take no longer than a few minutes. A third call would only be for the purpose of verifying their joint ventures.

Eddie liked the plan. David liked Eddie. David told him his bets

... 105

would probably not exceed $50 on any given game. Eddie said he expected to be wagering half-dollars and dollars—that is, $50 and $100—so they'd have to say they were both small-time investors with what they hoped to be big-time information.

After they met that first time, David was confident that his access to player information would be of tremendous value. Besides scholastic player info Eddie was familiar with most of the college fives in the East. Eddie's strength, of course, was the Philly area. The Big Five especially— Villanova, LaSalle, St. Joseph's, Temple, and the University of Pennsylvania. But he also knew the smaller teams in the Yankee Conference, and had an even stronger opinion on other Eastern and Southern teams. As an added bonus, he said he'd start developing his contacts in the Atlantic Coast Conference and start utilizing the ones he already had made in the Southeastern and in the Southern, where he said he knew most of the coaches and some of the black players.

Before parting Eddie told David he was hooked up with a Philadelphia lawyer, Mark Jagerman, in an agency business which represented athletes. Eddie's responsibility was to approach the youngsters during his Mr. Tom game and begin to pitch them a spiel on why they should think seriously of signing with an agent upon turning pro. Then he'd continue to develop his rapport with the boys through their college years and promote Jagerman. Consequently, if he did his promo job well enough, by the time the nattily attired, cigar-smoking Jagerman made a special trip to meet the prospect, he would have better than a fifty-fifty chance of signing him. Eddie, of course, would remain a silent partner and stay in the background.

At the very end of the evening Eddie Zeno told David that he was interested in getting Roger Brantley to work for him in the New York area. He had offered Roger 2 points of the standard 10 on any player he would be able to bring into the company, and he even got Jagerman to throw in an extra $25 a week for Brantley's expenses; but it was all to no avail, as Brantley had refused the offer.

Roger said he didn't want that kind of money, that he wasn't a flesh peddler, and that he wouldn't get involved in selling out on his kids.

Roger elaborated that he didn't trust Jagerman and therefore he wouldn't recommend him. Zeno tried like hell to promote Roger, but he couldn't. When David told Zeno that Brantley didn't need the 2 points or the $25 a week, that he was scalping tickets and earning over $1,000 tax-free a week, the agent gasped.

By the time David got home it was about five in the morning, but rather than go to sleep, he started to scribble down as much as he could remember of the conversation that had to do with basketball. The next morning, Sunday, as soon as he awoke, he typed everything on loose-leaf paper and transferred all the material he deemed pertinent into his notebook. He began a separate file for the information Zeno had given him on high school and college players and teams.

Later that same day he telephoned Nathan Rubin and asked him if he thought it would be a good idea for him to subscribe to the Gold Sheet or any other handicapper's newsletter.

"I gave you some of Olshan's sheets, didn't I? It's a good reference for you to use. The sheets are crammed with records, schedules, and stats." Nathan Rubin stopped. "But as far as picking winners, be a loner. If you lose you have nobody to second-guess but yourself. Besides, kid, the way you're cramming, you certainly should be as up on the game as anyone else."

David advised Nathan Rubin that he had begun to develop his own power ratings for every college team in the country. He told him how slowly it was going and how much research and preparation had to be done.

Rubin suggested that if David had trouble, he should use Mort Olshan's Hoop Ratings as a guide, as it was still about the best one he knew. They made a date to meet later that week for lunch, and David thanked him for everything he had done for him. Before Nathan Rubin hung up, he said, "The difference between opinion and information and balls and instinct and winning and losing on any given day or week very well might be luck, kid, but money management is never luck. . . ."

DAVID MET Nathan Rubin at the Young Men's Philanthropic League (all the members were past sixty), where he was playing cards with half a dozen rapacious gentlemen, including Sidney Feld. Rubin was winning; he was anxious to leave. Sidney Feld was losing; he wanted to stay.

David and Nathan Rubin grabbed a cab and headed for Jack Dempsey's restaurant. Once there, David nonchalantly mentioned Arnie Feld. It triggered Nathan Rubin, and he immediately countered, "You don't have to tell me about Arnie. I know him since he's a baby. I even went to his bar mitzvah. He must have cost Sidney over a hundred thou in gambling debts in the past ten or twelve years. Why the hell do you think Sidney had to sell his business and why do you think he drinks so much?"

David studied Nathan. "Can't you do anything for Arnie, Mr. Rubin?"

"I can't do anything," Rubin answered, almost violently. He downed a shot of Calvados, meticulously returned the espresso cup to the saucer, and then, exhibiting great patience, said, "You gotta understand something, David. No one gives you anything in this world. You gotta grow up and start understanding reality. Your mother and father aren't always going to be there to pay your rent and tell you how wonderful you are and make you feel like a king. One day all the nursery rhymes disappear and you have to go out and earn a living on your own. It's the guys who can't distinguish between the ego trip they're on as babies and what the real world really is who get in trouble. They keep thinking that the world owes them a living, that whatever they do it's going to work out fine. Well, it doesn't. They're suckers. They end up getting buried."

Once again Nathan Rubin went through his ritual of sipping his espresso and returning the cup to the plate. Finally, in a more gentle voice, he said, "Two years ago Sidney begged me to do something for Arnie, and I did. I got him a job as a runner for Tony Giardello's office." He stopped and knocked nervously with his knuckles on the table. "The kid swore to me he'd never make another bet, and he didn't, for two lousy weeks! He could have earned thirty thou a year as a runner for Fat Tony." He stopped again. "He would have had it easy. I lined up plenty of customers for him. I even had Fat Tony start him out on a thirty-seventy split, and convinced him to throw in a couple of hundred a week extra to tide Arnie over until he started earning a living. That's damn good for a guy just breaking in."

Nathan Rubin frowned and started tearing a paper napkin into strips. He neatly arranged the strips into a rectangle and placed his cup of coffee in the center, as if it were a helicopter and the paper a landing strip. He gazed at a couple of people walking by, and for a second David suspected he recognized them. But he didn't. His attention returned to the helicopter and the landing strip, and he crumbled the latter with his huge hands and then his attention returned to David. "Imagine that dumb kid screwing up a deal like that! Within two weeks that sucker was into Tony G. for twenty-one hundred." He paused. "I had to tell Tony to let him go, and when Arnie couldn't meet the obligation, Sidney asked me, and I made it good." Nathan Rubin slowly continued to sip from his cup.

"I started to tell you, Mr. Rubin," said David, "when I met with Arnie last week it was about gambling. Sidney told him I was studying up on college baskets. He must have made it sound as if I were a genius or something."

All of a sudden David felt the need to confess, as if he were speaking to his father. "I did sort of brag to Sidney about how well prepared I thought I was. Anyway, Arnie wants to work with me now. He sounded desperate to work something out. He said that if I needed him to, he could take shots at Tony Giardello's office for whatever amount I wanted."

Nathan Rubin responded in a sullen voice, "Arnie Feld's a loser, David, and the thing you should remember is you either stay away from losers, or you use losers. That's it!" There was a moment of silence. "He's dead wrong if he thinks Fat Tony is the kind of guy to play games with."

David mentioned that Arnie had told Tony that Rubin was his godfather and that he'd make good anything lost to him.

Upon hearing that Nathan Rubin went out of control. He swore loudly, jumped up and down, pounded the table with his enormous fists, spilling his coffee, and flung his arms wildly in the air. Then, when a startled waiter stopped frozen, Rubin grabbed a bowl of thick soup from his tray and splattered it against the wall, all the time completely oblivious of the people seated around them, staring and scurrying.

At last, breathing hard, he came to a halt, but then the very next second he flew to a pay phone and telephoned Tony Giardello and screamed at the top of his lungs that he wouldn't make good one penny for Arnie Feld ever again. When he returned his face was still flushed, but he didn't seem a bit self-conscious over the commotion he had caused. He simply sat down, knocked his bony knuckles against the table again, and asked the waiter to bring another espresso and some cheese Danish.

David kept quiet for several minutes, but finally, having a need to explain, he said, "I think one of the reasons Arnie's messed up, Mr. Rubin, is he's always tried to emulate his father as well as you. As far as he's concerned, Sidney's still the world's greatest gin rummy player and you're the greatest gambler who ever lived. He feels he has something to prove to both of you. Besides that, I think he unconsciously resents the time Sidney spent away from him when he was growing up."

David stopped speaking for a second and recalled what Doug had said after an evening with Arnie and him. "My brother read Arnie like an open book, Mr. Rubin. He spotted a million subconscious motivations eating away at him, and he's convinced me that he had an overpowering need to lose."

"There are two kinds of gamblers, David," Nathan Rubin said, "the suckers and the pros. They have nothing in common. Arnie's kind is unconsciously driven to gambling, while the pro consciously uses gambling as he would any other business."

"There's a third kind, Mr. Rubin."

"What's that?"

"The millions of harmless guys like Morty Lefko who play only for diversion or to fill up bitter hours or to be sociable."

Nathan Rubin's voice was testy when he corrected David. "They aren't gamblers, David. Not everyone who gambles is a gambler. Arnie Feld, he's a gambler!"

"My brother studied the psychopathology of that kind of gambler in school. You should hear him talk. He says Arnie's punishing himself for feelings of hostility he harbors toward his parents. From that comes his guilt and his self-punishment, his wanting to lose. Doug says for his entire life he'll be caught up in the vicious circle of rebelling, feeling guilty, and punishing himself."

"Stop psychoanalyzing it, kid. It's not going to get you anywhere. Arnie Feld's a born sucker. I just wish he had some real money so I could make him some propositions. That's the only thing you should be concerned about, kid." He stopped and grabbed a handful of sugar cubes. "In this racket, like any other business, you gotta take advantage of every sucker, not worry about their problems. Life's a simple thing." He casually tossed some sugar cubes onto the table. "Don't try to intellectualize it."

He picked up the cubes of sugar again and toyed with them. He fondled them in his large paws as if they were dice, and crushed them. Finally he looked at David and frowned. "Look, David, if you're really serious about gambling you're going to have to take all that book knowledge and whatever other crap you might have inside of you and lose it. You can't be a schoolboy all your life, and don't be a psychologist either. Just be a damn good gambler, that's hard enough." He stopped for a moment. "I heard about your brother from Solomon. He's some kind of intellectual, right? Well, let me tell you something about intellectuals." He snickered. "They don't make a dime. I never was detoured by all the garbage you find in books. I found out early that some guys waste as much time on the arts and learning as others do on gambling and whoremongering. To me it's all the same, David. One sickness is as bad as another."

His face changed and in a surprisingly youthful voice he said, "You know what I useta do in business whenever I had a problem? I useta go out and hire some brainy college boy from M.I.T. or Harvard for a couple of hundred a week. Remember that, David, you can always buy brains. What you can't buy is will and a sense of purpose and vision and whatever else it takes to be successful. What a businessman has to do is take those brains and use them as tools to reach his particular goal. Remember, David, brains are nothing but wings for you to travel on."

He laughed. "My whole life I've been on one nonstop flight. And, David," he added almost as an afterthought, "if you're going to use brains for any other reason, you're going to crash."

110 . . .

Suddenly Nathan Rubin was glancing at his watch and calling the waiter.

"Please, Mr. Rubin, do you have another fifteen minutes? I've brought my handbook with me. I wanted to show you some of the rules I've been working on. I want to know what you think."

David read off about thirty different factors to consider and then, half-teasingly, he said, "Why don't you let me handicap college baskets for you, Mr. Rubin? I'm sure we can work something out."

As he said it, a part of him was serious in spite of his teasing demeanor.

But Nathan Rubin only beamed in response and broke out in a large smirk and in a particularly malevolent voice said, "Not now, kid, maybe next year. Right now you haven't proved a thing either to me or to yourself. Once the season starts we'll find out real quick if you're a pro or just another sucker!"

Nathan Rubin stood up, and David helped him with his coat.

"Did I tell you I'm going to Boone, Texas, next week, David? I got some business down there I got to attend to."

David Lazar immediately associated Boone with Western University. "You know, Mr. Rubin, I have a friend, Roger Brantley. He just got Sky Davis, a great player, into Boone College's biggest rival. Rog and another friend of mine, Eddie Zeno, have access to high school players all over the country."

Nathan Rubin jerked his head up. "Ya mean ya got contacts that recruit high school players?"

David answered, "Roger Brantley recruits more kids than any man in the country. There's a gold mine of talent in New York's ghettos, Mr. Rubin. Roger says, and I agree, that he could turn a losing team into an NCAA tournament team in a year if a school looked the other way when they reviewed transcripts." David paused. "Take Boone, for instance. Last year they won four games and lost nineteen. But if they could hire a black coach like, say, Rodney Leland out of Louisiana, and if Roger could get two or three of his kids in the school, they'd turn the program around in no time. Right now he has one kid he says is as good as Sky Davis."

Nathan Rubin quickly asked, "What's the boy's name?"

David stopped and thought. "You know, Roger tells me about so many kids it's hard to remember all their names. Oh yeah, I got it, it's Stan Gibbs. They call him Swish Gibbs, Mr. Rubin." David paused again. "That's only one boy, Mr. Rubin. There are at least half a dozen of them around. Why, just yesterday I got a call from Eddie Zeno. He told me about one boy, Calvin 'Shrimp' Beasley, in Florida, whom he considers the best high school guard in the country. The trouble is the boy's flunked just about every course he's taken. He also mentioned another boy in Philadelphia, Johnny Lee Crawford, who he says is another Willis Reed. That boy was suspended by his high school for shooting up before a game. There isn't a school in America that's going to touch Crawford or those other two, Mr. Rubin. The NCAA would investigate them in no time."

Nathan Rubin's cold blue eyes hardened and his voice rose as he said, "Why didn't you ever mention those guys before, David?"

"I never thought it important, Mr. Rubin. Is it?"

Nathan Rubin looked pleased. His voice was incredibly calm as he said, "Well, ya see, David, I might be able to help your friends get those boys you mentioned into Boone. I know a fella who has some influence down there." Nathan Rubin stopped.

David Lazar's voice turned serious as he said, "If those three got into Boone they'd be one of the two top teams in the conference immediately. In fact, with the schedule they play, outside of Western, they'd have a good chance of going undefeated. But as I said, with the NCAA giving every school a hard time, not even an outlaw school like Boone would—"

Nathan Rubin interrupted. "You don't see the NCAA stopping all the schools, do you, David? Why, I just got a report the other day from Champ Holden that the University of Las Vegas is going to step up their basketball program."

Nathan Rubin smirked and then cackled. "I'll make you a bet, David. I'll wager you that in less than two years Vegas has recruited a great basketball team." With that Nathan Rubin took out a pen. "Give me the phone numbers of them guys, David." He jotted the information onto a memo pad. After that he headed for the cashier, and David Lazar noticed him examining the bill. Nathan Rubin didn't ask, but David sensed that he expected him to pay for his share. He reached into his pocket and took out what he had. He handed him a crumpled $10 bill and returned two crisp singles to his pocket. There was a smirk on Nathan Rubin's face as he said, "Thanks, sonny!" David swallowed hard and smiled engagingly as he said, "You're welcome, Mr. Rubin."

Outside, when stepping into a cab, Nathan Rubin grunted out, "See you when I get back, sonny!"

Minutes after he had left David Lazar, Rubin telephoned Boone College.

"Hello, Sam Boone, please. . . . Sam, this is Nathan Rubin. I want you to call a couple of men. One's a black guy, Roger Brantley, in New York. The other guy's name is Eddie Zeno. Ever hear of him? . . . Runs the Mr. Tom Tournament in Philly. Good! Both of them have access to some basketball players. Real blue-chippers. And the thing is, they can't get them into any college in the country. . . . Why? You know the reasons why. The kids are ghetto kids, fuckups!

"Now do this, Sam!" Nathan Rubin gave Sam Boone, president of Boone College, detailed instructions on how to approach Roger Brantley and Eddie Zeno. He was not to mention that Nathan Rubin was the chief

112 . . .

benefactor of the school; he was not to mention that the campus consisted of only two acres, that Boone was one hundred miles from Houston and had a population of less than a thousand, that it offered no nightlife, no movie house, no tavern, no blacks, no co-eds, that the social life—if you could call it that—was confined to the community store where old-timers sat gossiping.

Sam Boone was to mention to Roger Brantley that David Lazar had told him to call; that the school was pro-black; that it would be hiring a black coach, Rodney Leland, for the upcoming basketball season; that it could "adjust" transcripts and do any other damn thing necessary to get the right boys.

Rubin ordered Boone to tell Eddie Zeno that he, Rubin, was open to any kind of deal if Zeno could deliver Calvin "Shrimp" Beasley and Johnny Crawford. Crawford was the player Zeno described as a great ballplayer.

"Sam," Nathan Rubin added in a high pitch, "I want all three of those boys playing for Boone. *Get* them, Sam. Get . . . Wait a minute, Sam. I just thought of something. Call Josh Turner at the community store. Have him with you when you speak to that black guy Brantley. And whatever you do, take Josh along when you pitch the kids and their mamas." Nathan Rubin chuckled. "Josh is the best damn thing we got going for us with them black kids. Now remember, Sam. Get those boys. Get them!"

After finishing the work on his handbook, David thought of something Nathan Rubin had told him about Arnie Feld.

When Arnie was nineteen he had dropped out of college to join the army. He took his basic training at Fort Dix and one day received a telephone call from his father, who was on a junket to Vegas. Sidney Feld asked if Arnie could arrange to get a pass for the weekend and visit his mother. She wasn't feeling well, and no one was there other than the maid. Sidney Feld said he would be back on Monday, and if Arnie could arrange to stay the weekend, he'd appreciate it. He called Arnie "son" for the first time in years. That was the difference.

Arnie arranged for a pass and drove to Teaneck in his black T-bird. He hadn't seen his mother since he had begun basic training. He wanted to surprise her, so he wore his uniform. When he got home it was 11:00 at night and he knew the maid would be sleeping. He unlocked the front door and tiptoed up to his mother's bedroom. In his arms he held two dozen long-stemmed roses. He listened at the door and heard her put a book down and switch off the light next to her bed. Just as he opened the door and shouted, "Hi, Mom," the maid heard something creak and started to scream. In the confusion his mother must have thought he was a burglar, for she began screaming too.

She couldn't make him out in the dark. Besides, she was groggy from all the pills she had taken during the day. Arnie ran toward her to hug and kiss her; she was already gasping for air. Two days later in the intensive-care unit of Holy Name Hospital in Teaneck, New Jersey, Molly Feld quivered, convulsed, and died.

Arnie told David that after his mother's death, he and his father scarcely ever talked; his father blamed him for his mother's death. It was then that Sidney had started to drink. He said that he never asked Sidney to see a doctor, never even asked him to stop drinking. He noticed his belly and legs swelling; the sores on his feet caused by the poor circulation; his hands turning red, even the nipples on his breasts growing larger, or so it seemed. He noticed everything. What upset him most was: "He's becoming a pathological liar, David. I hear him on the telephone with Nathan Rubin and Sandy Rocca, and even my Uncle Leo. All he does is lie. I know he's sick, and I should do something, but I don't. I can't. He's always depressed, David. For days he locks himself in his apartment and refuses to go out. What do you think I should do?"

David had no answer.

The next day, David dropped his handbook off with Doug, who wanted to see how he was progressing. Doug called late that evening and advised David that he had read his notes and that he respected what David was doing and that now he was almost convinced that David was attacking gambling in a professional way. He said, "I'd like you to read a book I have on gambling. It's a classic in the field. You can't let yourself forget for a minute that you were in some ways the same kind of gambler the author's describing. Let me read you his definition of that pathological phenomenon, David."

Doug proceeded to educate David. He detailed the characteristics of the pathological gambler and said how afraid he was of David's inability to turn away from the tension and the thrill of the game itself. And for the millionth time he suggested that David not listen to or watch any games he'd be gambling on. "Don't try to derive pleasure from displeasure, David. That's sick."

David responded by telling him that the last thing he wanted was to be masochistic, but that he wanted to listen to as many of the games as he could. It was necessary, germane to the entire operation.

At Doug's place David mentioned that he was even pinching quarters so that he could buy the best shortwave radio on the market in order to pick up games played around the country. He explained how important it was for him to know how the games were going, how the coaches played their personnel, who substituted, who didn't, and on and on. Doug said it made sense and he believed David and that he would buy him a Nordmende radio as his contribution to David's profession.

At that moment the telephone rang and Doug picked up the receiver. "Hello? ... Hi, Solomon."

"Let me speak to him," David whispered anxiously.

Doug paid little attention to his brother. He continued speaking to Solomon, answering question after question concerning a business deal they were partners in.

The split second he finished, David grabbed the phone from Doug. "Solomon, David. Do you have a couple of minutes to talk?"

"What about?"

"About the progress I've been making in researching college basketball. I've—"

"Not now, Davy boy," Solomon interrupted. "Come into my office tomorrow afternoon, we'll talk then. Take it easy."

That night before David went to sleep the thought occurred to him that it was one thing to understand the holes in the gambler's psyche, but quite another to close them off. He turned restlessly in his bed and something said to him to go ahead and gamble but to make certain to do it perfectly. And then it said *sotto voce*, "If you can." He slept unsoundly.

14

DAVID VISITED Solomon Lepidus, and while waiting to enter the private office, he passed the time with the avuncular Ezra Bernstein, who for almost fifty years had been Solomon's closest friend. They had grown up together, had remained together, and now Bernstein was second in command in Solomon's basic businesses. Of all Solomon's friends, Ezra was by far the least flamboyant, and the most stable. He didn't share in any of Solomon's risky ventures, which ran the gamut from producing million-dollar Broadway musicals which inevitably bombed in a week or less, to absentee ownership in sports franchises which lost money every year.

Unlike Solomon, Ezra never dealt with the promoters of sundry shady business deals, nor did he wager and lose as Solomon did on stocks and commodities, at roulette, craps, sporting propositions, or coin pitching.

During all these adventures of Solomon's, Ezra was the one who stuck to the nitty-gritty of keeping Lepidus's multimillion-dollar business intact. He was the inside man who handled emergencies every day and who shouldered the ponderous business details. He was the most genuine, the most loyal, the best and wisest and kindest friend Solomon had. Solomon admired him, swore by him, considered him the one man he could go to with his most personal problems. David heard Solomon say a hundred times in his good-natured raspy voice, "I depend upon Ezra Bernstein almost as much as I do on my own right arm, Davy boy."

Ezra invited David into his office to wait for Solomon. There, as usual, he reminisced on "the good old days." When that was done, as usual, David asked Ezra questions about Solomon's background—his parents, how he met his wife, how he got started in business, what type of boy he had been. David asked a thousand questions, and before he finished, also as was usually the case, Ezra asked David what he was doing with his life.

David told him some of the plans he had for the coming basketball season. At first Ezra frowned and seemed skeptical, but soon after, he invited David to go to dinner with him the following Wednesday. At that point one of the secretaries who had been running in and out of Solomon's office called David's name and asked him to enter.

David walked into Solomon Lepidus's office and as always caught him behind his rosewood desk, hooked to the telephone, a dozen underlings surrounding him, waiting for him to get off, to sign papers and checks, to ask questions, to receive instructions.

As always David immediately felt that it was a privilege to be with Lepidus, to listen to him and observe him. He began to relax and become inundated by Solomon's warmth, charisma, and earthiness. David watched as the man bellowed and roared in a friendly but brusque voice and clenched his fist and related to everyone who was there in a harsh but natural manner.

Finally Solomon looked up in David's direction, his wide-open face breaking out in its special smile, and he waved to David and yelled, "What's doing, Davy boy?" Before David could even acknowledge his salutation Solomon had already turned to someone else. David sat in a corner and watched as Solomon received calls from all over the country offering a variety of opportunities and deals and propositions. There were calls from gamblers, governors, millionaires, professors, jailbirds, mayors, lawyers, bookies, and charity workers. They were all calling to speak to Solomon Joshua Lepidus. David sat in the corner for the better part of two hours, hypnotized.

Can you do this, Solomon? . . . Remember me, Solomon . . . I need a favor. . . . Handout . . . Tickets to the Ali-Frazier fight. . . . Can you speak at B'nai B'rith? . . . Can you play golf with Judge Henderson on Sunday? . . . I'd like to do an article on you, Mr. Lepidus, for *Newsweek*. . . . Useta play basketball with you in Brownsville. . . . Our organization represents . . . Frankly, Mr. Lepidus, we need a contribution. . . . Yeshiva University wants to make you man of the year. . . . "Geez, I never even graduated junior high." . . . We're forming that syndicate you suggested, Solomon. Do you think you can persuade Nathan Rubin and his Texas oil friends to come in on the deal? . . . Harold Wasserman's coming into town for the weekend. He'd like some company. . . . Nathan Rubin calling on twenty-three. . . .

"Hello, Nathan. I got a friend spending the weekend in the city. Who can you fix him up with?" . . . "That blonde, Sally Morrison? Nah, this guy's into orientals. Can you get him Susie?" Well, I got her a job in Orleans, but, yeah, I guess so. I'll send Sally down there and fly Susie up. But it's gonna cost him. . . . "Nathan, this guy likes a scene. Get him two girls. Wait a minute, Nathan, make it three and make 'em freaky." . . . Now listen here, Solomon, Susie's just a kid and she don't go in for anything too freaky. No golden showers. No tubes. No— "Don't worry, Nathan, my friend likes to be entertained, not mutilated. . . . What? Are you crazy, Nathan boy? Me? Join you with Kim and Odette? You know me better than that. I want nothing to do with tramps. Besides, Nathan boy, I would never cheat on Naomi. I love her. Take it easy."

Mr. Stern is on twenty-two, Mr. Lepidus. . . . "What's doing, Harv?" . . . I called earlier about the rock concert we're doing at the Garden, Solomon. I checked out everything you said. I think it's a good idea to add a few more groups for the evening. I can book anyone we want, that is, if you're still willing to go for top dollar. . . . "What do you think, Harv? . . . That's good enough for me—book 'em!"

Judge Henderson calling on your private line. . . . "Ask him what he wants, hon." . . . Lou Carlin on twenty-two. . . . "Hello, what's doing? . . . Now what do you want done about the problem? . . . Okay! Dem guys deserve it!" . . . Judge Henderson calling again on your private line. . . . "Listen to me for one second, Judge. . . . Judge, I don't want to mention what I've done for you, but . . . " You also have a Mrs. Adams calling. . . . "Tell her we'll mail her organization a check for a thousand. She's a friend of my wife." . . . Your wife's on thirty-two. . . . "Put her on hold. . . . What's the Jet game, Tony? . . . Give me two thousand on the Jets. Hold a sec, I got my wife on another line." . . . Solomon, you have to make a decision about this trip right now. I have to let Eva Rubin know today. . . . "Hold on a sec. . . . Tony, make it five thousand on the Jets." . . . Mr. Lepidus, it's the Mayor on your private line. . . . "Naomi, I'll call you back later, I'm busy." . . . Sol, last week you told me you won a few thousand dollars in

Vegas. I just heard you lost.... "Later, Naomi." ... Sol, don't you dare hang— "Hello, Mayor, what's doing?" ... Mr. Lepidus, do you want to speak to a Mr. Becker? He represents the Israeli Olympic team. I think they want you to be an honorary chairman.... "Mayor, will you get back to me on that? I'm a little tied up now." ... You also have your daughter on twenty-three, Mr. Lepidus. She says she has a problem. Do you have time to talk to her? ... "I always have time for my daughter! ... What's doing, Margot?" ... Nathan Rubin promised to take me to the Winter Olympics, Daddy.... "Listen, hon, I don't think it's a good idea for you to be hanging out with him so much." ... Oh, Daddy, don't be silly.... "Maxine, get me Nathan Rubin.... What's doing, Nathan boy.... Hey, Nathan, David Lazar told me that that Boone College of yours signed some pretty good ballplayers. How'd you do it? ... That's pretty good, Nathan boy. I guess next season you'll be lookin' to get even with me. By the way, Nathan, what's happening with Margot's modeling? And what's this I hear about your taking her to the Olympics?" ... You don't mind, do you, Solomon? She's a good kid. She'll get a kick out of the games.... "Nathan—just re-member—she's my daughter!" ... Harvey Stern again, Mr. Lepidus. He wants to know if you'd be interested in producing a film on Gorgeous George.... "Jesus Christ, I just lost three hundred thousand doing one on Julius Caesar.... Wait a minute, Maxine, put Stern on.... What's doing, Harv? ... Okay, let's go with Gorgeous George. What the hell, wrestling's in. It's all show biz." ... Your brother Jerry calling from Las Vegas. He wants you to send him ten thousand. He says he's going bad. "Tell him that ... no, wait, hon, I'll talk to him myself.... Hello, Jerry, what's doing? ... Okay, okay, I'm not going to give you a hard time, I'll send you the five thou, but why don't you ever listen to me? You know what I've always told you.... First you make a living, then you live your life.... Okay, okay, I'll send you ten, but just let's hope your luck changes. Okay? ... Take it easy...."

As David sat there waiting he recalled what Ezra Bernstein had said. "Sol-omon was all of twelve when he joined his father, Joseph Moses Lepidus, in the family business as a buyer of old clothes. His father pulled a pushcart like a stallion, David, and he cried out every day, 'Cash for old clothes ... old clothes ... cash for old clothes ...' Solomon joined him and began climbing onto the back of that pushcart at six each morning. There wasn't any more school for him. He assisted his father picking and loading the old clothes, and he watched his father bargain and cry and sweat for every penny. When Solomon was fourteen his father died of tuberculosis and he had to support a sickly mother and a younger brother and sister.

"Solomon survived by joining other young tough kids in learning and partaking in the ghetto game of fighting and stealing and hating. And there were no two ways about where he lived. It was a ghetto; it was a heterogeneous collection of struggling peoples with different clothes, different languages, different Gods, different souls, yet with one common bond, one idea—to survive! And the kike kids, like the wop kids, like the polack kids, like the Irish kids, and like all the other kids, quickly learned the law of the street—to survive they had to stick together, to create an army—and Solomon learned it best."

David sat there in Solomon's office, and before David could answer his "What's doing, Davy boy?" Solomon was answering another call and yet another. One after the other, they called, and most of the time Solomon was everyone's best friend. And that was no exaggeration. From where David was sitting, out of the corner of his eye, he could see a scroll signed by 632 of his employees, many of whom had been with him for ten or more years. The opening line read: "To Solomon Lepidus, who is 'Everyone's best friend' on his twenty-fifth year in business."

Finally, after two hours, between calls, Solomon asked David to brief him on what he had been up to. David tried to squeeze in everything he had felt, done, tried, and planned during the past several months. "Here's another fact, Solomon. I've checked back five years. I've gone through eleven thousand games. Of those games only twenty-seven percent were unpredictable. The other seventy-three percent all fell within twelve points of the official Vegas line. Furthermore, I think I can pinpoint and eliminate a great many of the teams that fall into that twenty-seven percent category. Most of them have these common denominators: terrible defenses, inexperience, and bad coaching. What I want to do, Solomon, is key myself to working with the other seventy-three percent."

"It's about time you started listening to what I always been trying to teach you, Davy boy. To first make your—" Another call interrupted.

When David finally finished explaining his plans to Solomon it crossed his mind that maybe he should ask him to get involved. Maybe he'd finance him? Become a partner?

David looked at him, and before he was able to half-finish his sentence Solomon casually placed his checkbook in his desk drawer and said, "Before I get involved, I want to see all you say by deed, not word, Davy boy. Of course, if you want to, you can use all my contacts and mention my name to whomever you want. In fact, I'm having dinner with Max Brown tomorrow night. He's the president of the New York Stars and one of the two friends I've made over a lifetime that I can turn my back on. I'll ask him if he can use you to scout college players or something." And a split second later Solomon was onto another call.

When Solomon finished his call he started speaking to David, but again he was interrupted. He had to attend a conference in another room, but before leaving he said David should wait. After he was finished, in an hour or so, he'd have dinner with David, and also he had someone he wanted David to meet.

Before Solomon Lepidus returned, he called Mustache Harry McDuff. "Harry.... Now what's this problem you have? Listen, McDuff, I'm not gonna finance your gambling, but I will do this. I'll give you a thousand if you keep an eye on Nathan Rubin. I want to know everything that goes on in his modeling agency. Especially anything concerning my daughter, Margot. Understand?"

"I gotcha, Solomon."

"Another thing, McDuff. You've been talking to David Lazar, haven't you?"

"Sure have. I've been calling the son of a bitch every day."

"Well, what do you think? Can he handicap?"

"I got to admit the kid's learning. He's working real hard, Solomon, but ... well, you know how it is, Solomon. He ain't gonna pick no more winners than the next guy."

"Take it easy, McDuff."

Solomon Lepidus and David Lazar went to Broadway Joe's restaurant, and as soon as they arrived a distinguished-looking man, about sixty, walked up to the table with his hat in his hand. It was a friend of Solomon's, Irving Tannenbaum, and as Solomon shook his hand, Irv said, "Who's gonna give me a shoot? Anybody winning? . . . Who's gonna give me a shoot?" Solomon laughed and joked around with him and reached into his pocket and took out a $50 bill and handed it to him. They talked a bit more but soon the man excused himself and left. Solomon ordered steaks for David and himself and explained that Tannenbaum was the man he had wanted David to meet. He knew Tannenbaum from Brownsville, where they had grown up together. The man had always been an inveterate gambler. He'd bet on anything. As boys they had shot craps together and Irv had yelled, "Who's gonna give me a shoot?" In his teens he went to the Bowery with Solomon and again shot craps and lost and again cried out, "Who's gonna give me a shoot?" When he reacned twenty he went to the Polo Grounds with Solomon and bet and lost on the Giants, and for the next forty years he bet a thirty-cent line every day, laying it on eleven-to-fivers during the baseball season, and he lost. He bet games of chance and games of reason; he bet with feeling and with opinion; he even bet games after he knew they had been rigged, though he didn't know which way.

In legitimate business, Irving was once a winner. He made loads of money and he always laughed at Solomon's pleas to quit gambling. He'd always say, "What am I gonna do, it's the only game in town." For forty years he lost. He bet and lost at tennis clubs, at country clubs, and on the French Riviera. He found crap shoots in midtown hotels and on Canal Street and in railroad flats and gyms and poolroom lifts, and at these places, too, he lost. For forty years he placed bets and he lost. Through his hands passed a fortune. He went through his business, his stocks and bonds, his diamond stickpin and rings, his $6,000 Bueche-Girod watch. He bet bill money, rent money, grocery money, and as things got worse and worse he bet money he didn't have.

As Solomon finished his soliloquy on Irving Tannenbaum he said, "Whenever he comes to see me now, Davy boy, we joke around and I laugh with him and he sticks his hand out and I slap it with a fifty. I throw him a fifty, Davy boy—a fifty!"

Solomon stopped talking, reflected, and soon his right eye was twitching and he said, "Now tell me, Davy, what's Nathan Rubin been up to?"

Hurriedly and compulsively David told Solomon everything going on between Nathan Rubin and himself. When they finished dinner Solomon asked David if he needed cab fare, and before David could say yes or no, Solomon put a $20 bill in his hand. Then he said, "Remember, Davy boy, I want to see all you say by deed, not by word, and remember you can use all my contacts. And another thing—call me anytime you get a game you think is extra special."

A few seconds after he left David remembered that Solomon had failed to mention Max Brown. He was disappointed.

In the middle of the night David awakened hot and feverish and sweating. He tried to go back to sleep but couldn't. He kept thinking of Irving Tannenbaum. Tannenbaum had done it all, but now he was boozing and borrowing and begging, losing and crying, "Who's gonna give me a shoot?"

David turned restlessly in his bed. He *knew* that Nathan Rubin had been in the same Vegas casinos, at the same crap shoots, bet the same ball games, but while Tannenbaum was blowing a million, Nathan Rubin was grinding out dollars and nickels and dimes. Something told him to go ahead and gamble but to make sure to do it perfectly, and it said, *sotto voce:* If you can!

As promised, David met Ezra Bernstein for dinner at Rosenbloom's Restaurant, a quiet Jewish deli which specialized in the old-fashioned dishes and virtues that Ezra prized. As soon as they sat down Ezra placed a silver yarmulke on top of his head and told David that Solomon needed some information about the city's medicaid program. Ezra wouldn't tell him why. Then he began to question David in a firm but gentle voice about his gambling plans, and his problems with Leslie. After a while David began to lose patience and said, "Look, Ezra, I don't want to be rude, but right now the only thing in the whole world I'm concerned about is gambling. What I want is to wheel and keep busy, just like Solomon does, and I want to be rich!"

Ezra replied that all David was doing was running away from himself, proving only that he had no faith left in himself. "As far as your wanting to be like Solomon, I love him, you know that, David. But the truth is, with all his wealth, he's not a successful man. From the time he first started making money until this very day, he's always been restless and discontented. His gambling's only one thing that reveals his torment. Believe me, David, he's not a guide for you to go by.

"Everyone thinks Solomon's the greatest because he does so much for everybody, and it's true, he's helped thousands of people. There's a lot of greatness in him, but he *needs* to do it. He's a driven man, David, because he *needs* so much. When it comes to Solomon's personal life he can't enjoy any of the simple pleasures anymore. He used to love to take in a ball game; now he can't even watch one unless he has a couple of thousand on it, and what's just as bad, he never has the time."

David couldn't help interrupting Ezra. "Why do you think I've always been so fascinated by the man, Ezra? It's just as Doug says. He combines what is great about man with what's not so great. Solomon's much more than just a multimillionaire, Ezra. He's both good and bad, success and failure. He's full of contradictions. He's . . . he's everything. You say Solomon's a failure, Ezra. I don't. I say he'll always have a following. How many times have you heard 'I'd do anything for Mr. Lepidus,' 'I love the guy,' 'He's not my boss, he's my friend,' 'He's the greatest.' He'll always be able to use men and abuse them, Ezra, and at the same time make them love him for it. The wretched of the earth need to follow, Ezra, and Solomon has the genius and the charisma to make them follow him! That's his genius; not the fact that he can toss five thousand down on a ball game. To me, he's like my wife, he has a genius for seducing men."

Ezra tried to interrupt, but David wouldn't let him. "Let me say something else about Solomon, Ezra. I've always thought he was a great man. If he was a boy he'd be leading a gang or he'd be the captain of the basketball team. If he were broke he'd find a way to make a million all over again, or if he were so inclined, he'd be a small-time rabbi in a shul on top of a candy store, but his congregation would swear by him. He's a great man, Ezra. And I'll tell you something else. It takes a great man to live life to the hilt though he might be a little bit lost while doing it. And you know what? I'd love to be just like Solomon Lepidus."

When David returned home from work the following day he began studying the handbook. After a couple of hours he became nervous, and an hour later he found himself extremely anxious and agitated. He forced himself to continue working, but soon he was overcome by demons.

Remember, David, for every dollar you make you should put away half. Remember, David, money doesn't grow on trees. Remember, David, you got to be sensible. Anybody winning? . . . Who's gonna give me a shoot? Hat in hand. I'll show her. If you can. . . .

The telephone rang. It was Nathan Rubin's friend Ursula Knutson. Ursula, a coltish nineteen-year-old with lovely tawny tresses, with enormous eyes that glinted like crystal balls and hinted of the arcane, with a body that was alive all over and with a baby-doll personality which was pliant and easy and also a bit freakish. When he had eaten her it was like scooping gobs of whipped cream from a spoon. He asked if he could come over.

By the time he returned home, it was 2:00 A.M. Half asleep, he sat on the edge of the bed staring at his book cartons. All of a sudden he felt a desperate urge to telephone Leslie. He reached for the phone, but instead he got into bed with his handbook and he cradled it, and slowly he drifted off to sleep.

15

AFTER ANOTHER NIGHT of intense research for his handbook, David returned to Harlem the next day only to find a fresh case transferred to him from the training unit. As usual in an instance such as this, the work done on the case was incomplete. David had to look up the caseworker to obtain some essential information that should have been part of the record to begin with, and it turned out that the worker was the same young man he had noticed with Debbie Turner months earlier. His name was O'Brien, a good-looking youngster with strong features, fair hair, and large friendly blue eyes. As David had suspected when he'd first noticed him back in September, he was fresh out of college, having graduated from Williams the past June. They got to rapping. O'Brien asked David about working in Harlem, and David told him about Harlem, where he had been mugged and robbed three times and two other times escaped by running faster than Jesse Owens.

"Thank someone, O'Brien, that the addicts didn't have shivs and that I had an umbrella. It made the two against one almost even. I had the advantage on one guy down below me on the staircase, and when I swung the umbrella and hit him clean he went head over heels crashing and careening all the way down. The other fellow I beat the living hell out of, but after my rage was spent, I realized he was just another addict who needed cash desperately for a fix, and I reverted to social worker type and took him to Harlem Hospital. Later on I talked him into going back with me to the welfare center, where I enrolled him in a drug-free program, and now Bobby Depree is a person and working at a job. He's one of the few victims I was able to help."

David looked into O'Brien's eyes. "You have to understand what you're dealing with. Almost every family you're going to visit has a legacy of brutality, someone who's either a junkie or an alky or a wino, or who's already OD'd, or had the cops on him. But don't think they're all losers. Most of them are tough. And sometimes you'll find a youngster with incredible potential. And sometimes you'll hit on a miracle like when a youngster is studying electrical engineering and his mother is working two jobs besides raising and caring for her six younger children and calling you and asking for their case to be closed." David paused. "If you like people, you have a chance at helping a few."

"It sounds fantastic. You must really get involved with your cases, David."

"I do more in an hour than most caseworkers around here do in a week, but I don't do the job I could be doing. I'm too involved in other things."

While O'Brien and Lazar chatted, David's new supervisor, Mrs. Roark, walked over to them. "Mr. Lazar, do you mind going down to the intake section and interviewing Mrs. Emanuelli? It'll only take a few minutes."

David nodded to Mrs. Roark. "Come on with me, O'Brien. I want you to meet one of the intake workers."

They took the elevator to the first floor, where David walked up to a Puerto Rican standing in a corner. The fellow had bulging biceps that he showcased in a sleeveless polo shirt, and an enormous black mustache and dark wavy hair. His velvety eyes were half closed; he looked sleepy or drugged. There was a pad and pencil in his hand. As David approached him he was reaching for a crumpled dollar bill from a welfare recipient.

"This is Hector 'Macho' Rivera," David said. "He's chief numbers man in the office. He takes from those that have nothing and gives back less." David smiled at Hector. "He doesn't have much of a brain, but Macho has one hell of an ego."

A black woman walked by, and Hector rubbed his biceps and followed her with his eyes. He grinned at her, and she smiled back. In a soft crooning voice Hector said, "Anything I can do you for, Mattie?"

124 . . .

She smiled. "Shee-it, Rivera, you've done it!"

Rivera glowed.

An old black woman came up to him. "You the numbers man, mister?" She opened her purse and searched for some spare change.

Hector quickly looked around, saw no one looking, and snatched the coins from the woman's wrinkled palm. He jotted the transaction down and handed the woman a stub. Instantly he transferred his velvety attention to an appetizing Puerto Rican recipient.

David said, "Hey, Hector, take some time off. I want you to meet O'Brien. He's new around here."

Rivera looked up quizzically. "Glad to meet you, man." He paused. "Say, aren't you in the same unit with that fine new fox?"

David pounced. "She's not for you Rivera. Stick with the ass down here and any of the other dogs in the office, but leave Debbie Turner alone."

Hector made a "who, me?" palms-up gesture. "Hey, man, don't get riled. Take it easy." Seconds later his eyes were undressing yet another female recipient, and seconds after that a tired-looking white man limped over and handed him a soiled single, as David went on for his interview.

The following day David was still unnerved and anxious. To get out of his depression he began to dwell on women—accessible Ursula Knutson, for example. But rather than call her, he telephoned Saskia Verdonck. She was the softest of his female friends and an artist in bestowing titillating pleasure to his most private parts. He enjoyed making love to her "the most." He thought of her as having oodles of tender flesh, perfumed holes, educated lips. She had graceful delicate hands, fingernails which sparkled like red rubies. She had the face of an eighteen-year-old, blue eyes that glistened like jumbo-sized agates. She had a steam-clamping vagina, a clit that was a delicious ripe berry, soft thighs, and an ass built for fucking. She drank Muscadet to Leslie's bourbon and was always hungry for jello or kissin', but when David wanted conversation she spoke in low mellow Dutch-accented tones that soothed his sores, his confusion, his helplessness, his loss. Burying his head between her thighs and nestling at her balmy nest was not the answer to all his woes, but for a few hours at least, it was a soothing hiding place.

"Hello, Saskia?"

The next morning David immediately walked over to O'Brien's desk. They chatted. David found himself enjoying the conversation. He was a good kid, open and trusting, not at all a New Yorker.

On that particular day, David was stuck in the office as emergency worker for the entire shift, so he suggested to O'Brien that they have lunch together. But O'Brien said that he had already promised to have lunch with someone else, and said that the someone else was Debbie Turner. When David asked him what she was like, the boy broke into a silly grin. "Debbie has a boyfriend and is. . . ." He didn't stop for half an hour. David learned about O'Brien's infatuation and got the facts. Debbie was "a good person, fun to be with." The most wonderful, most beautiful, most bosomy, most sexy girl in the entire world. She had slept with one boy in her entire life. In a dejected voice, O'Brien said, "She loves him and they're living together."

"So, what's the problem?"

O'Brien's face was sad as he told David of his tragedy. He couldn't get to first base with Debbie. She was the ultra-faithful type. They were friends, but unfortunately that was as far as it went. He shook his head despondently and said, "What a waste!"

David began teasing him. "She might come on like a Girl Scout, but none of them really are." O'Brien looked at David and his voice softened as he said, "Debbie's different from other girls, David. She really *is* a Girl Scout."

"Come on, cheer up. I'll call my brother and have him fix you up with one of his specials." David noticed O'Brien's eyes and ears perk up. One thing David had always wanted was a kid brother. Here was just that. David couldn't resist teasing him. "Believe me, O'Brien, there won't be anything old-fashioned about her." David smiled.

O'Brien looked at him with the kind of expression that said, "I don't know if you're kidding." Maybe it was mean to act that way with such a good-natured youngster, David thought, but he was suddenly in a foul mood, a mood brought on by the realization that Leslie wasn't and couldn't possibly be a Debbie Turner. Maybe David resented the fact that boys and girls like O'Brien and Debbie really did exist and that he wasn't and never could be one of them. Maybe he was envious of them and yearned for what they had.

O'Brien stood next to Debbie Turner's desk and waited for her to finish writing a telephone message on a history sheet. When Debbie finished, she immediately looked up and said, "What your friend David wants is an old-fashioned girl, the kind of woman who will be content to stay in the kitchen and have his babies. I don't think he's going to find that kind of woman in New York. The women who come to live in this city aren't anything like that."

"What about you, Debbie?" O'Brien said with a smile. "What kind of woman are you?"

Debbie chided good-naturedly, "If you think I'm that old-fashioned, you're dippy. I want a great deal more in a relationship than that." She stopped for a moment, and when she continued her brow was knitted and her voice rang with conviction. "And everything that I look for in a man I would want the man to look for in me." She stopped again, and then half apologetically, half seductively, said, "I hope you understand me and don't just think I'm another one of those 'aggressive females' you're always complaining about."

O'Brien wiped a mop of hair from his forehead, and his face broke into a wide grin. "I do, Debbie, but I don't think David will. Anyway, I've asked him to join us for lunch. I wanted you to meet him. He's a fascinating guy. I'm sure you'll like him."

David didn't really know how to describe Debbie Turner, but he tried to do so for Doug, who he hoped would not take him to task too severely for his sentimentality. She was in David's eyes a combination of innocence, gentleness, naiveté, and inner goodness, and all of it glowed. She had a shy grin, like a puppy, soft and friendly and sort of helpless. She was tall, with wide fragile shoulders and truly magnificent breasts, and she had slender sticks for legs and long delicate hands. Her face was that of a kid sister's, pretty and shiny and full of surprises, and she had wonderfully deep eyes which changed hues and looked like water colors on a palette, and with all that she was tender and shy.

Doug said, "Knowing you and your sickness, you're going to make that girl into a Jennifer with tits."

At lunch David found that her softness was almost touchable. He immediately took center stage. He spoke of his writing accomplishments, with a few embellishments here and there, and about some of the other highlights of his life, such as Leslie, and what he was going to do beginning December 1. He dominated the conversation.

Both of his companions were fascinated by this sophisticated, jaded, egocentric, cynical, obnoxious, ambivalent, and just a little bit crazy Broadway Dave. That was exactly how he saw himself. Debbie told him that she thought he must be very old, at least twenty-seven or twenty-eight—she couldn't think past twenty-nine. When he told them how old he actually was, he never saw such surprise in his entire life, and maybe, just maybe, a little bit of disappointment on Debbie's face.

It was true, he didn't look much older than twenty-six or twenty-seven, but was thirty-three much older? They were both twenty-two. The hour and a half flew by in what seemed like minutes, and before he knew it he was back in the office at his desk, feeling as if something was missing, and he knew that something was Debbie Turner.

At their next lunch David said, "You're my happiness pill. I want to take you and Jimmy to the ballet. I want to take both of you to dinner. I want to treat both of you to the theater. I want . . ." With each offering, he received the most delicious thank you, the most wonderful glow, the most appreciative gaze. Everything about Debbie Turner made him happy.

That evening, while he was studying his handbook, David's father came into the room. He said, "Doug told me you gave Leslie two hundred dollars."

"That was months ago," David answered angrily.

"Do you have any money, David?" he queried.

"What do you think?" David shot back.

"David," the cantor whispered, clearing his throat and spitting phlegm into a handkerchief, "I can't irritate my voice. I have to sing at shul tonight." He stared at David with heavy-lidded blinking brown eyes and said, "I went to the bank this morning and withdrew two hundred dollars for you." He handed him the money. David took it, suppressing a half-smile and not saying a word.

The basketball season was to begin in less than a month, but David figured for the next couple of weeks he'd loosen up and have some fun. Besides, he thought, he was caught up on power ratings, home-court advantages, player personnel, not to mention finding and listing telephone numbers of schools, coaches, players, arenas, newspapers, and TV stations. Everything. He was ready.

For the next two weeks, David took Debbie to lunch as often as he could. On one occasion he showed her some poems he had written for Leslie. After she finished reading them he said, "You're the first person I've ever shown them to, Debbie." She looked at him and blushed. He gulped hard, smiled, began coughing and turned away to cover his mouth. He reached for a glass of water on the table, and as he did, so did she. Their two hands clasped the glass, her warm hand brushed against his cool one. She looked at him and blushed.

Two weeks before the start of the season David made some arrangements with his "best friend" bookmaker, Johnny. He would call him every day at 5:45 for the line. He figured it would be easier to get through at that time. They also agreed to settle every Tuesday. Next he called Eddie Zeno, and they rehashed their arrangements for the season. He also contacted Ed Kashman and arranged for him to give him lines on an as-needed basis. His intention was to use him to place bets when his numbers were more attractive than Johnny's and Eddie's.

That entire week Arnie Feld kept calling him. If David told him he was busy, he'd call back in five minutes. If David told him he wanted to sleep on that weekend, Arnie would wake him up at 8:30 on Saturday morning. If David screamed and cursed and hung the phone up on him, he'd call back at 9:30, or at the latest 10:15.

Finally David broke down. He promised Arnie that once the season started he'd call him if he got any special games. But Arnie wasn't satisfied with that arrangement either. "No, David, that's not the way I want to do it." The way *he* wants to do it? "I want you to let me call you every day so that I know exactly what you're doing. I want to follow you on everything."

David was going to turn him down once and for all, but he couldn't. Instead, he told Arnie to call him at 6:45 every night, beginning December 1. He warned Arnie emphatically that if he tied up his phone before then, he'd change his number and make certain Arnie never got it again.

A few days later Champ Holden called to wish him luck. Holden told David he'd received a long-distance call from Nathan Rubin and they were both rooting for him. "Sometimes a word to the wise can be of help, Lazar, so let me tell you something. Don't be an obsessive-compulsive. It's not how many games you bet, it's how many you win! I'll call you from time to time to see how you're doing. Another thing, Lazar—don't lay points away from home. Those home courts are everything!"

Seconds after David finished speaking to Champ Holden, Mustache McDuff called. "Listen to me, Lazar. I know we haven't exactly hit if off, but maybe now we can help each other. I'm going to be betting games and so are you. What do you say we sort of get together and compare opinions every night?"

David Lazar did not take much time to give McDuff his answer. "I don't think so, Harry. First of all, I don't want to be influenced. The worst thing that could happen to me is to have another opinion influencing mine. Another factor to consider, Harry, is that you haven't won in years."

One week before the start of the season, David made his final decision on money management. He decided to risk $27.50 a week in his new undertaking at 11–10, $27.50 to lose against $25 to win. He determined he would begin his business with a $25 investment, and if that Tootsie Roll was lost to the bookies he would begin again the following week, and ultimately again and again, week by week. He would be holding $25 in his hand as he called Johnny or Zeno or Kashman or whoever else he was getting a line from and placing his bets. He was convinced Nathan Rubin's gimmick was a good one, and he wondered if Rubin really held thousands of dollars in his hand when he called. He realized Nathan Rubin didn't have to—dollars were and always had been in his hands, in his body and soul.

David was anxious and confident. The thrill of starting out on his venture turned him on as much as a businessman was turned on by an attractive new investment. He was nervous and high-strung, but in control and aware of what was expected of him. He was aware that his $25 was not Nathan Rubin's suggested hundred-to-one ratio of investment capital. In fact, it was exactly one-tenth of his entire bankroll. He had accumulated only $250 of venture capital. Still, he would have to make do. It was certainly less than he would have liked to work with, but a limit's a limit, everyone has one, and this was his. He didn't have any choice about that.

Around 6:00 every night he had to get lines, shop for the best prices,

...129

compare them with his power ratings, evaluate game-time information, rush everything through the proper channels, and funnel everything through his brain. He also knew exactly what he had to do in the afternoon: study each of the games on the schedule and reread and reconsider all his handbook notes, rules, and regulations—and synthesize everything.

David had transcribed every team and every player into his handbook, as well as all the rosters and schedules and pre-season power ratings from the Air Force Academy to Xavier of Ohio and Yale.

The key, of course, was to assemble as much information—inside information—as he possibly could on the more than two hundred college basketball teams Las Vegas put on the board.

Two fundamental guidelines remained as constants: (1) "Minimizing and maximizing" can overcome the bookmakers' 11–10 advantage; (2) College basketball is really a game of "hidden" information, and the conventional betting line does have flaws.

One week before his first season began, David Lazar decided to keep complete records on every game played so that by the end of the season he'd be able to tabulate results and see on how many games his line differed from the official one. He wanted to know his percentage of wins and losses for point differentials ranging from one and up between the official line and his unofficial line. He expected the differentials to be in his favor.

David vowed not to waver, to stick to his game plan and wager only when the disparity between the Vegas line and his own was flagrant. He was certain that if he stuck to his game plan and made his calls correctly he would be a winner. That week he also called his old high school friend Noah Weldon, in Los Angeles. He didn't tell him that he wanted information for gambling purposes. He told him that he was doing a book on basketball—on college basketball—and that he needed someone on the West Coast familiar with the players and teams out there to help him. Noah said he'd be glad to.

Five days before his first season he began calling everyone.

"Hello, Noah.... How's Doris? The girls? Fine ... fine.... What kind of team do you think Oregon will have? ... Washington State? ... Stanford? ...

"Hello, Zeno.... Let's go over some of the teams in your area again.... Will they hit their foul shots? ... Penetrate? ... Will they play a zone? ... Box and one? ... Man to man? ... Can they move without the ball? ... Are the guys in shape? ... How's their backcourt? ... Are they quick? ... Turn the ball over much? ... What about their big man? ... Is he quick? ... Their defense? ... Bench? ... Attitude? ... Is the coaching adequate? ... Are they going to play conservative? ... I want to know every player on the team, Eddie—let's go over each player again.... Now let's go over the Southeastern Conference.... Did you speak to Winfred Goyens? ... Oliver Valentine? ...

130 ...

"Hello, Roger.... How's Sky been doing in the scrimmages? ... How's the team look as a whole? ... What about their defense? ... What kind of shot selection do they take? ... I know Anderson's not much of a coach. You don't have to tell me that. Just tell me what he said about the other clubs in his conference and what he said he's going to do in the non-conference games during the first weeks of the season.... Say, Rog, doesn't Western open the season against Boone College? Well, what do you think?

"Hello, Zeno, let's go over Villanova ... St. Joe ... LaSalle ... Rhode Island.... Again!"

And on, and on. It all started coming together like a work of art. His handbook was ready. He was ready. It all started coming together a week before opening day.

DAVID WAS on a high. All week he had been having lunch with Debbie Turner alone, as O'Brien was copulating every free minute he had with a supervisor from the office.

By Friday, David said to Debbie, "You sure do have me talking. I've never talked like this to anyone." She smiled and blushed. David felt light, relaxed, and happy. He spoke about his friends. Debbie asked questions; David answered them.

"What are my friends like? Well, besides a few that are still around from the old days, most of my friends are either in their middle fifties or octogenarians."

"You're teasing me, aren't you, David?"

"No, I'm not, and what's more, they're mostly living contradictions. Vapid and vital at the same time."

"All of them, David?"

"Well, there are a few exceptions. You'd love the Colonel, and Solomon Lepidus is an unbelievable man. Of all the people I've ever met, and that includes men from all walks of life, from the arts to business, he's the only one I've ever considered great."

"What about Nathan Rubin, David? What's he like?"

"Nathan Rubin? He's also one in a million. But I don't think you'd like him."

"Why not?"

"Oh, a million reasons."

"Give me one."

"You're utterly pure, he's totally corrupt." David smiled and half-jokingly added, "I guess the same goes for you and me."

"Oh, David, people aren't really that different. You're always saying such nasty things to shock and tease me, but I know you aren't really the way you say you are."

"You wouldn't believe this about Nathan Rubin, Debbie, but he has a twenty-five-year-old girlfriend on the side and his wife's only about thirty."

"You're teasing me again, David. Aren't you?"

"No, I'm not." He laughed.

"What about those other wealthy men you spend so much time with?"

David thought of some of his other acquaintances, mostly men he had met through Solomon Lepidus and the Colonel, men so wealthy they could buy anything that they didn't already own, who continued to glut themselves by making more money and every now and then relaxing a little by playing cards and eating and maybe fantasizing about some young woman that they had screwed or almost had screwed or couldn't screw or wished they had screwed.

They were men with sons who didn't want to follow them into business and daughters who never came home except on rare occasions. For the most part they were terribly confused and lost and still chasing after something which could never be caught. They had never had the imagination to find out what was missing or where to start looking to fill their lives with meaning. He thought of the Colonel's friend Isaac Pizer, and remembered once posing questions to him as he spoke of business.

"Who is the most ignorant, Pizer? Is it the artist, the teacher, the theologian?" And before Pizer could wipe the sneer from his mouth and answer that it was those without a dollar, "No, emphatically not, Pizer. The ones most ignorant are the profit-seekers, for it is they who burrow into the filth, who dedicate their lives to a stool-stained dividend." Isaac Pizer didn't speak to him for days.

"About the only good thing I can say about them, Debbie, is that they're all self-made men, not corporate types, but still they're only businessmen." David stopped. "If I ever take you to dinner and we run into any of them, please don't be too disappointed."

"David, why do you hate businessmen so much?"

David snickered and smiled and said, "It's not only businessmen, Debbie, it's anyone who has a penchant for the metaphysics of comfort and indulgence, the soft chair, the cushioned couch, the pillowed bed, the warm bath. It's anyone sated by saunas, crystals, cocktails, or security."

In a carried-away, angry voice, David said, "I hate anyone who doesn't value the beautiful, Debbie. Anyone who ignores what is transcendent and holy."

"What is gambling really like, David?"

"What's gambling like?" David laughed softly and smirked, but soon he saw how serious Debbie was and he too became serious.

"You want the complete truth, don't you, Debbie?"

She nodded her head, and her lips puckered tight as if she were afraid to say anything else. He thought to himself that she had probably pondered the question for weeks and that it could very easily be the most important question, the boldest, that she would ever ask of him. It was more than being intimate sexually, more than even holding hands. She was asking because she wanted to know him. It was written on her face.

"What is gambling like? Let me see, how can I explain it? Just listen to me and don't interrupt."

He took the silver dollar out of his pocket and spun it on the table. He picked it up and flipped it in the air and caught it. He clenched it in the palm of his right hand and closed his eyes and reflected and tried to recollect everything. Finally, he said:

"You think to determine but you are yourself determined. You get a cold and clammy feeling. Your hands tremble, your face grows flushed, your lips turn white, you feel hot and cold, your veins bulge on your forehead, you sit up half the night reliving the game or waiting for the scores. You feel tension, dread, mystery, adventure. You crave it. Gambling becomes more necessary and better than sex. Sex can never duplicate or replace the thrill you get from gambling—that mania to live on the edge. You adore it; you dread it. You become overwhelmed by it. It's like being married to a woman who's a bitch, Debbie. In the beginning you're drawn to her, excited by her, you seek her out. In the end you feel bound and can't get away. Slowly it changes.

"Slowly you become a follower. Not choosing but being chosen. Somewhere, maybe hidden too deeply inside of you to ever surface, is a wound, a wish to be dominated, punished, and destroyed. The more punished you are the more you seek out your punishment. As I was with Leslie—symbiotically entwined. You never figure out all the answers, and you become confused and lose track of many you thought you knew. You get more and more caught up and more and more confused. You lose your balance and all sense of proportion, and money loses its value. You're always preoccupied, obsessed. More and more you're overwhelmed by the consistent ups and downs. Does she want sex or doesn't she? Can I pick winners or can't I? Should I take a shot or shouldn't I? What is enough? What isn't? You're always thinking of the game, the performers, the calls, the money, the time, the winning, the losing. Nothing else matters." He took a deep breath.

"You want to screw every girl, bet every game. You're lured by everything. Caught up in midstream. This one, that one. You don't give a damn. You do it to escape, out of despair. Out of frustration—out of being jailed, officed, clocked, enslaved, determined—you take a shot! You're your own worst enemy. You dream that every game is a potential winner.

"You plunge into one game after another, and deeper and deeper you go. It's like scuba diving, Debbie. The deeper you go the higher you get, but it's not the nitrogen going to your blood, it's the tension in your soul. It's gross, Debbie, that's the word you use, isn't it?" He took another deep breath before continuing.

"You daydream of being published, of making a million, but Monday through Friday you take that same M-20 bus to Harlem and clock in stoop-shouldered and you realize that here you're against another set of odds. Here life is really a gamble, with all the odds against you and addiction one of the few ways out. You shudder and ache as you realize how desperately you want to leave, but you can't. Instead, you're drawn to gambling as an addict to heroin. It's impossible to break out, so you wallow in self-pity. You destroy yourself with self-hate. You breathe in hope and exhale despair.

"You're in Harlem. You're not being published, you're despising your life, screaming at your wife, dying a little each and every day. Getting up impotent at twenty of eight every morning to go to nothing but a paycheck and another set of odds in an arena where oppression is literal, but you do it just the same. You come home, you sum up what's left of you, and you try to write again. You get rejected, you go unpublished.

"In desperation you call your bookie. 'Hello, Johnny!' You clench your silver dollar, you root for a team, any team you bet on. You take aspirin before, during, and after every game. Your kidneys rebel and you run to the toilet every half-inning. Your eyes twitch, your legs jerk, your heart pumps. You wring your hands, grind your teeth, bite your lip. You feel ashamed and hold everything inside when people are around. You despise them, wish they weren't there so you could listen to the game, get your scores, tabulate the results.

"But people are around as you watch the errors, the double dribbles, the fumbles, and though you feel like exploding, you lock your back teeth and hold your head down hiding the pain within. And as you agonize, your wife, child, friends, and relatives continue to chatter. They're in a different world, and after a while you stop pretending to be with them at all. You isolate yourself behind whatever walls you can build." He stopped and glanced at Debbie. Her look prompted him to continue.

"Your moods change, you throb and feel alive for a while. You hold your breath, you live, you die. Frazier has the ball, the Knicks are trailing by one, you have to win the game. It means everything, Debbie, more than three weeks' worth of paychecks. Do you understand? Eight seconds left in the game, Frazier has the ball, he hands off to Reed in the middle, and the team begins to work a basic play. You freeze in your chair. Clyde has the ball back and Willis sets his bulky pick. Bradley swings baseline and gets the ball in the corner. Dollar Bill shoots as the buzzer goes off. The ball goes swish.

"Yes! The Knicks win by one. Yes you're potent! You're alive! You're jumping in the air, trembling all over. For that second you've given birth. You're eternal. You hang onto it a day or two at the most. Then, inexorably, you again need another game and then another. 'Hello, Johnny.' You lose and lose and lose. You look for a way out, but there isn't any. You gotta do something, though, for you're still taking that same M-20 bus to Harlem, and now you're over thirty and Leslie's complaining. She's getting a pinched-up look. You're taking that M-20, clocking in and coming home and pecking away at a Smith-Corona, but most of the pages are crumpled into balls or remain blanks.

"And when you lose a game you die a little.

"Seaver's going into the ninth trailing one to nothing. I laid nine to five on the game. Seaver, he never wins the big ones for me, but I keep going back to him and laying those crazy prices. Why? . . . It's the bottom of the ninth and Fergie—you gotta be crazy to lay nine to five against Jenkins—looks like he might be tiring. Cleon's up, men on first and second and only one away. Jenkins hangs a curve and Cleon fouls it off. He should have murdered that pitch, it was high and out over the plate. Just where Cleon likes it. Jenkins pitches and hangs another one and again Cleon fouls it off. Please God, let the Mets tie it up. This is the game I need, just this one. Jenkins winds, pitches, it's a good pitch, low inside and on the corner. Jones can't do anything with it and he swings in self-defense and hits a measly ground ball off his hands to Kessinger, over to Beckert for one, back to first, it's a double play. The game's over.

"You don't get what you want—who knows better than me. You remain in your seat. You don't move for an hour. You stare at the tube and you feel cold death all over. At first you rage and scream, but seconds later you feel dead inside and you just stare at the tube. You just sit there replaying the game over and over; every inning, every pitch, everything that could have turned it around. Finally, you get up and go into the bathroom to urinate. You take three more aspirins. Nothing helps.

"The next day, Johnny's boss, Nino Tafuri, calls. 'Hello, Lazar, dis is

Nino.' . . . 'Hello, Nino. . . . Yes, I know who you are. Johnny had no right to give you my number. . . . So what if you're Johnny's boss, that don't mean anything to me. . . . Yeah. . . . Look, I'm going to pay you. I'm not looking for trouble. . . . You're wrong, I'm not a wise guy. . . . Yeah, don't sweat, I'll get the money for you. . . . You want to meet me downtown. . . . Listen, Nino, next week I'll give Johnny the money. . . . Yeah—next week.'

"And you say to yourself: What are you gambling for? Why don't you leave Harlem? Start clean? Why not take a job with Solomon Lepidus?

"But the next day you're again punching that fiendish clock, going into the ghetto, climbing the stool-stained stairs and stepping over fresh turds and sidestepping scurrying rats and avoiding barking wild-eyed dogs and scrambling roaches. You feel like puke and you know your clients do, too. But the amazing thing is, the tragic thing is, you still think only of yourself. You still only ask, Why is it you?"

David opened his eyes and gazed at Debbie. Her eyes were opened wide. She seemed completely involved, even thrilled. He flipped his silver dollar into his left hand, clenched it, and continued. "You go into a losing streak. Whatever you do, whoever you go to, it's wrong. It's murder, it's mayhem, it's pillage, it's rape. It tears and rents and pulls and storms. You find yourself lying to your friends, cheating your twin brother, swindling your father, robbing your mother, not loving your wife, losing and losing and being sucked in further and further."

David took a few deep breaths, swallowed a mouthful of water, and looked at Debbie's sweet face. He bit his lower lip, clenched his silver dollar in his right hand, and continued:

"Your twin brother loves you and says, 'You can't distinguish between winning and losing any longer, David. As long as you can get down a bet, that's all you want. I'm begging you to get out now, David. Don't stay around to find out if you can win—you can't.'

"But you don't. Instead you make one more bet, and you win! You make another, you lose. You make another, you win! You're exhilarated by winning, you're vindicated. You feel creeping beneath your flesh that feeling that this time you're going to win. You feel your luck changing. You make another bet: You win! Your emotions are electric; you're jumping out of your skin. You make another bet, you win. You're feeling great, playing with Jennifer, fucking Leslie good. Another bet, you win! Kissing and hugging and tickling Jennifer and pinching her tush. You're laughing and smiling and content and gay. You're embracing life, feeling like a winner, alive. You bet again; you win! It's the greatest. You can't lose. A gray day later you're losing. Your mood changes to dread. You're wretched with your second straight loss, crushed by your third, and by your fourth, you're dying, and by your fifth, you're dead. You swear to yourself a thousand times to stop betting, but you don't. You can't. You lose and lose and lose.

136 . . .

"You call your friend Ron Nivens: 'I probably won't need the money, Ron, but can I count on it if I do? . . . Thanks, Ron.'

"Later, you receive another kind of call—it's Nino Tafuri. 'I don't want to go through a whole number, Lazar. When can I have my money?'

"You stall Tafuri and you call back Ron Nivens and tell him you need more money, but rather than eight hundred, you tell him you need fifteen hundred. He pledges the money. You feel as if you'd received a reprieve. You call your 'best friend,' Johnny. 'Hello, Johnny, give me TCU plus the fourteen for twenty-five hundred. . . . What? I'll settle up with you on Monday. Twenty-five hundred, that's right. . . . What? Don't worry, Johnny, just tell Tafuri you'll see me on Monday.'

"You take your pocket radio with you to the movies and you watch the film with a radio plugged into your ear. Every half hour WINS comes in with scores. Finally you hear, 'Arkansas twenty-one, TCU six.' Rubber-legged, you walk out of the theater. Dazed.

" 'I don't want to go through a whole number, Lazar. I just want my money.' . . . You fill out an application for a loan at Household Finance. 'Why do you need the money, Mr. Lazar?' 'I want to take my wife and child on vacation.' 'How much do you want to borrow? How much do you earn annually? How long have you been married? Do you have any other sources of income? How many little ones did you say you have? What is your rent? Mmmmmm . . . How long have you been working for the department? This will all have to be verified, you understand, Mr. Lazar. Do you have any identification with you? Please bring your ID card with you next time and also your last pay stub and your W-2 form from last year.'

"You think to yourself: Dreary office, scum bag mentalities, morons. What am I doing here? The voice interrupts: 'Is this salary you put down net or gross, Mr. Lazar?' 'Biweekly, net.' . . . What the hell am I betting college football for anyway? What the hell do I know about football!? . . . I make a net take-home of three hundred and twenty dollars biweekly, I think.' . . . 'Oh, don't you know exactly, Mr. Lazar?'

"I look at the man, Debbie. The vapidity on his face enrages me. I hold in my anger. . . . 'I never look at my paycheck that closely. What's the difference? A few dollars more or less? . . . There is a difference, Mr. Lazar. You wouldn't want us to extend your loan for a few dollars less, would you?' . . . He smiles at me but every bone in his body is serious. . . . I think to myself: You creep. Don't you know there are guys making millions. . . . A few dollars more or less. . . . What the hell am I doing here?"

David is now talking as much to himself as to Debbie.

"I walk out muttering and raging but keeping it in. I see a newsstand. I'm lured. I spill over and buy the *Post*. I look up the pro basketball games to be played that night. I bet two thousand on the Celtics. Two thousand dollars.

"I lay seven and a half points. It's the biggest bet of my whole life.

. . . 137

And do you know what happened? John Havlicek, as great a player as ever stepped on a court, missed two fouls with a second to go and Dave Debusscherre hugs the rebound, falls to the floor as time runs out. The Celtics win, 107–100. David Lazar loses—by half a point. One half a point. Not even a basket. On take-home pay of three hundred and twenty-two dollars and fifty-eight cents every two weeks, I bet two thousand on the Celtics . . . and I lose. I must be nuts.

"Again I go to Ron Nivens. He hesitates—I feel uncomfortable—he starts to say no—I begin to plead—he gives me the money—again; to my father—again; to my mother—again; to my twin brother—again.

"As soon as I come home my 'best friend,' Johnny, calls: 'Listen, Lazar, I need the money. Don't give me any song and dance, I can't wait until Friday.' . . . 'If you want you can come over right now and I'll give you half the money.' He comes over: 'Look, Lazar, I've been dealing with you for years. You're intelligent and have class and I've always known you to be honorable. You've never been in any real trouble before. But you gotta understand something: I got other guys to pay.' . . . 'You'll get the rest of it on Friday, Johnny, but right now you have to do me a favor and get me down on a game.' . . . 'If I can accommodate you, I will.' . . .

"His voice is greasy, Debbie. . . . 'Give me three thousand on Arizona State, I'll lay the three and a half.' . . . He screams, 'Lazar, are you out of your mind? Tafuri's going crazy as it is. Besides, I don't take that kind of action on college baskets.' . . . 'Listen, Johnny, I'll give you eight hundred more tomorrow, and I swear, you'll get the rest of it on Friday.' . . . 'You're talking about three thousand dollars, Lazar, that ain't just a number, you know.' . . . 'Please, Johnny, get me down.' . . .

"That night I'm a wild man, Debbie. I jump on everything and everyone, including Jennifer, and especially Leslie. I pace the house as if it were a cage. I wait for the eleven-o'clock sports news. I don't get the score. I pace the floor. I pace and pace and take a million deep breaths, and I wait and wait and pace some more. Finally, at fifteen minutes after midnight, WINS radio gives the scores and I hear Arizona State, ninety-one—and before a fraction of an instant goes by I think, *Ninety-one's enough! It's plenty! New Mexico has no offense. They usually play pretty good defense.* . . . *Oh, that's plenty. It's a winner.* . . . *It's got to be.* . . . *New Mexico, eighty-nine. I lose!!!* I think of death, murder, robbery. I ache. My head throbs. My body collapses. I look at my desk and out of the corner of my eye I see my financial obligations to Beneficial Finance; Household Finance; First National City; Chase Manhattan; Municipal Credit Union. I look away, but as I do I think of what I owe my twin brother and father and mother and Ron Nivens. I sink into my chair, inert. Nothing can touch me except my own inner pain.

"I go over to see my twin brother—again! 'Do you know how sick you are, David?' . . . 'I know.'

138 . . .

"He stares at me and his face softens and his voice becomes tender. Very tender. . . . 'Okay, I'll borrow the money for you. But it's the last time, David. I'm not kidding, it's the last time.' "

David took a deep breath and a sip of water. He looked up at Debbie and saw she was no longer thrilled by what he was saying, but in her expression he read warmth and compassion.

"You asked me what's gambling like, Debbie—it's a disease! I've seen guys who've made millions and guys who haven't made a plugged nickel. Gambling is irrational. It's because we're scared to death and hungup over time and gold and power. It's because gambling is in our blood the same way needing, loving, and screwing a woman can be. It's more than sour grapes or self-destruction or fantasy. It's because I'm falling. It's because we're all falling. It's because it's something to grab onto and it's because there's death and because no one and nothing can help, not even winning!"

There was a lump in his throat, and perspiration beaded his forehead. Debbie gazed at him with innocent gentle eyes. Softly she said, "It must be awful to have lived through all that, David." She started to sob, really cry. She started to cry for him. Leslie had cried for herself. He looked at Debbie and at that moment he knew he had found the lighthouse in his own heart and he knew he would not have to wail or scream again about the cancerous things in his soul.

He wanted to say, "I love you." At the same time he was holding himself back with every fiber of self-control he had. He felt he could only hurt her, and he was afraid of hurting and being hurt again. And so he went on guard. He juggled and manipulated and mouthed all the platitudes that only expressed indifference on a male-to-female level, and yet he knew he had felt something that he'd thought he'd never feel again for anyone. He felt love.

He wanted to tell her that he loved her tenderly and needed her and wanted her. More than anything, he felt that need, that urgency, that agonizing throbbing of spirit and flesh, that hunger to share and be shared, care for and be cared for. But he left and didn't touch her. He never touched her. He didn't dare touch her. All of him was bursting to reach out, but he didn't dare move. All of him was screaming, but he didn't scream. He was silenced by fear. "Debbie, I . . . " He couldn't.

The night before the season began, Doug called. All week, David had discussed his power ratings with him. He rehashed the fact that he didn't intend to make any bets unless he found a mechanical error, or a spot where the Las Vegas line was in conflict with his own opinion by at least four and a half points.

"That's well and good, David," Doug said, "but you can't only think of it in terms of numbers. You have to integrate your numbers and your gut reaction. You have to have them working in harmony all the time. The error you find in the point spread is one thing, but you also need to have an intuitive opinion, and a strong one at that. The mathematical differential you discover is your cushion, but handicapping isn't only a number. It's both qualitative and quantitative. It's an art. And remember, David, in the long run it doesn't matter whether you pick sixty percent or forty percent—if you maximize and minimize correctly, you can make a living."

David agreed. Sometimes whatever the information you obtain, last-minute injuries or what-have-you, you still only have eyes for one side. You could make the game 6 and know that's the perfect number and Vegas could put it out at 12 or even 13 and you're still afraid to budge. You just can't go against that certain feeling, that special something. Sometimes you've got to go on something besides a number, on those games, and they do turn up, like love, when least expected. You'd better make damn sure you consider every reason for the feeling, and then think it through again, and then again. As far as David was concerned, he had already decided that if that kind of game appeared, he would play it by ear. Sometimes lay off completely. Sometimes go ahead and wager. Sometimes taper the bet.

Another thing he realized was that if he turned out to be the world's worst handicapper and picked only, let's say, three out of ten games correctly, maximizing and minimizing would save him from a Chapter Eleven, but it wouldn't make him a living. And, of course, he didn't feel he had done all his work to pick a mere three out of ten. Rather, he felt certain that if he capitalized by wagering on games that he power-rated as being wrongly priced by the Vegas price makers, he'd be able to pick at least six out of ten correctly. With six out of ten and with maximizing and minimizing, he'd be able to create a business. And that's what he told his twin brother.

That night David stayed up until 5:00 studying his handbook, as well as everything else he had accumulated in his library of sports gambling.

He reviewed Olshan's checklist, most of which he had already incorporated into his own, and went over every rule and regulation he had culled from sports betting guides, or thought of on his own, or had been told by Nathan Rubin, Champ Holden, or anyone else he respected. For every game, he would be checking individual circumstances on a day-to-day basis.

The first rule was: "Don't lay too many points against good defensive clubs and good ball-control clubs." The last rule was: "Remember, you are only as good as your character and your information. Don't go overboard on any one game."

At 5:00 in the morning he took a clean sheet of paper and typed out the following: "The moment you don't devote every minute of every day to studying all the rules and evaluating each of the thousand factors that go into forming an opinion, forget about handicapping!" After he finished typing, he took his scissors and cut the axiom into a smaller frame. Then he got some tape and taped it to his windowsill. Then he finally fell into bed, utterly exhausted.

At 2:00 the next afternoon, six hours before the college basketball season officially started, Nathan Rubin telephoned David from Boone, Texas. "Don't let anyone scalp you. If you're handicapping and giving games out, always keep the best numbers for yourself. Make the other guy lay the extra half a point. And don't tell anyone your business."

Nathan Rubin continued speaking to him for two hours. The last thing he said David wrote down in his handbook and underlined in red: JUST REMEMBER THE HANDICAPPING GAME IS PLAYED ON A FIVE-AND-A-HALF-INCH COURT—THE ONE BETWEEN YOUR EARS.

Exactly one hour before the season started, David got out of a hot bath and went into his unheated room. He switched the radio on. The song "Love Is a Many-Splendored Thing" was playing on WPAT. It had always been one of his favorites. He turned to WINS and started getting the day's sports news.

17

HE STEPPED ON some dandelions that miraculously had flowered in a crack of the pavement and crushed them. Back in Harlem he walked by a garbage can that was on its belly, its guts spilling out . . . portents of doom. . . . He continued walking through debris-strewn streets and tar-stained gutters to a building on East 111th Street, stepped over a junkie who had overdosed and was sprawled on the stoop, walked up the stairs, knocked on the door of Hilda Rosado, alcoholic husband, retarded child, pregnant again; crossed the street to Leticia Soto's, age fifteen, pregnant again, an infant child playing with rat droppings in its crib; to James Earl Carter, aka—above-knee amputation; to Arcadio Oquendo, jailbird. When he completed his field visits it was 1:00 P.M. and he was late for an appointment. He rushed home, like a horseplayer to a seller's window at post time.

David Lazar was ready to make his first bet. He had found a 5½-point differential between the Vegas line and his. It was the eleventh day of the college basketball season. All through the first ten, he had compared lines and gotten a feel for everything, but the biggest differential he had located was only 4 points. It was tempting and he would have won—whenever you laid off a game it invariably won. But he waited for something more secure. During that span, 171 games were played, but he had been unyielding and resolute—he waited. They were all without a perfect reason to wager; all potential losers.

Of those 171 games played, one was between Boone College and Western University. Nathan Rubin had propositioned Solomon Lepidus on it. David had been with them when they discussed it.

"Solomon, you know my team's opening the season against Western tonight."

"What do you mean, your team? Who's playing?"

"Boone College, Solomon," Nathan Rubin replied. "You know what I've done for that school. If it weren't for my money there'd be no school. Come on, Solomon, wake up. Both schools are gonna have great teams this year. It's gonna be a great game. I'm flying my plane down. Want to come along?"

"I don't think so, Nathan. Tell me," Solomon parried, "what do you have in mind?"

Nathan Rubin answered instantly. "No different than always. Ya see, I'll bet you man to man. We'll both be saving the vig by not calling it in to a bookmaker. And I'll be wagering on my boys."

Solomon Lepidus held his laugh.

"Listen, Nathan, I don't even know the points on the game. What do you say, Davy boy?"

"Western's got Sky Davis this year, Solomon. He's going to be an All-American. Boone recruited well also. They got Swish Gibbs from Brooklyn and a kid from Florida who might be exceptional. But the key to the team is going to be a big boy out of Philadelphia, Johnny Lee Crawford. Right now I don't think he's ready. He's got a lot to learn. But just the same, the game's being played at Boone and that's a hell of an edge."

"Come on, Davy boy, stop hedging. Who do you like?"

"Well, if you have to make a bet I'd lay the one point on Western. But it's not something I'd invest in."

"What do you mean, one? Is that what the game is with the books?"

"One in New York. In Philly it's one and a half. But I'm telling you, Solomon, it's not a good bet. The game could go either way."

Solomon Lepidus wagered Nathan Rubin $10,000 on Western University and gave Nathan Rubin 3½ points. Final score: Western 87, Boone 83, in overtime.

Now David Lazar was ready to invest $25 on his expert opinion. His bookmaker was still Johnny, who still called David his "best friend." David got the opening line from him at 5:45 and after shopping throughout the city for better numbers, David concluded that for his purposes, Johnny's line remained the best. At 6:15 he started dialing his number, and at 6:25 he was still dialing his number, but no matter how many times he tried, he kept getting a busy signal. David kept dialing.

On that day, the eleventh day, when Eddie Zeno called for the second time, David told him he was going to take Western Kentucky against Murray State; that he could get 4½ points on the game; that according to his own power rating he had made them a 1-point favorite. It was the biggest differential he had found since the season started. Vegas had made the wrong team favorite.

"Don't worry about it, Eddie," David said. "Just think for a second. When was the last time you were able to get points betting the Hilltoppers playing on their own home court? It's a great bet. . . . Yeah, I'm sure. Damn sure! . . . Your partner, Jagerman, is going to follow me? . . . I didn't know he was a player. . . . Damn right I'm mad. I don't want to tout for anybody. Okay, you give him my games, but make sure he introduces me to those people. . . . How much is he going to bet, anyway? . . . Pretty heavy? . . . Damn right, two hundred dollars is pretty heavy. . . . Does he know it's the first game I'm betting since the season began? . . . I know you're behind. I warned you that you couldn't win if you bet every day. You have to wait for games to come to you, Eddie, you can't go looking for them. It's all numbers, and these numbers are perfect. Western Kentucky will be running all night. You don't have to sweat. . . . Yeah, I'm sure!"

He kept dialing Johnny, but it was impossible to get through. You could call him anytime during his working hours—between noon and 2:00 in the afternoon; between 5:45 and 7:30 in the evening—and you'd most likely get a beep, beep, beep every time. You could go for a year before you reached Johnny on the first try.

He kept dialing. He wanted that extra half-point from Johnny. It could be a hell of a big half-point. It could easily be the difference between pushing and winning. The tension increased. But after each busy signal he got a fresh dial tone and began again. In his stomach he knew he was hooked. Dialing was the first kiss, the sweet promise. It wasn't a question of "should I" or "could I" or "would I." It was: "I have to."

As David dialed, he felt alive and hopeful, but grinding away at his optimism was the pessimism in his soul. It kept telling him that life was nothing more than decision, defeat, death. But he kept dialing, one more time, and one more time. His checklist was right in front of him, as was a list of his debts. He thought to himself, First you borrow, then you beg. Who said that? Was it Hemingway? Why the hell would he say something like that?

He clenched his $25 in paper and his silver dollar in his left fist. He continued to dial. He thought to himself, I can always call Kashman and get down with the four. I can call him as late as seven-twenty-five. Keep dialing. I want that extra half a point. What am I, a child that I have to close my bedroom door to make certain my parents don't know what I'm doing? My mother can drive me crazy; either she's indulging me or acting as if she were the grand inquisitor. I feel like a sneak. Is that what I am? I'm sneaking a call to my bookie. I'm forced to whisper at age thirty-three. God damn Jewish guilt. Why couldn't I be born Stanley Kowalski? A philistine rather than brissed and jewed. Who needs gefilte fish and a conscience?

It's ringing. . . .

"Hello, Johnny?" His stomach knotted. "Give me the college line again."

The voice came back rough, crude, churlish. He took down the complete line and compared it with his other lines and he noticed only a few changes. His game—thank God—remained the same.

"Give me Western Kentucky five times. That's right, Johnny, for twenty-five small American dollars."

Johnny's snarl and inference didn't intimidate him, and David asked him to repeat, and when he rushed and mumbled his words David asked him to slow down some, and mentioned his slurring lisp.

David told him to relax more and said that he sounded irritated. Johnny growled and before David could say thank you he hung up. David smiled, thinking that he had done a good job; that Nathan Rubin would have been proud of him; that he had passed his first test.

He was sapped. He shuddered as he jotted down the day's action in a special notebook he had purchased solely for that purpose. Afterward, he grabbed his coat and went to the movies to see John Wayne. As he stepped into the elevator, he felt as if he'd prepared all his life to get where he was. As the elevator descended, he felt a little more at ease.

Not for one minute in all of those 120 minutes of celluloid illiteracy was David able to stop thinking about Western Kentucky and Murray State.

He tossed and turned his reasons for making the wager over in his mind, and none of them digested too well. By the time he was back home with his cartons he felt nauseated. He had cramps as well as a migraine.

Timing it to the minute, of course, he switched on WINS radio and began getting the scores. His silver dollar tightly clenched in his perspiring right fist, he began the countdown. He held his breath, jumping inside, dying a little, blocking out everything else. He waited for the Western score; there could be an earthquake and he'd never budge.

At 10:47 P.M. the voice said, "Western Kentucky eighty-seven, Murray State seventy-six."

A winner! He exhaled slowly. He felt ten thousand percent more confident, and yet, as a reminder, he whispered to himself that they were the better team this time, on this court, under these circumstances, with those 4½ points, today. It was 10:48 and he was wasted. A few minutes later he began to relax and took out his handbook and waited for radio WINS' next sports repeat at 11:15. He had almost a half hour to cool it before he would start writing down all the scores of all the games. At least now he'd be able to concentrate. He had found new energy and could put new meaning, so much meaning, in what he was doing. It was more than a feeling of accomplishment or self-worth. It was more than the $25. He turned back to WINS at 11:15 and for the first time he was able to hear the other scores of the games played that evening. No longer preoccupied with Western Kentucky, he relaxed and could function. He scribbled down the scores of every game played, one by one. He transferred them into his handbook.

Later David made sure to get additional detailed information on as many of the games as he could. He found this information in newspapers, via telephone conversations, and through sports journal subscriptions and all the handicapping sheets he subscribed to—information he had learned to root up from every nook and cranny and which assisted him now in perfecting his constantly changing power ratings for all the teams in the country.

At 12:21 A.M. David finished. He gave a "God bless" to WINS. They gave the best and most complete rundown of college basketball scores in the Big Apple, and they had knighted him with his first winner. During the remainder of the season they would give scores every half hour. A quarter to and quarter past, every evening beginning at 10:15. During basket-dropping time they would always be his first contact with life and death.

He peered out the window at Emma's apartment, but there was only a window shade fully drawn. Emma had died in the middle of November. He thought about it. He winced. An hour later he thought to himself that through all the years he'd always retained hope and confidence. He'd never lost it. He had come close but never did. He had become more humble. He was softer but stronger. Things were kept inside more; there was still pride, but less arrogance. He was no longer all gloss and surface and poise. He wondered why. Was it because of the countless beatings he had taken? Was it because he knew a little bit more about what had happened to Emma? Was it seeing his mother in a wheelchair every day? Was it the effect Debbie Turner had been having on him? Was it because he'd lost Leslie? Was it because . . . he was a handicapper?

Then there was this feeling of flying. His brain was whirling high. It was giddy and warm and going around in circles. His head ached terribly, and he was weary. He was able to fight it off until he got his Western Kentucky score and completed his work, but now it hit him in the legs, in the arms, in the heart, in the mind. The body doesn't lie.

He was weary, but he would be back tomorrow. At early dawn the agony would begin again. He was a handicapper and he knew every angle and he had resolution. God damn! He had resolution. Now maybe besides doing the handicapping he'd get some luck. But who knew? Maybe the Vegas wise-asses would continue to be correct on the next 171 games, too. But he'd be scouting their trail better than an Apache. He'd be waiting to spot their errors, their 4½-or-more-point flaws. Resolution, confidence, pride, knowledge, hate. He had $25 that he hadn't had yesterday.

He woke up the next morning. The first thing that entered his mind was, Maybe today they'll make another mistake. The day ended. Vegas did not err.

He fell asleep holding his pillow and thinking about Leslie. Was she watering the geranium plant? The tomato plant? Later he turned over on his pillow and dreamed about Debbie Turner.

The season progressed. In the next two weeks, David found four games with 4½-point or 5-point differentials, and he made investments on each. He won all of them. He knew every angle and had resolution. He was undefeated. What could be better? He had bet $25 and $50 and $75 and $100 on each successive game. He had suffered for each dollar. Before each result, he had trembled and squirmed and felt pangs of fear. He had a million second thoughts. But his management was good and his handicapping was perfect.

The first four weeks of the college season were over and he was ahead almost $300. During the fifth week, he raised his basic bet to $50. He made his first wager of the new year on a Wednesday with the 4½-point differential between the Vegas line and his. He took Brigham Young minus 9½ over Utah. WINS gave the score in the same unbiased voice: "Brigham Young eighty-nine, Utah eighty-five." It was a loser. He felt a quiver. He felt dizzy. He didn't bet again until Saturday, and then he won. He practiced what he theorized. He recorded all his information and he got all his scores and he shopped only for the best lines. He waited for another flaw in the line.

He waited until Tuesday, when he found a 5-point differential on a Wyoming–Colorado State game. He won. Another $50. After every bet, before every result, his degree of concern was virgin-raw. Another bet he lost. Another bet he won.

18

ON SOME SUNDAYS, when time permitted, David would have lunch with Debbie Turner. He wouldn't see her more frequently. He claimed he had to do his handicapping homework. It was a noble gesture, an ignominious way of setting conscience at ease. He didn't want to take responsibility for ruining her life. He never asked Debbie what she wanted. He didn't give her a choice. He controlled the situation.

Doug saw right through him. "You know as well as I, David, that for every protective word you mouth, Debbie's only going to find you more attractive. You're being selfish. If you really wanted to protect her, you wouldn't see her, period."

He asked himself, Could I be that unselfish? Could I stop seeing Debbie? He knew he couldn't. It got to him and caused an ache.

In triumph David telephoned Nathan Rubin and bragged to him about how well he was doing. He also phoned the Colonel, Solomon Lepidus, and Isaac Pizer. Later that same day, Champ Holden called to congratulate him and to calm him down. While they were talking on the phone, his father banged on the door, opened it, and in a stricken voice explained that he had just finished reading in the *Daily News* that the Mayor intended to eliminate fifteen hundred jobs from the city's payroll, welfare workers included. With terror in his eyes, he asked David what would he do if he lost his job. How would he make a living? He commented that David had never had any sense.

Something inside David burst and he yelled out, "Damn your insecurity."

Seconds later, after slamming the door, he returned to the phone and continued talking to the Champ. He told him he didn't give a damn what the Mayor was going to do. He'd rather be broke and dreaming of winning and trying in his own way to make a million than losing a little as his father had done every God-fearing, dollar-pinching day of his sensible, decent, pathetic life.

In an unperturbed voice, the Champ proceeded to tell him a story about a friend of his who in the beginning of one college basketball season cached $40,000 in a safety deposit box in $5,000 packets. He further described how by the end of the same season, the only things left in the safety deposit box were rubber bands, paper clips, and empty envelopes. Finally he described how before the next season had begun, his now dismal friend had given back his box to the bank, not because the box was empty, but because he couldn't afford the $7.80 necessary to renew the lease. The Champ ended the story by telling him how *he* was that dismal friend. The Champ calmed him down.

A few days later Ursula Knutson called. She said she couldn't see David anymore. She told him she had taken up residence with some hairdresser. David wasn't concerned. He was into his handicapping, and for diversion he still had Saskia Verdonck, and, of course, for lunch he still had Debbie.

Yes, for lunch he still had Debbie. She was his happiness pill, the only woman since Leslie who made him feel more than lust. Much more. Jimmy, her boyfriend, didn't seem to mind their friendship. Whenever they were together, David took special pains to convince him that Debbie and he were just friends, that to him she was merely a cute, adorable kid sister. David was convinced that Jimmy trusted him.

But what Jimmy believed was quite different. He believed Debbie was a beautiful woman and an equal. As for Debbie, though for the most part she seemed to thrive on the way David perceived her, there were times when doubt appeared. For example, when responding to a friend's queries, she would say, "You know, I'm beginning to believe you're right. David doesn't see me for what I am. Sometimes I get the impression he only sees me for what he needs me to be."

And of course, to David, Debbie's reaction was just as fixed. She'd color, bloom, hang onto his every word. She was twenty-two, eager and wonderful. Her beauty was the kind that had all sorts of honesty; a higher and more perfect clarity; a more human quality; a softer aspiration. At least so it seemed to David. But when David arrived home the tension would begin, the tension which creates a rift between mind and body, the tension which caused strange stirrings, intoxicating thoughts. The tension over which he had no control.

His mother, hardly able to move a step, leaning on her walker, stood in front of the entrance to his door. "David, I want to speak to you. David, be a good boy and go to your Uncle Jake's anniversary party tonight. Your lousy father—he's too busy to take me. David, you want to make your mother happy and be a good boy, don't you?"

Safe in his room, David reached for his handbook and after thumbing through and locating the page with his current figures—he was already ahead $650 for the season—he grabbed the telephone and went to work. "Hello, Zeno? . . . You got anything to tell me? . . . Yeah, I've been doing okay. . . . I told you as long as I wait for their mistakes I should get my share of winners. I've been breaking it down statistically. Did you know that on my five-point differentials and up, my winning percentage has been fantastic?" . . .

"For the rest of the season I'm not going to touch anything unless I find at least a five-point disparity between the Vegas line and my own power rating. . . . What do I like tonight? . . . Well, if they give me about sixteen, with Alabama, I'll bet them. . . . You know what I've been thinking, that with all the games that come up on a Saturday, I should be able to find at least two that I can wheel. Most of the mistakes seem to come on Monday and Saturday anyway. . . . Of course I know why. That's when the majority of games are played, especially on Saturday. On those days the Vegas odds makers can't cover every game on the boards perfectly. What I'm going to do is start making 'if win only' bets whenever I find two teams I like as long as I'm ahead for the week. That way for the same basic investment I can win double what I invest. And if I get in a real strong position I'll make reverse bets. That way I can really make some money. It could snowball into something fantastic. . . . Of course I'm still going to apply my rules and regulations. . . . Look, Eddie, I don't want to be a candy-store manager all my life. It's time for me to start expanding, but you don't have to worry, I'm not going to forget any of my controls. Now, let's go over the Big Ten and Southeast Conference again. What did you say Oliver Valentine said about Alabama? . . ."

On Monday and Tuesday and Wednesday and Thursday and Friday and Saturday, team by team, roster by roster, coach by coach, player by player, gym by gym, with Eddie Zeno, with Roger Brantley, with Noah Weldon, with everyone and everything at his disposal, David went over everything.

"Hello, Zeno. . . . Roger's still very high on Sky Davis. I'm thinking he's too involved with the kid. Sky doesn't play any defense and he fouls like crazy. I've been watching Western closely since the season started. Look, Zeno, their fourteen–two won-and-lost record isn't really indicative of their ability. I just hope they make it to the NCAA tournament. If they do they'll get creamed by the first decent club they face. If they keep winning in their conference the points should be much lower than what their real value is. Everyone's overrating them because of their record and because of Sky. I just hope he keeps getting his thirty a game and leads the country in scoring. That kind of B.S. will influence the linemaker immensely. What I'd really like is for Western to win their conference championship and get matched up against a tough independent like Marquette or St. John's in the first round of the NCAA. If they do, they'll get blown out. . . . What? . . . Oh! Saturday. Saturday Michigan is playing Michigan State. They'll be making the Wolverines about sixteen over the Spartans. . . .

"I'm leaning to the Spartans. . . . You're crazy, Eddie, on my power rating I make the game eleven. It should be one of the best shorts of the year. Those State kids will be putting out a hundred and ten percent for the game. And remember, Michigan isn't that strong this year. They'll have their hands full just winning the game straight up. I'd love to wheel that game with Canisius if I can get a few points. They'll do a job on the Jaspers on that home court of theirs. I make Canisius a one-point favorite, and it should come up about four in favor of Manhattan on the official line."

It was David's best week of the season. He collected $400 from his "best friend" and $300 from Ed Kashman. He was ahead $1,500 for the season, and it was still only February. He reevaluated his financial situation and raised his basic wager to $300. He continued to hunt for 5-point differentials and more. He wasn't fooling around. He was looking for flaws. He felt strong, confident, and capable. He knew he was good, maybe the best in the business. In his gut he knew he was a handicapper. He felt the connection, that certain inner feeling that kisses and warms, that whispers in your ear and says you're the best. He knew it. He could feel it. Body and mind connected. He felt alive. He knew he was a handicapper. He just knew.

And when he wasn't handicapping he was either thinking of Leslie or Debbie, forcing himself to treat Debbie as a kid sister, but it was becoming harder and harder. Each day their relationship changed and grew. She was becoming bolder and brasher, more and more capable of holding her own. She was flourishing, contributing, communicating, and asserting.

"You know, David, from all you've told me about your friend Ronald Nivens, I think he's a man who's terribly disappointed in himself. I'm certain what he admired about you was the dream you had of being a writer and the strength you had in not compromising your goal. I'm certain it wasn't anything as silly as that Broadway Dave image you mentioned. David, why don't you try and write again? You must!"

"Debbie, the world doesn't admire those who struggle to be something pure like an artist. You know whom they admire? Those puny souls who succeed at being something decent—who look at teeth all day, who work machines all day, who sell anything at all."

"David!"

"Just listen to me. To be a writer, for that matter to be anything chaste and singular, requires a viciousness and a selfishness and an insolence which allows one to stand tall and fight and struggle. It takes integrity, Debbie, and arrogance. I've lost it. I've lost it."

"David, I realize how difficult it is to be a writer, but it's what you want. What you are!"

Debbie was flourishing. She was beginning to notice his erections when he sat too close to her or accidentally brushed against her. She gave him hints.

150 . . .

He followed them up with intellectualizations or sidestepped them completely. He juggled everything. Gave with one hand and took with the other. Told lies and confessed. Controlled and handicapped everything. Used his mind and experience and perversity.

Doug beseeched him to leave Debbie Turner alone. "Don't you see what you're doing to her? She's becoming more and more infatuated with you. What chance does that boyfriend of hers have? He's just a kid. You represent everything in the world she's never had. She's falling in love with you, David. You'll ruin her life. What will you do if her boyfriend leaves? Leave her alone, David. Leave her alone."

He didn't want to ruin Debbie's life, and he definitely felt that only as friends could their relationship remain perfect. He was afraid he'd start taking her for granted, become dissatisfied and bored with himself and with her, become angry and disgruntled and make her insecure. He was afraid that he'd start looking for distractions and start up with other women and that she'd never be able to handle it and that she'd live with nothing but pain. He was afraid that the only thing left would be those same complaints—"David, what do you want from me? What do you want?" and "You ruined my life. . . . You ruined my life"—and all because he did not know who he was, because he could not handicap his soul.

He continued to treat Debbie Turner as a kid sister. He was aware that one day she'd have to choose to leave or to stay. He tried to control every moment so that she would not have to choose. He wrestled with the idea of telling her two secrets he had harbored since the time she had asked him what gambling was like, but he didn't reveal them to her. He wouldn't say that he loved her, and that he'd marry her if she took the enormous responsibility of making all the moves.

During February, David told Debbie gently, very gently, that he thought it might be a good idea, because of her relationship with Jimmy, if she started seeing a little less of him. To his surprise she showed a strength he'd never thought she had. She said she had discussed the situation with Jimmy and they both felt that as long as it wasn't hurting their relationship there was nothing wrong with her continuing to see David. She said they had discussed it openly and had agreed that nothing would be accomplished by her not seeing him.

So he continued seeing her, but every now and then he said things that were cruel and hurtful. "Sex with Leslie was fantastic, Debbie. It wasn't like having sex with some Girl Scout from one of those preppy women's colleges."

At those times Debbie Turner would feel uncomfortable with David's fixed image of her.

"David, one of your problems is that you never are able to think in terms of someone else's needs. You think only about your own. And it seems to me that what you want is someone or something that can turn you on, something that you can believe in and care about and that would not threaten you. David, I'm not sure there's anyone, or perhaps anything, that fills the bill."

"I really don't know what you're talking about, Debbie," David would respond in an annoyed tone.

"You don't find me desirable, do you, David?" Debbie would counter.

David Lazar was hardly aware of his behavior, and even if he had been, he could not have helped himself. Increasingly, he seemed to become insensitive. Sometimes when he spoke he felt so overwhelmed by his defects he'd get carried away. Most of the time he felt as if his head were swimming, as if he had a bubble on his brain. At those times, his coherence and equilibrium were affected. Thoughts eddied in and out of him and swirled all over. It was only upon returning to earth after those euphoric trips that he'd realize how brutal he had been. He'd feel terrible and be at a loss to figure out why he'd lost control in the first place. At that point he'd make a clumsy attempt to apologize.

"Come on, smile. If I didn't have you to laugh with, I'd have to cry all by myself." Most of the time Debbie smiled. It would only take a word or two to change her mood. When he sensed how much pain he caused her by his insisting they not see each other, he tried to make light of it. He made a game of it. He called the period their S&S period—Silence and Separation. He even sent her a letter of instructions concerning the rules of the *game*.

The day after David sent Debbie an S&S letter, the Colonel's friend Isaac Pizer telephoned.

"Hello, David? I called because I want to do something for you. Howie Silver is the top editor over at Dellson Publishing and he's in trouble. His top college basketball writer had a heart attack last week, and he told me he hasn't anyone to replace him. The *Dellson Basketball Guide* has to be on the street in five weeks, and he needs a guy who can knock out some articles quickly." He stopped. "When you call, he already knows who you are." He stopped again. "By the way, the Colonel's been telling me you've been studying up on college basketball. Why don't you give me a call when you get something good? Maybe we can help each other then."

David called Howie Silver and made an appointment at his office that very same afternoon. They immediately came to an agreement. David would do two articles of approximately five thousand words each. One would be his selections for the post-season All-America teams and the other would be his ratings for the top twenty teams in the country. David would have some latitude. They discussed financial arrangements, and David emphasized the need for telephone expenses, as he would be calling all over the country for information. Silver obliged.

When David returned to his room, the phone was ringing. It was Eddie Zeno. He had been trying to reach David since three in the afternoon. David told him where he had been and why.

Eddie said, "Do you realize the opportunity you have for developing contacts? Every coach in the country is hungry as hell to get his players on the Dellson All-America teams, and if you promise them that, and put some of them into your top-twenty ratings, you'll establish a contact for life. Look, Dave, Ned DeFalco's club is beginning to make some noise in the Rockies, but he's still unheralded here in the East. I know for a fact that his university gave him the go-ahead to recruit like crazy. I bet if you called him and promised to give Hubie Lockwood, that soph guard of his, some consideration, you could pump him for plenty of information. In fact, if you want me to, Dave, I'll call him for you.

"Mark Jagerman's been after me to talk to him about Lockwood anyway. DeFalco won't talk to Mark because he's a flesh peddler, but with this, it's different. By the way, Dave, Mark's moved his offices to Chicago. He told me to tell you that the next time he gets to New York he wants to meet you. I think he wants to work some kind of deal out so he can get your games."

"Eddie, I don't want you to give Jagerman another game without first checking with me."

"Why?"

"Look, Zeno, someday I might be getting paid for handicapping games, and I don't want anybody to be able to say they got them from me for nothing."

"Don't get uptight about it, Davy, I'll do whatever you say. As far as the other thing goes, I think it would be a great idea for you to call some of the coaches who play a tough national schedule. Those independent guys should know a great deal about almost every team in the country. Another thing.... Oh, what the hell, you know what to do. You've been doing everything right."

David began calling coaches as soon as Eddie Zeno hung up. "Hello, Mr. DeFalco, this is Dave Lazar. I'm doing some articles for the *Dellson Basketball Guide.* If you have the time I'd like to talk to you about your team. What can you tell me about Hubie Lockwood and Rufus Champion? ... That game you had the other night went into overtime, didn't it? ... You had a scare from that State team. Do you think they're as tough as that game indicated? ... What clubs do you think will cause you the most trouble in the remaining games on your schedule? ... What about next year? ... Who have you lined up in your recruiting? ... How come you're not going after Rich Pokorski? Isn't he one of the best high school players in your area? ... New Mexico grabbed him.... Any junior-college kids you like? ... Any red shirts? ... Any guys coming off injuries that will surprise us? ... Any sleepers? ... How are your freshmen? ... Who do you think are the toughest teams you've played?"

Hello, Billy Williams.... Hello, Arch Kobell.... Hello, Lou Collins.... Hello, Duke Delsener.... Hello, Rip Kovalski.... Bobby Joe

Matfield. . . . Allie MacIntosh. . . . Aaron Thomas. . . . Hello. . . . Hello. . . . Hello. . . .

For the next two days David called coaches in every conference and many of the major independents. Some of them were the biggest names in the college ranks. He established contacts in the West, South, Midwest, Southeast, Rockies, Southwest, Deep South, Prairie lands, Missouri Valley—throughout the entire country. He got more and more information. He compiled it, evaluated it, and synthesized it. Ned DeFalco and Duke Delsener immediately came through with information which led to winners. David promised to include DeFalco's soph guard, Hubie Lockwood, on his honorable-mention lists at the end of the season. He also told DeFalco that if Lockwood finished the season strong, he'd probably be able to place him on his post-season All-America selection for 1971–1972. DeFalco's club eventually showed up nineteenth in his post-season ratings and Hubie Lockwood became an All-American. One hand feeds the other.

Later in the week, he told Eddie Zeno how friendly everyone had been.

"Geez, Dave, how are you going to make all those guys happy?"

"No problem, Eddie. I figure with five thousand words I can do a hell of a lot. If I can't fit the kids into my All-America teams I can always put them on my All-Sectional teams, and I can also give more clubs recognition by rating the teams in each conference as well as all the independents.

"I've also been thinking of doing an article on the top coaches in the game. That way I can really make the guys I contacted look good. Which title do you like better, Zeno—'Lazar's Top Twenty Coaches in the College War' or 'The Recruitment Jungle'? Don't worry, Eddie, I'm going to make every one of them happy."

Of the sixty-eight college coaches he had called up to that point, he made deals with seven. The other sixty-one were completely cooperative without his having to make any concessions or promises. Each of those seven made Lazar's top twenty coaches in the college war. Solomon Lepidus once said, "The good get buried and the bastards carry the caskets."

David was constantly amazed at the ease with which he was able to get inside information. He made certain to advise every coach he called that he would be calling again so as to keep a line on the progress of his team and players. The situation was a natural—it could only enhance his handicapping.

One thing he never lost track of was that most coaches, like most players, were little boys with little-boy mentalities, and if given the opportunity to express their opinion about their own teams would rant and rave. Yet he found that by listening carefully and by asking the right questions, he was able to decipher the facts and extract every useful tidbit. It definitely enhanced his handicapping. Besides, it was fun, and he enjoyed doing the articles and seeing his name in print. So what if it was a jock publication?

Because David wanted to secure his position with Dellson, he called Howie Silver. "I don't have time to talk to you now, David. How about if I meet you at the Spindletop for dinner? We'll have time to talk then."

While waiting for Silver to arrive, David flirted with the hat check girl. While she was taking what appeared to be a regular customer's coat, he noticed out of the corner of his eye his "best friend," Johnny. Johnny was standing at the bar conversing with a man he didn't recognize. David edged closer and listened to their conversation.

"I've had the same customers for years, Johnny. I'd like to get some new ones."

David quickly walked over to the bar. "Hiya, Johnny. What the hell are you doing here?"

After an exuberant greeting filled with crocodile smiles, Johnny introduced David to slack-jawed, sallow-complexioned Joey A. Joey A. was a dapper dresser, a cigar smoker, a bookmaker. Soon his "best friend" was telling Joey A. how David was one of his best customers. One thing led to another. "I can always use another bookmaker, Joey A. Do you have a direct number, or do you use a callback?" David had another bookmaker.

An hour and a half later, after Howie Silver had arrived and they were stuffed with good food, David told him that the money he was getting from Dellson for the articles wasn't that important to him—$600—and that he'd be glad to do them for whatever his telephone expenses were the following year. Silver loved the idea. He thought he was getting David cheap. David loved the idea. It legitimized his calling schools for another year and gave him last-minute information on games whenever he wanted. The thought struck David that he was beginning to build a business from the ground up. He also thought that the following year he'd ask Silver for a press pass to Madison Square Garden and for additional money for traveling expenses so that he could personally scout teams throughout the country.

When they were ready to leave, David volunteered to pick up the check. Silver insisted on charging it to his business.

David was always ready to commence scribbling furiously once the scores began coming in via WINS radio. He had developed a new ritual. First he clenched his 1887 silver dollar in his left hand; then he telephoned one, two, or three schools for the scores of the games he had wagered on. Then he held his breath.

Once he got the scores his tension disappeared and he was ready to receive the hundred or more other scores he needed every Saturday evening to complete his records for the week. He'd get most of them on WINS, calmly write them down, and transfer them to his handbook. And now, without the pressure of waiting for the results of the particular games he had bet, David made no mistakes. Also there was less fatigue and the work went much more smoothly. He had the technique down to a science. He was usually through by 3:30 on Sunday morning.

During the week it was even easier. He usually had everything recorded by a little past midnight. The results of almost every game other than those from the Pacific Coast Athletic Association, the West Coast Athletic Conference, and the John Wooden–led Pacific Eight were furnished by midnight. Those games on the Coast were the toughest. You had to wait them out the entire evening. There was nothing else you could do.

Most of the time the operators would give you the score, but if they couldn't because of a school ruling or policy, all you got was, "Sorry, we're not allowed to give out scores." Or if the school was already closed for the evening, a prerecorded "This is the University of Higher Learning. The University is open between the hours of nine and nine. If you have an emergency, please call . . . For all other business we will be open at nine o'clock Monday morning."

In such situations David would make the necessary adjustments and put into effect Plan Two. That is, he would call auxiliary numbers: dormitories, gymnasiums, school radio stations, TV stations, police security, fieldhouses, newspapers, sports services in the particular city, or the coaches themselves. He'd even go so far as to call the coaches' homes directly—and you'd better believe Mrs. Molson and Mrs. DeFalco and three dozen or more of their kind as well as their children knew the score.

On this particular evening David had won two and lost one. He had lost at Columbia, less than ten city blocks from his home, and he had won in Georgia and Minnesota.

"Hello. . . . How's the game tonight?"

"Sorry. The main switchboard closed down at seven o'clock. This is Security."

"Is there any other number I can call to find out the score?"

"Well, I reckon you can call the community store. Ol' J.T. has a room upstairs and—"

"Thanks, Chief. . . . Hello, is this the community store?"

"Howdy. This is J.T. How can I help you?"

"Hi, J.T. I'm calling long-distance from New York. Can you tell me how the basketball game went tonight?"

"Well, I truly can't tell you the final score, mister, 'cause I left Rubin Arena when it was ninety-eight to seventy-one against us. I sort of lost interest."

"Thank you, J.T. Thank you very much."

David's profit for the night was $270. Doug called while he was staring at his cartons and reflecting on what that one loss had meant to him.

"Hello, David. Did you get your scores?"

"Yeah, I got 'em. That damn Columbia team blew it in the last minute. I had seven and a half points and they lost to Dartmouth sixty-seven to fifty-eight. The other two won easy. The difference between a nine-hundred-dollar evening and a two-hundred-and-seventy-dollar one was one lousy basket."

"I told you not to bet Columbia. That Ivy League's the worst. How'd Davidson do?"

"They won."

"I told you to bet them. That Terry Holland is one of the best young coaches in the country."

David felt himself growing tense. He wasn't in the mood to listen to Doug's criticisms any longer. Whoever was talking was just doing so because they, like everyone else in this lousy world, had an opinion.

"I know what I'm doing, Doug. I'm ahead eighteen hundred and forty dollars for the season. Let's not talk about it, okay?"

"Well, are you coming to the party or not? Uptight Frohman's here. He finally worked up enough nerve to bring his girlfriend. He's been going with her for six months now, but he's so uptight this is the first time he's allowed me to get a look at her. She thinks he's an artist. He's been keeping her away from me like the plague. He's afraid I'll tell her what he really does for a living."

Jack "Uptight" Frohman had been a friend of theirs since they were in grade school. He had degrees from Columbia, Princeton, and M.I.T. and had attended a half-dozen other brain centers. He was a computer expert and had made some important breakthroughs in the field. He had gone on lecture tours across America for I.T.&T. and had achieved a prestigious reputation. But unfortunately he had been stunted in his youth. While they were playing in the streets, he was studying; while they were watching ball games on TV and going to Yankee games, he was studying. He didn't know the difference between Wilt Chamberlain and Willie Mays, and, what's more, didn't really care. At a dance he'd stand in back of David and say, "Make a move, Lazar, make a move." He never would. He'd stand frozen and stare.

At the Brasserie every time a girl walked by, David would say, "Look at that one, Jack!" and Jack would methodically turn around, put his glasses on, examine her, squint, turn his head and follow her, and stare.

He never got laid—other than once, while on a trip to Mexico with Doug, with some prostitute named Alicia—until he was twenty-three, and now at thirty-seven when it came to women he was "uptight" and trying to make up for lost time.

With females, Jack "Uptight" Frohman, from the top of his brainy head to the bottom of his callused soles, was one big horny shrivel.

Doug continued to give David the blow-by-blow. "Uptight has been telling the girl he makes the swinging scene here in New York. And get this one, David. He told her he gambles big. Come on over, we'll have some fun."

"No. I can't. I have too much work to do."

"Come on, David. This might be our only chance. It might be another six months before he brings her around again."

David was tempted. Not only because of the fact that Uptight was always good for a few laughs, but also because David hadn't seen him for a while and missed him. David recollected how Uptight had never forgiven him for stealing a blind date many years earlier. The girl, Linda Lurie, was a senior at Music and Art High School and Doug was supposed to have fixed her up with Jack, but when Doug described her, David quickly moved in. She proved to be a bigger winner than even Doug had forecast.

Where have you gone, Linda Lurie? Jack "Uptight" Frohman never forgave David Lazar. Filed away somewhere, in that uptight computer of his, was David's girl theft.

In spite of the temptation, David continued to say no to the invitation. Doug continued to apply pressure. "Come on, don't be a shmuck, David. You can catch up on your scores tomorrow. You already got the results of the games you bet anyhow."

"I can't, Doug. I have to get more than a hundred scores tonight. If I don't do it now, I'll be behind for a week."

"Come on. One night won't hurt you. Besides, there are some real freaks here."

"Did Debbie and Jimmy show?"

"No. Debbie telephoned and said they were sorry but they had to go out with Jimmy's parents or something. I don't know why you invited them anyway. They wouldn't fit in. O'Brien's here, though. The kid's been drinking beer since nine. He's already half drunk. Guess what?" He chuckled. "My friend Molina thinks he's adorable. She just told me she'd love to take him home with her. By the way, David, guess what Uptight told me?"

"Come on, Doug, if you have anything to say, say it."

"He's going to Abilene, Texas. He's gonna teach at Hardin Simmons."

That got a rise out of David. "What?"

"... This is Spencer Ross at the editor's desk and the time is now eleven-forty-five and now sports. ..."

"Here come the scores, Doug. I can't come over. So long."

"... It was a big night in college basketball. First on the local front, St. John's ..."

When David heard WINS announcing the scores there was nothing else he could do but pay attention. Just as his devout father, before all else,

158 ...

before shower and shave, before laying tephillin, before davening, vocalizing, eating his breakfast, rehearsing the Shabbos service, davening some more, vocalizing again, eating lunch, resting for an hour, testing his golden tenor voice one more time, before all else, went over his stock prices every morning, so David had to digest his scores. David got that wonderful feeling that there was no place else in the world he'd rather be than in the twins' room with his pad, pencil, and handbook, working. David felt as he did when he was first involved with Leslie, as he did when he was writing well, as he did when he won a bet.

The more David worked the more he realized that in some ways he was a great deal like Nathan Rubin, a driven man whose dedication to his work overrode everything else. On that particular Saturday night when he fell into bed about 5:00 in the morning he was utterly exhausted. But by the next morning when he awoke, since he had won for the week, he was completely refreshed and strong. He leaped out of bed, put on some clothes, went outside, purchased the *New York Times,* and came home and rechecked every score, as well as the ones WINS radio had missed the night before. By noontime he had all the games played the previous evening filed in his handbook. From that point on, at a flip of the page, he would know the bookmaker line on the game, the score, where the game had been played, what he had made the game on his unofficial line, and what, if anything, was unusual about the outcome.

After having accomplished this, and only after having accomplished it, he hurried over to the Colonel's for Sunday brunch.

ON THIS SUNDAY, Isaac Pizer was present. For almost half a century, Isaac Pizer and the Colonel had been friends. They had been schoolmates at P.S. 67 on Mohegan Avenue and had played together at the boathouse in the Bronx Park, where they would chip in—the Colonel always put up the extra penny—and for five cents would take a boat out for the entire day.

Pizer was a small man with enormous pouches under cold frigid eyes, which gave his narrow face a cadaverous phosphorescence. But if you looked closely you noticed soft gentle lines creasing his thin-lipped mouth and smooth purplish cheeks. Around his left wrist he wore a glittering Audemar Piguet watch. His voice was virile for a man past sixty; his ego was puerile. He was dressed in a plaid sport coat, blue shirt, and silk cravat, and his slacks were whipcord and of lighter hue. His clothes, his manner, his way of talking, the way he held a cigar, his jaunty stance gave him a certain youthful flair, but somehow the flair was in complete contradiction to another facet of his personality, something deeper and more profound. It was something about his cold blue eyes. It was necessary only to look at those frigid eyes, which tried to calculate everything, to realize that the secret strength that allowed this man to accumulate millions was an instinct for self-preservation and a shrewdness at manipulation.

The Colonel gave Pizer one of his "Nice to see ya, what do you say, Isaac" greetings, and commandeered his wife to fix him a platter replete with bagels, Nova Scotia lox, herring, whitefish, sable, cheese, tomatoes, and onions, as well as his choice of liquid refreshment, usually either coffee or tea.

After Pizer had finished eating, the Colonel escorted him to the living room, whereupon they both began noshing on some sliced melon, and for a while Pizer spoke with his profound sobriety of a restaurant he frequented with his wife and the gourmet food they had ordered and of the service they had received. And, with ill-concealed pride, of how much it had cost him.

The Colonel mentioned to Pizer the difficulty he had been having in getting a reservation at the Café du Parc. The cigar came out of Pizer's mouth and his voice rose. "I'll tell you what I'll do with you. You want to bet I get a reservation." The accent was on the "I." And five minutes later the Colonel was talking about a sellout he was having on some pocket radios. The cigar came out of Pizer's mouth, and again his voice rose. "I'll take a chance on those pocket radios," he said, "if they're the best you have," and the accent was on the word "best."

Finally the two men got down to business. They discussed their wagers of the night before. As always, there was a discrepancy in their figures.

"What are you talking about, Isaac? Rutgers was the favorite. You laid three points. You didn't get points, you lost. You have to give me fifty-five dollars. Look, Isaac, I care about the fifty-five dollars like you care about fifty cents. But it's the idea. You have to give me fifty-five dollars."

Pizer wouldn't and didn't. He insisted that he never would have bet the game in the first place if the Colonel had told him that the Scarlet Knights were the favorite. David laughed and mocked him. He knew Isaac

Pizer. He was cut from the Nathan Rubin mold. He couldn't help himself;
$1 or $10,000, he was deadly serious.

"I see the world as it is, Lazar, and I'm going to go on seeing it this
way, because some things never change."

The phone rang, and the Colonel's wife quickly answered. "It's for
you, Isaac. It's Harry McDuff."

Isaac Pizer shrugged as if to say, "What's that creep bothering me
for?" He stood up to answer the call.

"How'd you know I was here, Harry?"

Pizer listened for a while and then said, "I'm sorry Harry, I don't have
any cash to spare. Why don't you call your friend Solomon Lepidus? He'll
help you out, won't he? And as for you handicapping for me, well, I'm not
betting the way I used to. I really don't need a handicapper." Isaac Pizer
paused and glanced over at the Colonel. "Say, how'd you like to hire Mustache McDuff as your handicapper?" The Colonel ahemed and looked at
Rebecca sheepishly. "I'm not that kind of gambler, Isaac. You know me
better than that."

Isaac Pizer hesitated before he returned to the phone. He recalled
when he had gone to Mustache McDuff for help. It was for his son, Joseph,
who had been on the verge of becoming a gambler. McDuff had talked his
heart out to young Joe, and made him understand what gambling was
really like. Isaac Pizer owed McDuff for that. He looked around, making
sure no one could overhear him, and then he said in a very low voice, "Listen, Harry, I'm sorry your wife left you. I know how rough that can be.
But face it, Harry, it's been coming for a long time. You haven't given
Marsha very much, have you?" Isaac Pizer stopped and again listened to
McDuff's pleas. "Well, if that's the case, Harry"—Pizer quickly looked
around—"I'll loan you the money. Harry, I want you to know something.
I'm real sorry about Marsha. . . . And, Harry," Isaac Pizer whispered, "this
is the last time I'm going to bail you out. The last time." Minutes later
Isaac Pizer was telling the Colonel, "That McDuff's got some nerve. He's
cost me a fortune and he's asking me to loan him ten Gs for his gambling
debts."

On this particular Sunday, and at every brunch that winter, anyone
and everyone who visited the Colonel's was made aware that David was
gambling on college basketball, and winning. David owed the Colonel for
such publicity.

The Colonel promoted David as one of the world's greatest handicappers. If David picked a winner the Colonel made it five. If David won $300,
the Colonel made it $3,000.

Because of the Colonel, David was beginning to be thought of as a genius in college basketball. A handicapper. At the time David was only

barely aware of the implications of the Colonel's publicity campaign, or how he could exploit them.

At about 1:30 that Sunday afternoon Solomon Lepidus strolled in with a surprise visitor. David recognized him. He was a former next-door neighbor of Leslie's and his, Harvey Stern, a large man with little pig eyes in a dark boil-laden face. He had long straight fingers and a horribly crooked back. His soul was healthy, though, and he had a reputation for being one of the nicest guys in the music business.

David immediately squeezed Stern into a corner and began questioning him. "Harvey! I didn't know you were coming over. Tell me about Leslie, Harvey. Have you seen her? How is she doing? Does she ever mention me? How's Jennifer?"

"Wait a minute, David, just wait a minute." Stern stopped and looked at him. "To tell you the truth, David, I haven't seen very much of Leslie. She's been . . ." He stopped again.

"What is it, Harv? You can tell me. Come on, what is it?"

"You know how I feel about it, David. I hated to see you two break up."

"Come on, Harvey," David said in an agitated voice. "What is it?"

"She's been seeing an awful lot of some guy, David. I think it's serious." His tone was somber as he continued, "Are you still gambling, David?"

As David started to explain, Harvey said, "I always told you not to be like me, David, not to work all your life to end up rich overnight."

Harvey always had insisted that artists, gamblers, and promoters such as he had that much in common. He probably was right, though David didn't say so. What he did say was, "It's a lot easier to be smart for the other guy, isn't it, Harvey?"

As David continued questioning Harvey about Leslie, Isaac Pizer came over and interrupted them. He began complaining about his stockbroker, and David mentioned to him that his friend Ron Nivens was a broker.

The Colonel overheard and walked over. He took a deep puff on his cigar and, withdrawing it, said, "I never could understand how that friend of yours, Ron Nivens, ever became a stockbroker. He's such a lovely man, but a stockbroker?"

David was about to pull Harvey away again when Solomon Lepidus joined them.

"Hey, Harvey," Solomon said. "I haven't forgotten about that idea we discussed last week. It's just been a hell of a week. Tell you what, though. Give me a call tomorrow and we'll set up an appointment. I'll take you out to lunch or somethin' and we can get down to business." He grinned, his hand still on David's elbow. "I'd like to talk it over now, but would you believe I got an appointment. Davy has some business he wants to go over with me."

"Oh, well . . . sure," Stern said, smiling at David, nodding as if to apologize for keeping him from his business with Solomon. "Go ahead, David, I'll talk to you later." Stern stepped away from both of them.

Solomon called out after him, "And don't forget to call tomorrow, Harvey!" as he smiled across the room to an acquaintance.

"Listen, Davy boy," he said. "Sorry to interrupt, but I got some business and I got to get out of here." He put his arm around David's shoulders, smiled, and lowered his voice till it was almost seductive. David was getting the full treatment.

"Will you do me a favor, Davy? I got my chauffeur downstairs. Drive with me to where I'm going. We'll talk on the way and then I'll have my driver take you right back. You and Harvey can talk then." Solomon paused. "That okay with you, Davy boy?"

Solomon picked his moments for the full treatment, moments when he knew it would take full effect. David smiled and nodded.

"Sure, Solomon. I could use some fresh air."

"Good boy!" Solomon beamed. He left his arm on David's shoulder and walked him to the door.

As soon as Solomon had settled himself in his car, he instructed his driver, "Take us over to Cappy's Record Shop." The man nodded, asked no directions, and turned the limousine into the traffic. David realized he had driven with Solomon countless times and didn't know the driver's name. For a moment he wondered if Solomon did.

Solomon reached for the car phone and began making business calls, to people's homes, David guessed. He heard Solomon each time chatting with the man's wife, asking after the kids, chuckling and mentioning the last dinner or brunch or party, and how he would have run off with her "if that mensch you married couldn't straighten me out and hang me up to dry. Where is the son of a gun, anyway? He there? Sure, if I can't speak to you all day, I'll talk to the . . ." Five calls, and never for a moment did Solomon stop once to speak to David.

When the car double-parked in front of Cappy's, Solomon said, "Come on in with me, Davy boy; I'll talk to you there." Solomon didn't wait for the driver to open the door. He jumped out of the car and entered the record shop, David behind him. Cappy ran over from behind the counter and grabbed Lepidus's lapel.

"Solomon, thanks for coming right over. Like I told you, Solomon, I got this terrible problem. You know me, Solomon, twenty-six years in this business and I never fired anyone. But I caught this guy stealin' and I don't know what to do. I tried everything. When everything failed"—Cappy scratched the back of his salt-and-pepper scalp—"I couldn't think of anything else to do except to call you." Cappy again grabbed Solomon by the lapel. "What should I do, Solomon?"

"So what's this guy doin'?" Solomon was asking Cappy. "Liftin' stock or cash?"

"Both, I think," Cappy said, a little sheepishly.

"Okay, Cappy," Solomon said, nodding as if the problem were solved. "Tell you what. Does this guy like sports?"

"Yeah, he's crazy about hockey. But what's that got to do with—"

Solomon interrupted, "Give him a couple of tickets to a Ranger game and give him tomorrow off, too. You see, Cappy, it's better to give a man a day off when he's healthy and can enjoy it than when he's sick and can't."

"A day off will cost me a fortune, Solomon!"

"Cappy, I send over six hundred employees of mine to sporting events throughout the year." This was true, David knew. He'd been in the office with Solomon when some employees had come in and been handed tickets to Solomon's box at the Garden or the Stadium. They were sent out before they had a chance to finish thanking their employer.

"You mean you go for that kind of money, Solomon?"

"I'm spending it, Cappy. With you, they're stealing it." Solomon paused. "You gotta earn your employees' respect, Cap. Take that guy of yours to a Ranger game or to the fights. Spend some time with him, find out about his family, keep askin' him about his wife and kids. I guarantee he'll do more work for you next week, and every other week, than any other employee you got. Another thing, Cappy. How much did this guy steal from you? Now ask yourself, Cappy, how much did he steal that you don't know about? . . . The ticket and the day off just became a lot cheaper, didn't they, Cappy?"

David had been glancing at his watch every five minutes. A half hour later, Solomon was still talking with Cappy. David couldn't even interest himself when they began to talk over the college basketball season. David was still glancing at his watch, and stewing.

"Cappy," David interrupted, "do you have a phone I can use?" Without interrupting his conversation with Solomon, Cappy pointed to a phone behind the counter. David dialed the Colonel's, spoke for less than a minute, then walked slowly back to the two men. He looked grim.

"Hey, Davy boy." Solomon grinned. "You ready to go? I'll have my driver take you back to the Colonel's now." He smiled. "They'll just be getting to the real food. You can talk to what's his name, uh, Stern, the rest of the day."

"No I can't, Solomon," David said, sounding almost bitter. "I just called there. Harvey waited almost an hour, then he left."

Solomon quickly reached for his wallet. He peeled off a $100 bill from the top. "Here's a C-note, Cappy. Get David any albums he wants. This guy loves the classicals; show him what you got."

164 . . .

Solomon turned to David. "I got to get going, Davy. Geez, what a week. It ain't over and it's already the next one! Take it easy, Davy boy."

Solomon waved at David, squeezed Cappy's shoulder, and hurried out of the store. Cappy shook his head and smiled at David.

"Do you believe the guy, Davy? He's got twenty thousand things to do in the day, and he's got time for my problems. I call that class."

David was about to leave the store, a batch of record albums under his arm, when Cappy picked up the phone, waved his arm toward David, and shouted.

"Hey wait, Lazar! It's Solomon. He's calling from his car for you."

David laid the record albums on the counter and picked up the receiver.

"How you doin', Davy boy?" Solomon roared at him. "Listen, remember I had somethin' to tell you? Yeah. I must be getting senile. I almost forgot. Well, get a pen and some paper."

David picked up a pencil from the cash register, pulled his notebook from his pocket. "Okay, Solomon," he said.

"All right. I got three numbers here I want you to take down. These are guys I think you could use for some heavy bets you might want to make." Solomon dictated the three numbers, one of them a Brooklyn number. "The guy in Brooklyn is named Angelo Scarne, but actually, Davy boy, he's called One-Eye. I'll let you guess why."

Solomon went on to say that each bookmaker took up to two dimes a game, and that he might ask David to beard for him with any one of them.

"Oh, and Davy," he said, "there's one other thing. I told you, my friend, Max Brown. Well, we were talkin' yesterday and Max said he might give you a call. Listen to me, Davy boy. If Max has a proposition for you, listen to him. I guarantee you won't get hurt."

"Okay, Solomon," David said.

"Take it easy," Solomon said.

That evening David couldn't fall asleep. He kept thinking of what Harvey Stern had said: "She's been seeing an awful lot of some guy, David."

Finally he reached for the telephone and dialed Leslie's number. As soon as he heard her voice, he blurted out, "Harvey Stern told me that you're involved with some guy, Leslie. Is it true?"

For several seconds there was a blank silence, then she said, "Don't be silly, David, I'm not involved with anyone." He started to ask her how she was. "I can't talk to you now, David, I'm not feeling well." He was just about to say he'd call her in the morning to find out how she was when Leslie said, "I'd prefer your not calling here, David, it just upsets us both." And with that she said goodnight.

* * *

Nathan Rubin was in Sandy Rocca's apartment with Saskia Verdonck.

"I was always the smartest kid in grammar school," Saskia said. "Always nines and tens. That's why the other children didn't like me. Most of the time"—she frowned—"I was alone." Nathan Rubin fondled her calf as they sat on an upholstered white leather couch. Saskia continued to talk. "The first time, I was fourteen, Nathan, and it was not so good."

Nathan Rubin smiled. He took her hand and squeezed it. As he did Saskia leaned closer to Nathan Rubin and said, "Nathan, I would very much like it if you like me." Nathan Rubin peered at her and smiled. As he pointed to the bedroom he said, "Ya know, Saskia, now that Kim Colby's gone, I'd think it a good idea if you moved in with Odette. You'll like her. She's a good kid. Another thing, come over to my office tomorrow morning. I want to send you on a go-see for a lipstick commercial. I think you're perfect for it."

She entered the bedroom with a bottle of Muscadet in her hand. Nathan disrobed while Saskia stared at him, at his small, shrunken body with veins like frayed ropes, his thin arms and skinny legs; at his face, stained by greed and age; at his puny pink chest, with strands of gray hairs encircling the shriveled nipples; at his bloated, wrinkled belly. Saskia's undaunted eyes traveled below Nathan Rubin's navel, searched between his legs, and as she did, Nathan Rubin grinned and inched closer to her.

"Have some more Muscadet, Saskia." He placed his huge, rapacious hands around her long thin neck and cackled imploringly, "Suck me, Saskia, like a good little girl." At first Saskia resisted. "Suck me, Saskia." The hungry bony fingers gripped Saskia's head and neck, and applied surprising power to push her down. "Suck me, Saskia," Nathan Rubin hissed. Saskia's heavy lips parted, and her warm mouth and liquid tongue began caressing his aged organ. Nathan Rubin chuckled metallically. "That's good, Saskia. That's a good girl. . . . That's good. . . ."

An hour later Nathan Rubin was saying, "Ya see, Saskia, I can make you a living modeling, but first I want you to do something for me. Is it a bargain?" Saskia smiled and pouted pleasantly.

"Of course, Nathan. I'll be glad to assist you any way I can."

"Good," Nathan said abruptly. "Now this is what I want you to do."

Valerie Caldwell, a young woman with a body for sculpture and a mind for business, walked into Isaac Pizer's office. Pizer looked up and stared. He couldn't believe that this tall, statuesque huntress wanted a job designing jewelry. She had a chiseled, perfectly featured face and a curved, sensual form. Her chestnut hair was thick, draped down, and almost touched the curve of her backside. To Isaac Pizer she looked as if she'd be more at home and certainly more successful working as a fashion model for Eileen Ford or Wilhelmina.

"So you're the young woman that Lazar asked me to talk to. He seems to think a great deal of you, Ms. Caldwell."

Valerie Caldwell had met David only once, at P.J. Clark's. The first thing David had noticed about Valerie, who was standing at the bar with her back to him, was that she had a great ass, and second that she was carrying the *New York Times*. When he moved closer, he saw that the newspaper was opened to the employment section.

Isaac Pizer kept staring at Valerie. He couldn't get over her stunning looks, her poise. He intuited that her voice would match her style. He had a hunch about her from the moment she walked into his office. He noticed the sheer cream-colored dress she was wearing, which clung seductively to her arresting figure. Her jewelry was inexpensive but tasteful.

"The problem, Ms. Caldwell, is with your looks. My other designers would never be designing."

Valerie Caldwell spoke rapidly and with precision. "That's their problem, not mine, Mr. Pizer. Mine is, I need the job. I'm confident that within two years I can give you a line of jewelry that will sell throughout the country. Please, Mr. Pizer, just take a look at my portfolio." With that she brought her designs to Pizer's desk and laid them out in front of him.

Pizer casually lit a thick cigar and placed it in his mouth before silently leafing through the pages, examining each Caldwell design intently. Val Caldwell didn't move from the front of the desk, but as Pizer examined her work, her mind kept traveling.

She thought of how desperately she needed the job, of the bills she had accumulated since coming to New York, of what she might have to do if this didn't work out, of the small town in Oregon she came from, and the vow she had made herself never to return. She thought of her one-night stand with David Lazar. All he talked about that entire evening was his wife, handicapping, and that girl, Debbie, but he did get her this interview.

Anxious, but straining herself to the limit to look self-possessed, she stoically waited for Pizer's response. Finally, Isaac Pizer closed the portfolio, slowly took the thick cigar out of his mouth, and placed it in a marble ashtray. He stood up. Valerie Caldwell still towered over him.

"Your designs are very impressive, Ms. Caldwell. I'm going to give you a shot." He stopped before continuing. "Now let's have dinner, Val. I know a great little restaurant in Chinatown. We'll talk about your salary there."

Valerie Caldwell, relieved but anxious, and still all business, took a deep breath before saying enthusiastically, in a voice as pretty as music, "Thank you very much for the invitation, Mr. Pizer, but as far as I'm concerned, my salary can be set right now." She stopped and took another deep breath. She asked herself, I wonder if I'll be better off if I sleep with him? It's obvious that he wants me. He isn't that bad-looking that I'd hate myself in the morning. But then she thought, Let him want me. I'll get more out of him that way.

Valerie Caldwell smiled engagingly at Isaac Pizer as she said firmly, "I want to be recognized for my talent alone, Mr. Pizer, and for nothing else."

Isaac Pizer growled, "Your salary will be one eighty-five a week. See you Monday morning, Ms. Caldwell."

As soon as Valerie Caldwell reached the street, she walked straight to a pay phone and dialed David Lazar.

"Hello, David, I got the job.... I ... David, that's actually why I called you. I can't meet you for dinner. No, not tomorrow night either.... What? ... No, I don't think so.... David ... Look, David, it was fun, I had a great time too. But listen, David, I'm just not interested in dating. Right now the only thing I have time for is my career. And thanks to you, and Mr. Pizer, I think I'm going to get the chance I need to initiate one. I just can't afford to spend any time involving myself with anyone. Besides, David, you're already involved, with your wife and that young woman in your office, and with your handicapping. You of all people should understand."

Max Brown, president of the New York Stars basketball team, called David at his parents' home. As soon as David answered the phone, Brown hit him with a barrage of questions. What did he do for a living? What had he done in the past? What did he want to do? What had he written? What did his father do? Was he religious?

"Solomon says you're an expert on college basketball, David, that you know every team and every player in the country. What do you say?"

David explained to Max Brown about his basketball handbook and how he had prepared himself for the season and how well he had been doing. In a way it must have sounded as if he were bragging, because after several minutes Brown became annoyed.

"No gambler can ever win, Lazar. Solomon and I are living proof of that. If you gamble you have to lose."

Brown asked David to come to his office the following day, as he had a proposition he wanted to discuss with him. David didn't know what to expect. David began to think that Solomon had asked Brown to give him a job in order to get him away from gambling. He began to hope that Max Brown wanted him to do some scouting for Max's professional basketball team.

David became more than a little excited and started dreaming of coaching, assisting the team's general manager, even running a professional sports organization.

The next day David visited Max Brown. His office was as big as a basketball court. As David walked in, Moses Gerard was leaving. Moses was averaging 24 points a game for the Stars and was one of the few players Max owned, David thought, who could do well for the Knicks. On his arm was Linda Lurie, the same Linda Lurie David had known more than ten years back. She recognized him but gave a very hollow hello. She was still a beauty, a little plump, with crow's-feet starting to trespass around the eyes, but still a beauty. As they walked out together, David thought to himself that Moses must be quite a stud to be able to satisfy a woman like Linda. He would have loved to have gotten her phone number, but his timing made it impossible. As David ogled her leaving with Moses, Brown took his arm and pulled him into his office. He immediately shut the door and told his secretary—bleached blond, all blubber, mountains for boobs—that he didn't want to be disturbed by anyone. Half apologetically, David explained to him that he had known Linda many years earlier. Brown looked at him and said abruptly, "She's married to Moses." That ended their conversation about Linda Lurie Gerard.

Max Brown was a pink-faced, smooth-cheeked fat man with double jowls and a gigantic stomach. He was good-hearted, but abrupt and pulled no punches. Where one word would do, he'd never use five. He got down to basics as fast as any man David had ever known.

Without elaborating, he said that the following season he would have some special games both in college ball and in the pros, which he would want David to bet for him. He strongly recommended that David follow his selections whenever he called him. He also said that if David had a strong opinion on a college game he should telephone him. He wrote down his number on a memo pad for David. That was it. He didn't wait for David's answer. He just tore off the sheet from the pad and handed it to David and said, "Be talking to you, Lazar, and remember, anytime I call you in the future I'll only be saying, 'I'm cheering for these guys,' and that means that you should get me down six dimes on the game."

David was already halfway out the door when Brown called him back and reminded him to use Big Blake, Joey Zee, and Angelo "One Eye" Scarne, the same three bookmakers that Solomon had mentioned.

David was disappointed. He had fantasized getting a job with a professional basketball team. Why did he forget that no one gives you anything, that you never get what you want?

For all his resolves, David was again seeing Debbie Turner. The first time they were together he made an effort to tell her why he couldn't see her more than once a week, why he was afraid to see her more than once a week, but when he looked into her eyes, he couldn't. Instead he concocted another lie. A lie she of course didn't believe. As he thought she was going to burst into tears, he stayed an extra hour with her, saying nothing, just talking. The surest way of saying nothing is to talk.

After that, each evening while he waited for scores he thought about Debbie and hated his cowardice more than ever. Each evening, after having gotten his scores, he cursed and mourned Leslie.

Debbie Turner took David's lame excuses more bitterly than she ever let on. At home, for hours, she would talk to Jimmy about him, showing great concern with his handicapping plans, and more important, with the anticipated effects gambling would have on him. More and more she inveighed against the wasted days he spent preparing for the basketball season, and his ambiguous behavior toward her.

"David's incapable of leading a normal life, Jimmy. He'd be miserable if he were married. He needs the kind of intensity he finds in gambling, just as he needed the kind of intensity he found in his marriage. There are many things I'm beginning to understand about David, Jimmy, and I don't like them at all. He just isn't a well-rounded person."

DAVID LAZAR, novice handicapper, was coming down the home stretch of the season and was still doing well. Only once did he risk more than $400 on a single game. On one other occasion, just eight days before, when he was ahead $800 for the week, he made a reverse bet. He found two games with a substantial flaw—a 5½-point and a 6½-point differential from his line. He made two bets of $600 each. He won both games and as a result ended the week with a $2,000 profit. He didn't collect the $1,200 from his "best friend," Johnny. He did collect $400 from Ed Kashman and $200 from Arnie Feld and another $200 from O'Brien.

Weeks earlier he had started tutoring O'Brien on the ins and outs of betting. Soon afterward O'Brien found himself bearding for David and wagering $20 or $25 a game for himself. In those last three weeks, O'Brien personally pocketed $125. David allowed his "best friend's" office to hold his $1,200. "Once the money is in my pocket it's not for speculation."

David wanted to invest the money if he found a special game with a large enough disparity from his power rating.

The day after he made the reverse bet, when he phoned his "best friend's" service, Nino Tafuri called him back and growled that Johnny was not feeling well and was taking a few weeks off. "I'll be taking over the phones, Lazar."

After that, whenever David called Tafuri for a line he'd receive a caustic remark. He began calling just to hear how bugged he was. His $1,200 wasn't gathering interest, but annoying Tafuri was better than any dividend.

For the remainder of the season, David couldn't find anything larger than a 4-point differential. Consequently, the regular season ended without his making another wager. He went into the National Invitation Tournament and the National Collegiate Athletic Association tournament looking for opportunities. But the lines remained correct. The opening NIT games were appetizing. Almost every short deserved a play. But his power rating differed only by 3 or 4 points from the official line on each game. His rule remained steadfast. He wanted at least a 5-point differential from the official line for investment purposes.

On the first Monday in March, the NCAA announced its first-round regional pairings for the games to be played the coming Saturday. One of the games was to appear on television; it was Western University against a strong Midwestern independent. For the rest of the week he keyed himself for this game and hoped and prayed the game would be put on the board. He was afraid the linemaker would think as he did and keep it off the board entirely, or make it an astronomical figure. After all, his power ratings made Western a 31-point underdog. He spent the entire week praying that the linemaker would be duped by Western's 21–3 won-and-lost record, and by Sky Davis's 31.4 scoring average.

Sky had become a favorite of the press and the public, and the team had caught on as a Cinderella five. David hoped the linemaker in Vegas, as almost everyone else in America, would be conned by such gloss.

He touted everyone on the game: Doug, O'Brien, Jimmy, Debbie, Arnie Feld, Saskia Verdonck, Sandy Rocca, Nathan Rubin, Harvey Stern, the Colonel, Isaac Pizer, Eddie Zeno, Mark Jagerman, Max Brown, Solomon Lepidus, Champ Holden—just about everyone who had ever asked him for an opinion. He told each of them that Western should be blown off the court. Lose by 30. He said it emphatically, without a doubt in his mind. He told everyone that he didn't think there'd be a price on the game. "Just listen to me. Western's played a minor league schedule. The three games they've lost were against average teams. . . . Of course they went undefeated in their conference. It's a nothing conference. Boone College is their only competition, and that team's at least a year away." David said that if they did make a price on the game they'd have to make Western at least an unheard-of 26-point underdog.

Finally Saturday arrived. When he called Nino Tafuri to get the NIT and NCAA lines, he remembered holding his breath and clenching his silver dollar tight in his fist while waiting to see what he would do with Western. When Tafuri quoted them as a 16½-point short, he was thrilled. The 14½-point gap between the official Vegas line and his unofficial line of 31 points was the biggest differential he had found on a game all season. He figured he was in a position to maximize and at the same time to make a killing. It was the one game he knew would take care of the entire season.

Eddie Zeno and Roger Brantley both thought he was nuts. Sandy Rocca liked the other side. Mustache Harry McDuff called David for his opinion. When he got it, he said, "I don't agree, Lazar. I think it's a tap-out bet on Western. That sixteen and a half points will stand up till doomsday. The fact is, Lazar, I got a hunch Western's going to win the whole damn game. That Sky Davis'll be just too much for the other side." He stopped. "I've already called in a bet with Angelo Scarne's office. And now, after talking to you, Lazar, I'm calling them back to triple my bet on Western."

When David called Champ Holden he didn't say David was right or wrong. He offered no opinion on the game. He simply said, "If you think you got something good, play it. Without balls, you can't do anything in this world. And don't listen to anyone; they'll only have different opinions anyway."

For the season David was ahead $4,800, and all week he had planned on what he would do if they made a line on the game which answered his prayers. By Friday night he had gone over his power ratings for the game for the hundredth time and, as on each previous time, it still came out 31 points less for Western than for their opposition. He knew what he would do. He wagered $500 with Nino Tafuri, laying the 16½ against Western. Next he called Joey A. and placed $500 more against Western. This time he laid 17. After that he called Arnie Feld and had him get down for $400. This time he laid 17½. After doing that he phoned O'Brien and had him get down for $200 against Western. O'Brien called back and told David he was laying 16½. A few seconds later David telephoned Ed Kashman and had him call in a bet against Western for $250. He got David down at 17.

David had also touted Nathan Rubin on the game, and Nathan had said that he was following Sandy Rocca on the game and was betting $2,000 on Western. David phoned Tony Giardello's office and through one of the clerks called in $650 against Western minus 17. The clerk's voice was dull and flat. He didn't flinch one iota at the size of David's bet.

David isolated himself in his room. He sat on his bed. He got up and paced the floor. His mood had strayed from ecstatic, when he received the line, to apprehensive, to despairing. He waited for what seemed like hours for the game to begin. He couldn't eat lunch. He was nervous, hyper, manic. When he flicked on the TV he kept thinking of the numbers. If he lost it would mean $2,750 down the drain. If he won it would mean a profit of $2,500. He swallowed hard.

All pretenses were stripped bare. All theories and numbers could be thrown out the window. It was a game and he was gambling, nothing more. The 14½-point differential between his opinion and the linemaker's opinion was only an abstraction. It didn't have anything at all to do with reality. It wasn't reality. Anything could happen.

As they announced the starting lineups his throat went dry, his right eye twitched, his left leg began to jerk involuntarily, his hands became wet, and his kidneys rebelled. He went to the bathroom, urinated, and returned to the twins' room. He sat down on his bed. For a moment he cuddled his pillow and lay on his side, then he sat up and took the phone off the hook so that he wouldn't be disturbed. He was too overwrought to talk to anyone about the game, or anything. He was stripped bare of his handicapping cool. He was a gambler raw. He clenched his silver dollar. The game began.

Sky Davis opened the game by hitting a jumper from thirty feet out and putting him down 2-0. After that it wasn't a contest. He sweated for only the first sixty-two seconds. After that, he felt godlike. The final score was Western 71, Lazar's selection 105. Sky got 33 points, but he was horrid. A gunner, no discipline, no defense at all.

David's strong independent team cut Western to ribbons. They worked basic plays and penetrated and banged away at the boards for offensive rebounds. They scored at will inside. Tony Willis, Western's big man, was consistently boxed out by two giants three inches taller, and another giant climbed on their backs and dominated the boards. His team must have hit 60 percent from the field, most of their scoring being on easy lay-ups and good percentage shots. His team had five legitimate starters and three solid players coming off the bench.

Western had Sky and Tony Willis and a bunch of rink-a-dink kids who didn't know the first thing about basketball. His team did almost anything they wanted. It was never a contest. The thrill was a sick one for sixty-two seconds. The two hours of pleasure were better than sex. Much better. When the game ended he gazed at his silver dollar. It was smiling back at him.

Moments after the game ended, David's mother entered his room gripping her walker and stepping step by step closer to him. Her face was worn-out and shrunken from suffering.

"David, I want to talk to you," she said. "Why are you ruining your life? Why do you gamble? Wasn't I a good mother to you?" She clutched her walker with hands stained by black-and-blue blotches and half-cried,

"David! Talk to me; you're my favorite son; what did I do wrong? Didn't I love you when you were a child? Don't you remember how I took eyelashes out of your eye, splinters out of your hands? Don't you remember how I used to rub and massage your frozen feet after you played in the snow? David," she cried, "talk to me. I love you." She paused. "I taught you to love music and art and literature." She wailed, "You're a good boy, why do you gamble?"

As his mother spoke, he stared at her swollen body and suffering face. He understood her frailty and her terror, but he realized she did not know his.

"David, please, you have to stop gambling before it's too late." She paused and waited for him to say something. He bit his lip and remained silent. She let go of her walker and reached out with her hand to touch him, but he pulled back. His body became rigid, his face taut, his mood sullen.

She cried out, "David, I love you, I love you." And then she slowly turned, clutching her walker, and moved step by step out of the room.

David lay down on his bed and placed his hands behind his head, and his mind journeyed back to his childhood. He remembered his mother putting him down when others praised, lecturing him arbitrarily that he must respect his father. "David, you should be proud to be a Jew!" He remembered her "kvelling" and praising his As, scorning his Cs. He remembered basking in her adulation, being shaped by it. He remembered her all-consuming attentiveness and possessiveness, her nurturing him with an impossible belief in his ability to win at anything, whenever, however he wanted; distorting his reality; fortifying his megalomania.

He remembered how unprepared he was for life, for reality, for setbacks, for hard knocks, for earning a living, for giving, for being committed to anything, to anyone, to Leslie.

Of all those David had touted on the Western game the only ones who had bet his choice were Mark Jagerman, Arnie Feld, O'Brien, Saskia Verdonck, Doug, and Debbie. He had bet $25 of his own money for Debbie and told her so only after the game was over. Jimmy he told before.

Everyone else bet the other way or laid off completely. Isaac Pizer had dissuaded the Colonel from following him. He said that David was due to lose and that he had talked to some wise guys in Vegas who said that the word was that Western should win the whole game.

The Colonel followed Pizer. After the game the Colonel called and fumed and cursed and swore that he'd never speak to Pizer again. Sandy Rocca and Nathan Rubin also said that the smart money was bet on Western, that all the handicapping sheets had picked Western.

David slept like a babe with Saskia Verdonck in his arms. In the morning she smiled and said, "Last night with Nathan Rubin and Solomon Lepidus, I was stealing the show. I was the center of attention. I like them

174 . . .

to admire me, David. It's very nice." She paused. "But that Solomon Lepidus, he has windmills in his head, don't you think, David?" She mimicked Solomon. "Here's a twenty for the ladies' room Saskia. . . . Here's a twenty for a cab. . . ." She shook her head. "What a foolish man." David took her hand and squeezed it. Saskia leaned over and hugged David and whispered in his ear, "I'm very happy when I'm with you, David."

A few minutes later David told Saskia he had to go to the Colonel's for a victory brunch; she asked to come along. He told her he couldn't take her. She knew he just didn't want to. He had made feeble excuses many times before. Outside of bed he just didn't enjoy being with her that much. Still, she persisted. "David, did I do something wrong?" She kept up her questions as much as Leslie had kept up her recriminations.

"David, don't you like me anymore? Did I gain too much weight? Did I say something? Did I—"

David reacted. "Saskia, you might not understand this, but I have other things to do besides sleep with you." He went to the victory brunch at the Colonel's alone.

The same morning Saskia Verdonck received a telegram. She was fearful of bad news, but there was a chance it might be a go-see from Nathan Rubin's modeling agency. She slit the envelope.

"Dear Saskia, It is with deep sorrow that I tell you your father has died of cirrhosis of the liver. . . ."

Saskia knew only too well how few dollars she had left to her name. She had come to America with $1,500. Money earned by cleaning lavatories in a Dutch home for the aged. The only money earned by her since entering the States (excluding money borrowed from Lepidus) was $1,200 from Nathan Rubin, as payment for a proposition she had consented to. That money was all gone, spent on clothes, a movie camera, and rent.

Odette Bashjian had made it very plain. "Your share of the rent comes to two hundred and eighty dollars a month, Saskia. And it's due on the first. Kim had her telephone disconnected, so if you want a telephone you'll have to order it from the phone company. You'll have to put down a deposit and pay your bill every month. As for food . . ."

Just the same, Saskia decided to telephone Dr. Jan DeJong in Holland.

"Your father expired because his liver stopped functioning, Saskia. I knew your father for many years. May he rest with God. Don't think he didn't see me. You'd be surprised how many times your stepmother called my office about his drinking problems. He just wouldn't listen to reason. Since he lost his orchard, things went from bad to worse. The binge he was on these last four years would have killed anyone. I begged him to stop. Those symptoms I wrote you about—the swelling in his belly and legs, waterlogging, the punchdrunk effect, the mental disorders—all the same problem, actually. It was the alcohol, Saskia. When we finally got him in the hospital during those last few days we discovered more than eighty percent of his liver was bad. It had just stopped functioning. There was nothing to do."

After the call Saskia opened a bottle of wine, and when she finished the bottle she dialed the unlisted phone number of Nathan Rubin. She had put off consenting to one of his propositions for some time now, but times change, and so do plans.

"Hello, Nathan," Saskia said in a resigned voice. "Now I understand what you tell me. Life is hard. I've decided to do what you say. I'll remain here with your friend Odette and be available when you need me. Nathan, you should also know, I am not seeing David Lazar any longer. I like David very much, Nathan, but you can't force these kinds of things. It takes two people, right?"

"Ya see, Saskia, right now I know you don't think too well of me. But you will. I'm giving you a chance to earn a living. And once you earn a living, you'll see, you'll be grateful. Ya see, Saskia, independence is a wonderful thing. It gives you the freedom to do whatever you want whenever you want."

Nathan Rubin stopped, and then he said in his inimitable cackle, "Ya see, Saskia, the guys I'll be fixing you up with will be easy. They'll be generous. They're suckers." Nathan Rubin stopped. In a metallic voice he said, "Just remember our deal, Saskia, you see."

On his way to the Colonel's, David thought of something Solomon had once said to him when they were discussing one of his friends who had gone broke. He had said, "There but for the grace of my brain go I."

David knew exactly what he meant. Sandy Rocca had followed his own experienced opinion for the most part and lost a little. Eddie Zeno called every day, but followed his opinion only some of the time. He ended up about even. Mark Jagerman made a bundle on the Western game and had ended the year with an insignificant profit. Max Brown contacted him immediately after the game and berated Solomon and himself for not having had the Western game. Before hanging up he reminded David to call him next season whenever he had something good. Brown also reminded him that next year he would be calling him when he felt like "cheering" for certain teams. David asked him how he had done this year on college basketball.

"Are you kidding? I got buried."

David asked him about the way he wagered.

"I bet on everything, the whole board. But you don't have to worry. The games I give you to 'cheer' for don't lose!"

David asked him why he didn't bet only those games.

"Are you out of your mind, Lazar? That wouldn't be gambling."

There but for the grace of my brain go I.

21

DAVID GRABBED a cab and went over to Arnie Feld's apartment to collect the money he had won on the Western game. When he got to Feld's apartment the front door was half open. Arnie Feld had a smooth shiny face, a lecherous grin, small nervous hands, bony wrists, and crooked fingers, one adorned by a pinky ring. His nails were manicured and polished. Arnie Feld had followed David all season, had called him every day, and yet had ended up a loser for the season. David walked in and saw some pipsqueak in a fedora hat and mohair suit whining to him.

"What are you jerking me off for, Arnie? What did I ever do to you? Did I ever hold you up? Didn't you get paid every week when you were entitled? Did I ever blink, bullshit you, or make excuses? What do you think I am, an asshole? What are you trying to do, take a shot at me? The next thing you know you'll be pulling a claim."

Arnie snickered and continued to comb his greasy hair in front of a mirror, dandruff dropping on his shoulders. As the pipsqueak continued squawking, he waved his hands above his head, and every once in a while he'd remove his hat and twist it a few times and then stick it back on top. When he did, you could see he was wearing a cheap hairpiece. He kept squawking.

"I support four kids and my mother-in-law, Arnie. I'm not a bad guy. You know I can't make a living in anything else. I didn't even graduate high school."

Arnie pirouetted to face him, and as he did he noticed David. He was standing directly facing him. At first Arnie blinked in confusion, turned red, but slowly he regained his composure.

"I know I beat you for a lot of bread, Oscar, but I've been going bad in other places. You ain't the only guy I deal with. I just don't have it. Maybe next week I can pay you, but right now, I'm tapped."

Oscar snapped, "Maybe next week! You must be crazy! What do you think I am, some kind of putz? I want to get paid by tomorrow or else I'm calling in my boss. And I'm warning you, Arnie, once it's out of my hands, you'll be sorry. If you're looking for trouble, you're going to find it."

As Oscar turned his back to walk out, David thought of one of Leslie's conversations with Ron Nivens. "Did you ever see the kind of people

David mingles with, Ron? How can he let himself get involved with animals like that? Even if he wins, he loses!"

David followed Arnie, who ran after Oscar into the hallway and was screaming at the top of his lungs that he wouldn't pay until he was good and ready. David grabbed his shoulder, spinning him around.

"I don't want to have any trouble with any God damn office because of a creep like you. Now call him back in here and pay him."

Arnie spewed out, "Don't worry, David, I have the money to pay him. I just like to give Oscar a hard time."

He smiled, and the sickness of it revolted David. David waved to Oscar to return and said to Arnie, "If you want to continue working for me next year, Arnie, you pay off on time and you collect on time. Now give me the bread you owe me for the Western game."

Arnie reentered his apartment, walked to his dresser, opened a drawer, pushed aside a racing form, took out a wad of bills, and counted out $400. He was in the midst of paying David when Oscar walked in. His eyes popped when he saw the money. David told him to wait a minute, grabbed what was left of the wad in Arnie's hand, and asked Oscar how much he had coming. David counted out $300 and handed it to him.

As soon as Oscar left the apartment, David wheeled on Arnie, hitting him flush in the face. His knuckles did the job. Arnie dropped to the floor and started squalling, "Wha . . . what ya do that for?"

"Just to make certain you remember what I told you. I want you to collect and pay promptly from now on. Now wipe that blood off your mouth, creep, and listen carefully. I want to talk to you about some ideas I have for next year."

David Lazar had a business. He had made it grow. He had made $7,300 starting with a base bet of $25, and that was saying something. He had snowballed minimizing and maximizing to perfection. He had taken advantage of every damn mistake he had found on the official line. Not once had he made a wager where the difference between his line and the official line wasn't at least 4½ points in his favor. In toto, he had wagered on ninety-three games, winning sixty-seven and losing twenty-three. He had a winning percentage of 74.4 percent.

In his handbook he computed the final results of the 1970–1971 college basketball season. The results he shared with Doug.

"Vegas had an official line on four thousand, one hundred and forty-one games, and of those I found a hundred and sixty-three with a four-and-a-half-point-or-more differential from my power ratings. And I didn't even bet on all of those, Doug. I only made ninety-three bets for the entire season. Now listen to this. Where the differential between the Vegas line and my own was five and a half or six, I won thirty games and lost eleven. Where it was six and a half or seven, I won twenty-three and lost six. And

178 . . .

where I found more than seven and a half points to work with, I won nine and lost only one. The biggest differential I found all season was on that Western game in the NCAA tournament, Doug. It was fourteen and a half points off from my power rating. I'm telling you, Doug, numbers don't lie. In fact, I'll make you a bet right now. Next season I'll find just about the same number of games to invest in, and on those ninety games or so, I'll bet that I have just about the same winning percentage as I had this year. Listen, Dougie, I made seventy-three hundred. I started with a lousy twenty-five-dollar bet. What? . . . I won sixty-seven and lost twenty-three overall. . . . That's right. I said I bet on ninety-three games. . . . You're so damn picayune. Three games I bet on pushed! Tied! I didn't win or lose on them. That's why the're not calculated in my records. Okay? . . . Now answer me."

Doug only said, "How much are you going to make next year?"

For the first time in David's life he was able to plan for the future. First things first. He paid off his illustrious shylocks: Household Finance Corporation, Beneficial Finance Company, Chase Manhattan Bank, First National City Bank, The Municipal Credit Union of New York City. The total came to $7,168.26. He did this on the first Tuesday in April.

One day earlier he had done some master planning. On that day he jotted down what was left of his debts and made some calculations. After long and sober reflection, he decided to take a calculated risk. He would enlarge his enterprise beginning with the 1971–1972 college basketball season. His computations indicated he would be able to save $366.18 a month by eliminating those moneylenders from his payroll, and therefore he'd be able to accumulate between May 1 and December 1 $2,563.26 in cash. That wasn't the risky part.

What was risky was that he planned to apply for loans again: during the third week in November at HFC and BFC for $1,400 each; at First National City and Chase Manhattan Bank for $2,000 each. From past experiences he knew what to write down on the applications, what to say, what to wear, and how to act and cower when applying. He knew the kind of assholes he'd be up against and was certain that his loan applications would go smoothly.

The MCU loan he would finance for a period of sixty months and the others for thirty-six months each. That meant that his installment payment would total $343.94 monthly.

The $343.94 monthly installment total would be a decrease of $22.24 from the $366.18 per month he had previously been paying these pious-assed institutions. That was "making it"? With the $2,563.26 he'd be saving and the $6,800 he'd be borrowing, he intended to repay Doug his 2,000, Ron Nivens $1,000 of his $8,000, and his mother her $1,000, and to repay his father $500 on his account, leaving his obligation to him at $7,500. With all this accomplished, he'd be left with a balance of $4,868.26 in liquid assets—cold cash—American dollars to hold and gamble with. He would be ready.

The hardest decision was not to take the money and run—that is, to move out of his parents' home. He took a hell of a long time to decide on that one. In the end it took all his willpower, but he decided that business had to come first and that now was the period in his life to make a sacrifice. To make a life, one had to be ready to sacrifice a life, Doug had said.

The easiest decision was to lease a safe deposit box at the Manufacturers Hanover Trust Company branch at 2081 Broadway in November. He was looking forward to again having a box in which he could put his money and visit whenever he wanted to count cash in $100 denominations. He remembered how much he had enjoyed counting those Benjamin Franklins many years earlier when he was on a winning streak. He remembered visiting the vault every week and being escorted to a private booth that was locked behind him, and then taking out his lucre and counting and rubber-banding and putting the bills in clean white envelopes and sealing those envelopes and knowing what was in them was all *his*. It was a great feeling as long as the packets lasted. Losing was like having Mommy's nipple taken away. The world went dark.

During the first week in April, after having gone through all his statistics and all his results for the 1970–1971 college basketball season, he planned his basic betting strategy for the 1971–1972 season. On games where he found 4½-point and 5-point differentials in his favor he would bet $300. On games where he found 5½-point and 6-point differentials in his favor he would bet $500. On games where he found 6½-point and 7-point differentials in his favor he would bet $1,000.

On games where the Vegas linemaker made monstrous errors—that is, anything above 7½ points—he would bet as much as he could afford, as long as the point differential he discovered cushioned the same side he originally favored.

He always kept in mind that his power rating for the particular game dictated his opinion, but sometimes even with a perfect number which balanced out everything, he still had reservations, vibrations, and a prejudice. Most of the time, with the proper cushion, he would be able to overcome his gut reaction and invest, but sometimes no matter what differential he would find, he still only had eyes, faith, and soul for one side, and that was quite natural.

Many times during the 1970–1971 season David laid off games because his gut reaction was against the side the flaw had favored. In the short run, it might have cost him a few dollars. In the long haul, it definitely kept him whole.

During that first week in April, David discussed with O'Brien the possibility of O'Brien's bearding for him while attending law school in Indiana the following winter.

"That state is a hotbed for college basketball action, and bookies will handle dime and two-dime bets without changing the number on you. This could prove to be extremely advantageous to us, if I ever graduate to wagering important money; but even if I don't, it would still give me another out-of-state line to work with."

O'Brien became very enthusiastic about David's proposition, especially when David told him he'd be giving him his best games as a bonus. David wasn't only serious, he was cocky, too, that first week in April.

Another decision was not to work with Ed Kashman the following winter. Ed's wife, Maggie, had died. Ed blamed his wife's death on his gambling. He needed to blame something. He was a concrete man, he needed concrete reasons, and he had been gambling and losing consistently for the entire year and was becoming increasingly frayed and desperate. He wouldn't listen to David, and he wouldn't take a rest. It was obvious he was ready to crack. No, David would not be working with Ed Kashman the following winter. He would be working with . . .

"Hello Lazar? It's yer best friend, Johnny. I just got outa da hospital. I had cancer. It begun widda lotta pain and soreness in da chest. The pain was onda right side, aroun'da nipple. I couldn't touch dat side o'da body witdhout wincin'. For weeks I lived widda pain. Finally I saw a doc. Twenty-four hours later I was on da table. Da operation took nine hours. Dey took out a growth da size of a baseball. Dey tell me my lymph system was sliced into. I don't recollect nothin' about the week after that, Lazar. Dey kept feedin' me all sorts of pills. I was doped up all da time. The doc told me da odds against me makin' it was pretty steep. I guess he didn't think I was goin' to make it. It was more'n a month before I was able to sit up. After dat I went for chemotherapy treatment. I felt like heavin' all the time and my hair fell out and my fingers swelled to twice da normal size. Let me tell ya something, Lazar, it was a lot rougher'n any game you ever lost. I made it, though. I won! Now, take this number down, I'm workin' again."

When David explained his plans to Doug, Ron Nivens, and his other friends, they agreed without hesitation to wait for their money until the end of November. Ron, in fact, apologized for the little time they had been spending together.

It was also during that first week in April that David began working on his handbook for the 1971–1972 season. He again resolved to honor and obey his four private objectives, and again he wrote them down:

1. *To make money.*
2. *To beat the system.*

3. To show Leslie.
4. To be a winner!

He also added to his handbook his financial goals for the coming season. He wanted to make enough money to pay off every one of his installments debts—$10,800—and have approximately $2,500 left over. He calculated by the end of March 1972, his only remaining debt would be to his father, and then he would be able to take his own apartment and begin living like a human being again. He resolved that if he didn't screw up, did as good a job as he had done in the 1970–1971 season, and stayed lucky, he could do it. He would not allow himself to become lazy. He would never forget that the most unpredictable thing in sports, in the world, in life, is human emotion. It can turn on or off. It can run hot or cold. How many times in his past did he remember thinking, feeling, saying, "It's unbelievable! . . . It's incredible! . . . It's a miracle! . . . It could never happen again! . . . It just couldn't!"

But it did! It happened every day. With five minutes to go your team is ahead by 15 points and you're ecstatic; but from then on they don't hit a shot, they don't get one call, they miss out on every loose ball, and at the buzzer you're in agony! Divorced! It happens every day!

In his telephone inquiries to coaches and his other sources he never forgot human emotion. He always made certain to ascertain which team wanted it the most. The guys who wanted it the most were the guys he wanted to invest in. And above and beyond everything else, he would continue to maximize and minimize. He would be disciplined and be careful.

Another thing that was in the back of his mind was the Western basketball team. With Roger Brantley bringing Billy Duval to the school, and with Sky Davis, and maybe with Abdul (Tony Willis's new moniker) Azis returning, with a year's experience behind them, and with their having had their asses kicked on national TV, they might be ready to turn around.

David realized that they were embarrassed individually and as a team; that now the Las Vegas linemakers would probably underrate them. As David saw it, you never knew about human emotions. They might come out like animals, with a vengeance, with a will to win that could blow form and logic and class and all the other power-rating rationales right off the court. You never knew, he mused. Just let Sky and Abdul and Western get back to the NCAA and let the linemaker give him 16 or 17 points. He'd take it with confidence as long as they weren't playing against John Wooden. Champ Holden told him about John Wooden. "Don't ever let that bank-clerk appearance fool ya, David. Behind that bank-clerk appearance he is as cold-hearted a schemer as you'd ever want to meet. You know, in the old days his teams played in a hot box. One opposing coach even measured the temperature and found it to be ninety-three degrees. And don't think it was by accident. Wooden figured it gave him an edge. I'm telling you, David, he conditioned his players to play in that hot box. Hey, you should have seen him in the old days, David. He'd curse opposing players, scream at officials, give his own boys hell. I'm telling you John Wooden's a winner, David, and it doesn't depend on Sidney Wicks's having a good night. It depends on John Wooden making certain that Sidney Wicks has a good night."

David wouldn't bet Sky with 37 points against Wooden's American Dream, the Bruins. Besides, he'd been reading an awful lot about a red-headed freshman center he had that was going to make the world forget about Kareem Abdul Jabaar beginning in the 1971–1972 season. And David took that very seriously, because John Wooden didn't hype the press or rah-rah a boy to All-American. He didn't have to.

"Isaac Pizer is like Nathan Rubin, or, for that matter, your great friend Solomon Lepidus. You know what that Lepidus pulled on a friend of mine when he asked to borrow some money? He pulled out of his drawer a Chapter Eleven and had the nerve to tell him he was in the midst of declaring bankruptcy."

David instantly recalled that years before, when Doug had gone to Solomon to borrow funds for a business venture, Solomon had done exactly the same thing. Solomon did keep a Chapter Eleven form in a desk drawer for just such occasions. Of course, in another drawer he had hundreds of thousands of dollars for other purposes.

Howard Silver, editor of the basketball magazine, hesitated. "You know, a few years ago I had my own magazine. I went bust. I had to declare a Chapter Eleven." He hesitated for a long time. "I had a breakdown because of it. I was hospitalized for a long time. It was Isaac Pizer, David, who made sure my family survived. And I don't mean only with money."

In a gentle voice Howie Silver said, "You know, David, Isaac visited me every day at the hospital. Every day."

22

JIMMY WAS LYING on his back on the bed smoking a cigarette with Debbie Turner lying beside him. They had made love earlier, and Debbie, as usual, went right to sleep as soon as they had finished. The evening had started with dinner at a tiny Italian restaurant: checkerboard tablecloths, candlelight, a bottle of wine, and good talk. Debbie had been in a rare confessional mood.

Suddenly Jimmy felt restless and had the need to talk some more, to make love some more. He felt it was ridiculous. He was twenty-two, filled with love. It wasn't yet 11:00. He could make love the whole night. Yet they never had. He couldn't go on like this, fearful of demanding too much from her, frustrated by her. He had to talk to her. Get it straight one way or the other.

"Debbie? . . . Are you asleep? . . . Debbie?"

"What is it, darling?" she whispered in a contented voice.

Jimmy looked at her and melted. He couldn't think straight. He could only feel how much he loved her. "I've been thinking about what you said at dinner, Debbie. Are you sure you're all over David? Are you sure?"

Debbie reached for Jimmy's hand and gently kissed his knuckles. She propped herself up to a sitting position and pressed his hands to her bosom.

"I was infatuated with David, Jimmy. I never knew anyone like him. But I always knew it wasn't serious. Besides, I could never live his kind of life, without security." Debbie's face had a troubled look as she gazed at Jimmy for a moment. "I would never want to live in New York, Jimmy. You know how I'd hate that. I want a home. I want to travel. I want someone I can count on." She smiled and softly said, "I want you, Jimmy. You're different from David. I know I'll always be able to rely on you. You'll always be there. And besides," Debbie added in a coquettish tone, "you're going to be a great lawyer, and you'll become very rich and buy me that Mercedes."

She reached over and took a pack of cigarettes off the night table. She lit one and took a deep puff. "David could never be supportive of my work or encourage it. He would need me to be supportive of him. Need me to be there for him. But what about me? My work? My life?"

Jimmy started to say something, but Debbie continued, "I really believe I understand David, Jimmy. I know he needs to be free. Not because he needs to be free of a relationship, but because he needs to be allowed to find himself in order to be able to enter one in the first place. It would be impossible for him to give anything of value to another person now. Leslie's the perfect example of that." She paused. "It's really quite easy to understand how a relationship with David could turn into something malignant very quickly." She stopped and drew nervously on her cigarette. "Besides"—she frowned—"he's a gambler."

Jimmy gazed at her for a long while, then soberly said, "There's something very wrong with him, Debbie."

"What do you mean?"

"He doesn't see you the way you really are. Did you ever think why he has the need to project all those naive, virginal qualities onto you?" He paused. "You're the sexiest woman I've ever known, Debbie. The sexiest." He shrugged his shoulders. "David keeps denying it. All he ever talks about is how innocent you are. How sweet you are, how adorable. There's something very sick about that, Debbie. I mean, you're so much more. You're a beautiful woman, Debbie. A beautiful woman."

"Jimmy?"

"Yes, Debbie?"

"I love you," she whispered softly. Jimmy leaned over and took her in his arms.

"You're the whole world to me, Debbie."

"I know," she said soothingly.

He tried to kiss her passionately. She turned her face.

"Jimmy, let's go to sleep. I have to get up early. I've been late to work every morning this week."

Jimmy reached for Debbie's hand and tentatively placed it on his swollen penis. "I need you, Debbie. Now! Please!"

And so Debbie positioned herself. It was always the same position. She felt Jimmy knead her breast, suckle on her, but then, too soon, she felt him slip his hand between her legs. He elbowed himself down the bed, away from her face, away from her breasts, below her hips and teased her with his tongue. Her eyes were shut, not because she thought about it, or didn't think about it. It was simply involuntary, like her heavy breathing, like her erect nipples, which also stood up when she was chilled. And she thought, He needs me . . . he loves me. Just before he entered her, she thought, Then why do I feel this way? Why? Instead of . . .

She didn't know what. She didn't know. She'd only read about it in novels and her psych texts.

Jimmy lay beside her. He saw the tears still trapped in her glazed eyes. He didn't ask about it. He didn't want to pry. He just kissed her, kissed the tears, and said again, "I love you, Debbie." He heard her whisper, "I love you, Jimmy," and held her silently, while she cried.

Jimmy was still asleep when Debbie came out of the shower, dried herself off, laid the towel down, and stood before the full-length mirror. Every morning she would pause here before getting dressed. She would stand still and erect before the mirror, take one look, turn profile, and take another look. Could she just see her ribs beneath her skin, or had she put on the old two extra pounds? She checked her stomach, too. Then she would turn forward and study her face. Usually she'd then nod, or not nod, and begin to dress.

Today, though, she continued to stare at her face, then looked at her chest and her hips. For a moment she placed her hands just beneath each shoulder and pressed up, lifting her heavy breasts up and farther apart. She studied that effect. Slowly she removed her hands and looked at her natural figure again.

She said quietly, firmly, sadly, "He's crazy. There's nothing wrong with that. Any other man would jump."

Minutes later, as she was dressing, she began to dwell on the promise she had made Jimmy that night. Instinctively, she grabbed a cigarette. She knew she had a million things to do before June 21. But she just wasn't ready to start doing them. She kept thinking, What can I say to David at the theater tonight?

David had made arrangements to take Debbie and Jimmy to the theater to see *Abelard and Héloise.* As soon as they met in front of the theater, Jimmy said, "We're engaged." He was beaming.

David's heart hit bottom. He tried to conceal the pain he was feeling. He knew his voice would shake, so he didn't speak. He allowed Jimmy to do the talking. Debbie remained silent.

"We're getting married on June twenty-first. I finally got this person to agree." He looked David in the eye. "You know better than anyone how she's been giving me a rough time lately, David, but now she's finally come to her senses."

David had never seen Jimmy so relaxed or secure. He even managed to tease Debbie and to take her hand without being tentative. Before, whenever the three were together, Jimmy was always anxious. He never asserted himself and he was always self-conscious about expressing with a touch any feelings he may have had for Debbie. In his defense, Debbie had always pulled away from Jimmy when they were in David's presence, as if it were wrong for them to show any kind of affection. Still, Jimmy had always flinched. But now it was quite different. David was flinching.

As Jimmy explained their plans, David felt dizzy. He fought to keep his composure. He held his body erect, though his heart was fluttering and his legs were weak. Jimmy's words were coming through to David, but they seemed muted. From what he could make out of their plans, in the fall Jimmy would enter law school at Georgetown University, and they would set up housekeeping in the Georgetown area. Debbie would also be returning to school. She would go to Catholic University and begin graduate work in clinical psychology. Both of them would work evenings—Jim would drive a cab, Debbie would wait on tables—until they achieved their long-range goals.

When he recovered the smallest portion of his equilibrium, he said, "When did all this take place? I didn't even know you had applied to Catholic University, Debbie. And you, Jimmy? I thought you wanted to go into hospital administration?"

Debbie answered first. Her voice was soft and gentle. "We've been planning on this for the past two months, David. I guess you've been too busy to really listen to me. Every time I tried to tell you anything, you either changed the subject or ran away."

Jimmy added, "Debbie's going to quit her welfare job inside of a month." He smiled and playfully reached out to peck Debbie on the cheek. She blushed.

David wished both of them good luck, and as he did, he realized he would never now divulge his two secrets to Debbie. Neither did he peck Debbie on the cheek. In fact, it took every bit of the phony in him to shake Jimmy's hand. A large part of him felt as if he had run the gantlet, and an even larger part of him thought she would be a thousand times better off with Jimmy. The largest part of him, though, wanted to say, "I need you, Debbie. I love you. I want you to stay in New York and in my life and be my wife." But he didn't utter a sound. It took everything he had learned about controlling his emotions, about separating his feelings from his thoughts . . . about handicapping. And, again, he was successful. He didn't utter a sound. He wanted to look at her, but he couldn't. He lowered his eyes and said something flippant instead. Finally they became silent as the curtain went up.

The only thing David remembered about *Abelard* was that Diana Rigg played Héloise. After it was over David said he wasn't feeling well and went straight home. It was the truth.

Several days later he received a printed invitation to the wedding. It would be at the Turner home in Silver Spring outside Washington.

A week after the invitation arrived he finally arranged to see Debbie for lunch. They went to Friday's on Sixtieth Street and First Avenue. They'd gotten in the habit of eating there because it was only two stops from Harlem on the Lexington Avenue express and because it was convenient for both of them. David loved to browse in a bookstore that was a stone's throw away. Through the year he had purchased enough hardcover books on sale for a dollar to fill up at least two additional cartons. And while he was in the bookstore Debbie liked to run over to Bloomingdale's. On this particular day, they went straight to Friday's and talked.

"I'm sorry, David, if I haven't been a better friend to you lately, but you understand what a rush everything's been. We're planning to have the wedding on my parents' back lawn. I always wanted to be married there. It's beautiful with the trees all around, but I'm so afraid it might rain. Oh, David, I'm inviting Margot Lepidus to my wedding. I really like her."

She spoke in a high-strung nervous pitch, and he felt annoyed by the banality and snapped, "Don't worry, Debbie, it won't rain. Now tell me, what made you finally decide to get married?"

Her face became serious, and it was evident that she wanted to avoid the subject. But she didn't.

"I've been thinking about it for a long time, David. You know, your brother was a big help. He was very honest with me."

That shook David, and he responded pathetically, "When did you speak to Doug?"

She smiled as if she were being tolerant of him and said in a voice that sounded as if she were trying to pacify a small child, "Oh, David, where have you been? All through the winter I tried to explain to you about the problems I was having deciding what I wanted. You just never listened to anything I said. Every time I tried to tell you how I felt you'd keep finding excuses to see me less and less.

"I was very depressed, and I had to talk to someone about you, and I couldn't really talk to Jimmy, so I called Doug. We had lunch together several times, and he made me understand what a child I'd been. You must have thought I was retarded, the way I allowed you to relate to me." She smiled wistfully and said, "You know, David, I was so involved with you in the beginning I didn't even notice. But after a while I became so confused, I . . ."

Debbie nervously opened a pack of cigarettes and lit one. After taking a few puffs she continued, "It took Doug to make me really appreciate all the wonderful things I have with Jimmy."

David was upset at Doug's intervention. Doug always interfered when it came to the girls he genuinely liked. He knew why. He was his twin brother, that's why. He barked out, "What did he say?"

"He made me realize that almost everyone needs someone that they can count on when the going gets rough, and that I had found that someone in Jimmy. He said that's what Leslie didn't have with you. You were never really there when she needed you, and if you were, you always placed a value judgment on what her need was, and since her needs weren't yours, you resented them and thought them inferior."

Debbie looked at David and said, "That's wrong, David."

People walked by, and Debbie stopped speaking.

David could tell from her voice, which was thick with emotion, that she was being completely honest. For the first time he chose not to relate to her as "Jennifer with tits." He concentrated on what she had to say and listened to her as an equal.

"For some reason when you enter a relationship, David, you become paranoid. You feel threatened by almost everything, as if the relationship has to be in conflict with your personal freedom."

"That's a lot of nonsense, Debbie. Freedom's only an illusion; nothing changes."

"Oh, David, it's impossible to understand you. One second you say freedom is everything to you and a second later you turn right around and say it's only an illusion and that nothing changes. It's things like that which confused me about you for a long time. But now, thanks to Doug, I think I'm able to see you much clearer."

David began to play with some sugar cubes he found on the table. A little later he reached into his pocket and took out his silver dollar. He gripped it tightly and started to turn it over in his hand.

Debbie continued lecturing. "It's one thing to value your privacy and your independence, but it's something quite different to scorn everyone else. You're just plain antisocial, David. I guess now you're going to say that I don't understand the artistic temperament and how special a person you are. But I do. I'm only saying that loving a person doesn't have to take away from your own personal freedom. On the contrary, a healthy relationship should enrich it." David winced.

She continued, "Doug said that since you were a little boy you could never think in terms of another person's needs. That you always felt that if you did compromise you would be denying your own nature." Debbie hesitated. "He also said something I didn't quite understand, something about your searching for happiness in unhappiness. I'm not sure what he meant, David. Do you know?"

David glanced at the booth adjacent to theirs, where two women were being seated by the maître d'. One was a striking blonde who looked like Leslie. The other had stringy brown hair, a chalky white face, and a thoroughbred's fragile, knobby legs.

Debbie stopped speaking until she got his attention back. When she started up again, there was just a slight hint of irritation in her tone. "I really believe I understand you, David. I know you need to be free." She paused and enunciated clearly. "It's really quite easy to understand how a relationship with you could turn into something malignant very quickly."

David tried to stare her down. When that failed, his next effort was to growl, "Another one of Doug's brilliant insights, right?"

"No," she said, shaking her head for emphasis. "One of Debbie Turner's brilliant insights. The first. I have some more, if you're interested."

David was beginning to feel threatened by the conversation. Debbie sounded like Leslie in her more articulate moments, and like so many other women he'd known through the years. A thought flashed through his mind that all women must have attended the same lecture sessions and read the same women's magazines; that they all spoke of love and sex and marriage as if they were relationship handicappers. They were all so practical and knowledgeable and so damn pragmatic. They all knew what was perfect. Perfect, that is, for them. As if it were just a matter of handicapping. As if all you had to do was find a man who was willing to change. Willing to give up his star. Willing to commit himself and try. As if a man could be reduced to a handicapper's number. Didn't they know anything about erections, fears, longings, needs, dreams, despair? Didn't they know about the things of the soul? That men lived in their work, that men grew from their dreams? Didn't they know about the fragility of the human ego? Didn't they also yearn to leap and soar? Didn't they know what a blessing it was to write? To love? To create? Didn't they know that the aspiration in man was everything? That parents, livelihood, routine work, were an obstacle? That the mother's womb was warm, dark, and safe? That the world was cold, blindingly bright, and repugnantly sensible? Didn't they know what every man goes through in trying to sort it all out from the day he was born? Didn't they know?

"Come on, Debbie, stop dramatizing. Leslie and I weren't mutually malignant. We were just two complex people who weren't compatible."

Debbie looked at him and said in a somewhat disturbed, somewhat cool voice, "There's something about you that's fascinating and different, David, but there's also something about you that's dangerous and cruel. Many women find that combination exciting, but I think it's also very immature, and I question whether you'll ever be able to truly change. Doug says you won't, because you'll always be too busy taking your own needs more seriously than anyone else's." She reflected on her next sentence before saying wistfully, "It's funny how New York City makes you forget things you were born knowing."

David had dropped his silver dollar, and it rolled under the booth where the blonde was sitting. He walked over, stooped down, and retrieved it. As he stood up he smiled at her, and she, self-consciously, instinctively, crossed her legs, and her nylons hissed. He noticed it immediately but he didn't follow his blood. He returned to the table instead. As he did, something inside him made him say in an ugly voice, "Why don't you stop already?"

Debbie slowly drew on her cigarette, and in a controlled but friendly voice said, "I know this subject is irritating to you, but please, David, let me finish."

Debbie continued talking, and the more she did the more interested he became in the blonde whose nylons hissed. After a while he tried to hurt

Debbie by telling her how much the woman resembled Leslie and how attractive he thought she was. And it was true.

The woman had a way of crossing her legs so that you could see the flesh on the underside of her thigh, and that more than anything turned David on. He was also certain that she was coming on with him, as he could see her looking over at him out of the corner of her eye and wetting her lip incessantly with her tongue. He mentioned it to Debbie, but she was caught up in saving him and wouldn't be distracted.

"Honest conversation is crucial to a friendship, David. It's crucial."

For a second it crossed his mind that maybe Debbie had become engaged to Jimmy to shake him up, to get him to commit himself on how he felt. Then he thought he must really be paranoid, and he rubbed his eyes and continued listening. Little by little her words pierced his armor and hurt him more and more. They caused him to detach even more. She told him how throughout their entire friendship she had felt intimidated and manipulated by him. He was out of touch with his feelings. He was unaware of his real self. He was extremely defensive, and for that reason he would rather philosophize than feel. She pleaded with him to feel rather than think about what she was saying. It got to the point where he couldn't listen any longer and asked the waiter for a check.

"Please wait a few minutes, David. I know this is hurting you, but it might be the last time I have a chance to talk to you before I leave New York. You know I'd never have had the courage to talk to you like this if I weren't leaving the city. I've handed in my resignation, and I'm leaving at the end of this week."

"This week?"

"It's impossible to stay any longer, David; there are just too many things to do for the wedding." Her voice faltered as she said, "I probably won't be seeing you again for a very long time, except at the wedding, and we won't really have a chance to talk there."

He started to say something.

"Please don't say anything, David. Just listen. I can only say this now, and it's taking all my courage, so please don't interrupt. There was a time not too long ago when I was seriously thinking of breaking up with Jimmy so that I could be with you as more than a friend. I really felt that we had something special and that I was in love with you. You know, I even made a list of all the things I felt for you which I didn't feel for Jimmy. Would you like to hear the list?"

David started to say something, couldn't, and ended up nodding weakly. She burrowed for a wrinkled piece of paper buried deep in her pocketbook. She removed it, but paid it no further attention. She recited everything from memory.

"I feel happiest when I'm with you. I'd always be stimulated by you intellectually. I love doing things for you. It comes so natural." She hesitated and gazed at him and blushed. "I know sex would be wonderful with you, David." Softly she whispered, "I just know!"

She said it in such a way that he felt like crying. When he recovered sufficiently he interrupted her. His voice cracked a little as he said, "If you feel all those things for me, why did you become engaged to Jimmy? How could you?"

"I've always realized that I loved you, David. I've never told you that, and I never thought I'd have the nerve to ever tell you, but now I do. But I also have to be practical, and I do love Jimmy. I couldn't stand what I was doing to him."

Debbie paused to light another cigarette and to calm herself. When she continued she surprised David by saying something he wasn't quite prepared to hear.

"New York's only for the rich and the successful, David. If you aren't one or the other you only succeed in eating your heart out if you stay around. You have to have an exceptional talent to survive." She winced. "You've used yourself up completely by living in New York. Now nothing matters to you. You haven't enough energy left for anything but that gambling of yours and that dream of making it! Certainly not enough left for enjoying a relationship."

He didn't answer her, but he respected what she was saying. But almost simultaneously he thought, Why is it that most people feel the most important thing in the world is to enjoy yourself? He didn't say a word, though, and she continued her polemic. While she did, he detached himself and stared at the blonde and kept staring. Finally the blonde became annoyed and looked away. On her face was the same kind of hardness he had seen many times in the past on Leslie's face. When he turned back, Debbie was talking in a soft vulnerable voice.

"You don't even find me desirable, do you, David?"

He tried to deny it, but he had related to her as a kid sister for too long a time, and his attempts now at disavowal were futile.

"You made me feel so unattractive, David. At first you made me feel wonderful, marvelous, but before long you started taking me for granted and looking down on me and ridiculing me. With Jimmy it was always different."

A glint of satisfaction came to her face when she mentioned Jimmy, and David realized she was relieved that she had made a final choice. He continued to detach himself from her words, until the next thing he heard was: "Are you listening to me, David?"

He looked up and was a little taken aback as he noticed she was on the verge of tears.

"Jimmy's a wonderful person, David. He's not like you."

Instinctively David realized it was a perfect moment to tell her his secrets, but he didn't. He forced himself not to tell her that he loved her and wanted to marry her. Nor did he bother to negate anything she said. Rather he told her that he felt she was making a good choice and that he knew he would miss her a great deal. When he picked up the check, she was crying. She made an effort to say something, but her words were lost in sobs. He lit a cigarette for her. It calmed her down somewhat, and she said, "Even now I don't know what you really feel for me, David, or if you feel anything at all. Don't you know what you feel for me, David? Don't you?"

He didn't answer, but for the first time since he had known Debbie Turner he took her hand and held it. It was delicious. He swelled inside, but he didn't say anything. He just held her hand for a minute or two and closed his eyes and felt warm and happy. When he opened his eyes she had taken her hand away and lit another cigarette, and after taking a few puffs she stopped crying. She looked at him strangely, as if to say, "I don't know who you are." He got up and paid the check and walked outside. She followed closely behind.

As he hailed a cab for her, she again said, "You really don't find me attractive, do you, David?"

He smiled and said, "Of course, I do," but then, for some reason, he added, "You'd better hurry back to the office now, Debbie; you're late already. Look, if I don't have a chance to take you to lunch before you leave, I just want to say . . ." He hesitated. "You'll always be my best friend, Debbie. You are very, very beautiful."

He swallowed hard and took a deep breath before finishing, "I hope you'll be happy with Jimmy." He swallowed again. "Goodbye."

As the taxi disappeared in the city's traffic, he felt as if his last chance for happiness were disappearing with it. He began to cry.

That evening he telephoned Doug, who immediately took the offensive.

"Look, David, Debbie's much better off with that boyfriend of hers. She's a nice girl; I'm happy for her. You would've ruined her life. You know as well as I do that girls like that don't belong in New York. They're shaped by a different clay. They're not starved for what you are or I am. She enjoyed the city, like so many others. The same way they enjoy shopping and skiing and the Hamptons and Broadway theater and air-conditioned apartments. And that also goes for the way she felt about you, David."

"But—"

Doug continued talking. "Her type needs marriage and having children and buying a home and having some middle-class professional for a husband, and living sensibly ever after. That's where she and that fiancé of hers are coming from, David."

"But—"

"She's better off, David. Believe me, she'd never appreciate what you're all about. Do you think she really could understand the ideas you have? The passion? Oh, she might fantasize and fall in love with you for a while, but if she stayed around she'd end up despising you. People like her and that Jimmy of hers don't have or need dreams. They just need security and children to live for and through. Leave her alone, David. She's much better off without you. Much better."

"Doug—"

Doug screamed, "Damn it, David, you never saw her for what she is. You never see past your mother's nipple. It's your Jewish neurosis. You see women as either saints or sinners. You've made Debbie into an angel and Leslie's the bitch. Did you ever think, once, that both of them are manipulative bitches in their own way? Did you, David?" With that he hung up.

JUST BEFORE DAWN on the June day when Debbie and Jimmy were to be married, David Lazar, restless and depressed, looked out of his window and saw nothing but the black gutters that outlined the adjoining buildings.

He crawled back into the bedsheets. As usual during those bleak periods when he could not sleep, flashbacks of games he had lost took over his mind. Then came the gloom, and then came Leslie . . . and their interminable arguments . . . and her recriminations:

"I hate your vile temper, David, your snarling, your brutishness. I hate your vacillation and your feelings of superiority, when you're not superior."

This was often followed by whirling but sharp memories of better times, of the games he had won, and of loving Leslie, and her rejoicing.

"I love you, David darling. . . . I love the way you touch me. . . . I love it!"

And there were always memories of little Jennifer, pointing a tiny finger at the television set, jumping up and down with glee:

"It's Mickey Mantle . . . Mickey Mantle. . . ."

"No, Jennifer. I told you this is a Mets game. That's Ed Kranepool."

"But it's number seven. That must be Mickey."

And he held in his memory the picture of Jennifer in bed with her hands around her teddy bear . . . with her little tush sticking out . . . and then, somehow, he managed to fall asleep; but it was an unrestful, feverish sleep. . . . A gloating phantom visited him and hissed dark secrets and he spat back fire:

"You're impractical."

"I'm myself."

"You're depraved."

"I'm glorious."

"You're nothing."

"I'm many things."

"You're nothing."

"I matter," he shouted and sobbed, but the voice was unrelenting. It sounded like a howling wind.

"Who are you? What do you want? Why are you so ambivalent? So cowardly? So full of rents and tears? You must surrender, resign yourself, accept. It's futile to resist."

And he screamed, "But I cannot accept, and I cannot make myself whole, and I will not surrender. I matter. I'm a man. . . . I want everything! I've got to make it."

He awoke wretched and shaken. He opened the window and stared down at the black-silver gutters and while beginning another day, he mused:

There are black holes in the psyche of man. They are caused by fear, not by the finger of God, but by insecurity; not by the laws of the universe, not by the forces of good and bad, but by the very ice-tipped arrows we have fashioned, arrows which bleed and freeze our feelings. We seek or expect unwavering perfection, strength, and wise men to do us honor. Whenever we meet with strangers, we demand wholeness, warmth and virtue. Don't we know better? . . .

Lazar's thoughts drifted through the black mood until he forced himself out of bed. There was a plane to Washington, and he had a reservation. He dressed quickly, shouldered his way into the rainy morning, and hailed a taxi for La Guardia. He was on his way to Silver Spring, in Maryland just outside of the District of Columbia. Debbie's parents lived there.

On the flight to Washington National, David had the time to think about his family and himself. He reminisced: When I think of my mother I think of her courageous sad smile, her hollow cheeks and pinched mouth, her face with the year-counting lines crisscrossing, her thin, pale lips with a chronic cold sore on the lower one, her tired, sagging, weighted, milkless breasts. Lungs straining for air, swelling belly, warts on enormous haunches, withered legs, and her wanting voice, always wavering and un-soothing, tin-plated and dry.

And I think of her flabby, thin arms with black-and-blue welts, and hands and forearms also stained by blotches of ugly rashes, swollen too, and her frazzled, thinning, teased, oranged hair. How unsightly; how pow-dered and chalky; how green and sallow; how old and unlovely; how dry. She was a mother. My mother. And she was dying.

When I think of my mother I think of her struggling to get off her bed and never getting off the telephone. I think of her moans in the middle of the night. Her cane, her walker, her wheelchair. I think of her stabbing herself with insulin, with me wincing; her diabetes, my heartache; her pal-pitations, my fear; her gasping for air, my anguish.

When I think of my mother I think of oxygen tents and agony and my father's devotion. I think of her saying, "Do you love me?" to my father as he walked by her side weeping, always weeping, while she was wheeled into operating rooms and intensive care. "Do you love me? Moishe, do you love me?" And I think of his answer, "Yes," and her response, "Good," and I think of everything my father did for her. His commitment and his love.

When I think of my mother I think of the Beth Israel Medical Center and that Friday I had Solomon Lepidus and Margot and Roger Brantley and Harvey Stern and Betblood Willie and Ezra Bernstein and Ron Nivens and the Colonel and anyone else my father, Doug, or I could scrounge up, rush over to the Linsky Pavilion to donate blood for her. And I also think of the ambulance ride to the hospital and seeing her afflicted, shrunken face, worn out from trying, discouraged and frightened; her tired eyes with dark, foreboding, puffy pouches underneath; and though her eyes were uncomplaining, very deep within the pupils they did question: "Why me, I'm a good person, why do I have to suffer so?"—and while we were giving our blood I remember a suntanned, ghost-white-outfitted doctor walking into the blood bank room and announcing to us in a rehearsed subdued tone that my mother, Sylvia Eva Lazar, was dead.

I think of Doug sobbing and going to see her for a last time behind a pale white curtain and staying for a long time, and my father howling, and I, sitting there, not wanting to see her, dreading to see her, not able to see her, unable to cry.

And I remember gazing out the window and thinking it's a spring day, the Yankees are playing, the sun is shining, isn't it a beautiful day. And hours later, when I got home, alone, after trying in vain to sleep, I lay in bed and heard my mother's "What I got for you is a great big kiss" and her "I'm going to give you a piece of my mind" and her "David, I love you. I love you." I missed her and I missed her and I missed her.

Three weeks later, David's father joined David's mother. David was sad. David knew that for his entire life his father had been the kind of man who never understood other men, those who spoke in riddles, who spoke of the absurdity of life, who found levity in the human condition. They had all sounded like quitters to him, as if they were making excuses for failing. To survive and worship was what his father had been taught, and survival and worship were all that had ever sunk in. His entire life he had his nose buried in ritual and law. His eyes would squint and tear as he chanted from a prayer book. He had been a man of large opinion but little perspective, a man who had learned only to build in straight lines and who cared not at all about the curves.

The burden of his father's heritage, upbringing, and life-style had taken away his sense of humor, had depleted his ability to dream. He was ground and honed, pounded and pulverized, crippled and warped, from childhood to adolescence, from adolescence to manhood, from manhood to dust, by struggle and prayer—work/God; work/God—to pray to God; to get ahead—this was all that mattered. David's father, the cantor, under-stood this, and how to use his instrument—his voice—this and the "I don't want to die. I haven't lived." David's father had been terrified his entire life, and what made David feel even worse was not that his father had been blind to him but that he, David, had been blind to his father.

After his father's funeral, Doug deserted him to visit with friends in Venezuela. For days David was haunted by their growing-up years and how he had thought, Why can't I be free? Be left alone? Be me? Is he me? Am I he? For months David also was haunted by Doug's "I got a beautiful body odor, Colonel." And David recalled how he laughed and how Doug laughed and how the Colonel laughed. There's only one thing he never told Doug: If he had been able to choose his twin, he would have chosen no other.

I'm going away. I'm going away to be alone. I'm going away to write. I'm going away to try to write. I'm going away and just in case I cannot be sat-isfied with my art alone, I'm taking some pills.

David Bernard Lazar stood there, deep in the crowd of guests, watching Deborah Elizabeth Turner get married to James Franklin Edison. The ceremony was brief but poignant. The minister contributed a few well-chosen words. The bride wore a wide-brimmed hat, a dress that could have been a family heirloom, and a folded parasol. David wondered about that, this touch of the Victorian. Debbie looked radiant in all that nostalgic splendor. But when David finally confronted her in the receiving line, he didn't kiss or even hug her. He was the only person who did not. They exchanged looks in a frozen way. Debbie then smiled and asked him to write, promising she would reply. As he continued staring at her, someone in back of him called out, "Keep the line moving." He moved on.

Minutes later David felt unsteady and leaned against a tree. His thoughts wandered. Everything inside him was in fragments. He heard thunder and lightning and voices.

He heard Leslie's voice: "You're such a big-shot idealist. You've never practiced what you preached. You're nothing but a hypocrite."

And after hers, his own: "I love you, Debbie, I love you. Why can't we be together? Why can't my life be that simple?" And finally: "What am I doing here?"

He gazed up at the sky and could feel the warm June sun on his face.

This is a bitch, thought David. I should be working. I should be writing. I should be narrating the tragedy of my life with Leslie, with Debbie. I should be preparing my Handicapper's Handbook. But he couldn't hold a thought. They were all melting, oozing out of him. He asked himself, Why couldn't I be in command? Ordered and professional?

He recalled thinking that even though he loved Debbie, he would never, not in a million years, consider leaving New York. And that didn't go for only Debbie. It also went for Leslie or anybody else who might enter his life someday and ask him to leave. He would never make that concession for anyone. It wasn't that he was a typical New Yorker or that he needed his family for security. It was much more.

New York was his turf, his team. He felt that to be a winner in New York you had to be the best. And he still had to prove to himself that he was the best. He knew that he could be a loser again. But what did that matter? Where else could he play the game? He loved New York, its energy, its vitality, its real people and challenges and competition and culture. Where else could you go to great theater, dance, concert, film, opera, and sporting events every night? Where else could you challenge the infinite? What other city had such abundance? So much excellence, artistry, and genius? So many conquerors and dreamers? Where else?

When anyone said he was too insecure to leave, he would always retaliate by saying, "Maybe I'm too insecure to leave, but maybe I'm secure enough to stay."

David gave the same spiel to everyone, often to himself, on why he loved the city and why he wouldn't leave.

Lazar's personal conflict between staying and leaving was not quite that simple, but on that June wedding day, as he stood there in the Turner garden, leaning against an elm, objectively viewing the faces of the other guests, he let his thoughts bounce back to New York. Yes. It was true, he loved New York, even though he sensed it was an abomination. It was the Big Apple. He was too insecure to leave.

He watched Debbie's happy parents amid their splendid elms, dogwood, and birch, their private acre of freshly cut green grass and trimmed hedges. He envied them. His soul was in turmoil. He confessed a lot to himself.

Didn't someone once say that if people told the truth their faces would come off like masks? If not, he was saying it now. People didn't tell the entire truth; he certainly didn't. He had nothing to fear but himself. He thought, I have a hang-up over money and security and changing lifestyles. Nothing more. That's where I am at. It isn't my allegiance to the arts or my love of culture or my need for real people or challenge or even bookmakers or handicapping which has me jailed in New York. I could arrange to have most of that wherever I go. That is all mask. I am afraid to leave. When it comes right down to it, I don't have the guts. What would I do if I left? Wash dishes? Take a job behind a counter? Drive a tractor? Sell used cars? God damn it! I couldn't even drive a car.

And he heard his mother's voice: "I'm worried, Moishe. Have you noticed that Dougie takes great pride and works hardest in doing what he finds most difficult? But David, he's different? He takes pride in ignoring the work he finds most difficult."

It is true. I only like to do what I am good at. I always need encouragement, a pat on the back, someone to tell me how wonderful I am. Then my energy has no limits. My juices flow. But without it, I'm nothing. I feel rebuked, get scared, put on a mask.

He knew there was more than a germ of truth in what he was thinking. It was more than just a moment of weakness. He decided he should leave the shade of the elm and stroll among the guests. He noticed a skinny lad, the gawky type with face blemished and teeth still in braces. He was speaking to Solomon Lepidus's daughter, Margot, who had come down from New York the previous day.

Margot looked even younger than she was. She was a seedling, David thought, but one that had sprouted splender, supple limbs. Her breasts, in that lovely summer dress, were full of promise. She was going to be an exquisite woman.

"It's nice to have someone you can confide in, Margot," said the gawky one.

"I agree, Nelson," replied Margot. "That's the way I feel, too." At that point she spotted David, waved to him, and walked toward the nearby house with her friend, Nelson. David somehow felt rejected, but only for a moment, for he found himself quickly cornered by a girl with teased hair, lynx eyes, flabby arms, a double underchin—a cousin of the groom's. They spoke for a while.

"The way you quote Dostoevsky, Mr. Lazar, he must be your favorite author." There was something grating about her words, and her manner.

"That's not true. He was a gambler and he led a miserable life."

He didn't excuse himself. He simply walked away. He met a young mother, pipes for arms, no underchin, an aunt of the bride's. She had heard about him from Debbie. Soon they were talking about how she'd never live in New York. "It's not a fit place to bring your children up in. It's not . . ."

He smiled and agreed politely. Then he said, "Do you know any place in the world where you can get better delicatessen?"

For a while he listened to some of Debbie's roommates from college. Attractive girls with shiny childlike faces, innocent enough to cry at weddings. He wanted to talk to them, but he didn't. Instead he walked to the buffet and helped himself to some thin slices of pastrami and placed them between some rye.

An attractive brunette with a charming smile and green eyes addressed him. "Hi, David. Can I talk to you a minute? I'm Debbie's friend Myra Ross. Debbie's written me pages and pages of letters about you." She smiled. "You've certainly had an exciting life."

Debbie had mentioned Myra Ross to David. Myra had a wonderful marriage, according to Debbie. She and Harvey had married as soon as they graduated from high school. They lived in nearby Bethesda. Harv practiced law there and Myra worked for Senator Mitchell Cooperstock in Washington.

David noticed Myra with good reason. She was well built, with broad hips and long graceful legs. Over Myra's shoulder David saw a young man smoking a pipe and fidgeting nervously. When the man noticed David watching him he turned and walked away.

"What is it you'd like to talk about, Myra?"

She took a quick look around before she answered him in a whisper. "I really don't know how to say this, David, but I feel I know you intimately already." She hesitated. "There's something about the way Debbie describes you . . . your . . . sentimentality . . . that I find appealing." She paused and gazed directly into David's eyes. "Next week I'm going to be in New York, visiting my grandparents." She paused again. "Alone."

As Myra spoke she kept her elbows pinned to her sides, accenting her firm, full bosom. Her green eyes roved. Her black patent-leather shoe exhibited her large toe, which was painted a sensuous red.

David again looked over Myra's shoulder and saw the same young man, who had now switched from a pipe to a cigarette.

"I'd love to see you in New York, Myra, but unfortunately next week I'm going to be out of town. Say, maybe you and your husband—that's him standing over there, isn't it?"—David pointed—"can fly up together the following weekend and all of us can take in a show or something. What do you say?"

200 . . .

Myra Ross bit her lower lip. Then she turned and walked gracefully to her husband's side.

A young man with a rugged build and a wanderer's look put his hand on David's arm.

"Hi, David. I'm Terry Mennuti." David's eyes opened wide, and surprise showed on his face.

"You're Mennuti?" Debbie had told David about him. He had been her first on-campus boyfriend. He was a revolutionary and a freethinker. David grinned and shook Mennuti's hand.

"I'm sorry, Terry, but I expected someone quite different. Debbie told me you were an intellectual and a poet." He paused. "I expected some skinny guy with a beard. Know what I mean?" Mennuti nodded.

The two men spoke for a while, and before long Mennuti was waving his burly arms and orating. As he spoke, his eyes widened and he turned red. David's look was riveted on Mennuti's chin. He was fascinated by its cleft. He repressed a smile as he interrupted.

"I don't know how you can say that, Mennuti. It took them less than five years to break the spirit of you students. Now the revolt's over completely. It's the fifties all over again. Yeah, there'll be sporadic outbursts. You'll always have some youths with that rebellious spirit, but they'll do little good." He paused and looked angrily into the wild blue eyes of Debbie's first on-campus boyfriend. "Take you, for example, Terry. Don't you now look on your former conflict as something amusing?"

For a long time Mennuti just stood there without making a move. His eyes were fixed gravely on David, who did not lower his. Then Mennuti began to spit out some four-letter words.

"Now don't blow your cool, Terry," David chided in a controlled voice. "Just try to be honest with yourself. Didn't you just tell me you are returning to school to prepare for a career in corporate law?" David smirked. When he continued, his voice was light but direct. "And Debbie told me that after she wouldn't go for you, you went and found yourself some rich WASP's daughter, and that you ended up marrying her. Now tell me, is that rebelling, Terry?"

Mennuti's face went white, and his fists closed tight. Quietly, David said, "Keep your fists open, Terry. If you don't, I'm gonna break every bone in your body."

Mennuti stared incredulously into David's eyes, saw a warning, and slowly stepped back. He turned and walked away. As David glared at Mennuti's broad back he kept hearing Debbie's voice. "You wouldn't believe how attracted I was to Terry Mennuti, David. He had deep-blue eyes and a chiseled cleft in his chin. We used to park and kiss for hours."

The afternoon was turning into a bore. David decided he could use a drink, so he joined the crowd around the refreshment stand, where Debbie's young brother, Robert, was in charge.

Ahead of David, a man with a woman companion asked for small shots of Amaretto and vodka. The man, white-haired and portly, was explaining something to the tall, golden-haired, copper-complexioned woman: "In Arabia, Barbara, gasoline is given away, but you have to pay twenty-five cents for a glass of water."

Barbara suddenly noticed David staring at her. Her stare reflected her annoyance, but that was not enough to stop David. Barbara was just too attractive. She reminded David of Linda Lurie, the girlfriend he had known several years before. Linda had been a professional athlete, and she was not only athletic but sharply sexual. She enjoyed making love more than any woman David had ever known. He wondered if this were true of this woman enjoying her drink. After the couple left the refreshment table, David asked Robert Turner if he knew who they were.

"Yes, he's my father's friend Senator Cooperstock, and the girl is Barbara Amie. She's an Olympic diving champ."

As he sipped the drink, David spotted Margot Lepidus, now free of Nelson, sitting alone on the lawn. He decided to join her.

Margot was wearing a floor-length India print skirt. He noticed for the first time that she had warm, amber-colored eyes, thick auburn hair cut shoulder-length, a smooth and lovely skin, and a round face. Her arms were curled around her knees, and her chin promised still more beauty to come.

As he bent to her, she kissed him softly on the lips, a far warmer greeting than previously.

David began to speak to this lovely child. He tried the usual banal subject. What was ahead for her? Margot was silent. Then:

"Oh, David, you're just like my daddy. That's not what I want at all. What I want is to spend my life doing all sorts of wonderful things. Didn't you ever go hiking in the country in the summer and listen to the sounds? Sounds of wind and trees and leaves. Sounds of crows and squirrels. Sounds of birds, hundreds of birds. Did you know, David, that even clouds have sounds? Big, fluffy, cottony clouds; skinny, strung-out clouds; faraway, misty clouds. They all have special sounds you can hear if you listen."

Margot Lepidus, David sensed, was a kind of nature girl, that special variety bred in Manhattan.

"Didn't you ever go to the mountains to see a special waterfall? Didn't you ever go camping or fishing, or walk in a meadow that smelled of fresh-cut hay? Didn't you ever go mountain climbing? How about the sky at night? Can you identify the constellations?"

Then Margot came down to earth.

"Weren't you ever in love, David?" she asked quite suddenly. "It's such a wonderful experience. Everyone should be in love," she concluded.

202 . . .

David felt that might be the point to move on. That nature lecture had disturbed him. He found a convenient spot under a birch where he could be alone for a while. Gazing haphazardly about, he zeroed in on Debbie kissing Jimmy. He was jarred into less lyrical emotions and soberly pondered how much better off she was with her new husband. I can drive someone insane! he told himself.

Here he was at a wedding, in a lovely garden in Silver Spring, Maryland, but his mind was elsewhere.

Suddenly, he saw his father, the cantor. The cantor was in the synagogue, on the dais, leading the congregation in prayer. Cantor Lazar was wrapped in a prayer shawl with the traditional fringes. His head was covered by a yarmulke, a skullcap. Mused David Lazar: We know so little, we have to believe in something. Did God really exist for my father? What's the difference? He had his congregation. Cantor Lazar. They flocked around him with compliments pouring from their lips, with adoration in their eyes, with love and respect in their handshakes. He believed. What do I have? Nothing. Is that why I am what I am?

And while he continued to observe Debbie Turner moving about, receiving congratulations, being hugged and kissed by sincere friends and loving relatives, being pecked and limp-handshaked by thin-smiling envious enemies, he continued to feel left out, and his mind roamed.

Nathan Rubin keeps people down and makes no bones about it. He's gleeful about it, laughs at the way he swindles them. Solomon's everyone's best friend, but he, too, sermonizes and acts self-righteous and manipulates. No changes really ever occur. Accept life for what it is—manipulation and control and insecurity. The law of the universe is to feed and protect thyself. And God protect us from our parents, our children, our friends, our neighbors, our romantic notions, our lyrical emotions, and most of all, God protect us from ourselves!

Margot Lepidus came up to David. She was smiling.

"What's happened to you, David? You look like you've seen a ghost."

"I'm a gambler and rolling the dice, Margot, and I have one last throw and it's for my life and my arm is paralyzed."

"Oh, stop talking in riddles, David. You're just playing hard to get."

"I'm not playing at all, Margot, I'm serious. I have doubts about myself, God, existence, my parents, you." She smiled. "I have doubts."

She laughed. "A bunch of us are going to Nelson's house. We're going to turn on and have loads of fun. Come with us, David."

Margot took his hand and smiled in that trusting way which says, "Everything's going to be all right."

He pulled away and asked, "Whatever happened to that modeling career your wanted so much?"

"Oh, David, that was last year. It was just a phase I was going through. Daddy made me understand how silly it was." Her brow furrowed. "It was very important to Dad and Mom for me to go back to Yale."

David took her Yale telephone number and told her he'd like to see her again. She smiled at him once more and kissed his cheek before running off to be with her friends.

He watched Debbie saying goodbyes to the last of the guests. Jimmy looked in a hurry to leave. Debbie's eyes met David's for no more than a second. Her expression changed. It said everything. He continued staring at her, and he recalled what she had said to him the last time they were together in New York. "You've been hurt so much you refuse to feel. You do think logically about some things, I guess, but what does that mean other than that you might be able to handicap a ball game or two? I want to live my life with Jimmy, David. He's a wonderful person."

Jimmy was waving to Debbie, gesturing for her to come to the car. David felt that he was going to shout out, "I love you, Debbie! I love you!" But he couldn't utter a word. He couldn't even whimper. He couldn't do anything but stand there and watch Deborah Edison drive off with James Edison. Later, when he was alone, the tears which had been welling up inside him all day trickled down his cheeks.

That evening David took the Metroliner from Washington back to Cancer City. He tried to get some sleep, but his head felt as if it had been cracked by a lightning bolt. He almost did something rash. He thought about writing Debbie, calling her, going to see her wherever she might be. Telling her exactly how he felt. He didn't, of course. Who knows what would have happened if he had? He knew he should have at least tried.

In the middle of the night, still tossing and turning, unable to sleep, though the radio was not on he kept hearing WINS: "I'm Virgil Scutter with Bob Howard at the editor's desk. The time is now eleven-forty-five and now sports! It was a big night in college basketball . . . Brigham Young eighty-nine, Utah eighty-five. . . ." "This is Spencer Ross. This final just in—Dartmouth sixty-seven, Columbia fifty-eight. . . ." "Good evening, everyone. Time is now twelve-twelve and time for sports. This is Art Rusk, Jr. A lot of college basketball activity tonight. Texas seventy-six, Baylor sixty; El Paso sixty-one, Arizona sixty . . ."

There in the hours after midnight, he recalled how he met and fell in love with Leslie Kore . . . then the inexorable disunity. . . . The haughty, earnest, sober young woman's dissatisfaction with the struggling youth, with a boy who offered nothing but foggy visions and demanded passionate love. And now in the middle of the night he closed his eyes and he heard himself screaming at the top of his lungs, "Don't bother me, Leslie! Get out of here!"

And in his nightmare he saw her breaking into tears and racing into the bedroom and falling on the bed.

204 . . .

"I hate my life. I hate this fighting."

And he saw her hysterically continuing to sob, looking miserable and defenseless. And he felt his heart going out to her, and he heard himself saying, "I'm sorry, Leslie, please don't cry. You know I can't stand seeing you cry."

And he saw himself sitting on the bed next to her and putting his arms around her, and he heard her whispering, "Hold me, David. Squeeze me, David. Oh, David." And he held her, and kissed her cheeks and her hair, which dropped down at the side of her face, and her brow, and he comforted her, and not a second after her eyes were closed he rushed back to the radio to listen for scores.

The next morning, David grabbed the M-20, returned to the office, and felt it was completely nonsensical to be there. Nothing there had anything to do with him. Nothing. He looked around, all around; at walls, floors, forms, faces. None of it had anything to do with him. Immediately he took his field book and the forms he needed for his visits and left. As he walked through Harlem his mind returned to Leslie. She was his unrelenting yoke. "I'm dying, Leslie. I'm scared. I wish you were here. All I have is a mind that's painful and hopeless. I'm not brave enough or philosophical enough to change. I'm not strong enough. I'm a coward, Leslie. You know that, don't you? Is that why I love you? Because you're the only one who knows me? Who never really had to hear my words to know my thoughts? My needs? You were always right about me, Leslie. It was easy for me to be smug while you were there to hold me up. But what about now, Leslie? What happens if I pick losers? What do I do then?"

That evening he turned to the sports section of the *Post* and looked up the probable pitchers. But suddenly he remembered something Doug had repeated to him more than once—that there was a beast in all of us; that the most important thing in the world was to be able to stand up to that beast, not to be intimidated by it, to stand up to it as best we could. He did not make a bet. He remembered that he was a handicapper and that he was unemployed until December 1.

Debbie Edison was honeymooning in Paris. Emma Polanski was dead. Leslie Kore and Jennifer were gone. And with it all, in spite of it all, because of it all, his mind was a wanderer, and he got up in a fog and thought, New York has always been the place where you have to make it. A guy can be a winner in every city across the world but if he doesn't make it here he isn't a winner. It is always the last out you need to win the ball game. That's the toughest out.

He always felt that way. Always. And, always, he'd look out of his window and his mind would fly. And every day his soul grew darker, and every hour he dreamed new dreams of glory, of defiance, of showing Leslie. Always.

DAVID'S PHONE rang, and as soon as he heard Leslie's voice his heart began pounding. He became excited and felt alive. She asked him how he was and if he could come over to see her. She told him that Jennifer was at her mother's and that she would be at home alone; that she had problems and needed his help.

He rushed through dressing and with his heart continuing to throb he grabbed a cab and through the bulletproof shield shouted, "Sixty-eighth and Lex, and hurry, cabbie, it's an emergency." As the taxi crawled along in crosstown traffic he cursed the cabbie under his breath. He was overcome by the special New York paranoid suspicion that cab drivers purposefully miss every green and stop at every red.

Finally he reached his destination. The meter read $2.40, and he gave the driver $5. As the driver fumbled for the change David couldn't wait any longer and jumped out of the taxi, yelling, "Keep it!" He raced into the lobby of the building and, not waiting to be announced, dashed straight for the elevator.

As soon as Leslie opened the door, she gasped, "Oh my God!" He had let his hair grow long, very long, and in all the excitement he had forgotten to dress to her taste. He was wearing blue jeans, a flowered shirt, a beat-up leather vest, and sandals. In her eyes he must have resembled a hippie out of the 1960s.

David noticed that Leslie's face was fuller and her breasts larger, and he said, "You look rested, Leslie."

Leslie immediately began to explain that she wanted to see him because she had nowhere else to turn. She looked at him soberly and said, "You're the only one I would take money from, David. That's because I really loved you."

He laughed. "How about giving me some because you loved me?"

"That's another story." She smiled, continuing at once in the same serious tones. "I need the money for an abortion, David." She looked him squarely in the eye as she said it.

Now it was David's turn to gasp, "Oh my God!"

"I have to have it at once, David. I'm in my ninth week already. You're the only one I can turn to." She stopped. "Look over there." She pointed to a desk piled high with overdue bills—rent, phone, food, cleaning bills. The desk was littered with them.

"If you help me, David, I can stay with Aunt Jessie in Florida until after Labor Day."

She told David about the man she'd been involved with, a doctor, a general practitioner named Ralph Banks. They'd been engaged, and without warning one day he'd just called it off. She said it was just after that that she discovered she was pregnant. She said she'd rather die than ask Banks for help. She seemed defiant, almost hysterical, when she said it.

All the time they talked, Leslie's telephone didn't stop ringing. Each time she took a call she went into the kitchen and started whispering, or said to the person calling that she'd call back later.

David didn't say anything, but it hurt. On several occasions she mentioned the name of the caller. In those instances David knew the names.

Then another friend, Harold Freed, knocked on the door. He was short and burly and almost bald. David considered him one of those soft and gentle guys who sit around all day reading newspapers, watching TV, doing the chores, saying, "Yes, dear, I'll help you, dear, you're wonderful, dear, I'll do anything you wish, dear," and on those special and rare days of utter defiance, "I'll do it later, dear." Freed stayed awhile, and Leslie commenced to apply her charms. When he sensed that he was out of place, he excused himself and went into another room.

After several additional calls from girlfriends David only vaguely remembered, and other men friends he had never met or heard of, he began to boil. "Look, Leslie, it's impossible to talk with so many distractions, and I have to get home anyway."

She smiled and walked toward him and took his hand and leaned against him. He smelled her perfume as she gently rubbed her body against him. She laughed when she saw he was still pouting, and in a purring tone she said, "Believe me, David, none of those men mean anything to me."

"That's funny, Leslie, you said the same thing about Lou Cartel, and the next thing I knew you were living with him." He grimaced. "And then he got involved with that Swedish model, and then he was claiming Jennifer wasn't his." David paused and added, "Remember, Leslie? That's Cartel perfume you have on, isn't it, Leslie?"

Leslie's face softened, exhibiting fright, as she said, "Why don't you stay here for a few days, David? Jennifer's going to stay at my mother's until after I have the abortion." As David was about to refuse the invitation, Leslie gently touched his lips with one of her curved fingers.

"Please stay, David." She took his hand and lifted it to her cheek. Slowly she brought his fingers to her lips and kissed them. "Please, David," she whispered. "Please."

During the next twelve hours he fell in love all over again. He had forgotten how beautiful sex could be with the right person, how warm and how wonderful.

They made love and talked about everything. It was as if they had never been away from each other. It wasn't that they were only comfortable together; it was much more. Leslie told him that in the beginning she had adored him, believed in his values and thought he was brilliant; that what had destroyed it for her was the way he had acted, the pain he caused. Sometimes when he gazed at her he saw tears welling in her eyes, and at those times his too would cloud over.

It wasn't long before David told her about the different women he had slept with and about his handicapping. Whenever things were good between them he could never hold anything back. The words would pour out of him. He told her how he had made a net profit of $7,300 during the past season and how he had paid off some of his debts. He poured out that he had saved over $1,000 since the end of the basketball season; that he was saving $350 monthly of his salary. Leslie kept interrupting him.

"Believe me, David, I have nowhere else to turn."

They went to bed again, and while she stroked his penis, David began to confess how he was still hopelessly in love with her and how in his heart he had never stopped hoping or feeling that someday they would get back together again. He still related to everything about her with the same emotion, feeling, and openness as he had sixteen years earlier. He told her how difficult it was for him to hear about Ralph Banks and to listen to her speak about the other men in her life, and to realize that she had been sleeping with some of them. Every time her telephone rang he cringed.

That night when they made love it was everything that any man had ever known or experienced with a woman. She was a goddess, a whore, a mistress, a challenge, a toy, everything a man could ever want in a woman. When she relaxed and rested, David thought Leslie Kore was the most beautiful female, the sexiest woman, ever created.

The next morning when he awoke, Leslie had breakfast waiting. She smiled and kissed him as he sat down to eat. Soon he was saying, "Leslie, I want you to start thinking about us."

Immediately she began enumerating her bills.

"Don't worry, I'm going to help you as much as I can. That's one thing you have never had to worry about." He paused. "I'll be able to give you a thousand cash, Leslie, and I'll be able to send you about two hundred a month until December. That will give you five months to relax."

She took his hand. In a solemn voice she said, "I don't know what I feel right now, David. My feelings have been buried for a very long time."

Tears suddenly took over. He hugged her. He felt grateful.

Later that week when Doug and David entered Solomon Lepidus's office, a sad-faced man was standing in front of Solomon's rosewood desk and Solomon was pointing to some papers and saying, "See this here legal form,

Thurman boy? You know what it is? It's a Chapter Eleven. No one knows, this, but . . ."

Solomon looked up and noticed the twins and grinned. "What's doing, boys?" He quickly shoved the papers into his desk. "Listen, Thurm, I'll have to talk to you tomorrow. The boys and me got some business to discuss. That okay with you, Thurman boy?"

Later on, at dinner, Solomon mentioned to David that he had heard Sidney Feld had died the night before. David ignored that. He advised Solomon that he had been seeing Leslie, that she had financial problems and that he was going to help her.

Doug screamed, "You're an idiot to get involved with Leslie again. She's malignant! Utterly dependent!"

Solomon said it was better for him to keep his broken heart than to have her break his pocketbook.

On Wednesday morning David gave Leslie $1,000 and went with her to the abortion clinic. He waited nervously, pacing the corridors, the waiting room, and the reception area.

Abortion clinic—the name alone game him the chills. The place was overcrowded with men, women, boys, and many girls. He couldn't keep himself from thinking about Leslie and Ralph Banks, and soon he was woozy and feeling slightly nauseated. He leaned against a wall and minutes later found himself rushing outside into the street. With one arm braced against a car and the other holding onto a fire hydrant he vomited into the gutter. When he returned to the clinic, Leslie was waiting for him. He took her home and put her to sleep.

Several days later while he was having dinner with Ron Nivens, David said, "God, Ron, what a difference there is between Leslie and other women. Every night I go to sleep smiling and counting the days until she returns. It's a joy to be alive, Ron. All day long I feel uplifted and jubilant. I feel as if I were reborn, as if I could conquer the world."

Saskia Verdonck despised herself for living with Odette Bashjian. She hated being fondled and touched. She knew it was part of her bargain with Nathan Rubin. It was also part of the bargain to make love to Odette while Nathan Rubin observed. To allow Nathan Rubin and Odette, and sometimes Sandy Rocca, to perform together upon her body. To make visits to strangers was also part of the bargain. The escort service, thanks to her pleas to Nathan, demanded she make residential calls only two or three times a week.

Another part of the bargain were the go-sees she was sent on by the Rubin Modeling Agency. But jobs hardly ever materialized from them, and those that did were quite insignificant. So, in order to survive, to buy blue and green and yellow dresses, pretty things, expensive things, to pay her share of the rent, to take taxis, purchase cosmetics, go to the movies, buy Muscadet, live comfortably, she was dependent, so she felt, on the $500 to $700 a week she earned as a call girl. And so for months now she had smiled and chatted with strangers, sipped Muscadet, stared at ceilings, and obliged "suckers." And when she had time off she obliged Nathan Rubin and listened intently to his words and desperately tried to believe they were true.

"Saskia, it takes time. No one makes it in this city overnight. You've been here only a short time now. It might take another few months before anything important materializes. But something's gonna break for you. You're too pretty for it not to. Just be patient and leave it to me. Oh yeah, Sandy Rocca just got a call from Solomon's lawyer, Ben Tobin. He wants to see you tonight. Ya see, he's into Greek and other things."

On Sunday morning, the first week after Labor Day, Ron Nivens called David. Somewhat flustered, he managed to communicate that he had seen Leslie with some "fellow" at Michael's Pub the night before. They were holding hands. David's heart sank. Ron told David that Leslie looked great and that he had said hello. He stuttered, "I think she's engaged to the fellow, David. She was wearing a ring."

David hung up immediately and quickly dialed Leslie's number. A nasal-voiced operator intercepting the call said, "What number are you dialing, please? . . . Sorry, the number has been disconnected."

He had trouble breathing for a long while. He slumped back into bed and crawled under the covers and buried his head under a pillow, his entire body shaking uncontrollably with pain. Rather than go to the Colonel's for the usual brunch, he tried to sleep, but he was far too distraught.

An hour or two later he called Lillian Kore, his ex-mother-in-law. She intoned in a deliberate voice, "Leslie married Harold Freed Labor Day weekend, David. He flew down sometime in August and convinced her to marry him. The clincher was that he promised her twenty-five thousand dollars as a wedding present and that he would allow her to move wherever she wanted. She took both bribes, David. She's already found a six-and-a-half-room apartment on Fifth Avenue overlooking the Park. Harold says she can decorate the apartment any way she pleases."

"I . . . I don't believe it."

"David, I don't want to get involved in this. Call Leslie if you must. You certainly have the right."

"What's their phone number?"

"It's unlisted, but I'll give it to you just the same."

There was a long silence before Lillian continued. "It's all for the best, David. Maybe." There was genuine compassion in her voice.

His own voice was shaking and tremulous. It was impossible for him to control it.

"I'll talk to you later, Lillian."

He dialed Leslie's number until 11:00 that evening, but he failed to reach her. The only person he got was Jennifer's sitter. He didn't leave his name.

On Monday morning, as soon as he arrived at the office, he tried reaching Leslie again. This time she answered. As soon as she heard his voice, she whispered, "Don't be upset, David. You mustn't be. If you are, I will be. You have to be strong. I love you and I promise you we'll be together soon. Maybe it's a good thing that I married Harold. It made me realize how much I love you. I want to become part of your life, David. I want to share in your world. I know now I don't want to force you into mine. I wanted to call you, but I didn't know what to say." Her voice was sweet and alert, filled with hope and sincerity. He was overjoyed.

In a low hushed voice she said, "I can't talk to you now, David, but there's nothing to worry about. I was terribly confused and I made a mistake, but there's a loophole in the prenuptial agreement. The marriage can be annulled. I'll call you this afternoon." In an even lower tone she said, "Don't worry, darling, I promise, everything's going to be all right."

For at least ten minutes he sat at his desk without moving. After that he went straight home and waited for Leslie to call.

While waiting he reflected on what had happened. He remembered she had called him in the middle of August and while passing a joke about her tennis game she slipped in that Harold Freed had written to her, that he wanted to marry her. He flinched as he recollected how casually she had asked, "What would you do if I married him, David?"

Finally she called. She asked him to meet her for a drink. He suggested one of Doug's hangouts. It was small and dimly lit, and he figured it would give them a certain amount of privacy. It was on Second Avenue. It was Elaine's, a place for people in film, theater, and publishing. For people with dreams. For New Yorkers.

David was early. He was early because he was impatient and because Doug had told him how difficult it could be to get a good table. But Elaine, from her station at the end of the bar, spotted David as soon as he came in. She gave him one of her famous bear hugs, saying, "Hiya, Doug. How many you gonna be?"

"Just two," David replied, allowing for a mistake in identity, which he hadn't taken advantage of since he and Doug had stopped dating the same girls.

"Want to sit at the table?" Elaine asked, by which she meant the legendary Table Four, where you were still served, could talk to other regulars, or keep your peace and simply watch what Doug called "the passing parade."

"Thanks, Elaine," David said, "but I need a table in back."

"Hope it isn't another conquest from the Corso," she shot back. "Hey, Pepe, give Doug Table Nine."

Table Nine was a table for lovers and others who wanted to remain inconspicuous.

As David waited for Leslie he thought how odd it was that Doug should feel about Elaine the way he felt about Solomon, that for Doug she was beyond reproach.

When Leslie finally arrived she couldn't spot David in back, and so Elaine escorted her to the table herself.

"You guys are as hard to tell apart as the Sylberts," she said, referring to another pair of twins who frequented the restaurant, while throwing a quizzical glance at Leslie, who was garishly bedecked with jewels.

As soon as Leslie sat down, David noticed a certain fragility about her. It showed in the way she hugged him, the way she ordered, the way she rushed her words, the way she crossed her legs, the way her brow smoothed and ruffled. It showed despite the subtle glow of the lights of Elaine's, which lent everyone just the right touch of a classy tan no matter what weather they were under.

"I want to be with you every day, David. That's the only way I'll regain my faith in you." She stopped. "We'll move into another apartment when all this is over, one with a modest rental and away from Manhattan where all the sick things have happened to us."

And five minutes later, "I saw Jackie Onassis today. She lives in my building. It's fantastic!"

David grimaced. She noticed. She reached for his hand, lifted it to her lips, and started kissing his fingers. His eyes involuntarily began to water.

"I'm sorry, David, I made a mistake. I married Harold because I thought it could be a fresh start for me. Please don't be upset. I was confused and afraid to trust you. You know how you are."

He blurted out, "Leave Freed now, Leslie. Tell him tonight you made a mistake."

Leslie didn't agree. She turned adamant and rigid. Her entire appearance changed. Where she had been soft, she became hard. Where she had looked relaxed, she looked nervous.

"You know how I am, David. I can't function in a crisis. I'm afraid to rush into anything. I can't just give Harold up. First I have to believe in you completely. If I had to marry right now I wouldn't marry him. But, still, I'm only about fifty percent sure I'd marry you. Don't you see, David? I'm still afraid."

She reached into her purse for a cigarette, and Pepe magically appeared from nowhere to light it for her. She took several puffs before continuing.

"Don't worry, darling. We'll be able to be together now and then, and in time I'll be strong enough to leave him. Believe me, David, the money and the apartment don't mean anything to me." She stopped. "Trust me, David. Tomorrow morning I'll call you, and we'll meet somewhere for lunch." She inhaled deeply, smiled, and coyly said, "Now stop looking at me that way, David. You look like a little lamb, darling."

Fears quivered inside him. He tried to understand his ambivalences, his terror, and her instability. He thought, Will things ever be easy?

Leslie got up to leave, but he grabbed her arm and asked her to stay for another five minutes. He half saw, half imagined her shrugging her shoulders and sighing, as if she were exasperated with him. He gulped down a drink and then spoke.

"Tell me the truth, Leslie. What do you feel? Before you leave, tell me exactly what you really feel." His voice faltered as he spoke. Hers remained calm and smooth.

"I want to be with you, darling. Please just give me a little bit more time."

She glanced at her wristwatch. He noticed it was expensive and new.

"I have to leave now. I have to meet . . ." She hesitated. "Harold." She smiled. "Don't worry, darling. I'll see you tomorrow. I promise."

He didn't hear from Leslie for three days. He sat by his phone each day waiting for her call. Every time it rang, whether in his room or at the office, he jumped. Finally he couldn't stand it any longer and he called her.

"What happened?"

"I can't talk now," she whispered. "I have Harold's sister here. I can't talk." She hung up.

He called her back.

"I can't talk to you now, David." He could feel the irritation in her voice.

"What's happened, Leslie? What made you change your mind?"

There was a moment of hesitation. When she spoke her voice was cool and painstakingly clear. "I can't explain it, David. I don't know what to say. Harold comes home and he's so happy to see me." She stopped. "He loves me, David. He's been so kind. I do like him, not the way I loved you, David, but I do like him."

"What about me, Leslie? What about us?"

"I . . ." She faltered.

"Please, Leslie, you have to have the courage to trust me. You can't escape with a man just because he's gentle and kind."

"I can't live with the pressure anymore, David."

"You don't have to. I'll take over all the responsibilities," he broke out in a strong voice. "I'll meet you tomorrow afternoon at Doug's apartment. He's out of town."

She answered in a reluctant resigned tone, "All right."

Next day at Doug's he immediately pounced on her. "You have to leave him now, Leslie."

"I'm too old to begin again. I've been through too much." Softly she said, "I'm sorry, David."

He countered, "I can take care of you, Leslie. Please believe me, Leslie. You've got to believe me. This is our whole life we're talking about."

Leslie gazed at David's tortured face. For a brief moment she remained silent, and then she said in a bitter voice, "I've learned that the only one who can take care of me and who I can depend on is me. I do a better job than anyone in caring for me."

David said, "Do you think it's honorable to manipulate, lie to, and exploit a fifty-six-year-old man who is taking care of you? Don't you see what you're doing? I know you, Leslie. No one loves you or knows you like I do! You'll never have anything worthwhile with him. You'll be all alone. You'll have no one."

Leslie's expression changed. She became icy-eyed, and her body tightened. She seemed impenetrable as she said, "No one really knows me, David. You know more of me than anyone, but there are things about me that no one knows." She stopped. "Only a certain kind of man can protect me, David, and love hasn't very much to do with it." She stopped again. "I feel secure with Harold."

"He's a butcher, Leslie! A butcher!"

Mercifully and patiently came her retort. "I'm sorry, David, but I don't need to love or communicate with anyone. I don't need to be with an intelligent man or interesting people, or with . . ." She smiled fondly at him. "With a dreamer. I don't want to achieve anything, David. I just want to have some peace and quiet and a sensible life. Harold's given me that."

Her expression changed again and she looked sadder this time and her voice wavered as she said, "Don't think I haven't thought about us a great deal, David. I have."

He didn't say a word. He just listened while she continued to speak.

"For a long time I was dominated by you. I was in love with you and I admired your brilliance, but for too many years I was made its victim." She stopped and gazed nervously at David. Her eyes avoided his, and her voice became even more tremulous. "If it hadn't been that I was trapped with a child, I would have left a long time before I did. If I had my own money it would have been different. I would have been free. But I didn't have any money. What happens when I get old? When I'm no longer attractive? I need money, David. What happens if I get sick? It's very important to have the best doctors. I worry about getting sick all the time."

There was a long silence. Then she gazed up at David and seemed to be holding back some deeper emotion. Composing herself somewhat, she said in a loud whisper, "Once you were my whole world, my very existence; there wasn't a moment that went by that I didn't think of you." She paused and they exchanged looks. "Believe me, David, at one time I was completely ready to surrender myself to you, but . . ."

He took her hand and she stared at him and a strangeness came over her face. "You never really cared about me, David. You only cared about your own needs!"

She stopped, then pushed forward with even greater urgency. "I can't forget how cruel you were, David. You were my dream, my star, everything I wanted. Sensitive, romantic, wild, a stallion, a lamb, my everything. But now I'm too old to ride with you. I'm too tired to fight with you. I want something utterly safe and predictable." She smiled wanly. "I want someone whose ambition amounts to no more than selling some meat, who doesn't have to conquer the world."

She halted for a moment. Then in a voice which rose with resentment, "I don't want a man who will overwhelm me or want to change me, or be dissatisfied with what I am." She paused again before exploding in one last high-pitched bitter crescendo: "I don't want to be married to you. Of all the men in the world, David, I don't want to be married to you!"

He wanted to cry out that he'd changed, that he could change, that he would change, but he realized that it was futile. She gazed at his tear-stained face, and her bitterness subsided as she said, "Please forgive me, David. Of all the men I've ever known in my life you're the only one I've ever truly loved, or who really knows me at all. You must believe that. That's all we have left to share."

She moved closer to him and brushed some lint off his shoulder. Before he could react, she had kissed him and was walking out the door. Then she turned and said, "Both of us have been like children in a playground for a very long time, David. Now it's time for both of us to grow up."

She pressed the elevator button. He walked over to her, and she kissed him again.

The elevator door opened and she got in, and just before the door closed she said, "I want you to be happy, David. Believe that."

His heart collapsed as she waved goodbye.

25

DURING THE EARLY FALL of 1971, David spoke to Nathan Rubin almost every day. He told him everything he had discovered the year before. "I found a lot out, Mr. Rubin. First of all, it's impossible for Vegas to keep up with the whole board. I've found my line and theirs differed by four and a half points or more on at least one hundred and sixty games last year. That's one hundred and sixty out of approximately four thousand games, Mr. Rubin. Those games are the only ones worth touching. I should win at least seventy percent of them. I am confident that my power ratings will stand up."

David asked Nathan Rubin to finance him and suggested that they split the profits down the middle. David held his breath and waited for Nathan's answer. At first he just looked at David in that way of his, sneering and snickering. Then he controlled himself and said, "I'm not going to give you any money, David, but I will give you some advice. The thing to remember is that making a living on college basketball is hard because of the limits they put on you. Remember the bookie will change his number on you every time you make a bet of a nickel or more, and he has a pipeline, too. If any games are out of line, the vibrations are picked up immediately. Within ten minutes every office in the damn city will know about the game and take it off the board. They're not fools, you know; if they smell something fishy they'll react immediately. You won't be able to get down any important money even if you know something and want to. To do that you'd need beards all over the country."

"What about your outs, Mr. Rubin?"

"With the offices I use I might be able to get down four or five dimes, but that's about my limit on baskets, kid. You gotta understand only about three or four of the BMs I use deal college baskets. When it comes to college baskets, everyone's afraid." He paused. "If you really wanted to take advantage of your games, what you'd have to do is put together an organization. Of course, you're not ready for that, but if you ever get in a position to do anything important, make sure you have the people that can help you do it right. Remember, kid, you'd have to move your games fast, and you'd need men you can trust. You'd have to be careful and use codes for everything, especially if you're going to use the phone to call in your bets, with the federal laws as tough as they are these days."

Sometimes when Nathan Rubin spoke, his words were articulated perfectly but their meaning obscure; at other times his words came in a rush and were jumbled, but their meaning was crystal clear. On those occasions, he sounded very much like Casey Stengel. ("You fellas want to know about my team? Well, if my pitcher holds up and gives me a few good innings and if that second baseman of mine can make the pivot and if that Detroit team don't get too far ahead of us in the spring, and if . . .) You might have thought he didn't make sense, but if you listened carefully you could pick out the gems.

David interrupted Nathan Rubin's monologue. "That's the way I'd do it, Mr. Rubin. If I ever get in a position to invest important money, I'd have beards betting for me all over the country. If I do well this season, what do you think of this idea for next year?"

Invariably, Nathan Rubin sat back and let David pour out his own ramblings. As he did so, David observed by the look on Rubin's face that he, like Solomon Lepidus, believed in deeds, not words.

By the time David got home he realized that talk was sludge and that first he needed to make money. As he prepared his handbook he dwelled on how he could beat the bookmakers. He could stay within a bookmaker's limit, and not beat any one office for more than chickenfeed. To do more would take beards, money, telephones, organization, and his handicapping ability. He kept dwelling on that, and he recalled how bitter he felt because he didn't have sufficient money to execute his ideas. His mind wandered and he thought, Nathan Rubin made forty million—why him and not me? Harry Richardson made millions with his eleven–ten. I spotted ninety-three games last year. Definitely mistakes. According to my stats I won sixty-seven of them. Three were pushes. That's a winning percentage of seventy-four point four. If I wanted to, I could play it even safer this year and wager only when their point spreads are off by five or more from my own power ratings. Then my winning percentage should be even greater.

He had a godlike confidence, a confidence which buoyed him and told him he was as good as anyone who had ever handicapped a college basketball game. But he was also tense and utterly frustrated, because he only had $2,950 to start the season with. If he just had decent money, he could make a fortune. He really believed it. If only he had the right kind of money—that was the hitch. If he had the money, he knew how much he could make. Someday his handbook would be worth a million and would have to be placed in a vault, he daydreamed. That was his prevailing mood as he prepared for the 1971–1972 college hoop season.

A problem had arisen between Mustache McDuff and Angelo Scarne. McDuff owed Scarne $6,800, and neither Nathan Rubin nor Isaac Pizer would help.

Angelo "One-Eye" Scarne stared unbelievingly at the herculean forearms of the man sitting on the black leather Chesterfield couch and smiled to himself. He was confident that he had hired the right man for the job. He thought, Jesus! He has the body of a boulder. One-Eye raised himself with some effort out of his maroon leather desk chair and walked over to a hanging plant and reached up and started to prune it.

"This wandering Jew gives me nothing but trouble, Club."

The man was Club Collins, a gigantic florid-faced man with purple blotches on his nose and cheeks. He had whitish-blond hair, steel-gray eyes, a hooked nose, a frightening frame, and hugh rough-hewn hands. He was six feet seven and he weighed a rhinolike 285 pounds, and all of him was constantly gripped by an evil tension that he had discovered only one way to appease. He had discovered it playing baseball as a boy—physical assertion.

And now Club Collins pleasured himself as much maiming a man as other men did in making love to a woman.

One-Eye walked up to his custom-built buckeye wet bar and poured himself a drink. "That bastard McDuff made a bet with Tony Giardello's office last Sunday, Club. I think he's either holding out on me or he took a shot. Find out which. . . . And, Club, do whatever else is necessary. You understand?"

Collins rubbed his chin with his big hand and grinned. "Don't worry about a thing, Mr. Scarne. I'll take care of McDuff for you." He walked over to the wet bar and ran his fingers over the smooth buckeye. "This is beautiful wood, Mr. Scarne. It musta cost you a fortune, huh?"

One-Eye smiled and said, "One good football Sunday pays for the whole place, Club."

"Please give me another week. I'll get you the money, I promise," Mustache McDuff pleaded.

Club Collins looked at him and said indifferently, "It's too late, McDuff. I'm sorry, but you had your chance."

They were meeting on the tiled terrace of McDuff's home.

Mustache McDuff had nothing to say. He recollected how he had borrowed the money, and how he had lost it. Collins smacked a baseball bat he carried hard into the palm of his huge left hand and gripped the barrel with his right as he took two steps toward McDuff. McDuff instinctively lifted his arms, covering his head with his hands, and cowered against the wall.

"Please! . . . Don't!" McDuff whimpered.

Club Collins, with a sick grin on his face, slowly raised the bat above his shoulder, above his whitish-blond hair, high over his head, and held it there for what seemed an eternity to McDuff.

"Please ... please ... please," McDuff begged.

Before a fourth "please" was whimpered, Club Collins had clubbed Mustache McDuff to the ground. As McDuff cried out, Collins again raised his bat and again viciously swung, aiming at Harry's arms and again at his ribcage and again at his legs. Then Collins stopped and smiled to himself. He had heard the sound of McDuff's shinbone crack. As McDuff lay motionless on the floor, Club listened and heard a wheezing deathlike rattle coming from his chest.

Collins immediately shifted his stance for balance and flipped the bat over in his right hand. Again he slowly raised his weapon. This time he smashed it against McDuff's ankle, and then against collarbone and jaw. Blood gushed from Harry's mouth, nose, and ears, and two of his teeth rolled like dice on the smooth brick-tiled terrace floor until they bounced against a redwood planter and came to a stop. Collins suddenly felt the cold autumn chill and blew on his hands. He quickly turned and walked through the terrace door into McDuff's living room. He was going to head for the exit when he remembered. He walked over to McDuff's oriental desk and picked up the red touch-tone phone and dialed. "Hello? ... Give me One-Eye, tell him it's Club Collins calling.... You were right, Mr. Scarne, McDuff made a six-G bet with Tony Giardello's office last Sunday on the Knickerbockers.... Yeah, he paid off Fat Tony, I checked. And get this, Mr. Scarne—McDuff told me it was money he had borrowed to pay you off with, but the degenerate took a shot with it just as you figured.... Don't worry, Mr. Scarne, I took good care of him. He'll be in a hospital for months."

"Max Brown on twenty-two, Mr. Lepidus."

"Did you hear about Mustache McDuff, Solomon? One-Eye had Club Collins pay him a visit. Club worked him over with that baseball bat of his. McDuff'll be laid up in Lenox Hill Hospital for two to three months. He has a fractured pelvis and a fractured collarbone and fractured ribs. One good thing, though—McDuff's ex-wife, Marsha, heard about it. That broad's really got a heart, Solomon. She sold all her jewelry to Nathan Rubin and paid off One-Eye."

Isaac Pizer had been having trouble sleeping, though his bed was large and comfortable. Each night he had been tossing and turning and thinking of Valerie Caldwell. What did she do for sex? Who were the men in her life? Where did she disappear when she left the office? What did she like to do?

Valerie Caldwell's career had taken off. The Caldwell line was in demand internationally. And because of her looks, so was Val. For the first time in more years than Isaac Pizer cared to remember, he had a stirring in his breast. He felt silly, like a schoolboy. On the other hand, Val Caldwell had never encouraged him. He had never received anything more personal than "Goodnight, Isaac, see you in the morning" in the entire year she had been working for Pizer. Not once did she ever speak of a man. Not once did she seem to be rushing out of the office to meet someone special. Not once was there a hint of need or a suspicion of an affair. Yet Pizer couldn't believe that this beautiful woman didn't have a lover or desire a man. Isaac was not young, and he wasn't particularly attractive, but he was still good with women. He could be charming and generous, and, more important, he offered strength and style to the women he took into his life. But with Val, his thoughts went deeper. He felt something for her, felt the way she was, the softness he intuited underneath, and the sensuality that was evident. He felt something right about him and Val. Something he couldn't put his finger on.

And for some reason he believed that beneath her cool demeanor was more than a professional politeness for him. Fondness, friendship, and maybe even more. Nathan Rubin had gone out with Val and him on more than one occasion. It was strictly business. Nathan had mentioned to Pizer that he found her desirable. Yet when Nathan made overtures, Val seemed as indifferent as ever. All she spoke about were her designs. Whenever Nathan Rubin mentioned his modeling agency, his wealth, his possessions, his successes, Val Caldwell seemed bored. By the fourth time Isaac asked Val to join them for dinner, Val asked to be excused.

Isaac Pizer got out of bed carefully, so as not to awaken his wife. He stooped down, picking up his slippers, and tiptoed ever so quietly to his den. When there, he placed his slippers on his feet and a blue silk robe around his shoulders. Next he snatched a thick cigar from the top of his desk, lit up, and inserted it into his mouth. Then he sat down in his favorite chair and removed the telephone receiver to dial Valerie Caldwell.

He dialed. The phone rang. Valerie answered. "Hello? . . . Hello? . . . Who is this? . . . Hello?" Isaac Pizer placed the receiver back in its cradle. He puffed on his thick cigar. Minutes later, he slowly walked back into his bedroom to join his wife in his wide and comfortable but cold and lonely bed.

David Lazar continued to prepare for the 1971–1972 basketball season. By late fall Nathan Rubin was taking him very seriously. He was hearing things that made him begin to believe.

"Here's another thing Champ Holden never knew, Mr. Rubin. The home court doesn't mean beans for the weak teams. I've been keeping statistics, and I'm convinced the dog teams don't use the home-court advantage. Just listen to this fact. Over the past five years, according to my records, the thirty-five weakest teams have won five hundred and fifty-five games and lost eight hundred and twenty-two by the points. That's a losing percentage of over sixty percent, Mr. Rubin."

220 . . .

Nathan Rubin peered into his eyes and said, "Maybe it's time for you to become a professional handicapper, kid. Last year you weren't ready, but now maybe you are. What you should do is get yourself some good customers. I'm certain Solomon Lepidus and Isaac Pizer and at least half a dozen other guys would go in with you. They'd love the action. You probably won't even have to put up your own money. You could probably work out a deal where you'd get expense money and a percentage of the profit. Probably fifty percent!"

"What about you, Mr. Rubin?"

He smirked and crowed, "Well, ya see, it's always been my policy never to go into anything unless my partner puts up something on his side. In this type of deal, I'd expect you to put up a third. If you put up a third, I'd put up two thirds and we'd split the profit down the middle. That way you'd have almost a seventeen percent advantage, ya see."

"I've been trying to tell you, Mr. Rubin, I only have twenty-nine hundred and fifty dollars. What I need from you is financing."

There was a brief silence as Nathan Rubin squinted and peered at David. After what seemed like an eternity, Nathan Rubin said, "Let me see how you do on your own this year, David. And bear this in mind—everyone thinks they can win. Some guys bet systems, other guys follow touts, other guys think they can win by sorcery and voodoo. Some guys just get a feeling and some like to match the strengths and weaknesses of the personnel. They believe in cause and effect, ya see." He snickered. "Them guys should be writing about sports, not betting on them. What you have to do, kid, is remember one thing: It's all horse manure without money management. That's the only thing that's going to keep you around in the long run." He snickered. "That's what it's all about."

"My management will be perfect, Mr. Rubin, and I'm only going to invest in the games they mess up on."

"Yeah, sure," Nathan Rubin said, "but first you gotta make certain you know enough to recognize which ones those are. There aren't one hundred gamblers in ten thousand that know that much. Then you gotta be capable of getting down on those games—maybe ten percent of the hundred guys you got left have that ability. Then you need to have the discipline to only bet those games you're speaking about, and that's a hell of a job. Maybe five or six can do that. And last, and most important, you have to be able to back your opinion up with real money so that those games mean something more than just candy bars. Out of the half-dozen guys left, how many do you think have that kind of money? Maybe three guys in the whole freakin' country, sonny. Three!"

He chuckled and said, "Take it slow, sonny. Let's see how you do this year."

"Mr. Rubin, Sidney Feld said you started out in Scranton, Pennsylvania, as a coal miner. And Champ Holden told me that you gave sermons in the deep South."

Nathan Rubin's face became softer. He nodded his head a few times and remembered the old days.

"I useta sell land to the blacks down there. My gimmick was that I'd preach about the value of owning your own land and having a piece of the country. I useta put on a real minstrel show. Hire singers, dancers, everything. Oh, it must have been . . . well, I'll tell you this, I wasn't much more than a boy at the time.

"You know what the public needs, David? Someone with ingenuity. Someone to tell them how to do things. Most people are really like children. They're only good at following, being part of the herd. Ya see, David, the main reason for my success was that I followed no one. I was a lot like the blacks were in the South. Did you know that they weren't shattered and destroyed by the system like those up here? A lot of them, though exploited, remained strong, self-possessed, and unbroken. And I'll tell ya something else—most of the blacks I met in those days loved life and loved their wives and their children and the four or five dollars' worth of an acre that I sold 'em. Ya see, they took pride in the land. I might have made a few bucks, sure, but they had the land and they had dignity."

And then David saw a wry grin breaking on Nathan's face and Rubin raised his hands and shrugged. "They were probably as rich as I am today." Nathan's face had become kind and sincere. He took David's arm and said, "Ya see, David, the only thing that really matters in the long run is keeping your ego intact. Being your own man. Living your own life and not someone else's. Remember that, David.

"But I'm not here to philosophize. No, that's something I'm not, a philosopher."

He sat still for a while, and he seemed to be looking into the past. "There was one black, couldn't have been more than fifteen at the time . . . why, it must've been fifty-odd years ago. I think it was in some town in central Alabama. It was very late at night and I'd just left the home of some real estate agent with whom I had been playing cards. I was walking by an alley when I heard something. Someone said, 'Let's do it already, Bobby Joe, I'm sure he's one of them that sassed my sister.'

"I walked a few steps into the alley and I saw six white men with this one black boy. They were spreading his legs apart. One of them holding down one leg and another holding down the other. Two others were pinning his arms.

"'We know how to handle uppity niggers like you. We gonna cut your balls off, nigger.'

"Another white man, about thirty, climbed on top of the kid's chest and pressed a rifle barrel across his throat until the boy couldn't hardly breathe. And then one of them, the one they called Bobby Joe, took out a razor and got on his knees between the boy's legs and took the boy's testicles in his hand. He looked up at the others and grinned. I heard one of them say, 'Come on, Bobby Joe, cut the nigger's nuts off, we ain't got all night.' I saw him slash the boy's groin, David." He stopped and whispered, "He severed his scrotum."

Beads of perspiration appeared on Nathan Rubin's forehead as he said softly, "I can still hear the boy screaming, David."

Nathan Rubin didn't blink or look at David as he continued his story. "When the cutting was done, Bobby Joe held the testicles in the air and dangled them. Then he threw them in the dirt, and the other men ran after them as if they were dogs chasing a bone. When they reached 'em they started stomping."

In Rubin's face David saw something he had never seen before. Something soft.

"I couldn't do anything, David. I saw it happen, but I didn't even try to stop it. I couldn't move, David, I couldn't move. Bobby Joe yelled, 'Nigger, you make sure you don't talk to no more white women, and you make sure and tell them other highfalutin nigger friends of yours what happened here. You hear?'

"The boy was in agony, David, bleeding, but he refused to answer them. The one called Bobby Joe kept screaming, 'You hear me, nigger? You hear?' And he kept kicking him with his boot, but that boy wouldn't answer. Finally one of them bastards said, 'Come on, Bobby Joe, let's get out of here, it's almost dawn.' But that Bobby Joe, that cracker bastard, he didn't want to leave. He kept kicking the boy and screaming, 'You hear me, nigger? You hear?' Finally two or three of the other men pulled him away and they left."

Nathan Rubin took a monogrammed handkerchief out of his pocket and wiped sweat from his face and brow. He didn't speak for several minutes. He seemed to be returning to the past.

"Now I remember that black boy as if it were yesterday." He gazed at nothing in particular for a while, and when Rubin spoke again his voice was weak. "That boy had no people at all, David. His ma was an ex-slave and had died the winter before." He shook his head and when he continued he said in a stronger voice. "Well, after that, Josh Turner had somebody."

Nathan Rubin loved football—the confrontation of the men in the pit, the war of hitting, belting, beating, bruising, and maiming he found exhilarating. He ignored the artful dodging backs. He never noticed the fleet-footed mercurial athletes patrolling one-on-one in the corners. He cared little about the spiral pass.

What his eyes centered on was the combat of the awesome colliding

Goliaths in the trenches. What he relished was the goal-line stand. The men he respected most were those like George Allen, who had his Redskin team fight for every begrudged yard in a cloud of muscle and mayhem; Dick Butkus, a Chicago player of brutal strength and fierce competitiveness; Jim Taylor, a Green Bay fullback of vigor and courage. The more lusty, the more savage, the more devouring, the more wounding, the more carnal, the more Nathan liked it. The more jocks they carried off the field, the more he became enthralled. The game to him proved not who was the better team, but who were the better men.

Early that fall David began going to the New York Jet home games at Shea Stadium with Nathan Rubin. Each time clinging to Rubin's arm was a young woman named Harriet Barash. She bundled warmly to keep out the cold, packing for extra comfort a thermos filled to the brim with hot chocolate. Nathan Rubin explained to her how he felt about football. Nathan conveyed his thoughts with a brutal, animal sensual passion. Each time he did so, Harriet's physical comfort was affected. She became unsettled and ruffled. Her eyes took on a dreamy, willowy look. Her voice became huskier. Her breathing quickened and her breasts swelled to the rhythm.

On each of the Sundays they attended the football games, Nathan Rubin became ferocious. The more violent the games were, the more they excited him. And the more frenzied he became, the more he attracted Harriet Barash. Of course, David, too, was influenced by the games. It was all so carnal, so sensual.

Sometimes during those games Nathan Rubin discussed things other than gambling with David. On more than one occasion he discussed Harriet Barash. He bragged to David that she was fascinated by him because he possessed that peculiar paradox of almost being violent and always suppressing the violence.

At times during the games David noticed Nathan Rubin looking at her as if he wanted to make love, but then, after he got the message across, he'd return to the game. At other times he took Harriet's hand and guided it under his coat, but then he would push her hand away and, as always, return his attention to the game.

Many times during the week, for lunch mainly, Nathan Rubin would allow David to spend time with Harriet Barash without his being around. He never once let on that he considered David a threat to the relationship. Many times David wanted to come on with her, but he didn't. Most of the time he questioned her about her attraction to the old man.

"If Nathan accidentally grazes my shoulder or brushes against my breast, it makes me shudder. Just a glimpse of him out of the corner of my eye makes me feel all tingly and warm inside. Would you believe it, David, if I told you that sometimes I have an orgasm just by staring? I guess you wouldn't understand that, being the kind of person you are."

But, of course, David understood only too well. After all, during his early years with Leslie, hadn't he felt the same way a thousand times? Hadn't he had to hold himself back with a vehement detachment? Didn't he have to quench all his juices, suppress natural instinct? He understood only too well.

Finally one Sunday David propositioned Nathan Rubin.

"Mr. Rubin, let me make you a proposition. I'll bet you five hundred on the game and you don't have to put up a single dollar."

Nathan Rubin peered at David suspiciously. "Whaddaya mean, sonny?"

"Simple, Mr. Rubin. All you got to do is put up Harriet. If I win, I want to sleep with her tonight."

David didn't look at Harriet. He didn't know what she thought, what she felt, whether she wanted him. He didn't care.

Nathan Rubin smirked. David's face was tense and hostile. Nathan knew David was dead serious. He looked over at Harriet. He knew David recognized how much of a woman she really was. She was delicious—full, moist lips; a perfect straight-line nose; warm, large hazel eyes; thick brown hair; smooth, lovely skin; youthful, rounded limbs; firm, large breasts.

"I'll tell you what I'll do, kid. I'll take your proposition, but if I win, I don't want yer money, I want ya to handicap college baskets for me this season for nothin'."

David glared at Nathan Rubin. David glanced at Harriet Barash. He noticed her pulsating and inhaling hard.

He said, "No!"

NO ONE CAN lay the 11–10 and win consistently. Knowledge, information, opinion, all mean something—but not everything. Nathan Rubin kept reminding David of that. But what about David's ninety badly rated games a season out of the four thousand or more a line is put out on? That comes to less than 3 percent of all the games played.

What if those ninety or so games made David a better handicapper than the bookmakers and their official line? David was in on everything now in college baskets. He could build an organization. He would even be getting special games from Max Brown, games he wanted David to "cheer" for. He could call all over the country for information. He could utilize all his contacts: players, scouts, friends, everyone. He could pump and prime for more and more information; find out about coaches and player squabbles and last-second injuries; study press flashes and public relations tidbits and newsletters; use players; use scouts; use friends; use coaches. He started making some calls. Billy Williams stated he was going to use some new boys on his trip to the West Coast in the beginning of the season because he wanted to get a good look at everyone before his conference schedule got underway. He said he'd rather sacrifice an early win or two by looking at everyone. He also said his conference would be very strong and that State had two sleepers in Dexter Maxwell and Hollis Cimarron. And the day before, Ned DeFalco said he had two kids out of junior college coming around pretty good, that they were "tough old boys."

Earlier in the week, Noah Weldon said Oregon State was vastly overrated. And Bobby Joe Matfield said his team was very young, that they had good offensive strength but they weren't topflight competition. Their defense was ragged and they turned the ball over too much. And Eddie Zeno said Pennsylvania could play a zone or go man-to-man, and that they had the personnel to shoot over a zone and break it if they had to. And Roger Brantley said, "Sky Davis is playing super! He was threatening to quit Western last year, remember? All because of that Billy Duval. Right. Billy's at Boone now, but I had him all set up for Western and he went and got hurt playin' ball with some kids in the playground. Western wouldn't touch him, even though he's the best backcourt man since Tiny Archibald, and Sky got really down on Western. But I talked to that guy Sam Boone and bullshitted him into taking Billy down there. He's gonna make them into a winner. So now Sky and Billy are going to be trying to kill each other in the Boone–Western game this year, but everybody's happy. Sheeit!" And on and on—the phone calls were being made, the information was pouring in.

The last week in November, David made one more attempt to get Nathan Rubin to finance him.

"Mr. Rubin, I know for a fact that I could never beat Vegas because of the percentage and the limit and because I'm not blessed with your kind of genius. I can't beat football, hockey, or even baseball. The only gambling game I can beat is a game of opinion where I have the best opinion in the country, and that's college basketball. I'm studying it fourteen hours a day, Mr. Rubin, and I'm only concerned with the point spreads, winning and making money. My wife and I are finished, Mr. Rubin. I have no personal distractions whatsoever. The only competition I have is bookmakers, and they're limited creatures with limited intelligence and limited information. Last year I turned two hundred and fifty dollars into seventy-three hundred dollars, and I'm beginning this year with twenty-nine hundred and fifty in cash. By next year I might not need you, Mr. Rubin. I'll probably be ready to go for the big money on my own. But right now you can save me a year. Just give me twenty-five thousand to work with and we'll both make a killing."

Nathan Rubin said, "I got to fly to Houston tomorrow to see my old friend Lawson Monroe. We might go into the gold market together on a deal. Gold is going to be the biggest, kid, it's going to go sky high." He chuckled. "You remember those gold coins I bought from Morty Lefko. I paid him eighteen thousand for them. You know what they're worth today if I wanted to get rid of them? Thirty-two thou! Lefko must be dying." Continuing to chuckle and almost as an afterthought he added, "I should call him, he's really a nice fella."

But, then, in a flash, his nefarious mind changed subjects, and he geared his attention back to David. "Let me know how you do, kid. Keep in touch with Sandy Rocca while I'm out of town. He'll be talking to me most every day, and don't be impatient. Maybe next year if I'm still around I'll work something out with you." He stopped. "Let me see you put two good seasons together, back to back. Show me you can double your money, kid, then come back and we'll talk."

By the end of November, everything inside David was aching to explode. The tension was enormous. He knew only by challenging himself and working toward something and striving would he be kept alive. But sometimes he still felt something stirring in the blackness of his madness. Sometimes he felt something brewing inside him as though he were staring at the bottom of a cesspool. Sometimes he heard a voice within him revolting against the life he led. Sometimes in the night a voice spoke to him. Sometimes he muffled it with a soiled pillow and thought about settling for a wife and family, a job and security. But with the light of each new morning he felt renewed.

Nathan Rubin called the day before the season started. So did Solomon Lepidus and Doug. They wanted to wish David well. So did Champ Holden.

"The season begins tomorrow, doesn't it, David?"

"That's correct, Champ."

"If I were you, David, I'd relax the next couple of days. Why don't you meet me over at the City Athletic Club about five this afternoon? We'll take a steambath and play some squash. You got to keep yourself in the best shape possible, David. Eat greens and steak and get plenty of sleep. And . . ." He hesitated. "You don't drink a lot, do you, David?"

"I hardly drink at all, Champ."

"That's good. Everything helps." He paused. "I remember the first year I handicapped college baskets, David. I was livin' in Minneapolis and still married to Martha. Did I ever tell ya about Martha, David?"

"Yeah, Champ, you mentioned her to me. You told me she was the best woman you ever knew, but that she left you for some dentist because you wouldn't stop gambling." David paused. "You said before she left she went through some real hard times with you, Champ."

Champ didn't say a word for a while, and when he did his voice was emphatic. "Remember this, David. The difference between winning and losing is killing! And David, the only morality in handicapping is to win!"

The night before the season got underway, David tossed and turned and thought about a million things.

Maybe I'll open on December first, maybe a little later, but I'll open and I'll win. It'll cost—it always does, nothing comes easy—but I'll win. Whatever the price, I'll win. I'm going to make it. I'll show them what I can do. What pressure I can endure. Last year's profit means nothing now. I have to win again. Each time is a new time, and I can't dwell on yesterday. I'll reach my breaking point, again and again. My nerves will be raw, but I'll sustain myself. I'll keep my confidence and reach back for that something extra. The pain and the pressure won't matter. I'm a human being, and I don't want to be mediocre. I want to soar! I'll use everything and everyone I can. I'll cheat, lie, steal, claim, learn every angle and make deals wherever I can. I'll handicap better than anyone, and if I ever get the money, I'll set up an organization which'll make General Motors envious. I'll keep striving for as long as it takes, because I don't want to be mediocre, because I don't want to be sensible, because I want it all. I am a human being, and I have dreams of conquering, and a raging poet's soul. I'm going to make it.

With $2,950 in cash David began the 1971–1972 college basketball season. He had big ideas. He had the most complete handicapper's handbook anyone had ever created or ever could create. He had lined up all his contacts, and all his beards. He began to live on the telephone.

"Hello, Zeno, Isaac Pizer just called. He said the smart money boys moved Kansas State from seven and a half to nine. No, listen to me, Eddie, I'm going against the move. Grab the nine. Points are worth a lot more than opinions.... Hello, is this Kansas State? How's the game going tonight? ... State lost the whole game. Geez! That's too bad.... Hello, Solomon? Boy, it's hard reaching you. I must have dialed you ten times already. Didn't you get any of my messges? ... I just wanted to tell you I think South Carolina is a hell of a bet tonight. The game's fifteen. They're playing Boston College.... Hello, Solomon, Carolina romped eighty-six to sixty-four.... Hello, Coach Steinman, this is David Lazar. Can you tell me

228 . . .

something about ... Hello, Roger, how's Sky been doing? ... Hello, Johnny, give me Western for ... Noah? How are you? Tell me, Noah, how's Washington State been doing? ... Eddie, I want you to get me down on Washington State. It's a rivalry game. State's kids have been waiting for this game since the end of last season. ...

"Hello, is this Washington State? How's the game going tonight? Thank you, thank you very much. ... Hello, O'Brien? ... Listen, never mind school. This is important. I want you to get me down on Purdue and Marquette. ... Hello, Champ? How are you? ... I'm doing fine. ... The home courts are standing up, but it's not like it used to be. The refereeing's much better, and the players, too. It's not as one-sided as in your time. Even in the Southwestern Conference and the Southeastern. Nothing's that sure anymore. ... Listen, I can't really talk now. ... Hello, may I speak to Max Brown, please? ... Hello, Max? ... I just spoke to Duke Delsener. Did you know he's going for the one hundredth win of his coaching career tonight? ... Hello, Solomon? I just spoke to Roger Brantley. ... He says Swish Gibbs and Billy Duval are playing super. That Boone's a different team this year. Eddie Zeno says the same thing. It looks to me like Nathan Rubin finally has the makings down there. Yeah, I think you should bet them tonight. ... But Solomon, don't go overboard—remember, Boone's still a very young team. They've got a lot to prove. Besides, they're going against McDaniel State tonight, and they recruited three super freshmen. ... Oh hi, McDuff. How you feeling? Yeah, I know how rough you've had it. Isaac Pizer told me. He said you're getting out of the hospital next week and you're marrying Marsha again. Congratulations, McDuff. ... No, I don't think so, McDuff. I'm sorry, but I just don't like trading games. ... Hello, Eddie? Larry Hollerman just told me his kids are mad as hell. It seems one of the local papers reported he's going to be fired if his team loses any more games. You know how everyone loves Hollerman. His kids will go through a brick wall for him tonight. ... Hello, Mrs. Hollerman, is the coach home? ... Oh, well, how'd the game go tonight? That's great, Mrs. Hollerman, tell the coach I called. ... Hello? ... Oh, hi, Pizer. ... Yeah, I'm busy now. ... No, I don't have any special games for you tonight. ... Yeah, I've been doing real well. ... What? ... No, I haven't been doing that well. ... Look, you know the Colonel, he throws a lot of sludge. ... Okay, okay, I'll have dinner with you tonight."

David and Isaac Pizer had dinner.

"You know the kind of man I am, David. I'm the type of guy who either likes someone or doesn't." He paused and leaned forward. "And if you're my friend you can call me at four in the morning and I'll be there. That's the kind of man I am. A man of character." He puffed on his cigar. "Now, I can understand your not wanting to give your games to Nathan Rubin. I've met very few men in my life who didn't have at least one thing redeeming about them." He shrugged. "They're gentlemen with their mothers, or give charity, or are loyal to their friends, but that Nathan Rubin ..." He shook his head again. "He's drek!"

Isaac Pizer badgered David all evening for games. He kept asking for special favors, kept insisting he could be helpful. To David's mind he was very conscious of the fact that though they spoke in a friendly way, Isaac Pizer, like Nathan Rubin, was a killer, and had the sure instinct for the jugular, and that the friendly talk was not friendly but guardedly respectful.

"I'll call you if I get something extra-good, Pizer, okay? ... Yeah, I promise!"

"Hello? ... Mr. Rubin! Geez, I thought you were out of town.... You are! How's Harriet? ... Oh, I've been doing okay, but I'll tell you, I can use another out. Do you have anyone in the city you'd recommend? ... No, Mr. Rubin, I don't want to bet through Sandy Rocca. I want to be the one placing and moving the bets. I don't want to get caught by any wise guy, especially Rocca, with bad numbers. The only thing that would happen then is that he'd get rich by scalping points at my expense. Don't you have a regular BM you can recommend? ... Crooked Dollar Moishe? ... Okay, have him call me tomorrow afternoon.... What's that? ... That's right, I've been giving Solomon some games.... I know I haven't been calling Sandy Rocca. I've been too busy.... Okay, okay, Mr. Rubin, I'll call him more often.... Hello, Rocca? I thought I'd let you know I'm taking Dayton with the two. I think the Flyers will do a lot better at home tonight.... Look, Rocca, I don't have time to give you reasons now. It's Saturday! You know how much action there is.... Okay, okay, calm down.... One more thing, Rocca—don't bet with Crooked Dollar Moishe. I just did. He's probably knocked down the price already.... Give my regards to the old man.... Hello? ... Oh, hi, Pizer...."

Dialing area code 512 ... "Hello, is this Boone College?"

"Sorry, the main switchboard is closed for the night."

"Hello, is this the community store?"

"J.T. speakin', what can I do for you?"

"Remember me, J.T.? I'm the guy from New York. How'd the game go tonight? ... Thanks, J.T., thanks a lot."

"Hello, is this Villanova? How's the game going tonight? ... Hello, Zeno? ... Did you get the finals? ... Yeah, sixty-two to fifty-six, Villanova ... and Boone won also, eighty-seven to eighty-four in overtime.... Ya God damn right I know what I'm doing! Yeah, I'm sure!"

Every week he reorganized and expanded, and reminded himself that inside information on college basketball is meaningful. Unlike such information in football or baseball, the bookies do not ignore it, they run away from it. Those swine will take a hot game off the board in a minute, David thought. Many times they won't even deal them. They're more frightened of "hot games" than they are of the IRS. Bookies make their money not because they get inside information but because they get the 11–10.

230 ...

Screw Debbie, screw Leslie, screw everyone. I'm going to handicap, that's all I'm going to do. And I'm going to make money, real money. I don't need anyone. I told people in the beginning that I'd win, that I needed their help, that everyone involved would make a fortune. They smiled, snickered, nodded, mocked, chuckled, and didn't listen.

No one except Doug gave me a nickel. Not even Solomon Lepidus. Not even the Colonel. Everyone wanted proof of what I could do. Everyone adopted a wait-and-see attitude. They wanted guarantees. Doug said that when I sour-graped them, if I expected anything, I was still in need of "mommy's nipple"; and that whatever I did, I should do it for myself, and that went at least as much for my handicapping as it did for my writing or living in general.

Every Sunday David had his lox, bagels, and whitefish at the Colonel's. Every Sunday he told him how he was doing. Every Sunday the Colonel multiplied David's profit tenfold. If he made $1,000 for the week, the Colonel would make it $10,000. Inevitably guys began calling David more and more for games. Even Betblood Willie and Ben Tobin called. The more the Colonel promoted, the more calls he got. Guys he never knew called. Acquaintances of acquaintances started coming out of the woodwork. They begged, flattered, cajoled, bought him dinner, gave him presents, kissed his butt, did everything and anything to get him to give them a game or two. He began playing himself down. He changed his telephone number. He stayed loyal to a select few.

It was in mid-January 1972 when Max Brown began calling him regularly for games. By February, Max Brown had already returned the favor by telling David to "cheer" for a particular team. Usually that particular team won handily. When Max Brown called he was casual and smug. He acted as if the games had already been played. David asked no questions, bet on the games heavily, and would invariably win.

Unfortunately, Brown told David to "cheer" only four times during the entire season.

David Lazar was riding a crest. The bookies called him: not as the old days, to badger him to pay his debts, but to the minute at appointed times, to book his bets. He called the bookies: not as in the old days, to beg time to pay his debts, but to make arrangements to collect his winnings.

"Hi, Johnny, how are you? . . . Thanks! . . . Hi, Joey A., how are you? . . . Thanks! . . . Hi, Moishe, how are you? . . . Thanks!"

Did you ever splash along in the rain and laugh? Carry home a brown paper bag crammed full of money? Collect green every week? Did you ever shake crumpled $10 and $20 and $50 and $100 bills out of a bag onto a bed and count and count and count? Fling down piles of money and rake the bills in with your own two hands? Feel an indescribable glee? Did you ever see your brother with his mouth open, speechless, too flabbergasted to talk

. . . 231

about what you've accomplished? Laugh with him? Tease him? Did you ever win and win and win? David Lazar did.

He would shout to himself in his dreams, "Tell every godforsaken analyst I'm not looking to conform. I'm looking to express I'm me, God damn it. Me. I love it. I'm different. I'm original. I'm eccentric. I'm unique. I don't want to conform. I never did. I'm me, a handicapper. David Bernard Lazar. *The Handicapper!*"

27

IN MARCH, David had an altercation with Angelo "One-Eye" Scarne. The dispute was over an LSU–Tennessee game. One-Eye's clerk said David had bet $1,500 on Louisiana State, taking 1½ points. David claimed he had wagered $1,500 on Tennessee, laying the 1½ points. Tennessee won the game 78–66. The difference was $3,150 in cash, and David refused to pay. Since they both knew Solomon Lepidus, David suggested that he act as arbitrator. One-Eye agreed, and soon after the three of them met at Wally's Restaurant to resolve the dilemma.

One-Eye had a swarthy complexion, a heavy beard, and layers of loose flesh hanging from a massive frame. His voice was surly.

"The kid bet LSU, Mr. Lepidus. There's no question about it."

"That's not true, Solomon. There's no way in the world I'd have bet against Tennessee."

David turned toward One-Eye and said, "I wouldn't make a false claim, Scarne. I'm a professional. You can check me out with anyone you want. You'll find I'm as honest as you get."

One-Eye Scarne's brow furrowed; his face creased in a greasy smile. "Come on, Lazar, do the right thing. You know what's right."

"I'm telling you, Scarne," David yelled excitedly. "I had Tennessee."

Scarne stared at David, then turned to face Solomon. In a grim tone he said, "What do you think, Mr. Lepidus?"

"He's a professional, One-Eye. If it was a mistake, your clerk probably made it, not Davy."

Scarne's face flushed with anger. "My clerk is under strict orders to repeat everything. He only writes what he hears. If he didn't I'd rip his ears off. As God is my judge, Mr. Lepidus, I'm not out to steal from anyone."

Scarne glared at David, and David glared back. David couldn't take his two eyes off Scarne's one. Scarne looked at Solomon and said in a voice thick with repressed rage, "My clerks never make mistakes, Mr. Lepidus. In five years I've never paid a claim. This guy has to have made the mistake. He's into us for over three grand as it is. I want to get paid."

Scarne turned and glared at David again. David hated his coarse ugly face, the carnal superiority of his ignorance. David looked at him and egged him on. "I don't make mistakes either. I'm not paying a dime, Solomon."

At that moment David thought to himself, If I can't make a million off scum like One-Eye, what's all my handicapping been for?

And right then One-Eye screamed, "Who the fuck is this punk?"

And David yelled back, "I'm a man who's read Dostoevsky, that's who I am."

A moment later a thought crossed his mind, and David asked himself if beating this retard was really worth it. But he immediately eliminated that brain wave.

At the same time Solomon said, "In my opinion, One-Eye, you should take the loss."

One-Eye responded by turning toward Solomon and gesturing with his palms up, shrugging his shoulders a little. As he did so, he said, "What are you trying to do, Mr. Lepidus, stop me from making a living?" As if he were as innocent as a lamb.

David looked at him and thought, He's an animal, an animal! And a second later asked himself: What am I?

One-Eye continued talking to Solomon. "What's this creep got on you, Mr. Lepidus? Who is he?"

"I told you, I'm a man who's read Dostoevsky," David repeated, and as One-Eye pivoted to confront David, his one beady eye shining with hate, David got up and walked away.

Later that night, Solomon called and said he had settled with One-Eye by paying him $1,600. David told Solomon he'd pay him back the $1,600 and that he wouldn't deal with One-Eye's office again.

"Don't be silly, Davy boy, that's the nature of the business. Nobody's going to hold any grudges. Scarne's got a good office. Use it!"

"How can you have friends like that, Solomon?" David asked.

"What do you mean?"

"They're animals. They're not people, they're scum."

"You don't understand, Davy boy."

"What don't I understand, Solomon?"

"You don't have to marry a guy to do business with him. You never really had anything to worry about, Davy. Guys like Angelo Scarne are all mob-connected. What you have to do is learn how they think."

"What do you mean, Solomon?"

"Just this. They know screaming and threatening don't mean anything anymore. Nowadays the only time you have to worry is when they don't threaten you."

Before the conversation ended David found himself telling Solomon for the thousandth time, "Walk away from your business, rediscover your wife, spend time with your daughters, with your friends. Relax, enjoy."

"You don't understand, Davy boy. I got obligations. I got a business. I got employees. I got responsibilities."

"That's all sludge, Solomon! Face it. You're justifying what you are, rather than taking the time to find out who you are."

"You don't understand, Davy boy. You don't understand."

David's conversation with Solomon ended. For some reason, something Doug had once said to Leslie, after she had told him she loved David, popped into his mind. "You don't love him, you hate him. Your only problem is you're too much of a coward to admit it, even to yourself."

David began wondering if he felt that way about Solomon Lepidus. Soon he was thinking about how Solomon always cut him off whenever he started to speak about the fear and the humiliation and the squalor and the poverty of the people in the ghetto. Solomon wanted to know nothing of Harlem, where human potential was being wasted every day, where suffering was prolonged for a lifetime; and yet he was a Jew and aware of the Nazis and the camps.

Solomon asked David about the Boone–Western game. "Yeah, I'd lay the three and a half on Western. Boone's had a good season, Solomon, but Western is still a much better club. Remember, Solomon, they still got Sky Davis." David stopped wondering about Solomon Lepidus.

Solomon did not wonder about David; he acted.

"Hello, Nathan? What's doing? . . . Yeah, I've been kind of busy. I haven't made a bet in weeks. Well, I'm open to a proposition if you have one I like. . . . Oh, Boone's playing Western tonight? I didn't know. What's the points? Four and a half? Who do you like? . . . Okay, okay, I know who you want. How much you want to bet on Boone? . . . Fifteen thou? . . . Okay with me. I got Western minus the four and a half for fifteen thousand, right, Nathan? . . . yeah, you can come up to the office tomorrow and collect if I lose. Take it easy, Nathan."

And later that evening: "Hello, Davy boy, what's doing? . . . Say,

Davy boy, did you get a final score on the Boone–Western game tonight? I can't get it anywhere. . . . Ya did? Who won?"

"It's a funny thing your calling up at this time, Solomon. I just got off the phone with some guy called J.T. down in Boone. You wouldn't believe it, but the only way to get a score on the Boone games is to call him up at the community store. He clerks and boards there, I guess. He's a nice ol' guy, Solomon, and he attends every Boone home game."

"Who won, Davy boy? Who won?"

"Don't sweat it, Solomon. You won. The final score was eighty-three to seventy-four. Western was ahead by ten or more the entire second half. They were leading by sixteen with two minutes to go when they took Sky Davis out. That's when Boone cut it to nine. Ya know, Solomon, Nathan Rubin must be going crazy. How many times in a row is it now that you won taking Western over Boone? Say, Solomon, have you seen Rubin's new girlfriend? Isn't that Harriet Barash fantastic?"

"Talk to you later, Davy boy. Take it easy."

And as for Nathan Rubin . . .

"Leave me alone, Sandy. Leave me alone."

"What's the matter with you, Nathan? It's just one lousy game."

"Listen, Sandy, get Sam Boone on the phone. I don't care what time it is. Wake him up," Nathan snarled.

"Listen, Sam, I just got the score from Josh. What the hell's the matter with those jigs? God damn it, Sam, do you know how much money you've cost me? . . . What? . . . Hold on, Sam. . . . Yeah, Sandy, good idea, make me a whiskey on the rocks. And Sandy, call up Saskia and Odette. Tell them to come over. Yeah, right now!

"Sam . . . answer me this. Do you know how many games we lost to that Western team in a row? . . . That's right, Sam, *eleven!* Well, I want things to change, Sam, do you understand?"

It was around that time that Eddie Zeno's partner, Mark Jagerman, telephoned David from Chicago. "Listen to me, Lazar. I want you to call me from a pay phone later tonight. It's important!"

When David called, Jagerman told him about his "boys." He represented some of the prime meat in the pro marketplace now that he had merged with another flesh-peddling agency. He told him about his boys' domestic problems: wives who were ripping them off for large sums in alimony; girlfriends they had gone ape over and given more money to than they could afford. He told David about hushed-up paternity suits. Two of his boys in particular had fathered out of wedlock on more than one occasion and had paid the women off.

He told David about other boys who had mismanaged their money by pissing away thousands on cars, apartments, clothes, cocaine, and other costly habits, as if there were no tomorrow. He told David how they partied and made scenes and needed cash, how they always needed a lot of cash. He told David how most of them were getting fat and dependent on their $100,000-and-up life-styles. And finally he told David how some of them were "doing business."

"I'm telling you, Lazar, they're doing business! Now, let's make a deal. I can definitely help you."

"How?"

"I can give you the games. There's a lot of fishy business going on, especially now, with almost all the division standings clinched and almost everybody just waiting for the playoffs to begin. Let's get together. I'll give you *my* games and you give me *yours.*"

Mark Jagerman gave him two games. David invested and got buried. David told him to get lost. Jagerman insisted it wasn't his fault. He even went so far as to have one of his boys call long-distance to apologize. The man was a veteran player who in years gone by David had idolized. He was amazed. He guessed he was still a bit naive. The next day he recovered, got down to business, and made a new deal with Jagerman. David would get fifty cents on the dollar for every college game he touted.

David insisted Jagerman get down for the amount he dictated, anywhere from $300 to $2,000. In addition to that, David began using him as a beard.

One immediate advantage was that David started getting and using Jagerman's Chicago line every night. And though the regular season was just about finished, he was able to use it for the NIT as well as NCAA games. The best thing that happened, though, was that Jagerman's Chicago line differed from David's New York line eight times by as much as 3 and 4 points, and on each of those occasions David bet both ways and caught two middles.

By the time the basketball season ended, David had made "important money." He was able to pay off every debt he had. He took a one-bedroom apartment at a rental of $425 a month and furnished it lavishly. He purchased an expensive wardrobe and spent a lot of cash on things he had been deprived of his entire life. He bought presents and gifts for everyone. He gave a couple of thousand to Doug, and then when he looked in his vaults and other hiding places he found he still had $42,800 left.

Still, all the money he had made didn't change everything. Call it insecurity, fear, cowardice, habit, or whatever, each morning he continued to clock into Harlem.

Between nine and ten, while Hymie Rosenblatt did a *New York Times* crossword puzzle, he'd do his research, take notes, compare scores, go over his rules, and catch up on his *Basketball Weekly* and *Basketball News.* After that, he'd do a bit of social work and leave for the field. As soon as he got home he'd begin adjusting his power ratings for the upcoming season.

From his plush private office, Isaac Pizer watched Valerie Caldwell walk down the corridor, turn left, and disappear. He shoved his cigar into his mouth and took a deep puff. Feeling a little better, but still anxious and incomplete, he dwelled on the unapproachable Val Caldwell; on her cool starched flesh and her *Vogue* look; on her mouth; on her huge violet eyes that sometimes seemed intent on drowning him in their softness; on her slender sloping shoulders, her long legs, thick chestnut hair, and superb, youthful breasts. As Isaac Pizer closed his frigid eyes, he saw in his mind Valerie's nakedness, and the faint smell of her perfume came to him, and in his mind he grabbed out at her. He envisioned her biting him, scratching him, kicking, thrashing, and then submitting to him with a whimper. And he dreamed of Valerie using her tongue, lips, and fingers with the eagerness of a sweet sixteen.

"Goodnight, Isaac," Val Caldwell's musical voice sang out, shaking Pizer out of fantasy. His eyes opened wide and his thin lips clamped down on his thick cigar as he gazed at Valerie, who was leaning her svelte body against the rosewood door to his office. She smiled, and her dark fiery eyes seemed to be laughing and playing. "Did I wake you, Isaac?" Valerie smiled. "I just wanted to say goodnight and remind you that Gertrude Robbins is flying in from Los Angeles this weekend. I have an appointment with her Monday morning, nine o-clock sharp. I think you should be there, Isaac." She smiled and touched her upper lip with her tongue. "You sell my line better than I do."

Isaac Pizer gazed at Valerie and bit his stained porcelain teeth into his thick cigar and puffed it into a blaze. He growled irately, "Have a nice weekend, Valerie." She waved and disappeared.

Pizer returned his cigar to his mouth and took a deep voluptuous puff. He smiled to himself as he thought of something Valerie had recently told him. "I used to get up at three-thirty in the morning to get to the berry bus, Isaac. We had to be at work by five-thirty. And then we berry pickers would have to work until three or four in the afternoon, on our knees, hunched over. I didn't want to remain on my knees for the rest of my life, Isaac. My ambition was always to be a jewelry designer. It was never to be a berry boss."

Soon Isaac Pizer's calculating mind began to focus on how he could get Valerie to respond to him, to see him as a man. On the top of his desk, written on a memo pad, he noticed the name of the hotel he'd be staying at for the Basel Jewelry Fair in Switzerland. Valerie could go. It would be a business trip, another opportunity for—who knew what? Isaac Pizer continued puffing luxuriously on his thick cigar, blowing smoke into the air.

Meanwhile, Valerie Caldwell had hurried to meet her date. After cocktails at the Metropolitan Club and dinner at Perrotti's on Columbus Avenue, she and the man with the strawberry-blond hair returned to his apartment.

The man with the strawberry-blond hair stretched to open a night-table drawer to take out a box of amyl nitrates. He snapped one and carefully handed it to Valerie Caldwell. Valerie quickly held it to her nostrils and took three deep hungry sniffs. Within moments, she felt the rush to her head and was high. She began giggling uncontrollably.

The man grinned and quickly snapped another nitrate and sucked at it greedily. Soon he too felt the rush. His face began to flush. Valerie kneeled weakly and bent forward to rest her elbows across a flesh-colored hassock, and then the man got up and walked around so that he was in back of her. Raising her buttocks as high as he could, he spread her cheeks apart and then thrust his cock deep inside. Valerie gasped and gasped to the rhythm of his shaft.

Later, Valerie sniffed another popper and laughed. "I'm real high now. Let's do something kinky." She jumped off the bed and changed from the nude into a diaphanous black silk shirt, which she left unfastened except for a knot tied loosely around her midriff. And then she got into a lacy panty that covered her own silk and fur and rounded cheeks. Finally, adding the finishing touch to her outfit, she pulled on knee-high vinyl boots and fingered a bamboo whip in her hand. For a second she stood above the man, glowing in perfect enchantment. And then Valerie leaned down and struck him again and again on his bare flanks, until he rolled over and removed her flimsy armor and pulled her down, spreading her legs apart and licking her chestnut cunt. Then she took his face in her hands and kissed him with her open mouth, using her soft tongue, whispering, "Go inside. Go inside." The man leaned backward, using the king-sized bed for support. He snapped another popper and sniffed it, and then handed it to Val. Moments later, Valerie, with her lilac mouth opened wide and her violet eyes closed, reached for the man's penis, grabbed it, and guided it between her legs.

"Yeah, Nathan, Valerie went to Basel for the jewelry fair, and it cost me, all right. You're damn right she was the most talented designer I ever had. You know what the Caldwell line did for me last year? . . . What happened? She met this Lebanese bastard while she was in Basel and flew to Paris with him. They ended up getting married a week later. You know how it is, Nathan. The money these Arabs have is phenomenal."

Pizer flicked some ashes from his cigar. "The Arab's going to finance Val to an international Caldwell line. She won't be a designer anymore." He sneered. "She'll be a competitor." He shook his head and sighed. "You know Val—she was always all business. You could never get to her. . . .

Well, let me tell you, Nathan, Val Caldwell was one sharp dame. You know, four years ago she was pickin' berries on a farm in Oregon. . . . Nah, I never went to bed with her. You know me, Nathan, business comes first."

In the fall of 1972, David had dinner out almost every night with Solomon, the Colonel, Isaac Pizer, and Nathan Rubin. Usually he was escorting one or another of the women he considered trophies: a Swedish blonde who had finished quite high in the Miss Universe contest a few years back, or a West Indian woman with the most mellifluous accent he had ever heard. He was also becoming a real clotheshorse and regularly frequented St. Tropez, DeNoyer's, Madonna's, and Pierre Balmain. And for that little bit extra, he was getting razor cuts at Dominique's every week at $25 a shot. It wasn't long before he began to say to Doug, "Art doesn't pay, crime does!" Doug always answered him with the same Socratic broken record: "Is this what you won for?" Many times, while lying on his water bed with his hands behind his head, he would consider what Doug had said.

Beginning the first week in November, his telephone didn't stop ringing. Again guys he knew, and guys he didn't, started coming out of the woodwork to call. Each with one objective—to arrange a deal so they could get a chunk of his flesh. Some begged, some cajoled, some made subtle or not so subtle threats. All promised him a large percentage of the profits.

Each of these conversations ended with David's saying he wasn't becoming a broker. From complete strangers he demanded a $3,000 service fee in advance, win or lose. He also demanded 60 percent of the profits after the first $5,000 in winnings. He told each of them he wasn't looking for any other kind of deal. Some muttered under their breath, some thought he was crazy, some kept calling and trying to negotiate better terms.

By November 20 he had received more than three dozen such calls, and each caller cursed him under his breath. A few desperate ones who kept calling back time and again began to succumb to his extravagant demands. Each time they called they became more insistent and their offers became larger and larger. David continued to say no to everyone.

David made deals with only seven men. He arranged a fifty-fifty split on all profits with six of them, and discussed the management of their money in depth. Each had a particular philosophy of gambling which they expected him to adhere to, a particular financial goal. He demanded that each of them put up every dollar in advance. The seventh client he accepted was Nathan Rubin. He made a special deal with him.

Nathan Rubin would put up two-thirds of the money and David one-third, and their profit at the end of the season would be split down the middle. The percentage in David's favor would be approximately 17 percent. The reason he took the deal was ego. He wanted to be one of the very few, if not the only one, who ever got the best of a deal with Nathan Rubin.

* * *

From Solomon Lepidus David got $90,000 in cash on November 21. From Sandy Rocca he collected $25,000. From the Colonel, $10,000. From Isaac Pizer, $10,000. From Roger Brantley, $10,000. From Douglas Alan Lazar, $5,000. David told Doug that he didn't want his money, that he could stake him to his share. Doug insisted on putting up his own money. And from Nathan Rubin David got $66,665, which he agreed to put in the Colonel's safe along with his matching one-third obligation of $33,335.

David brought his share to the Colonel's office. Nathan Rubin was there. He grabbed the money, clutched it, counted out every dollar with his huge, greedy hands. It took him twenty minutes. The entire time his penurious eyes remained riveted to the bills and his lips quivered and moved to the rhythm of the count. It seemed as if he were capable of shutting out the entire world except for those dollars. After he counted David's share, David counted his.

David took twice as long as Rubin had, perhaps fifty minutes, and teased him and humored him all the way. At one point, David went too far, irritated him to such an extent that he was on the verge of calling off the partnership, but the Colonel came over laughing, and said, "Nathan, come on, where's your sense of humor? David didn't mean anything."

Nathan Rubin calmed down. The Colonel could charm anyone. Finally, after the tension was released, they all laughed and Nathan Rubin directed David to an empty corner in the office and suggested strongly that they check their games and the points every evening.

David suspected Nathan would watch him like a hawk, and he did. Solomon Lepidus, on the other hand, told him to do with his money as he wanted, and not to give him any figures until the season was over. He specified that at the end of the season all he should do was give him a bottom-line figure. David told him he didn't want that kind of responsibility. Solomon laughed. Solomon insisted. Solomon was that kind of man.

Thus, when it was all added up, David began the 1972–1973 college basketball season with a quarter of a million dollars. Almost every dollar other than the $100,000 deposited in the Colonel's safe, David vaulted. He got ready to invest for his clients. He got ready to win. He set up individual accounts in his notebook with individual ledgers and worked out wagering plans for each person individually.

Each person's goals were considered. Roger Brantley and Isaac Pizer told him to be conservative. Nathan Rubin said to check with him every day before doing anything. Solomon wanted him to go for broke. Sandy Rocca and the Colonel said to be careful and not to go overboard on any one game. His twin brother told him to do what he thought best.

David warned everyone that they would not necessarily be wagering on the same games. He wasn't taking any chances on losing for everyone as well as for himself on the same stupid games. David had six telephones installed in his apartment by the telephone company. Every phone had an unlisted number. David then proceeded to give out different telephone numbers to different people. Two of the numbers he kept for himself. The only people he gave those numbers to were Doug and Solomon. Finally, during the last week in November, he worked feverishly throughout every night. He organized, refined, and streamlined his entire operation. He completed his handbook. He primed and galvanized himself and at long last felt ready for the opening of his third college basketball season as a handicapper.

28

EARLY IN DECEMBER, David dropped in on Ed Kashman at his pharmacy. In the store with him were two large unsightly men. They turned toward David when they heard him yell, "Hi, Kashman." Then they turned back toward Ed. "Who's dat guy, Kashman?" one of them said in a dumb flat voice.

"He's okay, he's just a friend of mine."

The larger of the two walked around the corner to where Ed was standing and pointed a finger at him. "Get this straight, Kashman, we ain't just playing with you. You got one more week to come up with the rest of the money or else it's gonna be your ass."

David could hear every word, and immediately something began to churn in his stomach.

"Hey, Ed, who are these guys? What the hell do they want with you?"

Ed didn't answer, and David began walking toward the counter where Kashman was standing. As Kashman saw David coming, he motioned for him to stay where he was. "Don't worry, kid, they're just some guys I know."

The smaller of the two men pivoted to face David. "Stay out of this, buddy, unless you want your fuckin' balls cut off." As he said it, he glared directly at David.

David felt anger growing. "Who the hell are you?" he answered in a voice filled with disdain.

The smaller man slowly removed from his coat pocket a switchblade knife, which he snapped open. The glittering blade was at least five inches long. He continued to glare at David, and his facial muscles tightened as he grimaced. The veins on his forehead bulged. When he opened his mouth to threaten David, David noticed his many rotten teeth. As he cursed and spewed out abuse, David found himself fixing his eyes on his large Adam's apple, which bobbed up and down, and in and out. He pointed his knife within an inch of David's throat and ordered him not to move. His partner continued threatening Ed.

"Listen, Kashman, Carmine told us you never gave him any trouble before, so we're being nice to you, but you'd better come up with the six dimes or else your ass is in a sling." He stopped. "Another thing, if you ever try pulling a bullshit claim again . . ." The huge man hesitated for a moment before saying, "Just don't!"

David peered at Ed and noticed for the first time since he had walked into the store how much he had deteriorated since his last visit.

The vulture holding the knife in front of David returned the blade to his coat pocket and slowly walked toward his partner, all the time keeping a menacing eye on David. He advised him that they had another stop to make and that they were already late. The hoods exchanged nods and simultaneously began to walk out of the store. Only they didn't. The smaller one, the vulture with the switchblade, reached out instead and removed a bottle of aspirins from one of Ed's shelves. "All this garbage don't make you pigeon shit, Kashman," he snarled. "What the fuck, you might as well use it to feed the pigeons."

He opened the bottle, took out the cotton ball, and began tossing aspirins on the floor, acting all the time as if he were actually feeding pigeons. When the bottle was empty he looked at his partner and smirked.

"Where are all the pigeons, Russo? What the fuck, I'll bet they'd like these aspirins."

Both of them began to laugh. Then they continued to walk out of the store, and as they did, they both methodically stepped on and crushed all the aspirins in their path. Passing David in the aisle, the one called Russo pushed into him hard, and David stumbled against one of Ed's shelves. He couldn't regain his balance. Two shelves crashed to the floor, spilling pharmaceuticals all about and splattering bottles of glass.

"Excuse me, buddy," Russo said, then he wheeled and directed his gaze contemptuously at Ed. "You got a week, Kashman," and then both of them were out the door.

For a few minutes neither David nor Ed Kashman said a word. They just stood there numbly. Finally, because David felt it would do Kashman good to talk, he initiated a conversation.

"What happened, Ed?"

"I went over my head, kid. I became stupid. I didn't take a rest. I'll come up with the six thousand, though. I ain't fooling around with those guys. I should never have started up with that Carmine. I knew beforehand the kind of office that guinea runs."

Both of them walked behind the counter and sat down in the back of the store. "And you're the guy who always told me to deal directly with independents, and to take a rest whenever things went bad."

The second David said it he knew how foolish it sounded, and he felt bad, but Ed, who might have resented such a statement at another time in his life, now seemed crushed by it. All he could do was shake his head and wipe his brow and mumble forlornly, "I know. I know."

"I thought you salted away a mint through the years, Ed. What happened to all your stocks and bonds?"

"Are you kidding? Don't you know what's been happening in this country? I had so many margin calls I'm just about wiped out. I'm going to have to sell off the rest of my bonds just to pay off those bastards." He looked at David with a face filled with anguish and despair. "I got nothing left, kid. I'm as good as buried."

The resignation in his voice frightened David and also made him realize that he had to do something for him. He thought for a few minutes while Kashman served a customer.

When Kashman returned, David said, "Listen to me, Ed. A little while ago I got Vegas's opening line from one of my contacts. There's a game tonight I like very much. It's going to be six and a half or seven. I want you to take Tulsa with the points. They're playing the Billikins at St. Louis. At least you'll have everything going for you. When I find a mistake in the line this large, I win more than eighty percent of the time. I'll tell you what I'll do, 'Kash-Man,' " David said in a voice reminiscent of yesteryear. "I'll stake you to a ten-dime bet."

Ed Kashman looked at David as if he were crazy. He refused to let him go for that kind of bread. David told him how well he'd been doing and how he felt he owed a lot of his success to him. He spoke to him quietly for at least fifteen minutes, reminding him how close they'd been in the past, and how he had always looked up to him, and still considered him his mentor. David made him feel as if he owed him, and finally Kashman agreed.

That evening David called Ed Kashman at his home.

"Hello, Ed. Tulsa won the whole damn game. The final score was sixty-eight to sixty-seven. It was a close game all the way, just as I figured.

I'll come over to your place tomorrow evening to give you the ten thousand. But from now on, Ed, please, do me one favor?"

"What's that?"

"Don't make a bet on a college game unless I call you first."

When he went over to Ed Kashman's he arranged to have him beard for him. David insisted he use only independent offices. When David handed him his money, Ed's voice went soft as he said, "Thanks, kid."

29

WHEN HE was a boy, even when he went to college, David Lazar always was sure of what he didn't want, but never of what he did want: He was sure he didn't want to become a businessman. But during the 1972–1973 season he did nothing but think, eat, breathe, live, love, loathe business; that's all he did. He maneuvered, manipulated, exploited, "cheered," invested, picked winners. He reinvested, recapitalized, reorganized, expanded, ran a business. He was as profit-cruel as any tycoon, as mercenary as any Hessian. His actions in the war zone proved it every day. Assuredly, he was a businessman.

David was betting important money, and winning important money. As was his practice, he vaulted all profits and started each new investment cycle with the principal. Every day was collection day. Brown paper bag in hand, he met bookmakers in front of the Winter Garden, or at subway stations—Columbus Circle, Sheridan Square, Ninety-sixth Street and Broadway, DeKalb Avenue. He met beards at bars, in front of movie houses, at the Brasserie, at Radio City Music Hall, at the Gulf and Western Building, Chandler's, Mama Leone's, Elaine's, "21," at 118th Street and Lexington Avenue, under the clock in front of the Sherry-Netherland, at 115 Wall Street, at Alexander's in Forest Hills.

In the lobby of Mount Sinai Hospital, at the lion's cages in Central Park Zoo, he would pick up the money, stuff the cash in a brown paper bag, and quickly walk away. He would guard it, sometimes ducking behind a bush or tree or corner to hide it inside his socks or shoes. He got a permit to carry a .38 caliber revolver in a shoulder holster inside his jacket. A million times he would look over his shoulder.

He tried to make certain not to hurt any one bookmaker; to divide the action among as many books and beards as possible; to take every precaution to make no one suspicious. On the many occasions he used out-of-town outs, he would have money orders flying in and going out by special delivery, and sometimes he even made airplane trips if the situation warranted.

He took painstaking efforts to make certain that every book thought he was married to his office, that every beard thought he was one of his very few outs. He issued different phone numbers, different time schedules, different codes. He demanded that all calls be made to him on the minute. If a beard phoned late, he didn't remind him of his tardiness, he just stopped using him. As a rule of thumb, he changed most of his employees regularly. A few bookmakers, such as Tony Giardello, and "best friend" Johnny, and Johnny's boss, Nino Tafuri, knew David was big, but no one knew how big.

It all came and went so fast; the days, the weeks, the months, the entire 1972–1973 season. All of it went by like a jet. It was just a matter of doing his homework, following the formula that had proved so successful to him in the past.

First and foremost, David would spot the game which was out of line with his power rating and information. Then he would get money down; then he would collect; then he would enlarge the entire operation and redo everything again. It seemed easy. Ted Williams made hitting a ninety-mile-an-hour fastball seem easy.

David had never seen this kind of money in his life. This was cash money, nontaxed. The only catch was that he had to start betting more money than he wanted to with Angelo "One-Eye" Scarne and a great many other hard-core Syndicate men, and he could feel the slime beginning to stick. He tried to shower it off by answering his own as well as Doug's "Is this what you won for?" He told himself that one day he would walk away and do constructive things with the money he made. Maybe set up a foundation for the arts or a scholarship fund for starving writers.

"That's what I want to do, Doug—help people, help artists, help my friends, help humanity."

He found it necessary to daydream about doing a million things, and then he'd locate a mistake in the Vegas line and return to the realities of running his operation.

He continued to take every precaution. He changed his telephone numbers regularly. He had special phones hooked up by a friend of Solomon's at the nominal price of $500 per phone. He placed an order for a dozen installations at different locations and left instructions to increase that order on an as-needed basis. Solomon guaranteed him that the phones would be wired and that the telephone company would never bill him. As usual, Solomon was right. He coded his messages when he had to relay information to beards. He worked out of cheap railroad-flat apartments which he sublet from welfare clients throughout Manhattan, and he alternated his use of them regularly. He allowed no one, not even Doug, to know the size of his operation. He didn't want Doug to worry. He continued to find and train new beards. He tried to make every person feel as if he were a friend just doing him a small favor. He gave each one a soft sell in the beginning, but after they were hooked by that first taste of winning, he drilled each of them with the singlemindedness of a marine sergeant.

David made certain everyone in his organization knew his responsibilities, no more and no less. Then he used them on an as-needed basis and made certain to rotate them regularly. He also made especially sure that not one beard knew any of the other beards he was using; and he was doubly careful to make certain that he didn't get screwed on the numbers or on the collection of the gold.

He controlled everything, never gave any one beard or BM a wager of more than one or two dimes. He never told anyone which games were his hot games, double bets, triple bets, special games, very best bets, or "cheering" games. As far as anybody knew, his bets were always for the same amount. That way he made sure as hell no wise guy would be able to read his action. He learned that trick as well as many others from Champ Holden.

Of course, for the beards he used, it was a good deal, too. The reasons were obvious. First of all, the men he selected were pretty damn sharp. They knew how to shop around for prices. Second, they were usually experienced bettors in their own right, and getting games for themselves could only help. Third, the games he gave them were usually not hot games, because by the middle of January 1973, he wasn't concentrating his wagering in any one city in order to avoid the bookmakers' major weapon in college basketball: changing his numbers, limiting the bet, or taking the game off the board.

As usual, Nathan Rubin and Solomon Lepidus made their annual man-to-man wager on the Western–Boone game. Both men telephoned their handicapper for his opinion.

"I don't have any opinion on the game, Nathan," David said. "I know it's important to you. It's your team, but I just can't tell you I like one side or the other if I don't. Listen, Nathan, to me the line's right. It's a six-point game. You gotta understand, Sky Davis has turned into one of the most complete players in the country. He more than makes up for Swish Gibbs. Beasley and Crawford are good players, Nathan, but they're undisciplined. Billy Duval still does all that one-on-one garbage that belongs in a playground in East New York. . . . I don't give a damn what Sandy Rocca thinks. . . . Look, Nathan, I respect Champ Holden, but . . . Believe me, Nathan, if Solomon calls I won't tell him anything different."

"Hello, Solomon? . . . It's time for that little bet of ours. Western's playing Boone tonight. Now listen to me, Solomon, this is the proposition I'm gonna give you. Now remember, Solomon, the game's being played on Western's home court this year, and they're still only a seven-and-a-half-point favorite. Just the same, I'm gonna take Boone, but rather than give me seven and a half points I want you to give me twelve and a half. Ya see, Solomon, for that I'll give you seven to five for twenty thousand. Is it a deal, Solomon?"

"Hold on just a second, Nathan. I got to make one call."

"Hello, Davy boy? Who do you like tonight in the Western–Boone game?"

"I already told you, Solomon, the only game I'm betting is the Colorado State game."

"I know, Davy boy, but who do you like in the Western game?"

"Western's a six-point favorite, Solomon, and that's the right number. They're a strong homer."

"Nathan Rubin wants to bet me twenty thou, Davy. He's willing to lay me seven to five if I give him twelve and a half points. What do you think?"

"It's a sucker bet, Solomon. Just a tease. The odds neutralize the points. In fact, Rubin's getting much the better of the proposition. Don't bet."

"Take it easy, Davy boy. Take it easy."

"Hello, Nathan? You got yourself a bet. I got Western. I'm laying you twelve and a half points. And you're giving me seven-to-five odds on my twenty thou. Right?"

"That's correct, Solomon. And remember, if I win I'll be comin' up to your office tomorrow morning to collect."

"Whatever you say, Nathan boy. Take it easy."

"WINS news time, twelve-fifteen and time for sports! This report just in. . . . All-American Sky Davis scored forty-three points tonight leading Western University to a one-oh-three-to-ninety win over archrival Boone College."

* * *

Minutes after Nathan Rubin received the Western–Boone score, Sandy Rocca was saying, "Nathan, calm down. It's just a lousy game. Nathan! Remember what the doc said about getting yourself upset."

Nathan Rubin glared at Rocca.

Rocca walked over to the bar and poured Nathan a whiskey on the rocks. "Here's a drink, Nathan. Is there anything else I can get you?" Nathan didn't move. Rocca placed the drink down on a coffee table and quietly walked to the door, switched off the light, and left.

Nathan Rubin placed his hands on the arms of his Louis XIV tapestry chair and raised himself with difficulty. "Damn these old bones of mine." He limped to the bay window overlooking Fifth Avenue and Central Park. He kicked the radiator under the windowsill with his right foot. "God damn Boone." He peered into the park for ten minutes and watched the snow silently fall. He turned from the window and wandered back to the Louis XIV tapestry chair and sat down, placing his huge hands over the arms of the chair.

He sat without moving a muscle for two hours, just staring straight ahead, thinking, I lost that God damn Boone game for the eleventh, or is it the twelfth, straight time. To Solomon Lepidus." Losing to Nathan Rubin was Death, and winning was Life.

As the clock struck 3:00 A.M., Nathan Rubin began to resurrect himself. Out of his cadaverous mouth came murmurs, jumbled words, ideas, a plan. "God damn it, I ain't gonna die easy. If I got to die it'll be after living. I always said that, God damn it, and I'm still sayin' it. I ain't givin' in. I'm gonna go out a winner. God damn it, if it's the last thing I do I'm gonna win me a Boone–Western game and kill Solomon Lepidus. Everyone's best friend, my ass; he's nothing but a sucker." And then he roared, "God damn doctors. God damn time!"

Nathan Rubin was approaching his eightieth year, and two weeks before he had told his doctor, "I don't want to know what I got, doc, ya can tell my son Charley that. I just want to know, how long?"

At 3:30 in the morning Nathan Rubin began to calculate. "Boone College. . . . The closest coverage comes from the Houston *Gazette*, and that's a morning paper. The only other coverage of Boone's home games comes from the college newsletter and the college radio station. . . . The radio station's in desperate need of more of my money to keep operating. The Associated Press and the United Press don't even use stringers for Boone's games. There isn't even a telecopier on campus. The only way the AP and UPI bureaus in Houston can get the scores is through Sam's son, Billy Mack Boone, who is Sam's sports information director. Billy Mack's never at them games. He's always chasin' after tail. He don't even call them bureaus till the next mornin'."

Nathan Rubin stood up, walked over to the bay window, and peered out at the snow. "Fact: Sam Boone is president of Boone College. Fact: The college switchboard shuts down at six-thirty every evening. Fact: Security police officers man the phones for emergencies only. They have been given an ironclad rule—never give out any information to callers. They must refer all telephone calls to the community store. Fact: Josh Turner runs the community store. Fact: The community store is the only place an out-of-towner can call to get a Boone score. Fact: Josh controls the telephone at the community store. Fact: Sam, as president, controls Coach Rodney Leland, and I control Sam Boone!"

At six-thirty in the morning Nathan Rubin dozed off in his Louis XIV tapestry chair. Before he did he telephoned area code 512.

"Sam? Nathan Rubin. I ain't comin' up with any money for your radio station. Ya see, Sam, I don't need a radio station.

"I'm gonna wire you three thousand, though, for them typewriters you need and for the Nike sneakers you promised Coach Leland. Another thing, Sam—what time do the Boone boys put that newsletter of theirs to bed? . . . Sam, is that correct? The boy assigned to do the reportin' on the Boone home games doesn't phone in a story after the game? . . . No, I ain't angry about that, Sam. That's good news. Really, Sam, very good news. Sam, one other thing. Look up the scheduled date of our game with Western *next year*. And Sam, while you're checkin', make sure the game is being played at Boone. . . . December sixth, eight o'clock? At Rubin Arena? Very good, Sam. Night."

At the end of the 1972–1973 season, after all the baskets and all the dollars were recorded, all of David's people had won a considerable amount of money. Everyone, that is, except for Solomon Lepidus. He had lost. The one guy David loved more than anyone.

David told Solomon how terrible he felt. He told him he insisted on splitting his losses with him fifty-fifty. He paid him back out of his own winnings $27,000. It made him feel better. Much better. He was able to sleep without taking Seconal.

David spoke to his brother about it.

"I don't agree with you, David. Solomon took the same risk you did. You didn't have to pay him back. You know what your problem really is? You've always had a hang-up when it comes to Solomon. And you know Solomon—he takes advantage of everything."

"Listen to me, Doug. It was the only thing I could do. I felt I owed it to Solomon. Everyone else I represented won at least three times what they invested. I won big. You know that. Don't ask me how much. It's unimportant. The important thing is that I won.

"All my power ratings are holding up perfectly. Listen to this, Doug. I made eighty-two bets for the entire year. Nine of them were with a point differential of four and a half or five. Of those, two pushed, and of the remaining seven, four won and three were losers. Now get this: Of the remaining seventy-three games that I invested in I found a five-and-a-half-point differential or more on all of them. Of those I won fifty-eight games and lost only fifteen.

"You know what the winining percentage is on fifty-eight and fifteen? It's . . . What? Damn it! I know I shouldn't have bet on those nine other games. But Solomon talked me into most of them. You know how persuasive he can be. . . . I know. I know. It's bullshit. It wasn't because of Solomon. It was me. I got careless and fucked up a little.

"Now what else do you want to know? . . . The year before? You'll have to hold on while I look up the exact records in my handbook. . . . I was seventy-six and twenty-nine. And don't forget, last year I was still betting a lot of games with a five-point differential. . . . The winning percentage? . . . Wait a sec. . . . Seventy-two point four percent. . . . Max Brown gave me four games to cheer for that year, and we won all four. I am maximizing and minimizing to perfection. I'm finding between eighty and ninety games a year that are worth making a bet on. Listen, Doug, give me five and a half points or more to work with from the Vegas line and I'll make a fuckin' fortune. . . . Yeah, I know I made a lot of money, but I can make a lot more. . . . Quit? Are you crazy! I can make, God damn it, I can make millions! Just wait til' next year, Doug. You'll see.

"Oh, Doug, before I forget, I'm taking off for a week or two. I'm taking that girl I met from Holyoke, Thea Goldstein, to Cannes. I'll be leaving tomorrow morning. Take care."

When the season ended, David began to travel. He took a large black leather attaché case with him, and inside the case were eight large manila envelopes. In each envelope, neatly rubber-banded, were $100 bills. He traveled to eight different cities from Baltimore to San Francisco. He took out eight different safe deposit vault boxes, under eight different names. In each of the bank vaults he placed $100,000. He kept with him in New York City $150,000. David Lazar was certain he could live comfortably on that amount until the next college basketball season.

The evening David returned from his eight-city tour he went straight from Kennedy Airport to his apartment. He dumped the attaché case on the floor and the eight vault keys on top of his desk. He fell into bed fully dressed and was beginning to doze when the phone rang. It was Solomon Lepidus.

"What's doing? . . . I just got a call out of the blue from Esther Aroni. She's married to some fascist shipping magnate and is miserable. I'm meeting her for coffee at Rumplemeyer's in half an hour. . . . Tell Doug, maybe he'll want to come along."

Esther Aroni . . . the disquieting beauty . . .

David telephoned Doug. Doug tried not to show his excitement but immediately hung up so that he could dress and join Esther Aroni and Solomon.

During the off-season, David increased his plans for expansion. In June he traveled to the West Coast and arranged for outs in Los Angeles. While in L.A. he was so busy rounding up contacts and meeting strangers that he had only one free afternoon to spend with Noah and Doris Weldon and their two lovely daughters.

Doris looked the same as the high school girl David remembered. She had the same soft brown eyes, the same slightly weak chin, the same warm, generous smile. The girls were beautiful. Belinda was almost fourteen. Carol was fifteen. Both of them were happy, healthy, and bright.

Noah did not look the same. He was almost as gray as their old high school coach, Mickey Alonzo, and he'd put on about forty pounds. But in other, more important respects, he remained the same. He was still warm, sincere, and filled with life. They reminisced about many things.

"Hey, Noah, remember Arty Garcia?"

"Sure I do." Noah laughed. "He was a wild man. Remember when we went to the Garden and saw Robertson play for the first time? How every time Oscar scored a basket Arty stood up and saluted?"

"Arty died, Noah. I just heard it last week from a friend of Roger Brantley's. He had leukemia."

That news about Arty Garcia put Noah in a somber mood. He started telling David about his own heart problem, which was severe. But that wasn't what bothered him.

"It's getting to me, Dave. I can't sleep nights because of it. Them girls of mine deserve a college education, and I just haven't been able to put away enough. I got to build a nest egg for them and Doris, just in case something bad happens to me. And I got to pay off the mortgage on the house. I'd sure have a lot more peace of mind if I had that off my back."

Before David left, he made Doris promise to bring Noah and the girls to New York before thirteen more years went by. In return, he promised to take them to the theater and to the ballet.

From Los Angeles, David went to Las Vegas to meet with Solomon Lepidus's "friends," and through them he arranged for more outs. Then he visited Houston and Forth Worth, and from Forth Worth, he bused to Abilene to visit another old friend, Jack "Uptight" Frohman, who was teaching at Hardin Simmons University. While in Abilene David stayed at a seedy hotel on the outskirts of the city.

It was evening, quiet and dull. Jack had left David for his home-cooked meal and pregnant wife. David was in his room, alone, remembering when they were younger. After an hour of such retrospection, he rinsed his hot face with lukewarm rusty water and went down to the lobby. He approached the desk clerk, who had a cigarette stub behind his ear and was red-eyed. David bluntly asked for a girl and handed the clerk a twenty. With a light-hearted twang the clerk said, "Yes, sir." As he turned away, David couldn't help noticing the bemused glint in those bloodshot eyes.

A half hour later the "girl" sat in David's room. She was a big-boned woman with large cumbersome hands, thick ankles, horse-faced, with dirty brown hair swept back into a knot. Her pleated blouse opened at the neck, revealing an enormous silver crucifix. She wore a long cement-colored skirt. Her skin, though burned by the sun, still looked only dusty, blending in perfectly with the gloom of the dusty hotel. She edged toward him as he asked her about herself. She told him about her husband, the kind of man he was. She smiled wistfully. "He was a colored boy. . . . Useta play baseball in the black leagues. Josh Gibson was a teammate of his." She looked up and smiled and said softly, "He had tremendous shoulders, giant hands, but he was gentle." She removed from her purse his picture, still in a gilded frame. "So gentle," she whispered, and she closed her eyes for a brief moment.

When she continued, her manner had changed. She snickered defiantly and said curtly, "He was a colored man born in Louisiana who had been a black pimple on an all-white ass until the second he was slaughtered." She again snickered and rubbed the scarred knuckles on her left hand and said, "He never scratched anyone, but the rednecks slaughtered him. They butchered him, and then those same people looked me straight in the eye every day when I walked by. Finally I had to leave Alexandria and come here to live with my aunt. She died a few years back, and now I'm alone."

For a long moment she said nothing and just stared at the wall, looking hostile, but then she took a deep breath and sighed with fatigue and resignation and returned to her matter-of-fact way. She bent her head down and placed her hands behind the nape of her neck and unfastened the silver crucifix, placing it on top of the dresser.

Then she smiled at David, as if to say that she was all right now, and placed her hands once more behind her neck and pulled hairpins out of a muddy nest. She smiled again, an erotic smile on a plain face which was plain no more. The lust began to rise in David. The night began.

Her name was Nora Gynt Jamison. She was earnest, open, and bighearted. The softness of her body and the candor of her voice seduced David, challenged him, unmasked him, created a mood of warmth for him in that gloomy, dirty, arid inn. As she sat and smiled on the side of his bed he realized that he was not hard.

Nora grinned. She took one of her large, warm hands and reached out as if to shake hands with a casual acquaintance she might be greeting at a church meeting or on parents' day at the school. She tenderly closed her hand on his penis and started pulling in a slow rhythm, up and down, up and down. All the time she smiled, talking casually, openly, plainly, freely. Slowly she got him hard.

David took his hands, which were trembling, and unbuttoned her pleated blouse, and he saw her bra and unhooked it as she continued her ministration. The breasts were bountiful and spilled out of their cell, falling from a size forty D cup. They were freckled and soft. One nipple was maroon and looked like a purple grape; the other was concave and looked as if a pink dotted pit was at its center. He quivered. She stood up, and those enormous breasts rejoiced with life. His eyes were riveted to them, and she took his hand and motioned for him to lie down on the bed and relax. She excused herself and went to the toilet. Within minutes, which seemed like hours, she returned in wanton tender nakedness and immediately began her nourishing caresses all over again. She asked him in a husky whisper what he wanted her to do, what pleased him most, and just as he finished answering her she began to tell him what it was that she enjoyed most. She left out nothing. She told him what satisfied her as if she were shopping in a neighborhood grocery.

First she obliged him by doing everything he requested, then she motioned for him to mount her and penetrate. He obliged. Slowly she began to sway. He proceeded with a control and expertise which made it seem as if he had descended from stud heaven in order to please her. And she swooned and bellowed and moaned. And the more she moaned the more pleased he was with himself.

The next morning when he awoke at six he saw Nora Jamison sleeping restlessly. He showered, shaved, and dressed without waking her and left in an envelope under the pillow $1,000 in $50 bills, and he pinned a short note to them.

Dear Nora:
    If you ever get to New York, please be sure to look me up. I appreciate the person you are. Very much, I appreciate the person you are.
                                    David Bernard Lazar

David took his suitcase and moved on. To Chicago, Detroit, Cleveland, Paducah, Jackson, Pittsburgh, Boston, and Washington, D.C. Wherever he went he trusted no one. He found that he disliked almost all the men he met who were in the gambling business. He discovered that he instinctively saw them as competitors and opponents. On the nights he slept alone in hotel rooms he dwelled upon his loss of Debbie and Leslie and Jennifer.

He thought of his mother. Once, for a few moments, his mind flashed back to his childhood. He recalled his mother's enormous smile. He remembered being at the pool with her. She was a strong swimmer, and he recalled her teaching her "little fishes" the Australian crawl, the breaststroke, the dog paddle, and how to dive too. And then his mind jumped back to her wheelchair and her walker, and then it returned to the diseases within himself. Only if you have extraordinary courage can you take that kind of arduous journey and reexamine where you came from and who you are.

Something in me is not being fed. I'm hungry, I'm starving. I've been conditioned to believe that with success I'd get rid of the hunger, but it isn't true. The hunger remains. If anything the food I've taken in is unclean. It's spoiling everything.

He began to feel as if the earth was spinning beneath his feet, as if he didn't have faith in anything beneath the sky. Each day he felt such a pain in his head he had to take several Valiums.

From Washington, D.C., he went to New Hope Poll and spent a day with Eddie Zeno. From there he went on to Miami Beach and stayed the weekend as the guest of Allan Klein, a friend of Solomon Lepidus's, a bookmaker. Two weeks later he again took to the road and traveled to smaller cities and college towns and tank towns. He went to high school gyms, met coaches, scouted players, talked to promotion men, pumped sports reporters, and hired even more informers. He always used as his cover the pretense that he was a sportswriter for Dellson Publishing.

During that period he was approached by one of Solomon Lepidus's friends to do power ratings for a basketball trade paper for the 1973–1974 season, and again, because of certain fringe benefits, he accepted.

David took special precautions not to give away anything that might hurt him. He planned to give out bad games as well as good games and no games that he expected to be keying in on himself. He would stay a little above 53 percent in his winning percentage, sometimes even giving out special games in order to make lines move the way he wanted, and when they did, of course, he would go the other way.

One of the few things he did give away was the piece of information that hardly a single team posts a better record on the road than it does at home. He stated that in the 1972–1973 season, of the 177 teams he charted, only two recorded a better record on the road than they did on their own homecourt. They were Arkansas and Temple. He threw them in as a bone. He knew it didn't mean a damn thing when it came to handicapping the individual games.

All through the summer, David began forcing himself to "escape." He began utilizing his money to accomplish this. He rented a ten-room penthouse apartment on Fifth Avenue with a gigantic rooftop terrace overlooking the park. For his master bedroom he purchased a king-size brass bed, a four-poster with a canopy.

In other rooms he placed armchairs, sofas, and ottomans upholstered in luxurious suedes and rich leathers, and he covered the floors with rare skins and authentic oriental rugs. In addition, he commissioned a genius with wood, Fredrico Lavorini, of Compositions in Wood, to design cabinets, bookcases, shelvings, desks, and planters. Lavorini paneled his forty-eight-foot living room in rosewood and two other rooms in English walnut and American walnut.

David used the room paneled in English walnut as a library and the other room as a den. Another knotty-pine-paneled room he made into a projection room and stocked his film library with fight films and an entire repertoire of Bogart, Cagney, Muni, Davis, Gable, Hepburn, Tracy, and Charlie Chaplin. In all the rooms there were *Peperomia Grisso-Argentea* plants. When the Colonel first saw the place he raved. He said it reminded him of Le Club International in Fort Lauderdale.

By the early fall the apartment was completely decorated and ready for entertaining, and David began throwing parties. Almost everyone who was anyone came; Broadway actors and actresses, professional jocks, Hollywood types passing through, some Las Vegas showgirls and a couple of call girls from the strip, scene players, serious writers, hacks, pretty people, affluent people, empty people.

Harriet Barash, who had been dumped by Nathan Rubin, came by his special invitation, and several other friends, Saskia Verdonck, Ursula Knutson, and Odette Bashjian included. And when David insisted, Ron Nivens and his ballerina fiancé, Mellissa O'Neal, came.

David soon became one of the Big Apple's in people, and was looked upon with envy. Women propositioned him—many of them asking him to allow them to move in. Women, even Harriet Barash, and she tried, couldn't entice him. Somehow, somewhere along the way, he had lost the need.

By the middle of fall, thoughts again began to surface, questioning thoughts, such as: Had money changed everything? Anything? Nothing?

In the late fall David cut out the sludge and returned to work. He made deals with no one other than the Colonel, Solomon, and Doug. Nathan Rubin visited his place. He flew in from Palm Beach to persuade David to give him his games. He offered David the same proposition as before. David remembered how he had asked Nathan how he went about determining prices and odds on games the first time David met him and how Nathan had scowled and snarled, "I don't give lessons, sonny, and I don't take partners."

David remembered how Nathan had sneered when David asked him to finance him and how Nathan had refused. Now it was David's turn to refuse, and he grinned as he said, "I don't give my games out anymore, Pops, and I don't take partners."

Nathan Rubin argued himself into a blue funk, turned ashen white, started getting heart palpitations, and had to take some pills. Before he recovered, David had to call his son, Charley, to come pick him up.

Isaac Pizer also reacted badly to David's decision. He came over and cried, literally cried. Sandy Rocca threatened, but David held fast. His intentions were simple and clear-cut. He would work only with people of his own choosing and with his own beards and bookmakers, and he would only "cheer" for Max Brown's games, and his own, and for no one else's.

Weeks later, after Nathan Rubin had called and called and called, each time with a better proposition, David consented to phone him and Sandy Rocca whenever he wanted to get down very heavy and needed their outlets. Of course, whenever David would do so, they agreed to give him 53 percent of the profit.

ONE OF THE FIRST bets David made during the 1973–1974 season was on December 8.

"Hello, Arnie? Get me down on Boston College. Take the five."

"But, Lazar," Arnie Feld said, "Brown's got a hell of a club this year, and besides, they're a strong home team."

David said, "Arnie, just do what I tell you, take the five."

Two days later he visited Arnie Feld's apartment to collect. David gave him some important instructions. "Now listen to me carefully, Arnie. Here's a plane ticket and a hotel reservation I made for you. I want you to relocate in Cleveland for the rest of the basketball season. I'm going to give you the names of some people to contact there from whom you can get the lines. Here's another envelope; in it you have code names, telephone numbers, and any other instructions you might need. Now open up the envelope and start studying."

Beginning on December 16, 1973, David took a percentage of his profit and put it aside. With it he set a special goal of picking five winners in a row, of parlaying everything to the fifth power. He worked with increments of one dime or two or four as his initial wager. He sought out only perfect spots to invest in. Games where his inside information or Max Brown's tips gave him one hell of an edge. Sometimes he waited a week for the right game; other times for as long as a month. For every $1,000 invested, discounting vigorish, he would receive a return of $31,000 in profit if he reached his goal. Many times he'd take out a certain proportion of the profit if the first three games won. The amount he took out wasn't determined by mood, whim, or fancy. It was determined, like everything else, by calculation and number. On numerous occasions he won.

On one occasion both he and Solomon had $32,000 on their fifth progression. The teams were Texas A&M and Texas Christian University, and they had laid the points on the Aggies. The game was played on February 10, 1974. The reason he'd been so confident about the game was that earlier in the day he had spoken to Billy Williams, one of the coaches in the Southwestern Conference, and Williams had informed David that three of the starting players on the Horned Frogs were out with the flu. Of course, David also verified the information through other sources. It took him over an hour to get down for Lepidus and himself.

He had to span the country to do so, using fifteen bookmakers and ten beards in all, and he had to lay from 13 up to 16½ points on the Aggies in some places. He had power-rated the game at 19 before the special information. Now it was 26. And with all the effort and the extra points, it was worth it. The final score was Texas A&M 90, TCU 64. He was a big winner. Sometimes he got the feeling he was omnipotent. Of course, he lost games, too.

Debbie Turner had been in New York for three days, and not a minute had passed that she didn't want to call David Lazar. Her husband, Jimmy, was aware of it. He hadn't said anything, but after two years of marriage, he had become quite sophisticated in picking up the signs when his wife longed for "the other man." First her smoking increased. After that it was their conversations that suffered. Next it seeped into their sex life. And ultimately, those awful silences that stretched on for days. Once, out of anger or despair or courage, Jimmy found the strength to say, "Debbie, I think we should go for marriage counseling." And for six months, things did improve. But how many times, Jimmy thought, could he count on counseling? And why should he have to? Why couldn't they work it out? They were reasonable, rational people.

"You know, Jimmy," Debbie said, her voice tentative, "David lives only about five minutes from here. I'd like to see him. Would you mind?"

Quietly Jimmy answered. "Do you want me to go with you, or do you want to see him alone?"

Debbie hesitated. She drew on a cigarette she had just about finished. "Why do you ask?" She stopped. "If you're too tired to, I'll ..."

In a cold, strong voice, Jimmy responded, "We'll see David together, Debbie, as man and wife. But if we leave together, I don't want you to ever bring him into our marriage again." He paused and said softly, "I know it's wrong of me to act this way, Debbie. I'm not giving you enough space. But I can't help myself. I love you. You know that, Debbie. And I still think we can make our marriage work. But if you and I continue, it's going to have to be without David Lazar or his ghost. Understand?" He gazed at her with eyes that were almost pleading.

Debbie nervously took another cigarette out of her purse, fumbled for matches, and lit it. Taking a deep drag, she walked to the hotel-room window, looked out, and thought, How many times can I tell myself that falling in love is romantic and idealistic and a fairy tale, and that loving someone maturely is the only basis for a real relationship? How many times can I tell myself that the falling-in-love part wears away? How many times can I tell myself that Jimmy is loving, stable, and secure; that David's a gambler and a bad risk, self-indulgent and selfish? How many times?

"Hello, David? How are you? It's Debbie. I'm in town with Jimmy. We'll be in the city only tonight. Tomorrow we're leaving for the coast. We're moving to Frisco. I've taken a job with the Lindeman Clinic. Jimmy also found a job. He's going to be an administrator at the San Francisco Medical Center. . . . David, that's enough questions. I'm dying to see you. Is it all right if we come right over?"

The call upset David. He couldn't concentrate on what he was doing any longer. He put down his handbook and canceled his calls for the evening; he waited for Debbie. The Edisons never arrived. Jimmy called and apologized, making a banal excuse.

The following evening David listlessly made his telephone calls. He wagered on Tulsa. He lost. He wagered on Drake. He lost. On Tuesday he made a triple bet on Oregon State. He lost. He made an even bigger play on Fordham. The Fordham game was played at the Garden. He broke his cardinal rule: He went to the game. He lost. On Saturday he bet four more games. Three lost. He felt panicky. He called Doug.

"God damn it, David. You still have a million weaknesses. I told you that to be a professional gambler you've got to become what you're not, a killer. Just remember, David, every time you go to the telephone to bet you gotta make sure it's a perfect bet. Every investment can have a mushrooming effect, can snowball and cause a landslide. A small wager can be as dangerous as the biggest bet of your career. It can start you on a losing streak that before you know it will trigger your compulsiveness. If you don't control yourself by maximizing and minimizing every second, you're dead! And don't whine to me that without Debbie in your life it doesn't matter. You would destroy her. All your ambivalence would surface the moment you had her. You'd vent your frustrations on her. She's thin and flat. A fuckin' secretary mentality. You'd destroy her if she were with you. Count yourself lucky she's married to Jimmy. They deserve each other. Listen to me, David, she's got a good life. She's with Jimmy Edison because it's safe. Believe me, you're lucky as hell to be rid of her. If you were married to her you'd be bored to death. In six months you'd be destroying her rather than idealizing her."

Later that evening something inside of David began to surface. Something had begun to fight back, to salve what had been wounded.

I've got to remain calm or else I'll get buried, he thought. I've got to go into a shell and bet smaller and protect myself. I must look for larger differentials, bigger flaws in the line, and chip away at them like they've chipped away at me. I've got to ride this losing streak out—it'll die; the money'll start coming in again. I'll be collecting again. I've got to hold on and make it. I've got to win. Screw Debbie. Screw what I feel inside. I'm a handicapper. I've got a job to do. Screw Debbie. I've got to hold on. Make it. Win!

The world of David Bernard Lazar was a violent world. Not only were there the usual attempted rip-offs. Sometimes they succeeded. He was a consistent winner, and there were times when he would get involved in vicious arbitrations. Three times he was actually beaten; twice he was mugged. Once he needed hospital help. He had the reassurance of his gun, but he knew that was the bottom line.

One late afternoon, after he had picked up money from Angelo "One-Eye" Scarne's runner, he was suddenly confronted by a strange man on Eighty-third Street near Riverside Drive. The fellow came prepared for action. He held a baseball bat in his hand, though it was midwinter. David stepped back quickly, pulling his gun in the same movement. He pulled the trigger, a wild shot, before the bat could be swung. David didn't stick around to learn anything more.

The more successful he became, the more precautions he took. He began acting dumb, telling almost everyone he was losing. He started giving scroungers who wouldn't stop calling games he felt were bad risks. They soon stopped calling. He was only too aware that a winner's mystique leaves as quickly as it comes, and he was certain that he knew plenty of ways to get rid of the mystique, and with it the hangers-on. It just took some time, some cunning.

A thousand times he was asked, "What do you look for in a basketball team?" A thousand times he answered, "I look for speed and quickness, an easy, fluid, unselfish offense that hits the open man. A team with 'team' players who can move all night without the ball. A team that has poise and confidence, that believes in itself, that believes it's going to win!"

Then, if questioned still further, depending upon by whom, he would mention other, more important things.

When the season ended, David again began living a fantasy life. He was Sinatra, Gable, and Grant all rolled into one. He played the nightlife scene better than he had ever before. He was making it with beautiful women, but when he was alone and had a chance to reflect, he realized that nothing really had changed. Not in him. He was as dissatisfied as ever. About the biggest difference he observed was that the bar-scene women he used to unthinkingly call "nymphs" were now being called "liberated." As to the cost of this liberation, David noted that these new women didn't seem to feel as much, and for that reason "feeling" became an obsessive concern.

On an impulse David looked up Margot Lepidus's phone number at Yale and called her. He asked her to fly into the city for the weekend. When Margot arrived the first thing she said was, "My God! What happened to that little-boy look you used to have?"

They took a walk in Central Park. They went rowing. They went to the zoo. They listened to some Hispanics playing bongos and singing. They dodged cyclists on the bicycle path. They watched tired nags pull carriages filled with healthy-looking out-of-towners. They stopped for a bite to eat and some frozen custard at the Fountain Café. They held hands and laughed a great deal.

Margot kept gazing at him and smiling, and once she even stopped on an empty road and raised her face to his to be kissed. But they didn't kiss. He took her moist hand instead and continued walking.

A little later Margot telephoned her father.

"Hello, Daddy? Would you mind terribly if David and I didn't go to dinner with you and Mom tonight? David and I are up for a show, do you mind? . . . David, Daddy wants to speak to you."

"Hello, Solomon?"

"What's doing, Davy boy?"

"What do you mean, Solomon?"

"Well . . . ah . . ."

"Solomon," David said and laughed, "stop acting like a father. You got nothing to worry about. Margot and I are just friends."

"Take it easy, Davy boy."

When David and Margot returned to David's apartment, he mixed her a drink, and after several minutes more of casual talk, they walked into the bedroom. Somehow the top button of her blouse unbuttoned and he was able to see where her sun-nourished tan faded into the moon-white skin of her breast. He touched the moon, and she became a different person. First

260 . . .

she began stripping slowly, and then, suddenly, unashamedly, she stood in front of him, nude, nubile, wildly desirable. They fumbled with his clothes, then their mouths came together, and as he breathed her special smell, it reminded him of Leslie, and he became even more excited. He put his hands on her breasts, but then, out of nowhere, something made him push her away.

He gazed into her eyes and told her that he wanted their friendship to have more meaning than just sex.

"I'd like to see more of you, Margot. I want to get to know you better."

She nodded in agreement. But they began with physical knowledge first.

A half hour later, noticing her nipples were still hard, he said, "In today's world that's a miracle, Margot." She gazed at him with a shy smile and blushed. Later he told her he'd been thinking seriously about making a new life for himself and that he was even contemplating writing again.

"You know, Margot, for me writing was always a love affair between me and what I was creating. When I was involved in my writing it always became the most important thing in my life and took precedence over everything else."

Margot gazed at him and said, "Now you look like that little boy I knew, David." She smiled. "I like you better now."

A month later Margot and David were sitting with Ron Nivens and his fiancée, Melissa O'Neal. Margot was saying, "The other day David and I went out with a friend of mine and David was horrible. He didn't speak to my friend all night. When I said something to him later—in a nice way, mind you—you should have heard him. He sounded like a crazy man, yelling that he's a genius and that he couldn't be bothered with such trivia, and that if some little mediocrity took offense at his behavior he couldn't give a damn. How many times do I have to hear that he's a genius and that he couldn't care less about what my friends think of him? But you know, I think it has little to do with any of that. I think it was simply because the girl wasn't beautiful, because if she were, he would have been perfectly charming. Or if she had immediately made him the center of attention, he would have eaten it up. He claims that I depend on him too much, but in his own way, he's keeping me from developing my own friendships, or having new and different people in my life. Do you understand what I mean?"

Ron looked at David and said, "Are you aware of what you're doing, David?"

David laughed and turned his attention to Melissa. As he did, Ron said, "David, are you sure you want to pay the price again?"

David turned to him and said, "I'm sure, Ron, I'm sure.

* * *

By late fall a small circle of men were beginning to flatter David, calling him a genius; calling him the Handicapper. Some of them asked him to tout for them. When he refused, their musclemen tried to get to him. They threatened him, roughed him up a bit, warned him that if he didn't go along with them he would be spending the entire basketball season in a hospital. He ran to his surrogate father, Solomon Lepidus. Solomon intervened, and was literally a lifesaver.

David continued to run a one-man operation. He continued to shop for low-grade prices and to bet only prime lines. He worked everything to precision. Between 1:00 P.M. and midnight every weekday, and all day and night on Saturday, he was the consummate craftsman at work. He might have been bankrupt in other ways, but when it came to his handicapping, he was, he thought, the wealthiest son of a bitch this side of Nathan Rubin. In fact, he was even able to improve his winning percentage that year.

All David did was cut out games other than those where he located a 5½-point-or-greater disparity. He knew his probabilities backward and forward by then. He had every satanic statistic in his handbook. He knew just about how many he'd win and lose on any particular point differential he found between the Vegas line and his.

There are gamblers and there are gamblers. He, David Lazar, like Nathan Rubin, schemed, wise-guyed the wise guys, made deals, didn't make deals, stayed on the side of Napoleon ("Morality is the side with the biggest artillery").

He became bigger. Bigger meant money, "important" money. It meant nothing else.

And yet there were times . . .

"Hello, Zeno, I want to get down on Kentucky. . . . Yeah, it's the best bet of the night. . . . I know I had a bad week. God damn it, you don't have to remind me. . . . Yeah, I love Kentucky. Lay the nine."

When he finished with his phone call to Zeno, he called Tony Giardello and Joey A. Then he thumbed through his handbook and searched for other New York books that he used only for emergencies and for large wagers.

"Hello, this is Alex for Bummer. . . . Hello, Big Judy, this is Sid for Mr. Julien. . . . Hello, Serretta, this is Rick for Mr. Pollock. . . . Hello, Hunchback Bobby, this is Reno for Ninety-two. . . ." Then he searched for some of his out-of-state beards. He thumbed through dozens of them until he located the ones he wanted.

An hour before game time, Solomon Lepidus called. "What do we got, Davy boy?"

"We got Kentucky, Solomon. We're laying nine." He listened to Solomon for a while and then said sharply, "I know I had a bad week, Solomon. And I know you hate Kentucky. But I like them. That's who we've got. Goodnight." He slammed the phone down.

David nervously paced his rooftop terrace. His face was grim, his teeth chattered, his blue lips were sealed tight, and his right hand clutched his old silver dollar. His left hand held a pocket radio. His breathing was heavy. He paced back and forth for twenty minutes in the cold winter night before he stopped moving and jerked his head and riveted his ear to the tiny radio as it blasted out: "And now for sports." His feverish eyes twitched spasmodically as he instinctively clenched his silver dollar in his fist. "This final just in. . . . Kentucky ninety-one, Georgia eighty-eight in overtime."

"No!" he cried. His vigil was over; the winning margin was not enough. David numbly walked from the terrace back into his apartment and threw the silver dollar to the parquet floor. He walked to his desk, pulled a drawer open, and took out his handbook and a red Flair pen. Fumbling with the pen, he quickly wrote in the score of the game and next to it he wrote in bold letters: A LOSER, and the amount he had lost, $88,000.

It was half an hour before he moved. When he did, he returned the handbook to his desk and locked the drawer. He searched his pockets for the silver dollar. He couldn't find it. He was about to unlock the desk drawer and check it, too, when he noticed the silver dollar glittering on the floor. He picked it up and tossed the coin into the air.

"Heads," he called. The coin slammed into his hand. "Tails," he uttered mockingly. He stuffed the coin into his back pocket and shook his head. "What a week. Some fuckin' handicapper."

At three that morning, his phone was ringing. He raised his tired body out of bed. "Who the hell can that be?" He fumbled to pick up the phone.

"Hello? . . . Oh, hello, Solomon. We lost."

31

SASKIA THOUGHT of the time when she was new to America and had first met David. "I came here with fifteen hundred dollars, David, but money runs out of my purse. A work permit is very important. I can't get a job because I don't have the right visa. I have a visitor's visa. I have to show them a letter saying I can perform a special job that others can't. Then I have to hope they give me a new visa. It happens quite often that foreigners marry Americans, David. It would solve my problems immediately." And her mind jumped to the time David had introduced her to Solomon Lepidus.

"Saskia just arrived from Holland, Solomon. She hasn't any money at all. She'll have to return to Holland in a couple of weeks unless she gets some money and a different visa. Solomon, what Saskia really needs is a work permit."

Saskia recalled Solomon Lepidus shouting, "Maxine, get Vito of the IRS on the phone." He took out of his trouser pocket twelve brand-new $100 bills and handed them to her. When she told him that she did not know when she could return the money, if ever, he smiled and said, "Saskia, if you're ever in a position to return the money, find someone who needs it like you do now and give it to them."

Saskia thought Solomon had windmills in his head. Still, she never forgot him. But why was it that men like Solomon and David never took her seriously?

"Answer your telephone, Saskia," Odette yelled out. "It's Nathan Rubin."

"Meet me at Sandy Rocca's in an hour, Saskia," Nathan Rubin said urgently.

When Saskia arrived, wearing a green-and-yellow dress, Nathan smiled at her and pointed just as urgently to the couch. "Sit down, Saskia." He was about to pick up the phone. "If you want wine, Saskia, there's some Muscadet in the frig."

Nathan Rubin dialed area code 512. "Hello, Josh? Did you speak to Sam? ... Good! Now just remember your instructions, Josh. Remember, old friend, tell no one!"

Nathan Rubin slammed the phone down and walked over to Saskia. He sat down beside her on the maroon leather couch, slid his hand under her dress, and fondled her naked thigh.

"David Lazar once dumped you, right, Saskia? Well, now you can get even. And you can make yourself a hell of a lot of money besides. Ya see, Saskia, there's a certain game comin' up that I'm gonna put a lot of money on. And I'm gonna invest ten thousand on it for you too, ya see. Now what I want you to do is find out what Lazar's thinkin' is on the game. And this is how you're to do it."

Nathan Rubin drilled Saskia for an hour on what he needed done. He outlined bits and pieces of his plan to her. He gave away nothing that he didn't want her to know. Afterward, he took her hand and walked her into the bedroom and sprawled out on the bed. He closed his gray eyes and stretched out as Saskia started unzipping his fly. He cupped his hands around her neck and slowly pulled her head down until her full red lips were around his penis. As she sucked his penis he talked on and on.

After Saskia had relieved Nathan Rubin, she wandered into the bathroom to get a wet hand towel. As she carefully wiped Nathan Rubin off, he leaned over and reached for a bottle of Muscadet on the night table and poured wine into two glasses.

"Here's to Boone, girl."

She lay down next to him, and as he stroked and fondled her he said metallically, "I've done everything perfect, Saskia. I didn't overlook a thing. It's taken me thirteen years, but it's gonna be worth it. Ya see, I've been setting a certain guy up for this all that time. It's cost me plenty of dough, but it's all gonna be comin' back now."

On Nathan Rubin's aged face there was a rare aliveness and joy that had not appeared for a long time.

"All the money I spent fixing up Rubin Arena, on Sam, on the recruiters, that wop Zeno, that jig Brantley. All that money on them ghetto kids, Gibbs, Crawford, Beasley, Duval." He snickered. "It's all gonna be comin' back, with dividends."

A few minutes later Nathan Rubin dozed off and Saskia got up and took the bottle of Muscadet with her into the kitchen. She didn't know the full implications of what Nathan had said, but she knew someone was being taken for a great deal of money. She wondered who.

Minutes later she walked to the refrigerator and took out another chilled Muscadet and sat down at the kitchen table.

Two hours later when Nathan Rubin walked over to her and placed his bony fingers around her bare shoulders she was feeling very dizzy. Rubin patiently spoon-fed her some coffee and then insisted she call David Lazar. Saskia followed his orders.

"I've been thinking a lot of what I can do for ya, Saskia," Nathan Rubin said, "and I've decided. Besides the ten thousand you're gonna make on this deal I'm gonna do something else. This coming weekend I have to fly down to Palm Beach to be with my wife. Ya see, it's our anniversary, but as soon as I get back I'm gonna call Lou Cartel. I'll make him a proposition he can't refuse. You're gonna be the Cartel Girl, Saskia. How about that?"

Nathan grabbed at Saskia's waist. Saskia couldn't quite manage the show of joy she felt was demanded of her. She reached for the remaining Muscadet on the kitchen table and quickly downed it.

It was six days before the annual Boone–Western game. Nathan Rubin had gone over his plan for 358 days. He had filed dozens of tapes in his safe with notes, facts, and instructions. Each day he had added new ideas and erased and refined old ones.

Already much of the plan had been implemented. The college radio station was shut down in September. Stan "Swish" Gibbs, Johnny Lee Crawford, and Shrimp Beasley had with the inducement of $300 a week spending money attended summer school to make them eligible for the basketball season. One of their courses had been given by a sweating Coach Leland.

"Boys, ya gotta understand, the one thing you're here for this year is the Western game. We're gonna kick their butts this year. Understand, Swish? . . . John? . . . Shrimp?" Another player, Billy Duval, an exceptional student, had also been kept on campus all summer. He had been paid $400 a week to mow President Boone's front and back lawns. He too was under the tutelage of Coach Leland.

"Now, Billy, don't you go flying up to Brooklyn on weekends and screw yourself up playing in that Rucker tournament. Damn, Billy, you could get hurt. Damn, boy, you could get mugged up there in Harlem. Now, here's your four hundred smackeroos, Billy boy. Say, Billy, you know, I'm kinda glad you're staying down here all summer. Besides the fact I ain't losing sleep over you banging up your knee, I did like getting this chance to know ya. Now, Billy, I want you to get to know me too. What do you think is the most important thing in the whole damn world to me, Billy? No, it ain't my wife and kids, Billy boy, it's this year's Western–Boone game."

In August, Billy Duval had an accident in a routine pickup game. A doctor was flown in from Houston. "There's very little chance this boy's foot's going to heal by December, coach. Very little."

"Damn, doc, we're in trouble if it don't. There's no way we can whip Western without Billy. No way!"

Five minutes after the accident, the sports information director at Boone College, Billy Mack Boone, called the Houston *Gazette* and the AP and UPI bureaus in Houston and reported the unfortunate news. He did not report what Coach Leland had said to him: "It seems to me, Billy Mack, and I know enough about players to know, that that damn walk-on, Johnson, tripped Billy Duval. Where the hell did Johnson come from, anyway? I never saw him in the gym before. . . ."

* * *

Four days before the Boone–Western game, Nathan Rubin walked into Sandy Rocca's bedroom at 6:30 in the morning. "Sandy . . . wake up! I got a special job for you. I want you to make some calls and find out what girls we have available the next four or five days. Do it now, Sandy. I want the information in an hour. And Sandy, make sure they're our top girls. Of course you're one of my top girls, Saskia. I've already told ya what you have to do. Now get out of Sandy's bed and go take a shower. And don't start sippin' any Muscadet, Saskia. Sandy, get out of bed. Make them calls!"

An hour later Sandy Rocca walked into the living room. "Nathan, we got Ingrid, Brenda, Linda, Nancy, Maria, and, oh yeah, we also got Candice and Ginger available."

"Good, Sandy. Now let me think. Okay, this is what I want you to do. Get . . . ah, wait a minute, Sandy. What about Knutson? What's she doing?"

"Ursula said she's not gonna be available for the next few days. She's going upstate with her boyfriend tomorrow."

"Tell her Nathan Rubin has a special job for her. Tell her to get over here at once."

"Nathan, I just thought of something. Remember those two high school girls who worked for us two summers ago? You remember, Sally and Susie. We used them for guys who insisted on makin' it with kids. Don't you remember?"

"Yeah, sorta. What happened to them?"

"That's the whole thing, Nathan. They only worked that one summer. They planned to make enough money so they could go to college that fall. They needed to make tuition. Don't you remember, they were from Houston, and they enrolled at the university? What could be better? They're in Houston now. They're college kids. No one would ever expect they're pros. I bet if we offered them tuition for next year or something, we could work out a deal."

"Good idea, Sandy. That's using your head. Now, do you know where they're staying? What their phone number is? You don't! Well, what are you waiting for? Get to work. I want them here by tomorrow morning. Tell them Nathan Rubin got a proposition for them. Tell them anything, Sandy, but get them here. They're perfect for this job. Oh, and Sandy, don't forget to get Knutson, too. That's important. Ya see, Sandy, she'll do a job on Billy Mack like none of them other girls can. Get me Ursula Knutson, Sandy. Now!"

Three days before the Boone–Western game, three Boone College basketball players were suspended. Sam Boone refused the Boone College paper permission to print the reason for the suspension of the players. In fact, he refused to give the paper any information whatsoever on the suspension. The school's one reporter, a stuttering sophomore, was left in the dark.

But Sam Boone had Billy Mack Boone phone the Houston *Gazette* and inform them of the suspension of the three, and the Houston paper had an ambitious young journalist, Bobby Pearl, who convinced his editor to allow him to drive the one hundred miles to Boone to find out what was going on.

Sam Boone told the school security staff to keep the reporter away from the players. When Bobby Pearl was spotted by a security officer sneaking into the players' dormitory, he was immediately arrested and placed in Boone's lockup. The following morning Sam Boone went down to the jail and whispered to the angry journalist, "Bobby, it'll be bad not only for Boone, but for Texas, too, if we print what really happened. Take it from a man whose grandpappy was born in Texas, who loves Texas as much as his mother, it was just one of them things that happens when niggers spend time with white gals. You get my drift, Bobby?"

Sam Boone handed Pearl an envelope with a bundle of $50 bills inside. "Let's keep the damn thing in the family. Okay, Bobby?"

Pearl took the envelope and greedily counted the money. "Sure enough, Mr. Boone. I was born here too, you know."

The next morning in the Houston *Gazette* an article ran with Bobby Pearl's byline beginning: "This reporter has it from unimpeachable sources that Stanley 'Swish' Gibbs, Johnny Lee Crawford and Calvin 'Shrimp' Beasley were suspended due to charges brought by two Houston University coeds, Susie Nuyen, eighteen, a Eurasian woman, and Sally Morrison, nineteen, a white woman. These two women allegedly . . .

When Sam Boone read the article, he smiled happily and dialed area code 212.

"Nathan? Sam here. I reckon you're a genius all right. It went just as you figured. Every paper in this cotton-pickin' country is gonna be pickin' up on the story now. No way that game's gonna be on the board. Everyone and his grandpappy's gonna know them boys are out." Sam snickered. "The only way anyone's gonna be able to make a wager will have to be man-to-man."

Nathan Rubin nodded and sipped espresso with a calvados. "That's very good, Sam. You've been doin' a good job. Now, the next thing for you to do is to go down to the community store and remind Josh of his part. I telephoned him before, and I'll call him again, but just the same you go and remind him too. Make sure he has it right, Sam. Make sure. Go now, Sam. Right now!"

Thirty minutes later Sam Boone hurriedly dialed area code 212.

"Nathan? Sam. We got another break. I just spoke to Doc Henry. Billy Duval's ready to play."

"It's just what I hoped for, Sam. Have Billy Mack call up that reporter at the *Gazette*. Tell him we're giving him an exclusive. Might as well, it'll take all the suspicions away from the other thing. With that Duval running the show and with Crawford, Gibbs, and Beasley . . . This is it, Sam. You can bet on it. We're gonna make a mint. Oh, Sam, hold up on the other things till tomorrow. You got everything straight, Sam? Good."

It was sixteen hours before the Boone–Western game. Nathan Rubin sat in his Lous XIV tapestry chair. The telephone rang, and he reached for it instantly with his huge hand.

"Hello."

"Hello, Nathan? It's Saskia. I have to whisper. I'm still at David's apartment."

"Where's Lazar, Saskia?"

"He just received some late scores from the West Coast. He went into his study to record them in his handbook. Listen, Nathan, Solomon Lepidus called David a couple of hours ago. He talked to him about the Boone game. David told him that there wouldn't be a number on the game. Isn't that how you say it, Nathan? I don't understand the language, Nathan. It sounds strange, funny."

"Don't worry about language, Saskia. Just repeat to me what Lazar said, exactly as he said it. I'll take care of the rest."

"He said that with the three Boone players out Western would probably win by twenty or more points. Nathan?"

"Yeah?"

"I couldn't hear Solomon, but I think he asked David if you knew the Boone players were suspended. David lost his temper, Nathan. He said that you knew everything. That you would not be calling him to make a bet on Boone."

"We'll see, Saskia. We'll see. Say, Saskia, tell Sandy to take you off house calls tomorrow night. Odette too. Ya see, Saskia, I want both of you to stay home. After the game's over we'll all be going down to Solomon's new restaurant to do some celebratin'. Now, get back to Lazar. Ya don't want the poor little social worker gettin' lonely, do ya?"

Two hours and thirty-five minutes before the Boone–Western game, Nathan Rubin raised himself out of his Louis XIV tapestry chair and began to pace. All day he had forced himself not to telephone Solomon Lepidus. He waited and waited. If Solomon didn't telephone soon . . .

Rocca entered the room. "You want a drink, Nathan?"

"What are you bothering me for?" Rubin snapped. "Get out of here, Sandy. Go inside and call Sam. Make sure, double-check, do something!"

Two hours and fifteen minutes before the Boone–Western game, Solomon Lepidus unlocked his desk drawer and reached for his gold telephone. For weeks, maybe because it was the only proposition he'd ever bested Nathan Rubin on, he had been obsessed by the upcoming Boone–Western game.

"Hello, Nathan. What's doing? . . . Nathan, the reason I'm calling you is I want to know whether you made a decision about coming in with Jerome Vogel and me to help Dr. Green."

"Well, Solomon, I did. I'm gonna give ya a thousand dollars. What do ya say to that?"

"A thousand dollars. Look, Nathan, Vogel and myself are each contributing one hundred thousand. I want the same from you. With three hundred thousand, Dr. Green can set up a laboratory right in the hospital. The guy's a genius, Nathan. There's no tellin' what he'll be able to accomplish. Imagine, Nathan, you have a chance to help lick cancer. Come on, Nathan boy, come in for a hundred thousand with Vogel and me. It's a mitzvah you'll be doing."

"I don't think so, Solomon. A thousand is all I can give ya."

"Nathan, a thousand is insulting. . . . Say, Nathan, isn't tonight the Boone–Western game?"

"Yeah, I guess so, Solomon, what about it?"

"Well, I figured you'd want to make a proposition on the game, Nathan. Don't you want to bet Boone?"

"Come on, stop bein' a wise guy, Solomon."

"What do ya mean, Nathan?"

"Ya tryin' to tell me you don't know?"

"Know what?"

"Well, ya see, Solomon, it's like this. I'm being completely aboveboard with you. I wanted to make you a proposition on the game, but I figured it would be a waste of time. Ya see, Solomon, the fact is, the game isn't gonna be on the Vegas line tonight. Three of Boone's best players are suspended. Solomon, I just can't come up with a number for the game. Ya understand, don't you, Solomon?"

"Well, ya see, Nathan boy, the way I have it figured is as long as we both know what the facts are, we should be able to find a number that's agreeable to both of us. Shouldn't we, Nathan boy?"

"I don't know, Solomon, I just don't know."

"Come on, Nathan boy, you can make a number on anything. Make me a proposition on the game."

"Well, if that's the way you feel, Solomon, I'm willin' to get down to some serious talkin'. What do ya say about laying me twenty-one points on Boone for twenty thousand?"

"Nathan. Come on, stop fooling around."

"Well, I just don't know what to make it, Solomon. Say, why don't you give me a couple of minutes to figure out a proposition? I'll call you back."

As Solomon was about to hang up, Nathan Rubin, in an anxious voice, shouted, "Solomon . . . Solomon!"

"Yeah, Nathan, what is it?"

"I just want to make sure you're gonna wait in your office for my call, ya see?"

"I'll be here, Nathan boy. I'll be here. Take it easy."

Two hours and six minutes before the Boone–Western game:

"Solomon? I'm gonna make you a proposition. Now before you go gettin' suspicious I want to tell ya Sandy Rocca told me two minutes ago another Boone player, a player who's been out all year, name of Dubow or Duval or something, is gonna play. Now you see, he's supposed to be a pretty good player, Solomon."

"I'll call you right back, Nathan."

Solomon hung up the gold phone. He unlocked a second desk drawer and reached for his silver telephone.

"Davy boy? What's doing? . . . Listen, Davy, I got to call Nathan Rubin right back. What's the points on the Boone–Western game tonight?"

"Are you crazy, Solomon? I told you last night Boone's suspended three of their starters. There's not going to be a line on the game anywhere. I already checked with Joey Giardello's office and Dominic Denucci's. They're definitely not using the game. I also called Eddie Zeno in Philly, and that O'Brien kid in Bloomington. Neither one of them could find a line either. Solomon, no bookmaker in the entire country is gonna touch that game."

"What about this Dubow kid, Davy boy? Nathan said he's playin' tonight."

"It's Billy Duval, Solomon. I told you about that too. Why the hell don't you listen to me? That's the kid out of Boys High, remember? He's damn good, Solomon, but he's coming off a serious injury, and anyway, the other three kids are out. It's a shame, too, because those kids, especially Swish Gibbs, would've charged through a brick wall to win this game tonight. Roger Brantley told me they were psyched out of their minds for the game. With Duval back and Boone's home-court advantage, I probably would've made a big bet on them. The points would have come up at about two or three on Western, and I'd of made Boone four-and-a-half- or five-point favorite. It would've been a very strong play for me. Anyway, they're not playing. Western's going to wipe Boone out."

"Thanks, Davy boy. Now, don't go tying up your line or leaving the house. I'll be getting back to you right after I speak to Nathan Rubin. Take it easy."

One hour and forty-five minutes before the Boone–Western game:

"Nathan? Solomon. Let's hear your proposition."

"Well, ya see, Solomon, I'll take Boone as usual. Sandy Rocca says the team's better off without them three jigs. Don't you go thinkin' Rocca don't know as much as that wise guy Lazar. He's been around a lot longer. And, Solomon, don't think I don't know Lazar's been toutin' you on Western. I do. That's another reason I'm hot to bet you on this game."

"Well, what do you make the game, Nathan?"

"Well, let me see. Give me seventeen and a half points, Solomon, and I'll wager you thirty thousand dollars."

"Don't be crazy, Nathan, the game's being played at Boone College. Make it ten and a half."

"Nothing doing!"

"Well, Nathan boy, what do you want to do?"

"Let me think, Solomon, let me think. I'll tell you what I'll do. Give me them ten and a half points and three-to-one odds on the thirty thousand. What do you say?"

"I'll call you back, Nathan.

"Davy? Solomon. Rubin wants to bet me thirty thou. He's askin' me to give him three-to-one odds and ten and a half points. What do you think?"

"It's a hell of a bet, Solomon. I make the game nineteen or twenty with those three guys out, but something smells. Those guys might be playing, for all we know. Let me make some calls and get back to you."

"Ya gotta hurry, Davy boy. The game starts at eight."

"I know, Solomon. Don't worry. Just tell Nathan you'll call him back in ten or fifteen minutes."

David telephoned Roger Brantley.

"None of them are playing, man. The hearing isn't scheduled till next week. Swish and them other dudes are down, man. They were psyched out of their minds for this game. They were ready to play super."

David called Lepidus back.

"Hello, Solomon? Those kids are definitely out. It's a hell of a bet, but I still don't like laying ten and a half points, especially on Boone's home court. Tell Nathan you'll take his proposition, but only if he knocks down the points. Let him raise the odds if you have to. Hold on, Solomon. Do this. Tell Nathan you'll give him five-to-one odds for fifty thousand, but only four points. I just don't like laying points, Solomon, and I'll take ten thousand of your bet for myself."

Solomon picked up his gold phone again. "Hello, Nathan? Let's do this. I'll give you five-to-one odds for fifty thou, but you can't have ten and a half points. I'll give you five and a half. What do you say?"

"Well, I don't know. What time is it? We still got plenty of time till the game starts. Let me think it over. I'll call you back."

At one hour and twenty-four minutes before the Boone–Western game, Coach Rodney Leland knocked on the door of the Western University dressing room. Johnny Anderson, the Western coach, opened the door.

"Glad to see you, Anderson. I just wanted to tell you we're movin' the game up to seven-twenty-five. It's almost Christmastime and down here at Boone we have our exams before the holidays. Ol' Sam Boone don't want his student body stayin' up all night celebrating. Why, coach, I know we don't have a chance. I'm just jokin'. You don't mind about movin' the game up half an hour, do ya? Good luck, Anderson. Shee-it, it's us that needs the luck. See you courtside."

At one hour and twenty minutes before the scheduled Boone–Western game time, Susie Nuyen and Sally Morrison were marching up to courtside, where Bobby Pearl of the Houston *Gazette* was interviewing Billy Duval.

Sally Morrison said, "Excuse me, Mr. Pearl, can I talk to you in private for a minute?"

"Why, sure you can, sugar. I'll catch you later, Billy."

"Ya see, Mr. Pearl, we're them two girls you wrote about in the paper the other day. We feel terrible about what's happened to them boys. It weren't their faults. We'd been sniffin' coke, and we—"

Bobby Pearl grabbed Sally and Susie by their wrists and hurried them over to Sam Boone, who was conveniently standing a few yards away.

Thirty-nine minutes before the Boone–Western game:

"Solomon? I've been thinking your proposition over, and I'm not against it, but I think I've come up with a better one. Ya see, I want you to give me ten-to-one odds on a hundred-thousand-dollar wager, and for that ten to one you can make the game even-steven. You don't have to give me a point. It'll be pick 'em for both of us. What do you say, Solomon?"

"Hold on, Nathan.

"Davy boy? Nathan wants to bet me one hundred thou on the game. He's willing to knock the game down to pick 'em if I give him ten-to-one odds. I can go for a million, Davy boy. What do you think?"

"I don't know, Solomon. There's no way Western can lose, and yet . . . Solomon, let me get back to you in ten or fifteen minutes.

"Roger? It's David. Listen, Roger, I know it sounds crazy, but call Swish up one more time. I got to be positive those guys aren't playing."

"Look, man, they ain't playing. I just spoke to Swish's brother, Lenny. He's also down there. I got him in last semester."

"Rog, are you sure they ain't playing?"

"I'm trying to tell you, man. I woke Lenny and his girlfriend up. Lenny said Swish went to watch the game, but them three dudes definitely ain't gonna play. He guaranteed it, man."

"Thanks, Rog."

"Solomon? I just checked again. Those three kids are definitely out. There's no way Boone can win without them. But . . . wait a minute, Solomon, hold on, there's one more call I can make."

David Lazar reached for his handbook and thumbed through it until he came to Boone College. He fingered the pages searching for a particular phone number. Finally he found what he was looking for. He dialed area code 512 and the number.

"Hello, is this the community store? Is J.T. around?"

"Yes, sir, that's me, I reckon."

"Hi, J.T., remember me? I'm the guy from New York who calls you every basketball season. Remember? Tell me, J.T., what do you hear about the Boone game tonight?"

"Well, sir, our three best players have been suspended, and that ain't gonna do us no good, I reckon."

"Thanks, J.T." David Lazar was about to hang up the telephone when something triggered off his handicapper's mind.

"Say, J.T., what time is the game starting tonight?"

Josh Turner remembered every word Nathan Rubin had drilled into him. "Josh, if anyone calls you at the store you make sure and tell them those three boys of ours are suspended and that the game's on as usual at eight o'clock. And whatever you do, Josh, don't give out any score on the game or any other information until after ten-thirty. Remember, Josh, it's me, your old friend Nathan Rubin, askin' you for this one little favor. By the way, Josh, I also called to tell ya that what happened to you in Alabama is now all evened up. That Bobby Joe fella is in the ground now with them others. Ya see?"

"Game time's as usual, mister, eight o'clock, at Rubin Arena. I'm hurryin' over there right now to get to my seat. And them three boys, mister, they're definitely not playing. They've been suspended for . . . well, something bad. And, mister, I truly doubt if they'll ever play again for Boone."

"Will you be returning to the store after the game, J.T.? I'd like to telephone you for the score."

"Oh, I'll be back aroun' ten-thirty, all right. Ain't got nowhere else to go, I reckon."

Thirty-six minutes before the scheduled Boone–Western game time!

"Boys! I'm glad you all followed my advice and came down to watch the game. I know it took a lot of guts. And now, boys, I got some very good news for ya. You're *all* gonna be playing tonight. Them gals cleared you of them charges. You better hurry your asses and get dressed—the game's gonna be startin' in six minutes. Hey, boys, you gonna win?"

"Yes, sir!"

Eighteen minutes before 8:00:

"Solomon? I checked everywhere I could. Nothing's changed. Those kids are definitely out."

"Well, what do you think, Davy boy?"

"I still think Western should win by twenty or more, but . . ."

"But what, Davy boy?"

"I don't know. It's Nathan Rubin. And Nathan Rubin don't throw away one dollar. Damn it, Solomon, I don't like it. I don't want any part of the bet. In fact, go tell Nathan to shove it. It just sounds too damn good."

Fourteen minutes before 8:00:

"Nathan? What's doing? . . . I'm ready if you are to make that bet. This is what I'll do, Nathan. I'll give you your ten to one on the hundred thousand, but I want you to give me a point or two. What do you say?"

"Are you crazy, Solomon? Forget it. Not on your life. Forget the whole damn proposition, Solomon. You're trying to be a wise guy."

Sandy Rocca walked up to Nathan Rubin and handed him a piece of paper. On it was written in very clear print:

"Just got a call from Sam. With seven minutes and eighteen seconds to go in the first half, Boone's up 36–21. Also, Sky Davis is sitting on the bench with four fouls!"

Nathan Rubin shook his head triumphantly at Rocca as he said to Solomon, "Well, I'll tell you what I'll do, Solomon. Just a minute, Solomon." Nathan Rubin put down the phone and motioned to Sandy Rocca to contain himself. He then slowly sipped his drink and picked up the receiver.

"Solomon, I've been thinking it over. What I'm gonna do is take the ten to one on your hundred thousand. But I want you to give me one point, call it for old times' sake. What do ya say, Solomon?"

Solomon laughed. "That's okay with me, Nathan boy. You got the point." And Solomon roared, "And you got yourself a bet for one million dollars."

"Good, Solomon," Nathan Rubin said in his soft metallic cackle. "Ya know, Solomon, there's one thing I'm very happy about, win or lose."

"What's that, Nathan boy?"

"Well, I'm glad I told you about them suspended players and about that Dubow kid. I certainly was completely honest with ya. Now I'm sure there won't be no squawkin' if you lose, will there, Solomon?"

Solomon Lepidus roared, "Are you crazy, Nathan? I never squawked or welched on a bet in my entire life!"

"Good, Solomon. Say, are you gonna be at your restaurant later on tonight? I'm gonna be droppin' by with some friends. And Solomon, if I win the wager I'll be steppin' up to your office tomorrow at eight-thirty A.M. sharp to collect, ya see?"

"Whatever you say, Nathan boy. Take it easy."

Moments later Sandy Rocca had a wide grin on his face as he marched up to Nathan Rubin carrying a silver tray with two hand-blown Biedermeier glasses and a bottle of Dom Pérignon. He pointed to the year. "1935, Nathan. The best!"

Nathan Rubin chuckled metallically and shook his head. "Naah, Sandy, not to Boone, to Solomon Lepidus. The sucker!" Both men clinked glasses and drank quietly.

32

NATHAN RUBIN'S heart stopped on January 15, 1974. David remembered that date along with January 13, 1973, when Champ Holden died. But David remembered those dates not because of the deaths of Holden and Rubin, but because he won important money on each. On the Champ's judgment day he took 9 points on a very young and very talented Notre Dame team working on Marquette's home floor. They beat the Warriors 71–69 on a last-second shot by Dwight Clay.

On the night of Nathan Rubin's death, he laid 4 points on Duquesne as they were playing at home against a very erratic LaSalle team, and he remembered almost having heart failure himself. With ten minutes to go he got a phone call from Eddie Zeno telling him the score was tied. Sixteen minutes later, when he was anxiously pacing his rooftop terrace in the snow-flaked cold, Zeno called again.

"You're a winner, Lazar. Duquesne beat 'em eighty-one to sixty-nine. You're a God damn genius!"

He had won $38,000. He screamed out, "Yes!" as he ran back onto his terrace and slid in the snow. He made snowballs and heaved them toward Central Park. He enjoyed the wet flakes as they caressed his cheeks, eyes, and hair. He peered out at the dim lights on Central Park. He gazed over at Central Park South and shouted at the top of his lungs, "Fuck you world! Fuck you!"

Still exhilarated, he walked inside to answer the phone. It was Margot. She sounded miserable. "You haven't learned anything from your experiences with Leslie and Debbie, David." She stopped. David was too surprised to say anything. With bitterness in her voice, she said, "You have nothing to give to a woman, David. Nothing!" And with that she hung up.

David sat alone and burned some logs in his fireplace, and as he sat in front of the flames and watched them flicker, he heard Debbie Turner saying, "You've used yourself up completely by living in New York. Now nothing matters to you. You haven't enough energy left for anything but that gambling of yours and that dream of making it. Certainly not enough for enjoying a relationship."

For a while he thought about Margot, but it wasn't too long before the fire had died out, and as he rekindled the logs, he began thinking about the Duquesne game, and then his mind traveled to Nathan Rubin.

The last time David had seen Nathan alive, his face was bloated, and thin red veins were visible at his temples and at the corners of his dry mouth. His eyes also seemed different. They were no longer searing, shrewd, or discerning. They looked as though they were finally tired. Yes, tired.

He thought about the hundreds of telephone calls Nathan had made to him after he had begun to make important money, calls from Sandy Rocca's apartment and his son Charley's estate and his own home in Palm Beach and from Las Vegas and from a villa he owned in Madrid and from places where he was vacationing—the Riviera, Mexico City, Florence, Israel. And David thought of how on each occasion he called, after a quick hello and "how are ya," he would make a proposition. Always a proposition. David smiled, thinking how each time he had said, "No!"

There were probably a thousand people in the chapel at Nathan Rubin's funeral. None wept. They all were there—the brains he bought, marching in impotent sequence, wearing jail-striped suits and button-down shirts and horn-rims and $50 ties. And on their arms, decent unappealing wives. They all were there—the people he propositioned and screwed; the people he propositioned and hustled; the people he propositioned and suckered; the people he propositioned and hated; the people he propositioned and who hated him. They all were there.

It was a gathering of shadow people. They came from glittering drawing rooms and crummy back alleys; they came from swank offices on the sixty-fifth floor and from dim joints at the back of barber shops. In some way, Nathan Rubin's life had touched theirs.

Nino Tafuri was there, porcine-faced, with a grizzly's body and mud-colored velour suit.

"What do ya say, Lazar? Dat Nathan Rubin was something else, wasn't he? By da way, why don't ya come visit Johnny wid me tomorra?"

"How's he doing, Tafuri?"

"Well, I'll tell ya, I've been visitin' him every day but he doesn't seem to be improvin'. Dem doctors, I don't trust any of 'em."

"Call me tomorrow, Nino, I'll visit Johnny with you."

Ezra Bernstein, an old friend, was there, wearing his silver-laced yarmulke.

"Are the things I hear about you true, David? Are they really true?"

Irving Tannenbaum was there, smart-looking, subdued, hat in hand.

"Who's gonna give me a shoot? Anybody winning? Who's gonna give me a shoot?"

And the Owen Sadlers were there. Kim spotted David standing by himself and walked over. "Hi, David." David gazed at Kim's beautiful face and smiled. "How do you like living in London?"

"It's not New York, David, but it's exciting." Kim remained silent for a moment, and then a smile came over her face. "I guess you have the time to hang out at Elaine's nowadays, don't you, David?"

"I'm going to be there tomorrow night, Kim. Can you get away?"

Kim's eyes smiled. "It's a date, David."

Owen Sadler walked over. "Kim, darling, I'm getting awfully tired. Do you mind if we leave?"

"David, this is my husband. Owen, I think you've met David at a party at Charley Rubin's house."

David smiled as he shook hands with Owen Sadler. "That was a lifetime ago, Kim. A lifetime."

As David wandered off, Odette Bashjian was walking toward Kim. And at that moment Owen Sadler spotted Charley Rubin. "Kim, darling, do you mind if we stay another few minutes? There's good old Charley. I'd like to talk to him."

"Of course not, Owen, take your time."

Minutes later Kim Sadler was saying to Odette, "You're looking sexier than ever, love."

Odette glanced around and then whispered bitterly, "Can the big tycoon make you come, Kim, like I did?"

Everyone was there, scurrying around in a frenzied way and nervously whispering facts on stock deals and property values and the price of gold and grain.

The Colonel was there, head bowed, uncomfortable, sitting in a wooden chair. David walked over to him. As he did, Charley Rubin strode by talking about his costly new summer home. And then Irving Tannenbaum passed by with Nino Tafuri. They were talking about the fortunes Nathan Rubin had amassed in legitimate business. The Colonel remained quiet for a while, and then, soulfully, he nodded his head and said, "You know, David, there was a lot more to Nathan Rubin than just money. He was quite a guy."

Solomon Lepidus was there. He was speaking to Jerome Vogel in his friendly but harsh voice. "Listen, Jerome, are you chairman of the board of Kirkman and Watson, or aren't you? We've done business before. All I want you to do is study our rent roll, the potential of the location, the way the project was built, and our ability to pay the debt service, and then talk to me. I'll bet you right now that you'll tell me it's a cinch for you to get me the eighteen-million-dollar mortgage I want."

Minutes later Solomon was saying, "Oh, Jerome, I forgot to tell you, you better make that contribution to Dr. Green's laboratory one hundred and fifty thousand. I'm gonna have to do the same. Now that Nathan Rubin's gone, we're gonna have to do it ourselves. It's worth it. Saul Green is a genius. He's gonna be the one to discover a way of lickin' cancer. You think I'm backin' a quack?"

And of course Saskia Verdonck was there. She walked up to David, her large hips swaying, lips stained with lipstick, eyelids covered with shadow. Her blue-and-green dress was somewhat too tight for her now-maturing frame. "Hello, David. I guess I won't be seeing you again. I'm going home to Bergen. There's nothing here for me, David." Her voice grew bitter. "I'm glad he's dead."

And Mustache Harry McDuff was there.

David walked over to him. "Hey, McDuff, I hear your handicapping has really been suffering lately."

"Screw you, Lazar. Just remember I knew you when you were nothing, when you had to borrow forty-two hundred from Lepidus. And if Solomon didn't give it to you you would have been meat."

At that moment Nino Tafuri walked by.

"Hey, Nino, remember that time I owed you forty-two hundred?" David reached into his breast pocket and pulled out a wad of Franklins. He smiled and said, "I want you to do me a favor, Nino, and give this bread to your favorite charity."

"What the hell you talkin about, Lazar? I got no favorite charity."

"Then give it to McDuff, Nino." Lazar handed Tafuri the bills and walked away.

And Marsha McDuff was there. She was talking to Rebecca Lefko, the Colonel's wife.

"All Harry's friends play cards, Rebecca. See that tall man standing over there? Well, sixteen years and one hundred and eighty thousand dollars later he's finally learned how to play. I came back to Harry because I realized how much he needed me, Rebecca. It was that Nathan Rubin who ruined it for us. If it wasn't for him Harry would still have had Solomon Lepidus as a friend."

"I've always known Morty needed me too," Rebecca said. "I guess that's why I love him."

And Sally and Susie from Houston were there. Sally's long flaxen hair was tied in a bun. Susie's jet-black hair was pinned in a tiara. Each of them had an arm around Ben Tobin.

"That's right, honey, we flew in from Houston this morning for Nathan's funeral. After all, Ben, if it weren't for Nathan, we'd never have got to college."

And Ursula Knutson was there with her friend the hairdresser. When the hairdresser strolled away to talk to Sally and Susie, a stockily built young man came over. "Ursula, sugar. Remember me? Billy Mack Boone. Where'd you ever disappear to the next morning? I searched all over for you. I even checked the bursar's office. Ya know, sugar, they had no record at all of you ever attendin' classes. Boy, you sure enough got me in trouble with them wire service bureaus. I forgot all about callin' them shitasses with my report on the Boone–Western game that night."

And Betblood Willie was there.

"Got any good parlays, Willie?"

A chagrined expression came over Betblood Willie's face. "I got no luck, Davy. I had a perfect parlay going and I blew my money on food."

Arnie Feld was there with a racing form sticking out of his back pocket. Sidney Feld was not there. Champ Holden was not there. Harriet Barash was not there. Isaac Pizer was there.

Pizer's frigid eyes spotted David, and he walked up to where David stood and immediately began telling him about a surprise party he was giving for his wife at the El Morocco. He said it was going to cost him $100 per person, and then he told David about the elegant invitations, and after that he mentioned how sorry he was that his mother, Esther, was not alive to be there.

"My mother was the most wonderful woman in the world, David." When he finished telling David about his mother, Isaac Pizer had tears in his frigid eyes, but he wiped them away with the back of his hand and began bragging to him about his stock portfolio, and his winnings from the night before on his pro basketball selections. As he spoke he kept rubbing a birthmark on his hand. The more he rubbed, the more the mark seemed to turn the color of milk.

David kept nodding at him and saying, "Yeah, sure, Pizer ... that's interesting, Pizer." He kept thinking that when there's nothing else for men to talk about, they talk about elegant invitations, about profit and loss and winners and losers. David shuddered and thought, He's past sixty, I don't want to end up like Pizer.

As soon as David Lazar left, Mustache Harry McDuff walked over very slowly to Isaac Pizer. He spoke in a soft tentative voice.

"Isaac, I want you to know something. I appreciate everything you tried to do for me." He paused. "Listen, Isaac, all the times you visited me while I was laid up in Lenox Hill Hospital I wanted to tell you this, but I couldn't. I never told Marsha that you gave me the money to pay Scarne off. I pissed it away gambling. I was ashamed to. I guess you figured that out, huh Isaac? I'm sorry, Isaac."

Pizer looked around, making sure no one could overhear him. "You know, Harry, I was going to call you this week. I've had a terrible year handicapping for myself. Can you stop by my office tomorrow?" He paused. "I want you to be my handicapper, Harry. I'd really appreciate it if you'd help me out."

Mustache Harry McDuff looked into Isaac Pizer's eyes. He began to say something, but couldn't. He stood motionless for a moment and then lunged toward Pizer and wrapped his arms around him and hugged him and kissed him.

McDuff's gratitude got to Pizer. His cold eyes began to water.

And Hugh McDuff, Harry's seventeen-year-old son, was there. He was speaking to Ezra Bernstein and the Colonel. The Colonel had an arm around the boy. "When you finish up at St. Peter's, Hugh, what are you going to do?"

Hugh noticed Isaac Pizer walking by. "I'm gonna be a businessman, and make a million dollars like Isaac Pizer, Mr. Lefko."

Ezra Bernstein quickly responded, "You got to worry about making your first dollar, Hugh, before you start worrying about making a million."

The Colonel added, "Isaac Pizer. Heh! He don't have to worry about his first dollar. He still got it!"

Valerie Caldwell was there. Tall and statuesque and beautiful, she looked down at Isaac Pizer as she spoke. "My, Isaac, it's been such a long time since we last saw each other." Without warning, she leaned over and kissed Pizer lightly on the cheek and whispered in a voice pretty as music, "Remember, Isaac, that first day you interviewed me for the job?" She paused and smiled. "I really did want to go to Chinatown with you, Isaac. I really did."

A small man with a swarthy complexion and blazing narrow eyes edged in. "Isaac, this is my husband, Abdul Laham."

Minutes later, Valerie Caldwell Laham was on the far side of the hall conversing with David Lazar. "Come on, David, tell me, how successful are you?" Her violet eyes narrowed almost imperceptibly as she said, "How much have you made, David?"

On the other side of the hall, Solomon Lepidus was good-naturedly punching Isaac Pizer in the ribs. "Can you imagine the nerve of the girl, Isaac? She learns her trade from us Jews and ends up marrying an Arab."

Abdul Laham was standing unobserved in another corner of the hall, carefully listening to Jerome Vogel, chairman of the board of Kirkman and Watson. Vogel was choosing his words carefully.

And Coach Rodney Leland was there. He was huddled in a corner with Max Brown, the president of the New York Stars. Brown was speaking in a hushed voice, and Coach Leland was concentrating on his every word. "Well, Leland, is it a deal? Are you gonna be my coach next season or not?"

Rodney Leland paused briefly before answering, "Ya know, Mr. Brown, I've been hearing a lot of strange stories about you and your team down my way."

Max Brown looked around. "Listen, Rodney, I don't want any crap. You either take the job or you don't. Whatever you decide, just remember, I'm still gonna call all the shots. And that goes for who you play, when you play them, and for how long!"

"How much did you say you're going to pay me, Mr. Brown?"

Minutes later the two men were smiling happily and shaking hands.

And a happy-faced Thurman Tucker was there. He was speaking to Naomi Lepidus. She looked tired and old from a lifetime of trying to keep up with her husband. "I owe your husband my life, Naomi. I'll never forget it. Would you like to hear what he did?"

Quietly Naomi said, "You don't have to tell me about my husband, Mr. Tucker."

"No, Naomi, it's not that. It's just that I've never talked to anyone about it, and I'd like to. May I?"

Naomi Lepidus nodded, and Thurman told her about the day he visited Solomon to borrow money, the day Lepidus took out of his desk drawer a Chapter Eleven form and advised him in a whisper, "I'm in no position to loan money to anyone, Thurman. The best place to look for a helping hand is at the end of your own right arm."

"Well, Naomi, that's what I did. I was forty-one at the time and it wasn't until that day that I grew up. You see, I useta count on everybody. My parents, my wife, my friends. Now I count on myself. And," Thurman Tucker said confidently, "it's enough."

Solomon Lepidus joined them, vibrant and blooming.

"What do you say, Thurman boy?"

Before Thurman said a word, Naomi remarked, "Sol, Mr. Tucker was telling me about the day he came over to your office to borrow some money." Naomi paused. Solomon's face turned anxious. "He understands why you didn't loan him the money, Sol. He understands."

Solomon broke into a wide grin. "I'm glad for you, Thurman. You had me worried. Say, Thurm, how'd you like to go the Garden with me tomorrow night? I got ringside seats for the fights. And, Thurm boy, remind me to give you some phone numbers of guys I'm sure can help you with that deal you're working on."

And Fat Tony Giardello was there. He was a big man with a large potbelly. He was saying to David Lazar, "Nathan Rubin was the smartest son of a bitch in the world, Lazar. He suckered everyone and gave away nothin'." He shook his head with wonder and respect. "He was the smartest."

One-Eye Scarne complained to David, "When the hell you gonna lose some bets, Lazar? You're ruining me."

David grinned as he said, "By the way, Scarne, did you hear anything about who shot Club Collins on Riverside Drive?"

One-Eye shrugged his shoulders and gestured with his palms up. "I don't know what you're talkin' about, Lazar."

Crooked Dollar Moishe was there.

"The worst day of my life was the day Nathan Rubin gave you my phone number, Lazar."

282 . . .

"Come on, Moishe, I win a few, I lose a few."

And a man from Texas was there. He was speaking to Sandy Rocca. Rocca spotted David Lazar and called him over.

"I'd like you to meet the president of Boone College, David. This here is Sam Boone."

As David shook Sam's hand, he said, "Too bad about the way the NCAA came down on you, Mr. Boone. How long is the basketball suspension?"

And another gentleman from Texas was there. A black man, tall and thin, wearing a Sunday suit with a frayed white shirt. David spotted him standing in a corner talking to the Colonel.

"I reckon I'll be staying at Mr. Rocca's overnight. Mr. Boone and Billy Mack and me ain't got nowhere else to go, I reckon."

David recognized the "I reckon," and walked over. He noticed immediately that the man's face was different from those he saw in Harlem. It was more anguished, but at the same time more serene. There were deep furrows in his brow, and wrinkles creased his face. He also noticed that he had a farmer's hands and bowed legs. He walked over to him when the Colonel left and said, "Hello, J.T." He told him that he remembered his voice and knew who he was.

"You know, J.T., I never put the 'J.T.' together with 'Josh Turner' till now." David stood there puzzled and thought, How can it be possible that this man can even talk to a white man? How can it be possible?

When Josh Turner spoke it was with great calm.

"Ya see, if it wasn't for Mr. Rubin, I'd be dead now. He carried me in his own arms to Sam Boone's pappy's house. Must have walked more'n a mile to ol' Doc Sam's house with me bleedin' like a hog all the way."

David couldn't get himself to question J.T. about that day.

"Tell me what you remember about Nathan Rubin, J.T."

"Well, I'll tell ya, mister, I remember that you could trust him on his word, every word, and that he got the best surgeon in Alabama to look after me, and after I got well he furnished me land to work. He gave me a couple of acres and the money for a plow and a horse. And when I mended he moved me to Paducah, Kentucky. Ya see, mister, Nathan Rubin was the kindest white man I ever knew, and the strongest and the toughest."

David began to say something, but checked himself. Josh Turner looked into David's eyes and must have seen something he trusted, because he said, "Them that did that to me were townspeople, mister, and you know Nathan Rubin didn't let it go unsettled. No sir. Something terrible happened to each of them men. Nathan Rubin never went into it in detail, but just the same . . ." He shook his head. "I know it was him that evened things up. Yes sir, mister." He nodded. "I know it was him."

And Sandy Rocca was whispering to Solomon Lepidus in a corner.

"Do you understand, Solomon? You were set up. It was a scam. Nathan Rubin planned the whole thing. You were taken for a million dollars. I'm telling you because Nathan Rubin ordered me to. He said he wanted you to know. He said that you were his number-one sucker!" Sandy Rocca lifted a large attaché case and handed it to Solomon. "Nathan Rubin also ordered me to give you these tapes, Solomon."

As Rocca left him, Solomon Lepídus twitched uncontrollably.

And Helen Padrusch was there, a lovely woman, the Colonel's youngest sister. She was standing with her husband, Abe, a lean puny man, a little humped over in the shoulders. David spotted them arguing and walked over smiling.

"How's my favorite girl, Helen? Give me a kiss. Hiya, Abe. I didn't know you knew Nathan Rubin."

Abe Padrusch frowned. "Knew him? I knew Nathan Rubin for thirty-five years." He paused and shook his head.

"I never realized how crazy the man was until last year in Vegas. He was rolling the dice with at least fifty thousand dollars of his own money on the table and all of a sudden he hears these two ladies standing in back of us talking about needing watches. He stops the game, reaches into his vest pocket, and pulls out a couple of fifty-dollar watches and turns around and starts peddling them to these two ladies. I couldn't believe it, David. Imagine, holding up a game like that to sell a couple of fifty-dollar watches."

Helen Padrusch abruptly interrupted her husband.

"Do you hear anything from that friend of yours, Debbie, David? What a doll, and sexy!"

As soon as David heard Debbie's name his expression changed.

"You were crazy to ever let her get away, David. She wasn't just a beautiful girl. She was intelligent and sweet and—"

"Come on, Helen, mind your own business, leave the boy alone."

"I'm just telling him the way I feel, Abe."

"I'll talk to you later, Helen. I got to find Solomon Lepidus. Take care, Abe."

At the same moment Solomon Lepidus was saying to Doug Lazar, "Ya see, Dougie boy, Nathan Rubin mighta thought I was a sucker, and it's probably true when it comes to my gambling, although you gotta understand I have fun with that, too. And I'm not saying Nathan was a sucker either. You gotta understand that, Dougie. It's not a question of that at all. When we entered our business partnerships, Nathan didn't lose. He wasn't taken; he only gained. Both of us only gained." Solomon stretched and looked at Doug. "Ya see, Dougie boy, even Nathan Rubin and I, we helped each other."

Minutes later David walked over to Nathan Rubin's open casket, where Solomon Lepidus and Doug Lazar silently stood staring at the corpse. In an urgent voice David whispered, "Solomon, I'm sure Nathan Rubin set you up for that Boone–Western game. I've been talking to that black man over there. He runs the community store. He was under strict orders from Rubin."

Lepidus answered, "That's okay, Davy boy. Nathan Rubin made his last bet, and I'm still going strong."

David Lazar noticed Solomon's hand. It was clenching the strap handle of the attaché case Sandy Rocca had given him as tightly as David, many times in the past, had clenched his silver dollar.

David sat in the second row of the chapel with Solomon and Naomi Lepidus. Nathan Rubin's immediate family was directly in front of them. Rubin's appetizing Hungarian wife was dressed to kill. His daughter-in-law was arguing vehemently with Charley over an affair she wanted to attend that weekend. His granddaughter, Patricia, looked as if she had been hooked on uppers and downers for a long, long time. His other grand-daughter, Cynthia, was sliding her hand up and down the trouser leg of some long-haired, bearded youth, and leaning over, she whispered to him, "This is a drag, Julien. When it's over, let's fuck."

When the funeral services ended, David heard Arnie Feld say to Doug, "He was nothing but a prick!" And David heard his brother's retort, "Yeah, but what a prick!" He also heard Max Brown whisper to Solomon Lepidus, "That's one for us, Solomon. Now we won't have to pay the old bastard that two hundred Gs we owe him." David saw a flicker of light come to Solomon's face, but a moment later when Solomon turned to face Max Brown, the light was out.

After the funeral, David and Doug went with Ben Tobin to the Carnegie Delicatessen in memory of David's and Nathan Rubin's many meetings there. After lighting up and taking a few puffs on his cigar, Tobin began speaking about Solomon Lepidus. He told David and Doug that Solomon had been losing more cash than he could afford to bookmakers, to card sharks, to croupiers. There was a quality in his voice both of pain and pleasure. David wondered—was Solomon Ira Lepidus ready to fall? Minutes later Tobin changed the subject and told Doug and David that he had just returned from Israel, where he had run into Esther Aroni. She was separated from her husband and was visiting relatives in Jerusalem. He told them she seemed miserable and had asked about Doug. He said she was still an "unreal-looking" woman, but not close to the raving beauty she had once been.

Then he changed subjects again and this time began talking about campaign contributions and how well David had been doing. His eyes became slits and his mouth tightened as he waited for a reply. For amusement, David began throwing telephone numbers at him and hinted at the kind of bread he was making. Tobin became unnerved and bit right through his cigar.

After Tobin left, Doug fell into a dark mood. News about Esther Aroni did it. When David mentioned that, Doug denied it viciously and started lashing out at David. He said David was a very limited person and that he had lost all respect for him. He said David was glutting himself with things and possessions and that it was all shit, that David was filled with despair, that all his needs for "making it" were grounded wholly in despair. For several minutes Doug's harangue continued, then Doug calmed down, and when he spoke again, David could hear the concern in his voice.

"You're falling right into the trap those bastards have set for you, David. You've become just like them, like Solomon and Nathan. It's obscene. You work only for money, and you're a slave to success. Making money hasn't made you any stronger than you used to be. Only harder. You've got to get out. You've got to retire."

Though David felt that a lot of what Doug said was true, it still hurt, and he shot back angrily, "God damn it, Doug! Don't preach to me. I know what's important."

Doug shook his head from side to side with that ever-present concern and answered, "All you know, all Lepidus knows, all Nathan Rubin ever knew, is how to build more, fight more, run more, control more, do more. You've forgotten who you are, David, and anything else worth knowing."

Then it was David's turn to lash out, and he did. He called Doug a loser, reminded him that he, David, had made "important money," not Doug. That if it weren't for David he wouldn't have a dime. That he was speaking like that just because he had never "made it" and that Solomon Lepidus and Nathan Rubin and he had.

That night David could not sleep. His brother's comments kept whirling through his mind.

33

WHEN IT CAME to his handicapping, David Lazar hated to lose. He did everything his handbook said, and some things it didn't. As Nathan Rubin had once told him, "It's knowledge, it's art, and it's balls." In the back of his mind was the thought that if he went broke he'd be able to start again; that was one of the biggest differences, the biggest reassurances for him. He'd been broke before. He hated it, but it didn't terrify him. So what if he lost, so what! He thought about Solomon Lepidus, Nathan Rubin, and Isaac Pizer. He thought about what was in their black hearts. In his own heart he found boundless energy, immeasurable restlessness, frenzy, longing, and despair. Deep inside him there still was a lamp turned on. He knew there must be something more.

On Saturday, March 29, 1975, the NCAA semifinal game between the Kentucky Wildcats and the Syracuse Orangemen was to be played. In New York the points came out 8 and 8½ on Kentucky; in the Southwest it was Kentucky 10; in almost every other state it was somewhere between those numbers. David made the game 17½ points in favor of the Wildcats. It was one of the biggest differentials he had found all year. Kentucky was ten players deep.

David got down $388,500 on the game. It was the biggest single wager of his career. The final score was Syracuse 79, Kentucky 95.

UCLA was also involved in a semifinal game that afternoon. They won at the buzzer, whipping Louisville 65–64. Immediately at the game's end, John Wooden, the Bruins' coach and resident genius, announced he was retiring after the championship game with Kentucky on March 31.

Kentucky had won David a fortune, but John Wooden was tough to beat. He'd won nine national championships in the past eleven years. All year he'd been telling anyone who would listen that the UCLA team would run through a brick wall for him.

Anyone who had any sense knew that Kentucky was ten deep; that they'd wear the Bruins down; that UCLA would never be able to keep up with the pace of the Wildcats. Kentucky would be strong, physical, brutal. UCLA, in comparison, would be weak. The Las Vegas line came up: "Pick 'em." But David made it 3½ in favor of John Wooden. David figured the boys Wooden loved so much wouldn't let him down on this, his last day in the sun. David was sentimental, he was emotional, he was involved, he was vulnerable.

He staked his wager on Wooden. He decided to bow out with Wooden. It was his last bet of the year. The last bet of his career. He wagered $158,000 on UCLA.

The final score was Wooden's Bruins 92, Kentucky 85. The game was close, but David never worried. All the time he watched the game on TV he felt that talent would show, and it did. For the tenth time in a dozen years, John Wooden won a national championship. He was the most successful college basketball coach in history, and he retired with the whole nation knowing it.

On the same day, March 31, 1975, the most successful college basketball handicapper in America also retired, and no one knew about it except for the Colonel, Solomon Lepidus, and his twin brother, Doug.

David resolved when the Bruin game ended that he had done something, proved something, and now it was time to bow out.

David Lazar was aware that people wait for that moment when they can get even. The rise of a man is abnormal, euphoric—not human; and so other men do not taste or feel or touch it; but the decline of a man is normal, real—human; and so it sinks ineluctably into the psyche, into the heart and soul of every man. It makes them bitter. It makes them hate.

On March 31, 1975, David Lazar decided to pack it in. He quit handicapping. Bill Russell had walked away while he was still on top. So had Rocky Marciano; so had Sandy Koufax. David had been handicapping for five years.

In those five years David Bernard Lazar accomplished this: He started with $250 and won $7,300 the first year.

The following year he started with $2,950 and he made $109,500. With the quarter of a million he worked with in 1972–1973 he made . . . you wouldn't believe it. And with the "you-wouldn't-believe-it," he made, he still doesn't believe it, and with the "he-still-doesn't-believe-it," he made—Nathan Rubin, were he still alive, wouldn't believe it. No . . . Nathan Rubin *would* believe it!

David flew to Los Angeles to see Noah Weldon. He told Noah the truth about what he actually had accomplished and how much Noah had inadvertently helped by supplying David with information on West Coast players and teams.

Then David reached into his breast pocket for an envelope containing $100,000 and handed it to Weldon. Noah took the envelope, unsealed it, and saw the bills. His eyes widened. He began to stutter as he tried to say something, but he couldn't. He just stood there shaking his head and stammering. Finally, slowly, he composed himself and handed the envelope back to David and placed his hand in David's, and in a quiet determined voice told him he couldn't accept the money. They exchanged looks, and David knew Noah meant it.

Before leaving, David called to Doris, who was talking to Carol in the kitchen. "Hey, Doris, do you remember when you tried to teach me the cha-cha? Remember? Cha-cha, one, two, three." David walked into the kitchen and grinned at Carol and kissed her on the top of the head. Then he took Doris's hand and asked her to follow him into the den for a minute. When they were alone, David explained to her that he knew about Noah's bad heart and wanted to help. He then told her about the success he had had as a handicapper and how he had used Noah. He lifted the envelope from his pocket and handed it to her. Doris was more practical than Noah. She took the money.

From Los Angeles, David flew to San Francisco to visit Debbie Edison. He called her home, but an operator advised him that the number had been disconnected. He called the Lindeman Clinic, but was told that Mrs. Edison was on a leave of absence. They could not tell him anything else. He telephoned Silver Spring, Maryland, and spoke to Debbie's mother. In a shy and constricted voice Mrs. Kramer said that she had not heard from her daughter in recent weeks and did not know exactly where she was. Pehaps visiting an old college friend.

Psychiatrist Victor Matalon explored each soft hollow with unrestrained desire, every crevice with lusty affection. And Debbie Edison surrendered herself to him each time as if for the first time. It was more than anything she had ever experienced with her husband, Jimmy, or ever imagined with David. For the first time she surrendered herself completely to a man. In bath and bed, on soft earth and hard wooden floors, in motels and on yachts, in what she thought were the strangest places, she shivered, sighed, moaned, shuddered, and came as if for the first time.

For months Debbie had struggled to stay away from Victor Matalon. From their first harmless meeting at a psychiatrists' convention, in elegant Vienna of all places, she had denied herself this man. But he was always there, pursuing her, walking alongside her, smiling at her, asking her to lunch. He asked her to go with him to the Kunsthistorisches, Vienna's renowned art museum. He courted her with his psychiatrist's couchside manner and manly face and limitless confidence. And when she returned to the States it was no different.

Dr. Matalon pursued her again, with even greater urgency, with even more single-minded purpose. He flew to San Francisco every Wednesday for one reason or another and began seeing her again and again and again.

Finally she felt safe giving herself to him. She felt complete. Victor Matalon, virile, dynamic, confident, extremely successful in his profession, offered Debbie Edison all. And the inexperienced Debbie hungered for "all." In two months she stood in front of her husband, Jimmy, and in a soft, hesitant voice demanded a divorce.

Jimmy Edison stared at her. She gazed at him and involuntarily lowered her eyes.

"It's another man, isn't it, Debbie?" She stood, remaining motionless.

Jimmy thought her to be more beautiful at that moment than he had ever seen her before. She stood confronting him without a cigarette. She hadn't smoked in weeks, Jimmy noted. Raising her eyes, she gazed at her husband. She felt discomfort, a sense of wrongdoing. How could she do this to him? What could she say to her parents? Her friends? He hadn't done anything to deserve this. He was her friend. Her husband. She wanted to hug Jimmy and tell him everything was all right. She wanted to tell him that she would always share his joys and sorrows. But deep inside her she felt something larger than her guilt, something instinctive and self-ish and whole. Something all-powerful and brand-new.

She raised her face to his. "Yes, Jimmy," she said, almost triumphantly. He didn't say a word. He didn't ask her if the man was David Lazar. He didn't want to know. He stood there slumped and silent.

"Debbie's not as sentimental as you are, David," Myra Ross said in a vindictive voice. "She grew up and is living with a man in Boston. I'll make you a wager, David. I'll bet you the man's not sentimental either."

David paid back everyone. He had enough money to live on forever, but he was more alone now than ever before. Without Leslie, without Debbie, without Margot, and pretty much without Doug, who was involved again with Esther Aroni. David's mood reflected his abject misery.

The mountain climber in him was again beginning to gaze upward. He knew he had accomplished as much as he could have ever dreamed, and yet he still felt incomplete. Soul-searching was for losers, he told himself, but there he was, sitting alone in his bank vaults counting Franklins and soul-searching again.

What is the soul and where is its center? I am still flawed and human and pained. I still don't know who I am. A wound is still inside me. The darkness is still inside me. I am still conditioned, still unable to transcend my emotional fix. Some eminent doctor told me it would help if I exposed myself more. That way I'd develop my inner life, but I don't know where to start. I have the same fears, the same vulnerabilities, as before.

There are questions and there are questions. What's the price on New Mexico State? What should it be? How much is the game worth? Who are the best coaches in the college game? The best teams? For those questions David had answers. David had proved it during the past five years. Betting money, breathlessly waiting for the results, collecting bundles in brown paper bags, marching to bank vaults, opening safety deposit boxes, stacking 290 . . .

everything in. He knew that in business there wasn't a problem that couldn't be solved. But he had filled up his gut, anchored himself with gold and greed and flesh. And finally he had to admit to himself that there were problems inside him that should be unraveled and solved. A voice deep inside persevered, kept haunting him, kept saying that he should be interested in creating, not collecting. He had sold himself too cheaply. He still had the same values, anxieties, compulsions, and obsessions that he had always had. He merely felt that his core had deteriorated and that he was eons older.

Once, a long time ago, I opened up, and for a short while I knew warmth. I allowed Leslie to know me. She knew my insecurities, my ambivalences, my core. She knew the man I was and the one I failed to be. Now, in spite of all my success, I feel a cold chill. I still need her to hold me, to nourish me, to care for me, to love the man I am. Leslie was what I needed. Rather than go to her, I go back to my vaults and I count my Franklins.

David was wretched. He was miserable. He wanted Leslie. He wanted Jennifer. He wanted to play with his child and shoot hoops in his own backyard. He wanted to be lean and trim and youthful. He wanted to flirt with college cheerleaders and to write poetry and start over again. He wanted to take Jennifer to the zoo and watch her feed peanuts to the elephants and take her to a swank restaurant and feed her strawberries covered with whipped cream. And then take her home and hug her and kiss her and tickle her.

David's mind was filled with an imploring voice: I had wanted the impossible, to handicap and to create; to love and to use; to be whole and to be a machine. It is impossible. I am separated from my center. I am more than one self, I am split into many selves. And I am never more in one world than in another. How do you tie, clasp, brace, connect one world with another? How do you?

More and more Leslie loomed in his mind. Was it love? It wasn't love. It was the satisfaction of his own vanity, an ego trip.

More and more he felt madness seeping in, a strangeness overcoming him. Soul-searching was for losers, he told himself. But there he was soul-searching again.

From dungheap to glory he had marched, and yet he could not savor his success. His accomplishment was not sufficient. There was no need to bellow that he had *made* it, that he was content, that he was proud. There was no joy inside him.

Why is it in my entire life I never once found ultimate satisfaction? Why is it I have never known a time when the sweat and the tears and the blood of my dream coalesced into something more lasting and permanent than self-doubt and self-pity? Why is it?

He opened his volume of *A Treasury of Great Poems* and turned to

"The Lamb" on page 600. He noticed that Leslie had penciled in on the border of the page the date and "You no longer deserve this poem—Leslie." He had been married for less than seven months at the time.

He recalled Leslie's saying after she had read the first draft of his novel, "You get a feeling of being disoriented, David. People won't like that. It's not commercial."

"That's by design, Leslie. Stop looking at it as a commodity. See its potential as art. And remember, Leslie, it's just a first draft. What I need is feedback. I need an experienced editor to tell me what works and what doesn't. What to cut and what to change. What I need from you is encouragement."

"What you need, David, is an advance!"

He was sure the best businessman he had ever known was Nathan Rubin. He also wondered whether if Leslie had been a man she would have been better. If she were a man, would he have called her genius or sick? He recalled how many times when he was speaking to her in the middle of an afternoon he would get an urge, out of nowhere, and unzip his fly, walk over to her, and rub his organ against her face, her neck, her ear, and how she immediately responded.

He thought of a million and one things he should have said to Leslie in the beginning, and he realized he hadn't said one.

Doug, he thought, was the worst businessman in the world. Doug had always wanted to be a writer, and much of himself he gave to David.

One evening he had gotten into an argument with Doug on the telephone, and Doug had finally interrupted him. "David, I can't talk to you anymore. Esther Aroni just called. She just got a divorce, and I'm going to meet her. Goodbye." That depressed him.

The following day he telephoned Leslie and insisted she meet him for lunch. When she arrived, he immediately noticed a few silver filigrees in her hair and some fresh marks around her eyes, but rather than mention it, he told her that in spite of everything that had happened, he loved her, and wanted to be with her.

"I want to start over again, Leslie, and try to make you happy. I can give you anything you desire in the whole world. I don't blame you for anything. I blame myself."

"I'm content with Harold, David."

"But, Leslie, you don't understand. The money doesn't mean anything to me if I can't share it with you. I did it all for you. I love you. I always will."

Leslie gazed at him and smiled tenderly. She reached for his hand and took it and brought it to her mouth and kissed it and then held it to her cheek. As he leaned toward her, he was filled with the scent of her perfume.

292 . . .

When she started speaking, he detected an inner strength in her voice that he had never heard before.

"You need an entirely different kind of person, David. You need other things than what I can give you. You need someone much younger. Someone who can worship you and make your life her entire life."

She continued speaking calmly, and it was evident that she had found something with Harold Freed that she had never found with him. She seemed relaxed and satisfied with her life, not at all perturbed or flustered at being with or without him. She kept talking.

"Don't think I was horrible for the things I did to you, David. I was desperate and confused. I didn't mean to hurt you. I never meant to hurt anybody. I never felt I had any choice in anything I ever did in those days."

She smiled as if those days were gone forever.

"You know how I get when there's too much pressure on me. I just can't function. With you, David, I'd still be under too much pressure. All the money in the world wouldn't change that."

David's voice broke as he said, "It doesn't have to be that way anymore, Leslie. It's not too late for us. We can be happy now. We still love each other and we do understand each other. We can both try." He whispered, "Please, Leslie, come back to me."

There was a pained expression on her face, the same kind of pain he had witnessed many times earlier. "I'm content with Harold, David. I'm sorry for you, but it's too late for us. Please don't call again or try to see Jennifer. It's only upsetting for both of us. The truth is, we never were good for each other. We always needed each other and limited each other too much."

David bit his lip and gulped. The dryness in his throat made it difficult to swallow. He forced himself to hold everything in. He didn't cry.

There was nothing else he could say, and he wanted to say so much. He wanted to say, "But we still love each other, Leslie, and we're really so much alike. We've both constantly hit our heads against a stone wall trying to do something, and yet all we ever did was run around in circles and get nowhere.

"We've always known that we were losers in advance. Oh, Leslie, we are alike, to our very core we're alike. The only difference is that I refused to die. That I still have hope for the two of us."

But David didn't say a word. Instead he asked the waiter for the check and paid it. Then he stared at Leslie for what seemed like a very long time, hoping and waiting for her to say something, to change her mind; knowing that he would never see her again. Then as his eyes began to water he stood up and calmed himself and said, "I love you, Leslie, and I do want what's best for you, and now I realize that for you that means being away from me." Then he reached over and grazed her cheek with his fingertips and in a voice choking with emotion he whispered, "Goodbye."

From David's Handbook and Prayer Book:

"I'm trying to go through it all very quickly now because I'm still raw. I know if I don't spill it out quickly I'll start reacting again. Did you ever lose someone that you really needed? Did you ever feel real pain? The kind of pain that burns like a flame and flickers and will not burn out? That quivers eternally at the center of your soul? Did you ever come home when no one was there and just close the door behind you and cry out at the top of your lungs? Did you ever run into your bedroom and fall down and smother your face in a pillow and weep? Did you ever feel terror, real terror, and at the same moment feel weary, so weary that you knew you couldn't struggle any longer? So weary that you didn't care about tomorrow? So weary that you'd take some pills? Did you ever take those pills? I did.

"I hope I won't be permanently miserable. I hope I'm only feeling crushed and sad and alone today. I realize how childish it is, of course. After all, disappointments in one's life are a very normal thing. You might even say 'the way of life' But I can't help myself. I feel so tired. But even at the center of my fatigue I'm beginning to wonder if Leslie will ever call again. If I'll ever be able to salve my pain. Right now it's pitch black outside, the birds will not begin singing for hours, men are resting, but as I gaze out into the dark black-blue of the night I swallow hard and admit to myself that Leslie will never call and that I'll never be whole again. I just know I never will. What I'm beginning to understand is that the earth will always spin beneath the sky and that I'm healthy and that I'm sick. I feel so empty and no one cares. Oh, Leslie, I tried to convince you that I loved you, with all my strength I tried; but you wouldn't listen; and I took some pills and I didn't die, but whatever was left of me that was worth anything at all, did. What now, Leslie, what now? . . ."

Her voice, her sad and bitter feminine voice, was ringing in his ears. . . .

Leslie says I don't believe in anything anymore. She's wrong. I believe in something, all right. I believe in a holy cocksucker who dips his hand in bloody holy water and by so doing afflicts us with leukemia and anemia.

I believe in a pious pusher who drains our sense of humor and shoots us up with self-consciousness until we've been wiped out by self-pity.

I believe in a despotic deity who's obsessed us with making it so that we've become blinded to our egoism and taste only our own delusions of grandeur and hear only sounds of our own omnipotence. I believe in a sodomizing child molester who aborts our children and ravages our mothers and castrates our fathers. He's a joker who toys with our veins and souls and makes our minds into wandering Jews until there's nothing left but whines and poses, until we don't know who we are. I believe he's a gardener who plants by pissing famine, quake, and flood, and who packs the earth with evil seeds and stress that causes the seeds to mushroom wildly. And these seeds ejaculate a gummy pollen which drips from the sky and seeps through ceilings, soaking our brains and flooding our neighbors and impregnating our women and destroying everything. A charitable God—nonsense! He's a bookmaker who's shrewdly dressed us in the garb of insecurity and spoon-fed us anxiety and fear so that he can be certain to collect his vigorish. He's a shylock who's milked interest by squeezing men into a psychic ghetto so that they're satisfied just to keep busy. He's a pusher who's hooked the welfare mother into having baby after baby, and for that, that fiendish slaver hands out a public-assistance dole.

A spiritual God—he's a Mafioso who drowns us with kidney diseases. A pornographer who's invented osteoporosis to soften our bones. A seraphic God—not on your life. He's a consummate businessman who's ordained an obscene seraglio to seduce his chosen by giving them just enough brain power to entertain him. A miraculous God—don't make me laugh! He's made us fumble and err and lose our sight in the outdoor sun so that we now worship indoor TV. He's starved us for those games, as he knows. God damn him, he knows! That it's our only Home Relief! A smooth-cheeked tranquil beatific God—don't be naive! He nails us down with pussy-hate and penis-envy. And after we are nailed and helpless, this double-crossing fascist dives down on us in his Nazi Fokker and scoops us up and flies us into his demonic gale and soars and buzzes until we have bubbles on our brains and are out of control and ready for his next commandment. And, of course, it, too, is an addiction. An atrocity! Yes, he's a wise God for certain. And besides everything else, hasn't he used his munitions to blind our sight and cause rift and separation and pain? Hasn't he charmed us with hate and jailed us with haunting memories and psyched us with impossible dreams and isolated us by dehumanizing us into believing that we stand superior? Hasn't he butchered us still further from what is majestic by hacking us into Hebrews and Christians and Hindus and Muslims and Buddhists? And hasn't he divided us even more by bleeding us red and yellow and black and white and brown? And hasn't he caused us to become confused and alienated still more by taunting us, eon after eon, with worthless illusions which he jingles in front of us? And why? So that he, that Leader, can be entertained. So that he can muse over us. So that he can watch us, his fragile fuck bubbles, try to survive the warped, fleshy, fossilized beach of this, his besotted creation!

Yes, Leslie, I believe in that holy wonder all right. I say, Screw the son of a bitch; we'll survive in spite of him. In time we'll computerize everything and beat down myth and deity and all our other obsessions and become immortal ourselves. And we can do it, and you know why? Because he isn't a very godly messiah. What he is is "a game," and what we can do is research that "game" right out of existence. We have eons of time to achieve it. We have our own unsurpassed intelligence to help us learn how. We have our live bodies and hopeful instincts and marvelous brains to feel and probe and tinker with. And with all of that to power-rate with, we can handicap everything together. We can enlighten our darkest centers. Yes, Leslie, I believe we will become infinite and holy, so help my brain.

As for myself, Leslie, I am exhausted. What I need is to rid myself of my inner life, and that's something I have discovered but one way to achieve without waiting. For in the purest sense, what is death but the elimination of excrement—a lobotomy!

Now there was time on David's hands, plenty of time. Empty time. He tried to fill it up by buying things and chasing women. It didn't work. His deepest needs were not being filled. He was tired and depressed, but he kept collecting women and possessions and running from one party to another. For months he continued to find beautiful women for a day or a weekend or at most a week and then changed them as if they were one of his DeNoyer suits. After each experience he felt emptier, more exhausted, more severely depressed.

He realized that deep within himself he needed desperately to find something that gave his life purpose and meaning. And then he knew the answer. It had always been there. He would write. Not sports books, but a novel. A serious novel.

He was aware of how exhausted he was, but he commited himself to work. And David worked. Six hours a day in the beginning. And then that incredible energy of his surged and it was twelve to fourteen hours each day, seven days a week. And he forced himself to work on. Two hundred pages. Three hundred. Four hundred pages. It was definitely therapy. The get-it-off-your-chest kind of catharsis. He poured his soul onto the blank pages. Five hundred pages. Six hundred. A novel was being shaped. He wrote on. Did not show his work to anyone. His pain was being exorcised. He was writing. Authoring again. What he always wanted to do. What he always fancied himself as. An author. He wrote with a fury that was unbridled, and the words and confessions kept pouring forth onto the blank pages.

One morning, about three months from the day he had started, he began to read what he had created. It took him days to read his manuscript. But it was worth it. He loved it. He was sure he had written an important novel. A good book. He called up the biggest publishing house he could think of. Asked to speak to the senior editor in charge of fiction. Was passed on to a junior editor. Explained to the editor who he was, what his life had been like, and how he had captured it in the manuscript. An appointment

296 . . .

was made. The bulky manuscript passed hands. A decision was promised within a week. Three weeks later a rejection letter came. And a week later the manuscript.

David photocopied the manuscript and personally submitted it to ten other publishing houses. But within two months all of the copies had been returned. Rejected. He felt he was a loser. A loser! He jailed himself within his spacious apartment. For days he didn't answer the telephone. Mood black. He didn't read a newspaper. Exhausted. Didn't watch the sporting events covered on television. Depressed. With this uncontrollable darkness seeping into him, he remained within himself. A loser. . . . The days turned to months. . . .

There's now an attendant watching over David Bernard Lazar, handicapper, as he lies in bed without a life of his own. The attendant has light-brown hair and a fair complexion. He's tall and corpulent with a sullen face and a plump underchin. He, as most of the attendants here, is indifferent to David's condition.

All day and all night, David's brain continues to throb. David is certain some people have experienced days when they've been unsettled, have had experiences which unnerved them, but why is it that his entire life has been unsettled? That he's always been unnerved? Sometimes David experiences a false gaiety, but that's not who he really is. The real David is not provided with diversions of any kind. David always knew life was slipping away and he woke up every morning terrified of what was going to be. It seems his head has always felt itself to be a void where the darkness gathered, where the light never penetrated, a place both mysterious and sinister. He stumbled into the light but then fell back into the gloom.

He's much older now, but he's still certain it's not David who is odious. It's the darkness, the dark inside of him. He can't rid himself of it, and unless he does, how will he ever see? Sometimes he gazes at himself when the sun is warm and bright and he thinks he knows what to do, but then the darkness returns and he's chilled all over again.

Every dawn from his barred window David sees the bloody red come up over the dungheap in the east, but it swoops down so quickly. Then at dusk it disappears into the dark soft rot. The dark is inside him. It's impossible for him to see the way. He's looked a thousand times. He's searched. He's tried. But it gets so dark so quickly now that he does nothing. He's resigned himself to stay.

A very long time ago David was told by teachers that he was a gifted child, but that he was always daydreaming. He's convinced now that the only thing his handicapping did was give others the chance to admire him. Looking back, he thinks his handicapping success was the most grotesque of his failures. The dark is inside him.

It's dusk now and the bloody red is going down again. Many years ago

. . . 297

he walked in the snow with a girl, she pressed his hand and called him "a little lamb." He lived in the dark with her. He kept her there. It's the way it was; it's the way he is. He still wants glory, something so perfect that it could never be defined. Something as complete as a girl in the distance who appears idyllic, as a mistress whose very conception completes our quest.

Sometimes he pried himself open for a little while. Maybe a few times he had the taste of life, but each time he closed even tighter than before. He doesn't want to be hurt anymore! He's not seeing the light anymore! He's resigned now to living in the dark. That girl once whispered to him that she would live inside him if she could. That she'd make love to him, inside of him. That's what he needed, she said. But she couldn't. And, of course, he never really loved her for herself alone, only what he wanted her to be. Today he would hold his breath until his lungs burst, just to see her the way he first envisioned her. The truth pours out of him. The dark is inside him.

I'll probably remain here for the time I have left, he thought. I want to talk to someone about Leslie, but now I realize I'd only talk the same way today as I talked yesterday.

One hour before Doug stepped on the plane with Esther Aroni I spoke to him. He said my problem was that I knew enough to suffer anguish but not enough to be redeemed. He said I was an excellent handicapper because I didn't participate in the playing, but that life cannot be handicapped, that it must be played. Courageously, gallantly, breathlessly played. Why can't I obey? That dark is inside me.

Sometimes when the darkness went away David was accursedly perceptive. He saw roads it would be disastrous to follow, but then it was dark again and he pursued them anyway. He was seldom able to unite his perceptions as an artist with his feelings as a man. The artist in him was always wiser than the man. Now, looking back, he realized that it was true. For him life had been a disease, and art a hospital. Unfortunately, many times he would never go to the hospital. It's still a quantum leap to the hospital.

He took a walk with his hospital attendant yesterday. While he was out he saw some children playing. He saw them strike a match to a puppy dog. The puppy began running in circles and screaming. It went on howling and howling. The children jumped up and down laughing. Their laughter reminded him of Nathan Rubin, their screams of Leslie Kore; the puppy was he. Jennifer Cartel is a beautiful young woman, he's heard. His only joy was Jennifer.

To this day his voice still quickens when he says Leslie's name. To this day he is frightened. To this day he feels a tinge of "I want to get even" creeping around in his soul.

He's having a visitor later today: Ron Nivens. He thinks he's coming to take him home today. It's light outside now. He can see a tight-lipped grimace on his male attendant's dark-chocolate face. He's sure he's well enough to go home today. But still, he's tired. He's always tired. That dark is inside him.

Briefcase in hand, he walked onto Madison Avenue and thought, What am I supposed to do now? Go to my vault and count Franklins? But he didn't go to his vault. He walked west to Fifth Avenue. And then paced north. When he stopped walking he was one hundred feet from the entranceway to Leslie's luxury apartment house. He waited. Hours later a beautiful young woman stepped out of the building. Immediately, joyously, he knew it was Jennifer. Frightened but compelled, he followed her. As he did he kept hearing Nathan Rubin's words: "What really matters in the long run is keeping your ego intact, remaining whole." And also ringing in his ears was something Doug had once said: "Time is as life, David, it's round and full. It isn't meant to be conquered, it's meant to be lived. You shouldn't be hung up on making it, or scared of the time you have left. That's absurd! Comical. That's exactly what death is!"

As he walked along the street he continued to reflect. A terribly long time ago I wanted to change the world by my writing, but all I ever did was change my own life by handicapping. What I have to do now is start over again and change. I'll start over again. I have possibilities. Choices are available. It was a comforting refrain.

As he kept walking and observing Jennifer, he thought how many years he had wasted. She stopped for a red light.

He had succeeded in acquiring money, but there was never anything enriching or fulfilling about that. The best he could see using all those Franklins for was fertilizer so something of value could grow. From now on he was going to make every effort to overthrow the dark inside him. He was going to start by scraping off the slime. By doing that, maybe he could find out what had been lurking in the dark. He was going to work harder on his inner life than he had ever worked on his handicapping. He knew it would take a great deal more courage, but maybe then he'd be able to relate to someone with genuine love, and maybe someone would love him, too. If all went well he might even try writing again—he did try last night—and he might just try going to Harlem again. Maybe now he could be of help there; if not, maybe his Franklins could. Choices are available.

Jennifer had stopped walking. She was standing in front of a Japanese restaurant and seemed to be searching the street as if she were looking for someone. He walked up to her.

"Pardon me, miss. I don't know who I am, my mind has been a wandering Jew. No, it's not a gag. Maybe you can help me to find out. Can you answer this question? If I'm not going to be the Handicapper any longer, who am I going to be? Oh, you're smiling, that's good. That means you know me, doesn't it? Then you know I won't doff my hat to anyone, but I'm still willing to give my seat to a person in need. Oh, you're laughing, you have a sense of humor. That's wonderful.

"We're going to be friends, aren't we?" he went on. "Is that a nod? Good, now I can tell you without frightening you that I've been following you for blocks. I've been observing you. I've noticed that behind that exquisite face of yours is someone I feel I know. You are a little like me, aren't you? Just a little bit sad. I noticed that immediately. It's something about your eyes and your mouth. You're a complex person, aren't you? Does that nod mean I'm correct? I thought so."

David could not stop. "I can tell you more about yourself. Want to hear what else I noticed? You're lonely and a little bit afraid of everything, and you write poetry, don't you? Boy, we really are communicating. Maybe we can help each other. Come on, don't stop now, smile, it isn't that bad, you have a great deal to be grateful for. Why, in my day, by the time a woman reached thirty, it was tragic. Every wrinkle was considered a wound. Today a wrinkle is no more than a crinkle. So, come on, smile. Why, you have a beautiful smile."

Intrigued by this talkative man, a stranger she seemed to know, Jennifer said, "What do you mean, in your day? The way you speak you'd think you were an old man."

"I mean . . . Hey! I have an idea. Let me take you to dinner. I know a fantastic restaurant not too far from here. We'll have dinner and I'll tell you about myself. I'll even tell you about the woman I loved."

He watched her lovely young face break out in a marvelous smile, and then, in a more serious voice, he said, "Is it possible you know that my wife was the only person who ever made tears come to my eyes?"

Jennifer continued to be amused. Her face broke out in an even wider smile than before, and in a soft voice, a voice which reminded him of his youth, she said, "Who are you? You must tell me who you are." He smiled, collecting his thoughts for a moment before he replied.

"For a time I was a child, and for a longer time a little boy, and for an even longer time a bully and a dreamer. But now, I think, I'm ready to become a man."

She asked again, "Seriously, who are you?"

With a laugh David tried to cover his fear of losing her interest. There was genuine concern in his voice as he said, "Don't be impatient. I'm going to tell you everything, young lady, but it's got to be in my own way." And in a hopeful voice he added, "Okay?"

She took a step backward and gazed at him, and as she did her face changed. No longer was there amusement in it. Her eyes were wide open now. They were clean and intelligent eyes. She hesitated before speaking. Finally she smiled and with real affection answered, "Okay."

300 . . .

He felt something inside himself break free, and as he looked at her for a long time he found himself becoming more and more convinced that she was not only physically beautiful but also sensitive and intuitive and loving and whole.

David took from his briefcase a sheet of typing paper and said, "Let me read something to you. I wrote it last night. It's the beginning of an idea I have for a novel."

She nodded enthusiastically, and he read what he had written.

" 'When I think of who I am, I think for years, each day, I made plans that had no chance of being realized. . . .' "

As David read he looked up more than once at Jennifer.

" 'But now I've finally discovered that what I need is someone pure who can help me to heal my wounds and bring solace and richness to my life, someone who can help to nourish me. Someone to give me clean, sturdy, whole human feelings. Light in the place I am dark. Sinew and backbone in the places I am weak. And I also realize that the best I can hope for is some knowledge of where I've been and a glimpse of where I am going, and to be pleased with where I am.'

"That's what I wrote, young lady. And now, can I take you to dinner?" He smiled engagingly. "By the way, my name is David."

She gazed at him and answered in a youthfully apologetic voice, "I'd really like to but I can't. I'm meeting my mother here for dinner." She paused as she noticed he was genuinely upset. "Perhaps you'd like to join us. My name is Jennifer."

Out of the corner of his eye David saw Leslie walking down the street toward him. She was no longer windburned, youthful, ageless. Time had touched her heavily. She had aged beyond years. She had gone from the perfect girl, from a sensuous vital woman to one whose face was lined, shadowed, caked, and gaunt. The splendid lips were no longer inviting, the sparkling green eyes were now faded and dull, and sunk deeply into their sockets. The health of her rich blond hair was also gone. It was now only bleached and dying. The graceful neck was now stringy and veined; the delicate arms now lumpy; the entire body violated. Time, the immortal champion, the conqueror of all who contested her, had ravaged Leslie Kore.

He stared and thought, We get to look like what we've suffered. His initial response was a longing to comfort her, to run up to her and to tell her that he still loved her, to surround her with his arms, to kiss her temple, hold her hand, whisper into her ear, make her smile. Then Leslie saw him and stopped in her tracks.

She stood still, and they stared at each other. Before he was able to do anything she turned away, ashamed of what she knew he saw. Quickly she started walking back up the street.

Jennifer was saying, "What's wrong, David? What are you staring at?" And then she turned around and saw her mother walking away and started calling, "Mother . . . Mother!"

At that moment something inside David Lazar, something bolted shut for a long, long time, broke completely loose and the door to all his feelings swung open.

Feelings of love poured out, and he wanted to scoop them up and bring them to Leslie. He wanted to tell her so many things he had felt in the stillness of the night for years and years and years. Why had he held onto her so desperately? Because he loved her! Why was she his everything? Because he loved her! Why couldn't he leave her? Why did he always return? Because he loved her! Why was he obsessed? Because he loved her! Why did he reach to other women? Because he loved *her!* And at that moment, more than ever before, he wanted to be with her. Not to wail or scream at her, but just to be with her.

Someday there won't be any you-know-who-I-am how-do-I-look mirrors, and no penis-pussy-putdowns and no mommy-daddy needs and no handicapping for externals, and on that sporty day there won't be a man-woman left who thinks as a stallion-mare-stud-nymph.

There won't be a jock-strap-g-string, or a piston receptacle, or a prick-cunt around.

And on that day the women will be wanton, the men will be wild, they'll fuck and fuck, and laugh and laugh, and love and share and love and share, and help and help each other. Someday . . .

He wanted to climb up the hill after Leslie. He wanted to grab Jennifer's hand and climb after Leslie. He wanted to shout out, "I love you, Leslie. Wait! I love you." He couldn't climb up the hill. He couldn't risk climbing up the hill. He was too depleted to climb anymore. He stood there unable to move. He stood there gripping his silver dollar.

From the top of the hill Leslie turned toward him, and he knew she wanted him to come to her. She stood there waiting, beckoning for him to come to her. He couldn't. He handed his silver dollar to Jennifer. "Jennifer, give mommy this silver dollar. Tell her"—he hesitated—"it can't smile anymore."

Gamblers' Argot

BACK-TO-BACK BET   A conditional bet on two teams that is reversed. X bets on team A; if X wins the bet, winnings are placed on team B. Simultaneously, a bet on team B with the same instruction.

BEARD   A friend, acquaintance, or other contact used to place bets so that book-makers will not know the actual bettor's identity.

BOOKMAKER   One who takes race and sports bets—for a price (vigorish).

CHALK PLAYER   One who bets only the favorites.

CIRCLE GAME   A game on which the bookmaker limits bets.

CLAIMER   A bettor who claims to have bet on the winner when the bookmaker claims the reverse.

CONFERENCE PLAY   Play between teams in the same conference. There are at least twenty major basketball conferences in America right now. Some are the Ivy League, Mid American, Southern, Big Ten, Big Eight, Atlantic Coast, Southeast-ern, Metro-Seven, Missouri Valley, and Ohio Valley. The number of conferences and the names keep changing.

COVER   To win by the required number of points. When you lay 5 points and the team wins by 6 they "covered."

DIME BET   A $1,000 wager.

DOING BUSINESS   Dumping.

DOLLAR BET   A $100 wager.

DOUBLE BET   A game that warrants twice the usual bet.

DUMPING   Doing business. Selling out your school or teammates for a payoff.

EASY PIGEON   A sucker. A naive gambler.

EVEN-MONEY BET   Odds of one to one; a bet in which neither side gets odds.

EVERY-DAY ACTION   A guy who bets every day.

FLASHES   Radio, TV, and phone reports, telling how you're doing.

FORM   A combination of elements such as what the team looks like on paper, how it's been performing, how emotions are, if it's playing a weaker team, and the odds.

GARBAGE   A garbage team is the kind that never makes the money; a garbage player is the kind who sits on the bench or, if he gets into the game, screws up.

GETTING DOWN   Registering a bet. When you call the bookie, he writes down and repeats your bet; then you are down.

GOING FOR THE VIG   The player makes decision to accept the loss of bookmaker's commission.

GOOD GAMBLE   What seems to be a sure win.

HANDICAPPER   One who makes a career of selecting the probable winners in sports events.

HEDGING   Player bets on opposite side to cut possible loss.

HOLDING YOUR OWN   Breaking even.

HOME COURT   The court where a particular basketball team plays most or all of its games.

HOST TEAM   The home team. Usually during Christmastime, tournaments are held and the school that invites the other teams is the host team.

HOTDOG PLAYER OR TEAM   A hotdog player is a showoff, a clown, a guy who likes to do his thing for the fans. He can be a good player or a garbage player—but he does have flair. A hotdog team is one that has caught the public's fancy. Frequently an overrated team, not as good as the record would indicate.

HOT GAME   A game in which one team attracts a lot of bets.

HUNCH BETTOR   One who places his bet on impulse, feeling, intuition, or compulsion.

HUSTLER   Anyone who takes advantage of the ignorance of his victims. There is an exception—a man who can take advantage of a bookmaker. He's a professional.

IF MONEY BET   A bet on one game with the provision that if the bettor wins a bet is placed on another game.

INDEPENDENT TEAMS   Teams that do not play within conferences. In college basketball there are many major powers that are independents, such as Notre Dame, Providence, Marquette, Holy Cross, Detroit, De Paul, and on and on. In all there are about seventy-five of them worth power-rating if you are a handicapper. Also, it is possible that in any given year some of them will join up in a newly formed conference.

JOURNEYMAN BALLPLAYER   A professional athlete with experience. A veteran who has been traded from one team to another.

JUICE   The interest rate. The vigorish. The commission. The 11–10 or more that the bookmaker is charging you.

LARCENY GAME   A game on which the bookmaker, suspecting a fix, will not take a bet. The player, on the other hand, suspecting a fix, is anxious to get down a bet.

LAY   Same as laying odds. To bet a larger number of dollars against a smaller number. Such as when you make a wager on a class pitcher against a garbage pitcher.

306 . . .

LAYING POINTS   Betting on the favorite team in a sport in which points determine the odds. If you lay 6 points against the underdog, your team has to win by 7. If they win by 6 you get a "push" (a tie). If they win by less than 6 you lose.

LIMITS   The maximum bet a bookmaker will take at given odds or points.

LINE   A sports bookie's lay-and-take odds on a sports event. Same as betting line or price line. When you make a bet, remember to get the complete line. Don't let the bookmaker hurry you.

LINEMAKER   Odds maker or price maker. The person or persons or gods or devils who make the price line or odds.

LONG SHOTS   Odds may seem good but chances of winning are poor.

MATCH GAME   The last and deciding game when a series is played and each team has won an equal number of games. In the World Series it would be the seventh game.

MIDDLES   Betting the favorite with one bookmaker who offers a small point spread and reversing the bet with another who offers a larger point spread. If the final score falls between the two, you've got a middle.

NEUTRAL COURT   Suppose the game between St. John's and Northwestern is played at Kentucky's home court. It is a neutral court for both teams. Neither one has the advantage it would have if the same game were being played on either home court.

NEWSPAPER LINE   The point spread or odds listed in the paper; not an official line.

NICKEL WAGER   A $500 wager.

ODDS   The way in which a team's, player's, boxer's, or horse's probability of winning is stated, as calculated by the handicappers, the linemakers, and the betting public. The correct odds are actually the ratio of the unfavorable chances to the favorable chances. The relationship between the favorable and the unfavorable chances a bettor has. The figures used (6–5, 11–10) by linemakers, bookmakers, handicappers, and bettors.

ODDS MAKING   The business that provides odds. The bookmaker who tells what the odds (including his commission) are on an event.

OFFICIAL LINE   The line that the bookie gets and uses. He can make adjustments as he starts getting his action for the day, but he begins with the opening line he gets—it's the official one!

OFF THE BOARD   When the bookmaker won't take a bet on a game it's off the board.

ONE-TIME BET   A "time" in the argot of the bookmaker is five small dollars. Therefore one time is $5, two times is $10, three times is $15, and so on.

OUT   A bookmaker; a beard.

OUTLAW LINE   Sunday night the line comes out of Las Vegas for special (wise-guy) football bettors.

OVERLAY   The sucker will do it most every time—lay more or take less than the official line. He'll bet a 6-point favorite on the official line and lay more. He'll bet a 7–5 favorite and lay more.

PARLAY   The bettor bets two teams to win; both must win to collect. While the usual straight bet pays even money, parlays usually are paid at odds of 12 to 5.

PAST PERFORMANCE   The records of the teams in previous games.

PAYING AND COLLECTING   "P&C." Bookies usually arrange with customers to collect on Monday and pay on Tuesday.

PAYOFF   When you get paid or when you pay off. Collection time.

PICK METHODS   In sports betting, when the odds are even in a baseball game. You still are being charged with the vigorish, though—regardless of which side you take. In sporting events, with lines rather than odds, when the line is zero points and you just have to select a winner. Again you will be charged with the vigorish whichever side you wager on. Of course, if you win, you don't pay the vig.

PIPELINE   Grapevine through which game and betting information runs. A good organization funnels you information through its pipeline.

PITCHER'S LINE   The ten-cent line in baseball. You can specify the pitcher or pitchers you want.

POINTS   The predicted scoring difference between two teams in a game. The bettor's odds are equalized with the point spread.

POINT SHAVING   When a team cuts the margin of victory below the predicted point spread.

POINT SPREAD   The predicted point margin intended to equalize the teams in a game.

POOLS   Office pools, football pools, baseball pools, basketball pools—a form of betting. Always with the odds tremendously against the fellow doing the wagering.

POWER RATING   Arbitrary numerical weights determined by a formula that includes records, statistics, and whatever other factors the rater feels are necessary to rate the teams.

PRICE   The odds; the point spread.

PROGRESSION BETTING   Setting a formula to increase the size of bets. Usually very dangerous. If you keep increasing long enough, or doubling, you'll run into a pretty big number before too long. Progression betting after winning is a form of money management (for some wise guys). Just don't ever forget to take out some of the profit before you increase your bets.

PUSH   A tie, not actual, but resulting from point spread. If the point spread is 6 and the game ends 96–90 you neither win nor lose. Of course, if one bets the short, the sucker would take 5½ and the handicapper would've shopped all over town for 6½.

RED SHIRT   A player who has been kept out of school for a year because the team is already well stocked with fine players. If you keep him out of school, he won't lose his eligibility; he won't have to sit on the bench; he won't put another player on the bench; and he'll make your team stronger the following year when other players graduate—and you really need him. So he's "red-shirted."

REVERSE BET   The same as a back-to-back bet; always involves more than one if money bet.

ROUND BALL   The hoop game. The city game. The game known as basketball.

ROUND ROBIN   A bet placed with a bookie on all possible two-or-three-sports parlays on three or more teams. Only for the sucker, only for the profit of the bookmaker.

RUNDOWN   The current bookie's line on the games of the day.

RUNNER   An agent for a bookmaking office. Runners usually are carried by the office until they get ahead. Then the arrangement generally is 50 percent of profit to runner, 50 percent to office. Never does the runner get more than 50 percent. A good runner is worth every penny he hustles. His customers are honorable—they don't make claims and they don't cause problems when it comes time to pay. He can do his work on the phone or give out the telephone number to his office, where a clerk will be waiting with the line. There are many varied ways of working as an agent in this most illustrious business.

RUNS GAME   In baseball when a game is quoted by runs rather than by price odds.

SCALPER   A ticket engineer. A guy who buys tickets or gets them for nothing and then sells them at a profit. Definitely a hustler.

SCALPING POINTS   When a bettor finds a better point spread and uses it to his advantage.

SCORE   Could be the score of the ball game; could also be "a score"—winning at gambling on sports.

SCRATCH BET   To remove the bet by washing it. If you can't wash it, reverse the bet and lose only the vigorish.

SERVICE LINE   The line made up by unofficial sources that is discussed, debated, and given out. Never an outlaw line.

SHARKS   Crooks, wise guys, hustlers, sharpies, guys who carry notebooks and pencils around to figure out the odds on every proposition. They try to know everything. They flock to Vegas. They usually end up broke!

SHARPIES   Sharks.

SHEET   A list of a bookie's customers.

SHORT END   The lesser risk in any bet. Obviously it would have to be a bet in which there are odds or points, not even money.

SHORT PRICE   The odds keep moving down and down and down.

SMART BET   A bet on an unofficial line better than the official line.

SMART MONEY   Bets based on handicapper or inside information.

SPECIAL GAME   Hot game. Larceny game. Fixed game. Special information is received on game.

SPECTATOR   A fan who does not bet.

SPECULATOR   One who loves to bet. He speculates on everything.

SPREAD   The points. The odds. The price.

SPORTS LINE   The information kept about teams by the handicapper, the bookie, and others.

SPOT PLAYER   To a bookie, a customer who bets occasionally but not every day.

STANDOFF   A tie. Deadlock. Dead even. A push.

STRAIGHT BET   A single bet on a single team to win or lose.

SUCKER BET   A bet which, considering odds, points, and vigorish, the bettor has little chance of winning.

SURE THING   A bet which the bettor has every chance of winning, even considering the vigorish.

SYSTEM PLAYER   The guy never follows a hunch. He only uses a method that is based on some kind of mathematical formula. He'll stick to the formula the whole year. He never relies on chance.

SYSTEMS   Methods of handicapping and betting.

TAKING ODDS   Take the short end of the odds. The short. The dog.

TAKING THE SHORT   Taking odds. Taking points.

TEN-CENT LINE   If you lose you pay the bookie $1.10. If you win you collect $1.

TEASER BET   You get points to play with but must pick two or more winners to collect at even money. In Las Vegas the sports books such as Churchill Downs offer 6-, 6½-, 7-, 10-, and 14-point teasers. This means you get the number of points specified in the bet to add to or subtract from the point spread. The tease is you must pick both games. If you want 6½ points you must lay 11–10 odds; 7 points, you must lay 6–5 odds; if there is a tie the bet is off. With a 10-point teaser you must pick three winners and lay 6–5 odds, and on a tie you lose the bet. With 14-point teasers you must pick four winners and lay 6–5 odds, and on a tie you lose the bet.

TOSSUP   Both teams have an equal chance to win.

TOUTS   Tipsters. A wise guy who sells supposedly inside information. All gamblers should be cautioned to make sure the wise guy is trustworthy.

TRIPLE BET   A game worth three times the investor's usual wager.

TWENTY-CENT LINE   Differential of 1 point between bookies' lay and take odds. Example: 6–7, 7–8, 7½–8½. Also, a baseball line for the general public. Those who bet into this line are suckers. The bookmaker gives one no choice if bets are less than $1 a game. What it means is they can't specify pitchers, and that they are laying $1.20 to $1 in vigorish. Too much to overcome.

UNDERDOG   The dog. The team picked by the linemaker to lose.

UNDERLAY   Opposite of overlay.

VIGORISH   Juice. Commission. The charge of the bookmaker for handling bets. The term originated in England in the eighteenth century.

WASHING BETS   Calling it off. Betting the other side when bookie won't let you call it off. If you lose your vig it's still better than losing the bet. If you don't have an opinion, or if it's changed by good information, you'd better wash the bet. Don't give in to any bookmaker.

WHEELING   System of betting when you take any three or more teams and combine one with all the others. You hope to cover every possible way to win. It's a multiple betting situation and very risky. Reverse bets are much safer and give a better return.